Far from
the
GATES *of* GOLD

Laura K. Weld

Copyright © 2021 Laura K. Weld

ISBN: 9798506100102

DEDICATION

For my husband, without whom I would not have persevered to finish this book. His loving hounding compelled me to see it through.

For my grandmother, who always hoped I would one day write her story.

And for my Lord and my God, the Shepherd and Overseer of my soul, who pursued me and brought me home.

CONTENTS

There Were Ninety and Nine

Elizabeth C. Clephane

There were ninety and nine that safely lay
In the shelter of the fold;
But one was out on the hills away,
Far off from the gates of gold.
Away on the mountains wild and bare;
Away from the tender Shepherd's care.

"Lord, Thou hast here Thy ninety and nine;
Are they not enough for Thee?"
But the Shepherd made answer: "This of Mine
Has wandered away from Me.
And although the road be rough and steep,
I go to the desert to find My sheep."

But none of the ransomed ever knew
How deep were the waters crossed;
Nor how dark was the night the Lord passed through
Ere He found His sheep that was lost.
Out in the desert He heard its cry;
'Twas sick and helpless and ready to die.

"Lord, whence are those blood-drops all the way,
That mark out the mountain's track?"
"They were shed for one who had gone astray
Ere the Shepherd could bring him back."
"Lord, whence are Thy hands so rent and torn?"
"They're pierced tonight by many a thorn."

And all through the mountains, thunder-riv'n,
And up from the rocky steep,
There arose a glad cry to the gate of heav'n,
"Rejoice! I have found My sheep!"
And the angels echoed around the throne,
"Rejoice, for the Lord brings back His own!"

For you formed my inward parts;
you knitted me together in my mother's womb.
I praise you, for I am fearfully and wonderfully made.
Wonderful are your works;
my soul knows it very well.
My frame was not hidden from you,
when I was being made in secret,
intricately woven in the depths of the earth.
Your eyes saw my unformed substance;
in your book were written, every one of them,
the days that were formed for me,
when as yet there was none of them.

Psalm 139:13-16

Prologue
Carmel, California 1969

It was evening and the fog had once again settled on the bluffs. An old cypress outside her window feasted on the briny air, the comforting drone of a foghorn sounding. Beyond the low, stone wall of the inn, time and people proceeded as they always do. But here, with his name staring back at her, everything had stopped—her breath, her heart. She was far too old to be this sentimental.

Age had taught her that the past was a fragile thing. The memories she had of him now were not the truth; they'd grown discolored from her repeated handling. Each moment, each picture had been damaged and washed with her own longing, hurt, and disappointments—fingerprints dirtying film. Was that truly the sound of his laugh, his voice? Was he ever the man she remembered him to be? Yes, there were still scenes from their time together that the years had not corrupted; their vividness had not been polluted. When he'd first taken her hand overlooking Repulse Bay—the heat in her cheeks and pounding in her chest. Reclining at his side on the boat's deck as they motored towards Macao, the warm triangle of sun on her legs and the salty breeze, the rolling of the ship as he read to her those shocking verses from his Good Book. His face and sweet words when she'd confessed her secret.

She could taste the brackishness in her mouth when they'd said goodbye and the scent of his skin as he'd held her in the Peninsula Hotel lobby. But where there should have been a lifetime-worth of reminiscences, there were only a handful. To put it simply, she had regretted getting back onto the *Asama Maru* at the end of that lush, miraculous summer every day since. She had missed him more than she

1

missed her youth, her parents, her husband—all buried long ago.

At some point over the years, the quarantined memories of Willem began to escape their early entombment and fight once more for her attention. They seeped back out to entertain her through slow, shadowy evenings when the children were playing at the neighbor's and Charles prepared for the next day. After he'd died, she'd put away the picture of their honeymoon and hung a photo of Willem on her office wall. She'd wanted to look at him, to live in the past, to be reminded of a short time when she'd had everything she'd wanted.

Peg stood and carried the phonebook to the dresser, setting it down, and looked at her reflection in the mirror. She brushed her hair with Mam's sparrow-handled brush, worn smooth and dark from decades of use, and put on lipstick, as though Willem would be able to see her through the phone line. She stared back at the sixty-three-year-old woman and wondered what she had done with her real self, that girl with the large brimmed hat who had stepped so expectantly onto the wooden docks of Hong Kong a lifetime ago.

Peg glanced at her watch and reached for the phone but drew back before she touched it. He would not be the same man, and she surely was not the same woman. Really, she'd known him for such a brief moment, that one distant, exotic summer. Would he even remember her name, this old lady whose young heart he'd broken? She'd always longed for an explanation, for the truth to at last be spoken aloud. No matter how preposterous, the last vestiges of a forlorn hope remained, that perhaps he had, after all, truly loved her. She could not snuff it out, despite the compelling evidence to the contrary.

She sat down once more on the bed and lifted the heavy telephone onto her lap, raising the receiver and dragging the phonebook closer to her leg so that she could easily see his number. She put her index finger in the round groove next to the first digit, turning it all the way to the right, and then did the same for the remaining numbers. Peg sucked in her breath before dialing the last, the hand not holding the receiver clenched in a tight fist.

For thirty years, she'd searched, even when it was wrong for her to do so, even when her husband had still been alive. She'd looked for his name in every phonebook in every city she'd visited, and she'd traveled the world—from Kenya to Nepal. How could she have found him in a town but hours from her home?

She prayed then, without meaning to, for the first time in years. She prayed for the right words, for the man she was never able to leave behind to answer and to know her. Her spirit cried out without her consent for God to rescue the years eaten by longing and confusion, for another chance.

With the first ring, she remembered her father and how they'd feasted together amongst the wild plum trees when she was still small enough to ride on his shoulders. The second evoked her mother's face, broad and warm. With the third, she thought of Mam, her stalwart and extravagant kindness. The fourth sang of Willem and his proposal on the balcony of The Peninsula Hotel, the earnestness of his voice and sincerity of his words. As she waited for the fifth to chime, her eyes filled with tears. Her throat constricted so that she did not know how she would speak.

The last ring was interrupted by the unmistakable sound of a receiver lifting, of a phone call answered.

Margaret

Helena, Montana
1903-1904

CHAPTER 1

The train swayed across the uneven tracks, but Judith's hands shook from something other than the locomotive's rough progress. She held them tightly together in her lap to stay their spasms and watched the flickering light gild the compartment's upholstered walls. Focused solely on her face, the illusion of composure and femininity was impregnable. Only her tidily gloved hands, unruly beneath the white lace, betrayed her nerves.

The clothing and bearing of her traveling companion were equally fine, but whereas Judith's complexion was opalescent, her servant's was the same shade as the tea she sipped. Tall with broad shoulders, her knees beneath the folds of her silk, plaid dress knotty and immovable, she was a formidable woman—even seated. A thin cross pendant, half hidden by lace, was her only adornment. She noted Judith's trembling but said nothing.

A redheaded woman and her precocious little boy, who insisted upon knowing the train's every bolt and lever, joined them in their cabin. He had with him a small picture book on the subject matter, which he consulted whenever his mother did not supply a satisfactory answer. Judith found him charming and let slip a wistful smile at his innocent prattling.

"Ruth, I'm awfully thirsty. Do you think I could have a sip of your tea?" Ruth passed her the cup, but Judith, despite her proclaimed thirst, only lapped conservatively at the beverage.

"How much longer, do you think, until we're there?" she asked, blowing across the drink's surface. The redheaded woman chose this moment to lift her son from the floor onto her lap, who flailed and kicked with all the substantial force his pudgy legs possessed. Despite his struggles, the delicate mother was soon able to subdue the raging beast with a whisper and a few strokes of his hair.

"An hour or two more," Ruth answered. Judith nodded her acknowledgement and set the tea and saucer down in her lap. The little boy stared unashamedly at Ruth from the safety of his mother's arms, his curious young brain whirling with questions. When he opened his mouth to speak, Judith interjected to prevent the inevitable affront.

"—And how old are you, my little sir?" she asked kindly, catching him off guard. He gazed now at her, taking in all her finery and perfume with awe. Tilting his head back so that it rested against his mother's stomach, he looked up into her eyes, seeking confirmation that the stranger was safe.

"Go ahead, answer the pretty young lady," she nudged, kissing the swirl of hair on the crown of his head.

"I'm four," he answered proudly, grinning when Judith's eyes opened wide in disbelief. The boy squirmed in excitement, anticipating what the elegant girl might say next.

"My goodness! Such a grown-up little man you are. I bet you even know how to count to twenty, don't you?" His face lit up with pride.

"To fifty! One, two, three..." he continued into the teens, rattling off his knowledge with glee, stumbling once or twice until he reached the limits of his familiarity. His mother corrected his missteps gently and congratulated him with a loving squeeze.

"Ruth, did you hear that? How impressive!" Ruth turned her head to look the boy in the eye. She leaned forward.

"That is very good, young man," she said with authority.

"Papa says I'm the smartest boy he knows!" he blurted out.

"Ah, I see. Well," said Judith, playing along, "I've met a few lads in my life, and I'd say your father's estimation is quite accurate." The boy grinned and kicked his legs with pleasure.

"Do you want to see my book?" he asked, now thoroughly enamored of his traveling companions.

"Teddy, I think we should let these ladies sit in peace," instructed his mother. Teddy's bottom lip protruded.

"If you don't mind, Madame, I was hoping he would ask. I'd wager that the book's replete with important facts about trains I've always wanted to know."

Teddy looked at Judith as though she were made of sugar. He slipped from his mother's grasp and slid down into the narrow space between the two seats, using his feet to lift his treasured book from the floor. Without waiting for further permission, he flipped open the pages and began to point out his many favorite parts. They spent the remainder of the ride this way—Teddy blissfully displaying his mastery of locomotives, and Judith observing his unmitigated enthusiasm with tenderness—until the wheels slowed and the train came to a halt.

Momentarily, Judith was disoriented. Peering through the dusty glass, the station at Helena looked much like the one at Great Falls. She followed Ruth down the narrow aisle and stepped tentatively onto the platform, watching gratefully as Ruth orchestrated the removal of their trunks from the luggage car. They had indeed arrived at their intended destination. She held her breath and then exhaled slowly so that the tears in her eyes would not brim over.

Teddy and his mother passed Judith, and the two women warmly smiled their farewells. Suddenly shy in the bustle of the station, Teddy held his mother's hand tightly and turned to wave. Judith quickly dabbed at the corners of her eyes and the tip of her nose with the heel of her palm and then winked and wiggled her fingers playfully. The little boy covered his smile with his hand as he was pulled along.

Judith moved to Ruth's side and readjusted the hat pins in her hair while two men carried their heavy belongings and set them down at their feet. Ruth inspected the trunks just as a carriage rolled to a loud stop before them. Judith felt lightheaded and grabbed onto Ruth's arm to steady herself. There was no lettering on its side, but both women knew instantly that the carriage was theirs. It had only one small window placed higher than would be expected; Judith blushed at the need for the alteration. An older man who kept his gaze lowered hopped nimbly down from the driver's seat and held open the small door, helping them into their black leather seats.

Once inside the compartment and the door was shut, Ruth saw that two veils hung on the wall. She handed one to Judith, whose pallid face appeared ghostly against the darkness of the carriage's interior. They stared and one another pensively until Ruth broke the tension with a nod, indicating that Judith was to put it on.

She'd understood the meaning of the veil immediately and clutched it in her lap as she'd previously clutched her shaking hands. Her vision grew blurry before she blinked back the rising tears once more. Ruth secured her own veil, but panic seized Judith's throat, and she could not bring herself to do the same. Ruth took it from her and carefully arranged it over her hat and face.

"It's for the best, Judy." Judith swallowed and nodded her head quickly in agreement. Traversing the narrow distance between their kneecaps, Ruth squeezed Judith's hand. From the brief touch, the girl drew courage and sat taller in her seat. "I don't know what I would do without you," she said, humbly accepting the limits of her own strength. Ruth gave a slight smile and sighed quietly, leaning back and closing her eyes.

Now and then upset by rocks or an uneven patch of road, the carriage jangled and lurched. "It's not far. A quarter hour," proclaimed Ruth, answering Judith's unspoken question. To a woman eager to arrive at her destination, such statements would have been assurances. But to Judith, they served only as unwelcome reminders of the bleak future into which she descended.

Too soon, the carriage's wheels slowed and then were still. A polite knock rapped on the door. "It's time," said Ruth.

The women emerged into the dry, radiant heat of the mid-July afternoon like two Italian widows on their way to mass. The edges of their bodies undulated in the direct, high sun. Through the heavy veil, Judith saw the Rocky Mountains rise ungracefully with brute force over a vast, thinly stretched basin below. Low and cottony clouds cast great blue shadows on that distant plain. The yellow of the dead grasses and the gray of the precarious boulders pierced her temple as though she had been stabbed there with a needle. The land was barren, desolate. Unconsciously, she rested her hand on the small mound of her abdomen and held her breath.

Judith crossed the open space and followed the carriage driver into the home directly before her. She did not lift her head and so did not know that they had entered through the back door. She saw only the dusty road change to failing grass and then to wooden stairs. All the while, there were her neatly shod feet in the latest fashion, shuffling along obediently.

CHAPTER 2

Ruth liked the veil. It was dramatic and made her feel mysterious. She peered through the black lace at the patterned interior of the carriage. She was protected, for a time, and so was Judith. She squeezed the girl's hand to let her know that she understood her fear. Mrs. Frisk was right; Ruth had failed her. She should have watched for the signs more carefully. She should have known what loneliness and a boy would breed. She'd forgotten that Judith was a daughter of Eve, too, with flesh that told her to do things she should not.

The Eleanor Barrett Home drew fallen women from across the West. They came for the haven, to learn a trade, and to grow large far from wagging tongues. They were willing to stay shut away for their pregnancies because they had nowhere else to go; they knew that the matron would protect their secrets at all costs.

At first, the socialites of Great Falls hadn't known what to think. They'd frowned and shaken their heads—the state of the country that such a place existed! But then a few had dared to donate to its cause, and helping the fallen soon became fashionable.

Mrs. Frisk had not been immune to Barrett's popularity. She wanted to be modern, and maybe she even cared a little for those unfortunate girls. It was a large sum, Ruth knew, that she donated each year. She knew because Mrs. Frisk had told her the exact figure. She told her with pride how much she was willing to give to save a few souls. Now, she even ran the Eleanor Barrett Circle of Great Falls, raising money for the Helena chapter and referring girls to its doors. She'd thought herself broadminded and stylish for her involvement in the cause, but she hadn't been so broadminded when she'd learned her own daughter needed its services.

When Ruth had told her, the color left Mrs. Frisk's cheeks completely, and she'd thought her mistress might faint. She'd moved to her then, in case she fell, but Mrs. Frisk recoiled. Her hands shook, and then her arms, and then her entire body. When she'd clutched the chair for support, it rattled against the floor. "With child? With child?" she cried. She reeled and faced Ruth. "You, where were you? How could you have let this happen? I trusted you with my daughter, and you've ruined her!" The sunlight caught the droplets of saliva that sprayed as Mrs. Frisk spat her accusations, and her neck bulged and turned purple with rage. She'd lunged at Ruth with her finger as though it were a sword.

Judith hadn't protested when she'd learned her fate; she'd bowed her head with shame and accepted her punishment, humiliated. She would wait out her pregnancy in Helena. Despite her transgression, Ruth did not think that Judith should be forced to give up her own flesh. What was better, what was holier than new life? Ruth had told her this, and she'd smiled at her like she was a child, like she didn't understand the simplest things about the world.

If it were up to Ruth, if she were Judith's mother, she wouldn't have sent her away. Ruth didn't care what people thought; let them whisper, their luncheon invitations dwindle. What were the opinions of such women worth? Not even the price of the expensive clothes on their backs. It was wrong the way girls like Judy were hidden, out of sight, as though pregnancy were a catching disease.

When the time had come to leave Great Falls, Ruth had helped Judith pack her bags. She brushed Judith's hair and made sure she looked like a lady. She wanted her to know that she was not ruined, that there was still hope. Mrs. Frisk did not say a word to Judith after announcing her banishment, and Judy suffered from the silence. Ruth's growing contempt for her mistress came in waves, but she reminded herself that without the Frisks, she might have ended up on a poor farm. She'd been with them since before Judith was born. She was fond of all the Frisk children—Jack and Phillip, the younger brothers—but she loved Judy like she were her own.

Neither Ruth nor Judith had ever been outside of Great Falls, but Ruth read everything she could to prepare for the journey. She knew that linens were provided, and that Judith was only permitted one trunk. She'd taken all of this into account when she'd packed their things, selecting the right dresses and making sure to bring a few bright pieces to lift Judith's mood. She would never have thought of this, and so Ruth thought of it for her.

She'd thought of other things too—paper for letters and a large straw hat for shade when she sat in the yard. Judith was white like eggshells, and Ruth didn't want her to lose her complexion, to turn leathery and wrinkled. She wanted the best for her, the best of everything. Once her time at Barrett was spent, Ruth most of all wanted Judith to know that she was not ruined, that there was still hope.

When the carriage came to a halt and Judith and Ruth were escorted inside, a thin woman greeted them and introduced herself as the matron. She gave them permission to remove their veils.

"—A precaution," she explained, smiling at Judith while taking her hands. "Welcome to the Eleanor Barrett Home." Ruth looked at her and nodded her greeting. "It is unusual for us to have a chaperone escort an inmate," she continued. Ruth said nothing. The matron cleared her throat. "My name is Ms. Wendell." She was no more than thirty, had a very small nose and eyes set too closely together. Ruth noted that she smelled of starch and violets. Ms. Wendell took from the folder under her arm a piece of paper and handed it to Judith with great efficiency. "These are the rules of the home, and as long as you are here, we expect you to abide by them. I assure you that they are for the common good of all the girls. You will see rule number three states that all new arrivals must submit to thorough inspection upon admittance to Barrett." She looked up from the paper and blinked. "I know it sounds unpleasant, but it is a necessary practice, I'm afraid. It is for everyone's bodily and spiritual safety. No liquor, no weapons, no opiates, no inappropriate reading materials."

"Judith has none of these," Ruth said, wishing to spare her the embarrassment.

"I trust that she does not—nevertheless, she must still be searched as all other twelve inmates have been searched. I'm sure you'll agree it's only fair. I will take you to your room, and we will conduct the procedure there." Ms. Wendell took a break from her speech, and her voice softened. "Judith," she said, "I hope you will be content here. I find it is best to be upfront about these things, no matter how unsavory, in order to avoid problems later. If you know what we expect, it is easier for you *and* for us." She smiled again, broadly, but Judith and Ruth only stared.

Ruth knew that she herself would not be given room and board at the home. Barrett was for the girls themselves, not for friends and family. She would only be allowed to stay until Judith was shown her quarters. Ms. Wendell took them to it, and they saw with mutual relief that she had the space to herself.

"May I stay for the search?" asked Ruth, standing in the doorway. Ms. Wendell paused, collecting her thoughts.

"It's unconventional, but yes, I will allow it." She opened Judith's trunk and pulled out each item of clothing. When she found the paper and pencils, she stopped.

"You will see rule number eight states that all letters to and from inmates will be read first by myself." She rattled off the rule as though it were the most normal expectation, and Ruth was too surprised to comment. She frowned. Ms. Wendell continued her search and asked Judith to turn out her pockets and purse, finding nothing. "Very well," she said. "I am pleased to say that you have passed inspection!" She clasped her hands together with excitement. "Now I did not see a Bible in your belongings—do we need to furnish you with one? There are scripture readings every afternoon before the evening worship." Ruth smiled for the first time. She spoke for Judith.

"Yes." Judith watched her interlocked fingers and said nothing.

"Very good," said the matron. "We are family here, Judith—a tightly knit household. Think of me as your mother while you are with us. We have your best interests at heart. You must keep your person and your room neat, and profane language is forbidden. You will do your share around the house. Bedtime is ten o'clock, sharp, and you must be dressed and washed in the mornings by seven. Leaving the home is not permitted without prior approval and only for exceptional circumstances. We will always do everything we can to ensure your anonymity. All of these rules are found on the sheet I gave you. You should know that privacy is of the upmost importance to us here. You will find the other inmates come from all walks of life, and some are rougher around the edges than others, but the Lord loves them all, and so do we." She paused to allow her words their full impact. "Do you understand and agree, Judith?" Ruth began to answer for her, but Ms. Wendell interrupted. "Judith," she stressed the name, "do you understand and agree?"

"Yes," she replied, quietly.

"Good. Very well then, let me show you to the door, Madam. Judith, you can put away your things." Ruth watched Judith's bravery rally but quickly fail. She collapsed on the bed, fighting back tears as the trembling from the train returned. She needed Ruth to stroke her hair and sing to her as she had when she was a young girl. Instead, Ruth kissed the top of her head and told her that she would be back soon. Ms. Wendell faced away to give them privacy, but Ruth did not wait for Judith to say anything more, for her to plead that she stay. She left and shut the door behind her so that she would not be tempted to turn back around. Her ribs were tight as she and the matron walked together down the stairs.

"I trust that Judith's mother has provided the twenty-five-dollar maternity fee?" Ms. Wendell asked. Ruth could tell that she disliked the mention of money. She withdrew the envelope from her handbag and placed it in the matron's outstretched hand. "Thank you," she said, tucking it inside her own pocket. She was more comfortable once the envelope was out of sight. "Because of Judith's family, you have been granted special privileges afforded no one else. You may visit every morning at eight if you so choose. But I should warn you that I or another employee must be present at all meetings. It is in the home's rules."

"Yes," Ruth said, "there are a great many rules for such a small house." Ms. Wendell's cheeks flushed pink.

"Indeed, there are, Madam. And I firmly believe in each and every one. Not all the girls are as...*cultivated*....as Judith, and they need discipline. In my experience, discipline has never harmed anyone."

"Nor in mine, Ms. Wendell. Nor in mine. Take good care of her," Ruth said, earnestly.

"We would not dream of doing anything less. We are all accountable to these girls and to God. There is no higher standard," she said. "Madam," she added, her voice softening, "If I may make a recommendation? Stay away for a day. Give Judith a little time. It will make the adjustment easier. It is, of course, up to your discretion; I only give my professional opinion." Ruth nodded but did not commit herself either way. She would decide what was best, not the matron.

The carriage that had brought them to the home that morning waited dispassionately in the dusty road. Ruth said goodbye and stepped lightly inside without the driver's help. She instructed him to take her to the Helena Hotel, which Mrs. Frisk had only reserved at Ruth's insistence. Seeing no point in her staying, she'd wanted Ruth to drop Judith at the home and return to Great Falls, refusing to fund any extended time away. Ruth would be paying the entirety of her hotel and food expenses from her own savings.

The horses leapt forward, and Ms. Wendell's small frame disappeared from view. Ruth listened to the horses' pitiful whinnies and stomping feet; they did not want to take her to the hotel. They must have known that she didn't really want them to, either. What Ruth wanted was for them to charge through the doors of the Eleanor Barrett Home and set all of the somber girls free—ants scattering from a sieged hill. She would scoop up Judith, the queen, and take her away where no one would force her to make unholy sacrifices.

Ruth imagined Mrs. Frisk's expression when she learned that her very own servant had destroyed her anthill, and she chuckled. Ms. Wendell was so sincere, and here Ruth was wearing a veil again. Everything that was happening was not at all funny, but she laughed out loud, regardless. The wheels on the gravel couldn't drown out the sound. The driver must think her insane! She sat back and grabbed her sides, tears coming to her eyes. She could hardly breath. The image of Judith sitting on her narrow bed in that dingy room, her lip trembling, interrupted her fit as the carriage threw her to one side. Ruth hopped across the seat, losing her balance, nearly tipping over.

CHAPTER 3

It was dark when Judith awoke. Alone in the sparse room, only the outline of the furniture was visible. She could feel the heavy, swollen flesh of her eyelids each time she blinked. Although she made out the shape of a lamp next to the bed, she did not reach to turn it on. There was no hurry to greet the day, for there was nothing in it worth welcoming. She would wait for the sun to force her from her bed. The ticking of a clock was the only discernible noise, and she was pleased for the distraction. She counted each second until she'd accumulated hundreds, and then the numbers lost their meaning. A final sob shook her frame.

Judith rolled over onto her side to face the window and watch the shades of black grow lighter and lighter still. She wasn't sure how many hours had passed when she detected the first change in hue—from black to blue to pink and, at last, to gold. Any other morning, she would have admired the delicate progression.

When there was enough light to clearly see the room, she was indifferent to the sight. Everything was just as utilitarian and drab as it had been the day before. Judith still wore her traveling clothes, which were now wrinkled and stale. After Ruth had gone, neither Ms. Wendell nor anyone else had come to check on her. During the height of her misery, she'd opened her bedroom door an inch and peeked out briefly before quickly shutting it and returning to bed.

A high-pitched voice called her name, interrupting her pitiful thoughts. Judith rolled toward the noise and found auburn hair within inches of her face. Disoriented and alarmed, she sat upright abruptly and nearly knocked heads with the woman leaning over her.

"Well, you looked like a broken doll lyin' there like that in all your clothes! Deary, it's well past seven. If you don't hurry, you'll miss breakfast," said the petite woman, regaining her balance and wiping her hands on the rag that hung from her apron. "What's that now, can't you talk?" she asked teasingly. "Come now, Miss, it will do you no good to give me the silent treatment. I'm nobody! Save it for the matron." She stood now with her hands on her narrow hips, her pointy elbows jutting out at threatening angles. "You'll need to change your clothes and wash your face. You look rumpled." When Judith still did not speak or move, she grew irritated. "See here, I have other ladies to attend to! I can't spend my whole mornin' tryin' to lift your spirits." Judith turned her head so as not to have to look at the demanding woman. There was no power on earth that could coax her to join the other girls at breakfast.

"I'm not hungry, thank you."

"Ah, then, I knew you could talk," she said. "But, I didn't ask if you was hungry, I said you have to get dressed and head downstairs. It's the rules! Everyone eats together every mornin' at half seven. Period. You don't want to start your stay off here on the wrong foot." When she saw that her warning did nothing to convince her, she turned to leave. "Suit yourself, but don't come cryin' to me later for somethin' to eat." When she was through the doorway, Judith called to her quietly.

"What is your name?"

"Fiona Nearbonne, but everyone here calls me Netty. I'm not sure yet what *you* can call me."

"I'm Judith. It's a pleasure to make your acquaintance," she muttered, ignoring the woman's contentiousness and turning once more to face the window.

Judith slept the rest of the day and following night, waking only once to use the restroom. She preferred unconsciousness to her grim circumstance. The next morning, Ruth's dark visage replaced Netty's. Judith wanted to slap the familiar face, to scream and tear at its skin, but before she could rally the strength to do so, Ruth hugged her fiercely and kissed her hard on the cheek. In Ruth's embrace, Judith found it impossible to be anything other than comforted.

"You've not eaten or washed since I last saw you," Ruth whispered tenderly, shaking her head. "You must take care of yourself. You are going to be here for a long time, Judith." Ruth walked to the window that looked out over the garden and gently pushed the white curtain aside. "It's a nice day. We should walk in the yard and get some fresh air before it's too hot." She turned back around and came close again to Judith, touching her hair with the tips of her fingers. The sensation traveled the length of each strand to her scalp.

"I don't mean to be difficult. It's just that I can't seem to bring myself to do anything except lie here." Even as she spoke, Judith stood up to find her clothes, drawing strength from Ruth's presence. She saw then that a uniformed woman waited in the hallway, doing her best to be attentive yet unobtrusive. They briefly locked eyes before the onlooker cleared her throat and glanced upwards at the ceiling.

"Where are my things?" Judith asked, ignoring her and looking around at a room devoid of her belongings.

"I put them away while you slept." Ruth walked to the closet and opened the door to reveal her neatly hung dresses. "Your hat is on the chest. Would you like me to help you?"

"No, thank you. I can manage."

Now upright and moving, the narrow bed covered with its yellow quilt stood out against the otherwise innocuous furnishings. Judith did not want to imagine the other women who had slept beneath it, and so she hastily chose a dress and preoccupied herself with its many buttons. Ruth poured water into the basin for her to wash, handed her the towel to dry her face, and then brushed and braided her hair. Judith grabbed the sunhat, and the two walked down the narrow stairs, their chaperone trailing behind them at a polite distance. As they passed through the doorway and out into the garden, Judith wanted to reach for Ruth's hand. She fought the urge and kept her arms close to her side.

Walking the grounds together after breakfast became their routine. Ruth arrived promptly at eight each morning and stayed until ten when the matron escorted her from the grounds. As forewarned, Ms. Wendell or another Barrett employee was present at each meeting, quietly busying herself in the corner with some sort of needle work. For Judith, it was an unwelcome reminder of her confinement and darkened what otherwise was the brightest part of the day.

When the conversation between the women faltered, Judith turned to her sewing and to her laundry, mundane tasks that distracted her only because of their novelty. While her scholarly education surpassed the other inmates, her domestic skills fell far short of the average ability.

Her participation in these common chores provided an invaluable service; they kept her hands and her mind preoccupied. Her head tilted, her eyes narrowed to better see the thread's path, the bulge in her waist became nothing more than a utilitarian mound upon which to rest her diligent wrists. With her ear close to the fabric, she coaxed the needle through each tiny hole with quiet encouragements.

Ruth often observed her silent industry from the wingback chair across the sitting room and knew that those things Judith truly needed to confess might never be spoken aloud. If her heart's language had been translatable, she might very well have shared its burden, but instead she turned inward—an insect curling to protect its underside—silent and armored. She would not share her grief, even with Ruth.

CHAPTER 4

Strong winds had arisen suddenly in the morning, keeping the women from their walk, and so Judith and Ruth gathered their yarn and knitting needles and sat down in the parlor instead. One of the older inmates strode unexpectedly into the room and joined Judith with a heavy descent onto the worn, blue-velvet sofa, making her arm wobble. Judith's mouth pursed in annoyance, but she smiled politely.

"What are you making?" asked the intruder, leaning in closer to see, ignoring Ruth entirely.

"It's a blanket, for the baby." The woman raised her eyebrows and nodded.

"That's fine work. I'm Emma, by the way."

"Hello, Emma. I'm Judith. Yes, you sit behind me in the classroom."

"You're an awfully pretty, young thing to end up here, aren't you?" asked Emma. Judith could not tell if she actually expected a response to her vulgar question.

"When are you due?" Judith asked instead, changing the topic.

"Next month, and then I'll go back to my family."

"Your family?"

"Yes, I have five other little ones. Four boys and a girl. My sister is watching them now." It was Judith's turn to stare.

"I don't understand, I'm sorry," she said. "Then why are you here?"

"My husband has a fondness for the bottle, that's why, and I've got to learn to do somethin' other than sell my womanly wares to feed us all. I can only count on my sister and her husband so much. I kept thinkin' Frank would turn things 'round, but he ain't. I see that now. We've been married for eleven years, and he's had twice as many jobs. There ain't many people left who'll hire on a man with his reputation. Half the time, he doesn't even come home at night. Likely asleep in his own piss in some ditch. So the matron's been teachin' me how to read. I'm going to get a job teachin' or maybe as a secretary," said Emma proudly.

Judith flinched at the woman's vulgarity and doubted her ability to

19

secure any kind of respectable employment. Thankfully, another of the girls called for her unwelcome companion from the other room.

"Coming!" Emma yelled, lifting her large backside off the sofa and rising slowly. "Sorry to leave you here yourself, but I have to go." Ruth looked down with raised eyebrows at the scarf she was knitting.

"Yes, please, go right ahead," Judith said with understanding, relieved and happy to be rid of her. As Emma left the room, Judith stared at Ruth and exhaled loudly before turning again to her own knitting.

Her fellow "fallen angels," as one of the nurses referred to them, were not what Judith had expected. She'd thought they would all be young and pretty—refined and unfortunate and from wealthy backgrounds, like her own. Instead, they were mostly like Emma, living at the home out of necessity rather than disgrace.

Unlike her fellow inmates, Judy had been horrified when she'd gotten pregnant—the evidence of her indiscretion on display for all to see. Had she waited until she were married, had she not strayed so markedly from the straight path that was hers to walk, her pregnancy would have brought joy, gratitude, and blessing. And yet there were moments when she went over her moral fall with pleasure, when she relished the illicit sensations she knew she should not. Such wicked thoughts alarmed her, and she longed to distance herself from the influence of these dissipated women, women like Emma, whom she irrationally blamed for her own turpitude.

As her needles hooked the yarn, she thought back on Emma's words. It shocked Judith that the state of marriage did not protect women from evil and suffering. Before Barrett, she had not known life contained so many possible variations of tragedy.

CHAPTER 5

"Good day, Miss," Netty said gruffly, bobbing her head sharply in greeting as she waylaid Judith in the hall. Pulled back severely beneath a bleach-white nurse's cap, her hair looked more orange than before. "There's something different planned for you today. You'll skip the sewin' lesson. I'm to give you the *grand tour*," she said facetiously, "though I don't see the use. You've already been here long enough to know what's where, but I don't ask questions and I do as I'm told. We normally show girls the first day, but you had your difficulties, and well, being as busy as we are, these things happen. You must be somebody awfully important—the matron wanted to take you herself but couldn't. She asked me to do it instead." Netty stuck her hands deeply into her apron pockets and shrugged her shoulders. "Well, shall we get started?" Judith did not want to see the rest of the home but was grateful for the change in routine. She followed Netty as they walked down the hallway and began to climb the central staircase.

"Still tightlipped, are we?" The shuffling of their feet against the thin green carpet scantly protecting the wooden steps replaced her response. "I've seen you talking with that servant of yours," Netty said over her shoulder, accusatorily. "You must be someone special for the matron to allow her to come see you every day," she prodded again, hoping to induce an explanation. "If you ask me, I think it's strange. It's not right that you have a visitor and none of the other girls do. Makes them feel downright lonesome. But I suppose it doesn't matter what I think." They had reached the landing, and Netty moved to the side to allow Judith to pass.

"Here we are. That room there is for nursing. There's one on both floors, and the rest of these doors are inmate's quarters."

"Nursing?" asked Judith blankly.

"Why the little ones have to eat, of course, and the matron wouldn't have it done out in the open. This is where I do most of my work. I'm a wet nurse but help out in other ways as I can. When you have your girl, you'll come here to feed her," she said decisively. Judith winced and looked at her with alarm.

"—My girl?"

"Oh, well I have a knowin' for these things. I'd bet this month's salary that you'll have a lass come February." Judith's hands hovered over her abdomen.

They resumed the tour, walking further down the hallway, past Judith's quarters and around to the other side of the home. Here, a single door led to a room with two rows of bassinets. Judith saw a nurse pass by and then the unmistakable fingers of a newborn reach spasmodically above the bassinet's edge. Netty approached the door and Judith hung back, leaning against the wall for support. She shook her head with panic.

"It's a room full of babies, not lepers, for Pete's sake! You won't catch anythin' you ain't already got." She beckoned Judith with a forceful wave and a tap of her booted foot. When she did not move, Netty stomped towards her and grabbed her arm, yanking her forward. Dragging Judith inside, Netty stood closely behind to prevent escape.

"You, my dear, will have one of these, too. You're with child, just like *all* the others. There's nothin' I hate more than the girls who pretend they haven't gotten into any trouble, like that swollen belly comes from eatin' too much bangers and mash. You walk around never lookin' down except down at the other ladies, thinkin' you're so much better than the rest, your eyes on the sky and whistlin' dixie. I don't mean to be cruel, but it would do you good to face what's comin'." Netty spoke into Judith's ear in a low voice, no less fervent for its diminished tone.

Taking in the full view of the infants in their grid of cradles, Judith covered her mouth with her hand. Peach feet bottoms and pudgy knuckles grasped the air. Disembodied smacks and shrill cries emanated from beneath blankets and echoed off the wooden sides of the cradles. There were no more than five babies, and yet their synergistic howls created the impression of at least twice that number. Judith stared with wonderment.

"What's through there?" she whispered, pointing to a door on the far side of the room.

"The solarium. The cradles get moved out there for an hour each afternoon to give the babies their daily dose of sunshine. This whole wing is brand new, just built last year. It's the matron's pride and joy. The home got a big donation recently from a muckity-muck in Great Falls, and there's enough space now for thirteen little ones," Netty said with satisfaction, proudly surveying the room. "Would you like to see?" she asked eagerly.

"No, no. That's really quite enough. I'm not feeling well. I think I'll lay down for a bit before lunch if the tour is done." Judith stepped back into the hallway, dizzy, her face ashen.

Netty frowned. "No, it's not done. We've not seen half of it." Judith's knees buckled momentarily, and Netty reluctantly yielded to her demand. "Well, I suppose there's no good to come from your faintin'. I'll take you back to your room, and you can rest until the bell. You'll come across it all at some point. Just don't tell the matron." She took Judith's forearm and led her down the stairs. The girl was compliant and did not try to shake free. It seemed that the sight of the babies had been a shock, and as much as Netty knew that Judith needed a jolt, she still worried after her health.

Netty left her at the door and so did not see Judith ignore the bed altogether and choose the stool in the corner instead. Alone, she unbuttoned her dress and pulled her arms out of their sleeves so that the garment hung down around her thickened waist. Her back against the wall and her feet squarely on the floor, she inspected her changing body, fearfully touching the unwelcome bulge at her middle. She was being shaped as though spun on a lathe, her sharp edges rounded to smooth, fleshy moons. She was one of them now, a drone among drones.

As the lunch bell's metallic reverberations spread through the floor and up through her legs, Judith slid from the stool and buttoned her dress, catching a glimpse of herself in the small oval mirror on the wall. The sight arrested her, and she felt her mind clearing, as though awaking from a dream. How could this have happened? What was she to do?

CHAPTER 6

A month passed, ushering in the advent of cooler evenings. A single orange leaf on the tree outside Judith's window decried September's end. Despite Ruth's efforts to combat her melancholia, the passage of time only worsened Judith's spirits.

Netty's tour had produced a dramatic effect, and Judith could no longer deny that she carried Andrew's child. Her acceptance of the situation brought unexpected consequences. Judith found herself growing surprisingly attached to the daughter she had accidentally conceived and never met, coming to love her without reservation—as though she had been conceived in purity, as though she would be there to tuck her in each night or when she lost her first tooth. When she was alone, she spoke softly and sang to her, savoring the kicks and punches she received in response.

As Judith tried to find an answer to her impossible predicament, she often thought of the clever toy her aunt had brought back for her from one of her trips—a shadow lantern that told the spinning, wordless story of a little girl lost in the woods. Judith twirled and turned like the paper girl as her own wretched story unfolded across Barrett's filigreed walls. The ending did not change, no matter how desperately she tried to rewrite it. She strove to appear normal, to at least present a peaceful façade, but her efforts were futile. Ruth knew her far too well.

Ruth continued to speak of a time after Barrett when Judith would reenter society and carry on as before, but Judith now knew that such a thing was impossible. She would never be the same, and she would never marry. Saving her reputation was a futile exercise, as she would surely do nothing with the esteemed possession once she returned home. It was all a waste. How could she dare eke out any sort of normal life when she would never know if her daughter was safe, happy, loved? Her innocent child would be the one to pay the heaviest penalty for her trespasses—a truth that possessed her bones and gave her no peace, clawing at her heart incessantly.

And what of Andrew? She may not have spoken of him aloud, but Judith did think of him. She relegated these thoughts to the evenings, to those heady moments just before sleep. He came to her naturally then, without effort or conjuring—his reddish hair, the freckles on his cheeks, his laugh. He existed in her mind in treasured pieces. Fragmented, he was a great work of art.

She had known him since she was three, and there had scarcely been a day that they had not seen one another. In their explorations, they'd unearthed wart-covered newts, sparrows with one eye, and hissing snakes coiled beneath rocks. Ruth had been their guardian and chaperone, and she'd let them alone for hours. They were, after all, happiest when together.

If she were not a Frisk or had Andrew's family been better off, she could have kept their baby. But Judith was a Frisk, and Andrew's father, though a respected lawyer, was still far below her own family's standing. Her secret had posed such a virulent threat to their reputation that it had been kept even from her own father. He had no reason to distrust his wife, and she had told him—as she had told everyone else—that Judith was spending the winter in Italy with the same aunt who had gifted her the shadow lantern. Believing that such an experience would surely be edifying, Mr. Frisk had not asked any questions.

As Judith lay in bed and gently stroked her stomach, she supposed that Barrett was likely the place on earth least like Italy. She wondered what her father would say if he knew the truth.

CHAPTER 7

R uth noted the wet that seeped through her boots, soaking her stockings and chilling her toes. The lawn in the garden was green and thick, the rains during the night plumping each blade of grass to its fullest. The late October downpour refreshed Barrett as it washed away the stale sorrow that coated the walls like paint. Judith's mood, however, remained unimproved.

Ruth watched her closely as she paced the garden. Her skin was sallow and the bones of her hands prominent, the dark circles beneath her eyes, deep. Judith leaned down to whisper to her stomach, now rounder and high. When Ruth asked how she felt, she only shrugged. Ruth frowned, concerned.

When she visited, Ruth sometimes brought something with her to distract Judith and remind her that there were places beyond Barrett. She'd brought chocolates once and a newspaper another day. This morning, she carried with her a little toy she'd found at the store across from her hotel. It was a tin soldier painted red, blue, and yellow that marched when wound. Because Judith was the only person she had to give things to, she wanted her to have it, but it was something Alex would have loved. Ruth tucked the toy inside her dress pocket for another time.

When Ruth was not at Barrett, she was alone. For the first time in fifteen years, she was alone. As she sat in her hotel room or walked in the hills behind town, she tried not to think about the past, but the past came anyway. In the forest, alert for the signs of mountain lions and grizzlies, Alex returned to her. He was not her Alex, for she had sacrificed him, and he did not want her as his mother. She didn't blame him. She was not to be forgiven for what she'd done. The priest had told her that Jesus died even for this sin, that the very Son of God had forgiven her. Jesus may have, but Alex had not. Ruth didn't forgive herself, and she didn't think Alex should forgive her, either.

Ruth had something of his still, a piece of his scarf she kept pinned to the inside of her dress. It no longer held his scent, but she knew that he had once worn it around his neck, and this was a comfort. It tickled her skin and sometimes itched.

It has been years since she'd seen him, but now he came each day and night, walking with her and sleeping beside her. Ruth feared that if she reached out to touch him, he would vanish, and so she did not try to hold him. He had been so small when she'd lost him. Even in heaven, he must have wanted a mother.

Her people did not believe in heaven or in Jesus. Ruth's ancestors, her family, did not exist. No Blackfoot man or woman had stepped forward to claim her. A white woman and her husband who reeked of whiskey had brought her up until Alex was born. Then the woman had told Ruth she had to leave her home because she wasn't that kind of woman and what would people think. Ruth had thought she was her mother, which was foolish. Of course she was not her mother. She was short and round with blond hair and green eyes, and she did not love Ruth. Ruth had not loved her, either.

There was one memory of her Indian mother, but it was broken. It was only the smell of her hands, like moss, and the sound her soft shoes made on the floor. It did not even last as long as it took for her to think it.

When she was young, long before Alex, there had been a man. They were related, somehow. Not close like brother and sister, something more like cousins. Caleb. She remembered his long hair and the words he'd spoken in a language she couldn't understand. He'd come to the house every now and then, after she went to live with her white family. They always talked out on the porch, and he brought hard candy with him that tasted like oranges. He was the one who'd told her she was Blackfoot.

When Ruth though of Caleb, it made her wish that Alex could have known him. The house she'd lived in after Alex was born had belonged to him. The last time she'd seen him, he'd given her a key and a few papers and told her that if he passed, she was to have his home. There never was any funeral, but he must have died, because that was where she'd gone when the blond woman told her she had to leave.

Alex was born with grey eyes. When he'd first arrived, she'd been amazed. Her eyes were black. His skin, too, was lighter than hers, more like dry sand than wet. She knew why, but she liked to pretend he was special, magic. Ruth did not want to think about the man who had made those tiny eyes a different shade from hers. She had only been fourteen, but she'd known what to do. She'd put him to her bosom, and he'd sucked until he was so full with milk that it dribbled out of his mouth onto her blouse. Ruth had loved him even before she held him; this was how she knew that he was hers.

Twenty years had passed, and yet even her arms and back remembered his weight. There were times it was as though she'd just set him down for a nap. Judith was her only family now, and Judith's child would not know its mother. Alex had known his mother but would have been better off had he not, if someone who did not drink bourbon and fall asleep midday had raised him. Long, long ago. Ruth did not recognize herself in her memories. The Lord had given her a new life, but there were times she could still taste the old.

She remembered perfectly what Alex looked like after they'd pulled him from the river. She could never forget. For so long, it was all she could see. He was blue and rigid and his mittens were glued to his hands —the mittens she had knitted in one of her rare moments of sobriety. His eyes were open, staring up at nothing, filled with no tears and making no demands. What had he seen as his spirit rose to be with the Lord? Did he wonder where she was, why she had not rescued him from the deadly river? Had he seen her on his way heavenward, unconscious on the sofa with the empty liquor bottle cradled in her arm? Did he call out, even though that freezing water must have stolen his words, his breath, so soon?

Even though it was winter, she had been wearing only a slip. The liquor heated her so that she did not feel the cold. She'd opened the door like this when they'd come with his body—no shame, no sense. She'd been too drunk to save her son, too drunk to be any kind of mother, but she was not too drunk to howl, to scream, to claw at her face and clothes and tear out clumps of her hair.

Most of the women at Barrett looked at Ruth as though they suspected her of something. She thought so often of Alex, she wondered if they could see what she had done. Had the sin seeped through to the surface of her skin? She'd worked so hard to kill the feral girl she used to be, to yield to the pruning of the Holy Spirit, to be more like Jesus and less like herself. When people saw her now, they never would have guessed what she had once been. Her hats were fine, and so were her dresses. She was articulate. She was a new woman, but she was also the drunken girl who had murdered her son.

CHAPTER 8

As a reward for her obedience to house rules, Judith was granted a nightly walk in the garden, which she took every evening without fail, regardless of the weather. The sunless air was bracing, the early stars bright and large. She looked briefly at the moon as she paced the perimeter of the yard. Judith knew that Ms. Wendell watched her from her office window. She heard the tree branches scratch against Barrett's walls and the low music of hardy insects. With each step, the baby within her kicked and wriggled relentlessly. The growing child pressed uncomfortably against her diaphragm, obstructing her breath so that she became winded.

Judith looked down at the path before her and sighed, resting her hands on her stomach. "My darling girl," she whispered, "I'm sorry. I'm so sorry. I've been such a fool, and I've ruined your life. I've ruined my life. I've ruined Andrew's life. Andrew! I'm sorry," she cried out into the night. Covering her face with her hands, she sobbed, overcome with regret and self-pity. "No, I can't. I cannot do this. There is no point" She shook her head vigorously. Her nose ran from her crying and the cold, and she wiped her face with the sleeve of her sweater.

The baby kicked again, and Judith wanted to scream. There was no escape, no reprieve. Facing Barrett, she watched as the inmates inside closed their curtains and turned off their lights. She seethed with hatred for the home, despising it not for its confinement, but for its refusal to allow her to forget her transgression, her stupidity, and the consequences she must endure come February. Impetuously, she picked up a stone and hurled it at the house. It missed glass and hit the brick harmlessly.

Ruined. Sullied. Worthless. Shameful. Her mother's barbed words tore through her mind, inflicting further injury. The walls surrounding the home were tall enough that they could not be scaled, but even if the garden were fenceless, she would not have tried to flee. She was too worn, too hopeless to fight. Judith thought of Ruth and how she always prayed when situations were hard.

"Lord," she began quietly, "save me. I can't do this. I'm only fifteen. I should not be here. I should not be pregnant. Save me! I want to keep my child, but I cannot. I want to marry Andrew, but I cannot! Do *something*. *Help* me!" she pleaded hysterically. She waited, counting the moments, unsure what she expected to happen. Her her meager faith evaporated altogether as no response came. Her anguish mounted.

An angular shadow cast by the full moon dissected her boots and drew her attention upward to the roof high above. It was a much taller building than she'd realized. She counted four stories to the top gables where one of the windows reflected the night's silvery light, signaling to Judith below.

Her crying subsided, and she wiped her face again, her breath calming. There *was* an escape. She could change the ending to her story. She could turn off the lantern show, forever.

Judith's heart thudded in her chest as she considered the possibility. The desperation of her spirit startled her. The depth of her own selfishness was sickening, but the allure was undeniable. It could all be over. She could be with her daughter, in whatever afterlife awaited—heaven or hell or the dark, hushed grave.

Her tears ceased altogether, and a resolve and compulsion unlike any she had ever known overtook her. She needed only to find the staircase to the fourth floor. Judith ended her walk early and climbed into bed without changing or washing. For the first time since arriving at Eleanor Barrett, she slept soundly.

CHAPTER 9

Before the Frisks, Ruth had made hairbrushes for a living. She carved the handles with pretty things the women in town all seemed to like. She never could have afforded to buy one of her own brushes, but the ladies of Great Falls could and did. Ruth had learned to carve while Alex grew inside her. Her hands and mind were so restless then, and she'd discovered in trying to keep busy that she had a gift. It wasn't prideful to say so; it was the truth. God gives everyone gifts to use in His service, and she'd looked at the plain wood and turned it into something beautiful.

Mrs. Frisk had visited her stall one Wednesday afternoon and bought a brush. She thought they were clever. She told her friends about them, and then she'd decided that she also wanted Ruth. She was different, "a novelty," Mrs. Frisk said. She would pay her twice as much as she was making selling her brushes if Ruth would come work for her. But Ruth had said no. She didn't want to work for anyone. This was before Alex was pulled from the river.

After she'd seen his body and knew that she'd killed him, Ruth shut all her doors and windows. She could not feed or bathe herself. She forgot how to speak in any language. She'd finished the bourbon that was left in the house and laid in bed, not sleeping, staring blankly at the ceiling, her feet, the floor. As the alcohol left her body, she shook and sweated. Ruth searched for Alex in her memory, but there she found only a scream. For weeks and weeks, she did not leave the house. She did not change her clothes. When the hunger pains became too great, she ate the food she'd canned that summer.

The priest was the first person Ruth had seen since the policemen. After months of silence, there was suddenly a sound, a loud knock on her front door. It echoed through the house like a clap of thunder. She wasn't sure why she'd opened the door, but she had. Ruth stood behind it, and the stranger walked into her house without a word. She did not say hello, but she'd turned to face her visitor. Too sad to care about her appearance or her stench, she didn't know the man and didn't care if he meant her harm. He was dressed all in black except for a bright white rectangle around his neck. It suddenly occurred to her that this meant he was a priest. He was tall and broad-shouldered with a thick beard and hands like a bear. He looked as though he spent his days cutting down trees in the forest, not on his knees in prayer. When he spoke, Ruth couldn't understand his words, but his voice was low and heavy, soothing. He handed her a bottle of milk and a loaf of bread wrapped in a towel. When she did not reach for them, he set them down in the kitchen. He watched her, said a few more things, and then he left.

Ruth was too lost to think much about him, to wonder about who he was or why he had come. But she did eat the bread and drink the milk and then vomited most of it in the sink. The next day, he'd knocked again. When she opened the door this time, he had a basket of fruit in one arm and a dark leather book in the other, tucked in the crook of his elbow.

It was the second of many visits. He came every day for three months, and each time, he brought food and his book. They sat together through the afternoons, reading together from its pages. He asked her about herself, which no one ever had. Eventually, her tongue was loosened and her words returned. Even though he was a stranger, Ruth told him all that she was and all that she had done. She did not trust the man; she simply split apart, her pain ripping through her chest out into the surprised daylight. She couldn't have stopped the confession had she tried. Each day before he left, he would ask if she was ready to repent of her sin and trust in Jesus. Each time she responded the same, "Jesus doesn't want me, Father."

Until one day, he asked Ruth if she wanted to accept Jesus as her Lord and Savior, and she found that she did. She knew that everything the priest and his book had said was the truth. Ruth had not known she would say yes, but there she was on her knees next to him, praying out loud to God, telling Him how she was a sinner who deserved to burn in hell—which was the sure truth—and asking Jesus to save her. Ruth told Him she knew now that she needed Him, that she needed Him desperately. She cried then, talking to the Lord for the first time, because He showed her He was real and He was good. It was His grace that made her cry out. In her wretchedness, she was too broken to try, to live, to want anything other than to stop breathing. Jesus Himself must have put that hope in her.

The next morning when she'd opened her eyes, nothing looked the same. When she'd gazed out the window from her bed, she'd seen the sun rising, and it meant something more than it ever had before. It meant that God had made her, that God had made the world, and there was a place for her in it.

When the priest visited that day, he'd looked her in the eye. "Yes, indeed," he mumbled, shaking his head. He brought Ruth her own Bible. "Every disciple needs one," he'd said. 'Read it. Read it every day and pray," he told her. "You are God's now, His daughter, and He has His plans for you. You've been bought with the Son's blood. Walk worthy of your calling." She'd taken the heavy book with awe, not understanding most of what he'd said.

They continued to read the Bible together, and Ruth read it on her own as well. She had no formal schooling, and so she read slowly and carefully, soaking up each word. She prayed more than she did anything else. She found she had so much to tell her heavenly Father. She awoke in the night praying to him out of her dreams.

The priest's visits thinned to only twice a week. "You have to go back out into the world," he'd told her. "God calls us to be salt and light. You can't be neither holed up in your room."

The last thing he ever said to her he said after removing the stiff piece of white cardboard at his throat. "Ms. Ruth, all this collar means is that I've given my life completely to God." He'd sighed and looked tired. "You do the same. It don't give me no special powers or authority, and anyone who tells you different don't know what he's sayin'. I figured it all out a little too late, or I might have walked a different road. You remember it ain't about fancy buildings and Ave Marias. Don't get turned around." When she thought of the priest now, Ruth smiled. He'd showed her what it meant to listen and obey and to seek the lost. He'd showed her what humility and love looked like. She still thanked God every day for sending him to her.

It was after he'd stopped visiting that Ruth decided to take Mrs. Frisk up on her offer. She washed herself, gathered her brushes in a basket, and went into town. After months of being away, she set up her stand again in the same old place in front of the post office, and Mrs. Frisk walked by not fifteen minutes later. She barely recognized her. If it hadn't been for the brushes, she wouldn't have known her. Ruth tried to smile, to be pleasing, but her mouth was stiff. She'd forgotten how. She blurted out that yes, she would like to come work for her. Mrs. Frisk was confused, as it had been so long since she'd offered.

"Let me take a moment to compose my thoughts," she'd said, squinting. "I will give you my answer in an hour when I am done with my errands." Ruth waited for her, and when she returned, the answer was yes. "Although your appearance is greatly...*altered*...I still have a need I believe you can fill."

At first, Mrs. Frisk had dressed Ruth up in the latest fashions and had her trail behind her through town. She introduced her to acquaintances they passed, inviting them to speak with her "savage servant." The women were shocked and in awe of Mrs. Frisk's courage to keep such a heathen under her very same roof. They spoke as though Ruth could not understand them. Of course, she had understood every word, but she'd said nothing.

Mrs. Frisk hadn't learned about Alex until after Ruth was already in her employment. She'd feared firing her, lest people think her uncharitable. She'd had no children then. It had been only Mr. and Mrs. Frisk and an echoing household of servants.

But after a few years, Mrs. Frisk gave birth to Judith, and then everything had changed. Her mistress did not know how to be a mother, and Ruth did not want to hold the pink baby. She was afraid she would hurt it, like she'd hurt Alex. But Mrs. Frisk had insisted, and so she'd become the nanny. At first, Ruth hated her new position, and she'd hated Judith because she had soft blankets, because she was alive, because her mother did not drink bourbon, because she was not Alex. She was afraid that if she loved her, she would erase him. Ruth sang her the hymns she'd learned from the priest and made up other songs. She learned that she had a sweet voice because Judith smiled and cooed whenever she sang.

Judith knew nothing of Ruth's past. She did not know that she'd had a son or that she came from ashes, how the Lord had raised her from the dead. She did not want her to know and would never tell her. Even though Judith would also lose her child, even though Ruth could see that Judith was failing, she would never tell.

CHAPTER 10

Having tended to a colicky infant and her exhausted mother through the night, Netty was thankful to have finished her shift. Bone-tired and blurry-eyed, she scarcely heard the footsteps and door creak open far overhead. She put away the bleached sheets she had carried into the linen room, rubbed the small of her aching back, and despite her fatigue, went to investigate. It was too early for any inmate to be awake, and they were not permitted on the fourth level. Yet it was from these forbidden hallways that the sound had arisen.

Netty took each step quickly, lifting her skirt with both hands so as not to trip. When she reached the abandoned floor, she could hear nothing over her own labored breath. She walked forward and was rewarded for her tenacity with the sounding of a single disembodied sob. Netty ran towards the forlorn cry and threw open the door. On her knees was a girl, her head bowed, with one palm pressed against a sealed window.

"What in heaven's name?" asked Netty loudly, alarmed. The girl's head whipped around, startled. "Judith?" she implored.

"It's painted shut," Judith cried, distraught and unconcerned that she had been discovered.

"The window? Yes, they all are. We wouldn't want anyone getting any ideas," she said without thinking. It wasn't until Judith turned and sat with her back against the stubborn window that Netty realized her intentions. "Oh Judith! No! No, my girl." Netty hurried to her side, knelt before her, and took her hand. "It's not as bad as all that, I promise you. You mustn't let the devil play tricks on you, Judith." Netty's eyes were fervent and filled with concern, but Judith stared blankly without emotion. Netty was at a loss. They sat in silence for several moments before Judith finally spoke.

"Please don't tell the matron," she pleaded, "and you mustn't, for any reason, tell Ruth. She'd never forgive me." Judith wiped her cheeks with her slender fingers and attempted to compose herself. "I couldn't have done it regardless, you know. Even before I tried the window, I knew I would never be able to jump from the ledge. I don't have it in me," she said with perverse dejection.

"Well thank heavens, deary. Now, come with me. We have to get you back to your room before anyone sees you're gone." She lifted Judith by the elbow and helped her stand. The girl was spoiled and foolish, but Netty cared for her. She put her arm around her and guided Judith back down the staircase to her room. While Judith sat on her bed, Netty unlaced her boots for her. "Rest now. I'll be right outside your door."

"That's unnecessary," said Judith.

"I'm sorry, Miss, but you must understand if I don't quite believe you." Judith shrugged her shoulders and crawled under the covers.

Netty walked outside and shut the door, exhaling and sitting heavily on a chair in the hallway. Telling no one would be a mistake. She would wait for the Indian and let her know that Judith had tried to take her own life. Her mind raced as she thought on what might have happened if she had not heard those footsteps, if the windows had not been sealed.

Ruth arrived at eight and headed upstairs. She unpinned her hat as she took the steps and thought on how she did not fully trust Ms. Wendell. Rounding the banister, she came upon a softly snoring Netty perched inelegantly on a chair outside Judith's quarters.

"Mrs. Nearbonne?" she said quietly. "Netty?" she repeated, softly touching the woman's arm. Netty's eyes flew open.

"Miss Ruth! Thank goodness!" she proclaimed.

"Has something happened? The baby?" she asked with alarm, brushing past the woman and opening Judith's door. Her pulse slowed when she saw Judith safely asleep in her bed, the mound beneath the blankets rising and falling gently.

"I've been waitin' for you. She's not well, Miss Ruth. Do you know where I found that silly girl earlier this mornin'? I'll tell you where! At the tip-top of this very house about to jump to her death, that's where!" She hissed. "Somethin' has to be done, Miss Ruth. She didn't want me to tell you, but I figured you ought to know."

Ruth sat down heavily on the chair Netty had vacated and covered her face momentarily with her hands. She looked steadily at the wet nurse. "Would she have done it? If you had not been there, would she have jumped?" Ruth felt hollow and defeated. If the truth had not been so conspicuous, she might have tried to deny it.

"She says no, but she's broken, that one—an everlovin' mess. Even though she's got so much more than any of the other girls, she's worse off than them all! I can tell you I've not pulled anyone down from a ledge other than your, your *charge*," she said, struggling to find the right word to describe their relationship. "I don't know what's come over her, but she's sinkin'."

Ruth listened carefully to Netty's assessment. "When I asked the doctor last week, he said she was fine," she muttered crossly to herself, angry that she had listened.

"Dr. Gibbs is a nice man, but he couldn't find chocolate in a candy store. He can't see it because it ain't her body that's sick," said Netty.

Ruth nodded. "She's rotting—she's too still, too confined. She sits all day long with her own thoughts, like a large dog in a small kennel, chasing its tail. What do you expect in a place like this? She's watched after as if she were a lunatic or criminal! She doesn't speak to anyone other than to you and to me, and to the baby. She speaks too often to the baby." The two women stared at one another in silence. "She doesn't want to give her away!" proclaimed Ruth, throwing up her hands in exasperation. "She wants to keep her little girl." Ruth paused. "She can't keep her," she added firmly, as much to herself as to Netty.

"Why not? Why couldn't she?" Netty asked with frustration. "I have six children and enough money for one. If we can manage, so could she."

Ruth sighed and shook her head. They were both quiet. "I wish we had never come here," said Ruth. Netty's eyes opened wide and her face brightened.

"My father-in-law has a cabin, an old miner's cabin. He never found a lick of anythin', not even fool's gold—though heaven knows he was a first-class fool! It's a bit run down, but with a little help, it'll do. He was a far better carpenter than miner." Ruth stared at her blankly, not understanding. "She could stay there!" explained Netty with annoyance. "She'd be out of sight, and I could bring her food," she whispered, conspiratorially.

Ruth raised her eyebrows and tried to hide her contempt for the ludicrous plan.

"No, it's too dangerous," said Ruth, irritated. "And why would you want to do this, why would you want to help?" she asked suddenly, the woman's eagerness perplexing.

"Oh, I don't know. I suppose I have a soft spot for the cast-offs. Does it matter why? I'm willin', ain't I? You have any other offers?

"Where is the cabin?" Ruth frowned. Despite her initial dismissiveness, her curiosity was piqued.

"Past Last Chance Gulch, a few miles or so. There used to be a road, but it washed away years ago. She'd have to go in on horseback, but there's no one 'round for miles." Ruth watched one of the other inmates step fully dressed from her room. She stopped when she saw the two women speaking but then quickly lowered her gaze and headed down the stairs. Ruth thought over the rickety plan. The morning light filling the hallway hurt her eyes and made her head throb. She looked once more at Netty.

"She needs company and happiness, to know that the rest of her life will not be like *this*. She won't find that hiding in the hills. And winter will come soon. What will she do then? She can't stay in a miner's cabin through the winter. She and the baby would freeze to death!" Ruth spat out the last words, exasperated there was no better alternative.

"No," Netty persisted, "she wouldn't. The hut is sealed, and there's a stove. As long as we kept it lit, she and the baby would be right as rain. And for company, she'd have you and me—that's more than her fair share. I know it's not much, but it's somethin'. It's better than all these sad-faced girls and their woeful tales. Mark my words, Barrett is killin' your Judy, Miss Ruth. You can't keep her here."

Ruth had heard enough for the time being. Without saying goodbye or thanking Netty for her generous offer, she abruptly went inside Judith's room, shutting the door behind her.

Netty stood dumbly in the hallway for a moment until her weariness and frustration pushed her towards the exit. She needed to get back home to her own family. She thrust her hands into her apron pockets. "Let them sort out their own mess!" she said aloud, sighing audibly and clucking her tongue.

CHAPTER 11

J udith did not rise when Ruth met her in the garden the next morning. She acknowledged her presence with a furtive glance, but she did not smile, nor did she speak. The front of her dress was dirty, and so were her fingernails.

"Netty was right; you truly are not well," began Ruth, clearing her throat as her voice broke. She was weary and burdened. "You were sleeping when I visited yesterday. I didn't stay because—"

"—Netty swore she wouldn't tell you! I wasn't actually going to go through with it." Judith interrupted, embarrassed and furious. "I do *not* wish to discuss it."

"—And neither do I, Judy." Ruth had not intended to mention their primitive plan, but the words poured forth nonetheless. "It may be time for us to leave this place." Judith looked at her with interest.

"What do you mean? There is nowhere to go. Mother…" she began, her mind stalling on Mrs. Frisk.

"—Netty's family has a cabin. She's offered to let us live in it for the rest of your pregnancy. I wasn't sure if we should until this very moment. I prayed all night, but the final decision is yours. There *is* risk involved. You would be far from a doctor, and it will be *rustic*, to say the least. I would be with you, and Netty would help." Judith scowled and then sat up in her seat, leaning towards Ruth.

"You're serious?" Ruth nodded yes, gravely. The flush that spread across Judith's cheeks was the answer. She smiled for the first time since Ruth could remember. "Fine, then. Take me to the woods!" A thin chuckle escaped her tight chest, and she leaned back again in her seat. How changed she was; a wiry, cynical woman had replaced the young girl Ruth accompanied on the train just a few months before.

"First, I must meet with the matron. Netty will ready the cabin so that it's safe, but it will be another few weeks at least. Until then, you must try to get better. This gloom is not good for you or for the baby."

"There is nothing wrong with me," answered Judith, stubbornly. "I'm happy as a lark," she sneered. Ruth sighed and folded her arms across her chest. She stared at Judith until she fidgeted beneath the scrutiny.

A few other wards wandered out of the house and into the garden, taking a seat at one of the picnic tables near the pond. Their skin was ruddy, their hair unwashed. Ruth frowned. "I will do what I can to make things go quickly," she stated with confidence. A chill spread across her back as a cool breeze picked up and blew loose strands of hair across her forehead. She wrapped her shawl more tightly around her arms. The fall days had already begun their slow decline.

Judith stood up from her chair and took Ruth's hand. "You see, I am better already!" Her reformed countenance was perhaps only partly forced. Dormant joy sparked alive behind her sunken eyes. Ruth patted Judith's hand and spoke softly.

"Judith, even though we are leaving here, you know you must still give your baby to Ms. Wendell, to Barrett." Judith withdrew her hand and turned sharply away.

"Why yes, of course I know it! Do you think for a second that I could forget?" She stood at an angle so that only her cheek and eyelashes were visible. The wind thinned her voice, and the sting of her words was carried away toward the Rockies. Ruth was insistent. She knew she seemed cruel, but it would be crueler still to allow ambiguity. Judith turned on her heels so that she stood but inches from her friend. She stared up into Ruth's eyes with unrestrained animosity. Losing her courage, she looked down at the ground. When she raised her head, her eyes wavered with tears.

"No tears, Judy," said Ruth, touching her lightly under the chin so that she was forced to hold it up. Judith's jaw clenched and her nostrils flared as she fought to suppress her indignation. Her eyebrows raised and twitched with helplessness before she pulled away.

"Fine. Of course you are right. I will do whatever you say. Speak with Netty, please, and I will take better care of myself—I promise."

Ruth put her long arm around Judith's shoulders so that the shawl covered them both. Judith was tense and rigid, but soon the proximity and protectiveness of Ruth's close body relaxed her.

As they traced the garden's edges, Judith grasped this last alternate ending to the eternal lantern show with white knuckles. Her mind had been filled with unholy lies, with poisonous thoughts. She had felt herself twisting, the blood she shared with her daughter growing thick. She had seen thriving trees grow brown and then grey with blight, their sap murky and frozen. Now, there was a small reason to move, to resist that slow petrifaction. It was nothing, this cabin, this scant freedom, and yet it changed everything. She'd only needed the most infinitesimal grounds for hope, for renewed resolve.

The cabin would be a refuge, a place for restoration. While living beneath its humble roof, she might find a semblance of peace; she dared not hope for more. Wilderness would surround her. It would instruct; perhaps its guileless ways would seep into her. Maybe her daughter would learn the sound of flame catching and ice splitting before she was ever born.

CHAPTER 12

R uth delayed meeting with Ms. Wendell. She prayed and waited for the right moment to tell her they were leaving but trusted that she would, in the end, give her permission.

It was close to a month before Netty declared the old miner's cabin fit for occupancy, and she relished every moment of her role in their harrowing escape, sneaking clandestine trips to the cabin in preparation whenever possible. She insisted on doing all the work herself, refusing Ruth's help. Ruth saw how important the task was to her and capitulated, supplying only the necessary funds when an item could not be borrowed.

Netty explained her absence to her family by telling them that Barrett was temporarily short-staffed; she would have to take on more shifts until it was able to hire another wet nurse. Although the deception was distasteful, she spoke it anyway. Her husband's assistance would have been helpful, as he certainly was handy with a hammer and saw, but Netty dared not divulge her secret. Edgar was generally an even-tempered man, but there were certain incendiary topics that sparked his anger and made him unpleasant. She did not think he would approve of her involvement with the fallen girl and her servant, especially when it jeopardized her own livelihood. He would tell her to mind her own business and look to her own family.

When Netty was satisfied and at last agreed to show the cabin to Ruth, the women rode two hours on a Saturday past City Hall, through the narrow Last Chance Gulch, and up into the foothills. Netty prattled on about the town and businesses as they passed by.

Ruth only half-listened, paying attention instead to the terrain and markers she would later need to find her way alone. The crude road ended, and they kicked their horse's ribs to lift them onto the hillside where deer and other game made narrow paths. The women did not bring weapons with them, an oversight Ruth noted and would later correct.

Once they were amongst the trees, it took over an hour to reach the hut. The way was sparsely vegetated, the evergreens tall and old but sporadic. They were almost upon the cabin before Ruth saw it, for its color and angles blended uncannily with the forest and boulders. Her first impression was that it was much larger and sturdier than she'd imagined a miner's hut to be. Edgar's father had indeed been a skilled carpenter.

"Here we are," said Netty, dismounting her horse and leading it to the post she had pummeled into the hard ground the week before. She had paid special mind not to decorate the house's exterior. The repaired shutters covered the blue trim of the interior curtains so that no bright patches would draw the eye. Netty wanted Ruth to know that she had thought of every detail. Holding the door open so that she could see inside without obstruction, Netty stepped aside.

Ruth noticed immediately that the floor did not creak. The boards were dark and smooth from wear. Following the planks to their natural end, her eye met the opposite wall, which was unstained but cut from the same wood. Upon a small nail above the fireplace hung a crude landscape painting. To the right was the kitchen, and to the left were two beds made neatly with triangle-patterned quilts. There were also two windows, both paned with glass, one in the kitchen and one near the hearth. The air in the cabin smelled of the pinewood used in its construction and of the lemon oil recently rubbed into the kitchen countertops. Ruth could not help but smile.

She turned to call Netty inside and found that she had slipped in quietly beside her and stood already in the kitchen.

"Well, will it do?" Netty asked with nervous expectation. She turned the fabric of her dress into a tight knot as she awaited the verdict. Not given to effusiveness, Ruth responded with the truest thing she knew.

"Judith and the baby will be happy here. This is far more than a hut, Ms. Nearbonne." Netty's cheeks flushed with pleasure, and she smiled broadly, finding the pot and pan she had sacrificed from her own home to preoccupy her hands.

"Did you see these? You can fry eggs with 'em, or dough," she said, letting them clang heavily upon the counter. "Those mattresses have fresh straw, and there's firewood stacked outside under the hutch. Everythin' you see works, even better than in my own home!" she declared. "I chinked the logs myself. She'll be comfortable." Netty kicked something with her foot. "There's a bucket for water and maybe for milk, if we can manage. There are dairy cows over the ridge. We might be able to bargain." Netty put her hands on her hips and surveyed the cabin as though it were a palace.

"We should unload the horses," said Ruth, everything left to do at the forefront of her mind. As she untied the saddle bags and carried the food and blankets inside, she thought of the simple life she and Judith would soon enjoy, the improvement in Judith's temperament she hoped to witness. Ruth would take good care of her, and the few cracks between the cabin's logs would let in enough mountain air to revive them each morning. It would be a simple existence, yes—quiet and devotional.

CHAPTER 13

Ruth walked towards the matron's office and steadied her breath, standing outside the cracked door and whispering a prayer. "Lord, give me the words that will move her heart," she said.

There was a small window in the door, but she could not see inside. She avoided it so that Ms. Wendell would not know she was coming until she was ready to enter. She knocked on the door softly, and then because she did not think Ms. Wendell had heard, once more. A muffled voice answered.

"Come in!" Ruth pushed open the door and closed it behind her. "And to what do I owe the pleasure, Miss Ruth?" the matron asked, not altogether pleased to have been interrupted. Her eyes drooped with weariness.

"Good day, Ms. Wendell," said Ruth. The matron motioned for her to sit, and so she lowered herself onto the chair and settled on its front edge. "I would like to discuss Judith."

"—Before you begin, let me be forthcoming," she interrupted, holding up her left hand as she spoke. "I *have* been quite worried about Judith. But these past few weeks, she has rallied. Two nights ago, she actually participated in Bible study! She is just as thin, but her spirits have improved. Don't you agree? I think she may be turning a corner."

"Ms. Wendell, you are a good woman and do these girls a great service here. I will be honest with you," Ruth said. "I have been planning to remove Judith from Barrett and take her elsewhere to wait out her pregnancy." Ms. Wendell sat forward in her seat, resting her elbows on top of the giant book, an expression of consternation spreading across her face.

"Leave Barrett? But whatever for?"

"A month ago, Judith tried to take her own life." Ms. Wendell's jaw hinged open in disbelief. "Frankly, she has only been in better spirits because she knew she would soon leave. Barrett is a fine place, Ms. Wendell, but not for Judith. I am deeply concerned for her and the baby."

"—This is my concern, as well," she interjected, shocked. "Her physical, moral, and *spiritual* wellbeing," she said, her voice tightening.

"Ms. Wendell," said Ruth, "I assure you that I will do everything I can to guard Judith from harm. But she must leave Barrett. May she leave with your blessing?" Ruth asked directly, growing frustrated and not wishing to prolong the conversation. The matron's many concerns flashed across her eyes. "I will not tell her mother," Ruth said. "I vow to you that Mrs. Frisk will not know that Judith has left the home."

"And how can you possibly guarantee such a thing?" she asked. "This is the first I have heard of Judith's alleged suicide attempt, and I am chagrined, to say the least, but I do not know if the answer is for her to leave our sanctuary. It seems rather hasty."

"Ms. Wendell," Ruth said, plainly, "if Judith were to die here, it would go badly for Barrett. Your reputation would not recover. You and your staff misunderstood her sickness, and she nearly jumped from the roof." The matron leaned further forward, analyzing which was the smarter wager.

"Where on earth would you take her?" she asked, needing more information before she could furnish a decision. "It would have to be someplace safe where she would not be seen. Word could not get back to Mrs. Frisk," she said, urgently.

"Yes," Ruth agreed, "the place is secluded. No one will see her. But I don't think I should tell you where. It is better if you don't know." She was careful with what she divulged, not wanting to give Ms. Wendell any further grounds for objection.

"And what if something were to happen with the baby? Or what if Judith needs medical attention?"

"Judith will have everything she needs," Ruth said definitively, not explaining further.

Ms. Wendell removed her glasses and rubbed her eyes.

"Ms. Ruth, it is not our policy to hold anyone here against her will. Habitation at the Eleanor Barrett Home is entirely voluntary. The truth is that were she anyone else's daughter, I would have no reservations. But Judith is a *special* case. Do you know how great a responsibility rests upon my shoulders regarding this girl? I must do everything within my power to see that her time and labor here are successful, Lord willing. We have already bent the rules for your daily visits and in allowing her to give her baby up for adoption. What you are asking now would be granted at an enormous risk to the home, to all the women and girls we help. If anything goes wrong, I will lose my post here, and Barrett will lose a large portion of its funding. Do you understand? I must know that

46

you fully understand what you are asking," she implored.

"Ms. Wendell, I do not ask lightly or without having weighed all possibilities before coming to you. I respect the work you do here, but Judith is my priority. She can't stay here, and we are agreed that Mrs. Frisk must never know. Your risk may be great, but it is nonetheless the right thing to do."

Ms. Wendell stood up abruptly and went to the window, staring through it at nothing for several moments, perturbed. She turned and stepped closer to Ruth, who could see that she'd reached a conclusion.

"Very well," she said with solemnity, "Judith may go. I will be praying for her and for you."

Ruth stood abruptly. "Ms. Wendell, thank you. I *will* keep her safe. And come February, we will still need Barrett to help find a family."

"Ms. Ruth," she said, "we do what we can to find good homes for the orphans, but the truth is that we do not have the resources to look very deeply into the lives of those who wish to adopt. We cannot guarantee anything. It is far better for you to find a couple you know desirous of an infant. At least, then, you will be certain that people with good intentions will raise Judith's child. It is sad to say, but I have seen many cases of neglect, and worse. We live in a fallen world, Miss Ruth, and nowhere is it more present than in the mistreatment of our children. You may bring the baby here if you must, but I would advise against it." The matron clasped her hands behind her back and sighed. Ruth listened and absorbed the warning, her own childhood a dark testament to the truth of her words.

"Thank you, Ms. Wendell. With your permission, I will fetch Judith early tomorrow morning before anyone is awake," she said.

Ms. Wendell eyed Ruth and then stepped forward to walk her to the door.

"I will send the carriage to your hotel at four-thirty. Please use the back entry. I'll leave it unlocked. Barrett is in your hands, Miss Ruth. I hope you are worthy of my trust and able to carry the burden." Ruth nodded and shook the matron's hand, passing into the hallway without looking back. Ms. Wendell watched her turn the corner with a sense of foreboding.

With each step, giddiness replaced Ruth's sobriety. She had never spoken in such a way to anyone in all her life. At Judith's door, she did not bother knocking but threw it open and shut it quickly behind her. Judith lay on her bed in her clothes, staring at the ceiling. Ruth's blood rushed through her ears. She hurried to Judith's side and whispered loudly, "It's done. She said yes! We leave tomorrow." Judy sat up slowly and smiled. Although she knew she should not, Ruth reached out and touched her belly, bringing her head close and whispering. "You are going to a new home! You will be born in the woods!"

Judith looked at her with surprise and then amusement. "Yes, she knows. I told her while I was waiting. I've told her everything." She watched Ruth, tilting her head. "I've never seen you quite so animated," she said without exaggeration. As Ruth's heart quieted, she regained her composure.

"It is good, good news, Judy, and I am very pleased for you," she said. Her face was flushed, and her eyes flared. She stood up and walked to the door. "I will be here before five, and you must be ready. It's a two hour ride to the cabin. You need a good night's rest tonight."

"What is it like? Have you seen it?" Judith asked eagerly. Ruth ignored the question.

"I will help you pack your things now and then be on my way." Judith blinked repeatedly and pulled on Ruth's sleeve, pleading for assurance. "I *have* seen it, and it's actually quite *nice*. Netty has done wonders." Judith took Ruth's arm again and brought her close against her side.

"Thank you," Judith said, exhaling. The two women moved towards the closet and pulled out her trunk, folding and storing all but three dresses that Judith would bring with her. Ruffling through her clothes, Ruth's hand brushed against a hard corner. Her fingers touched a picture frame gently and withdrew. It held a photograph of Andrew. She shut the lid without comment, an aching in her chest. The trunk would stay behind. Ruth kissed Judith on the cheek, squeezed her arm, and left to return to her hotel.

CHAPTER 14

In the dark after supper, Ruth paced the room in her nightgown, braiding and unbraiding her hair, humming to herself. Small doubts began to work their way into her mind. "Ruth!" she yelled aloud, trying to stop her spinning thoughts. The word was uncomfortable in her mouth. She said it again, until it was once more recognizable—a name and not just a sound.

Lowering herself down onto her knees, she thanked the Lord for this chance. She asked for their safe travel and praised Him for his wisdom and goodness. She prayed for Ms. Wendell, too, and asked for forgiveness for the lie she would tell Mrs. Frisk.

She at last packed her things when the dark first gave way. It was time to think of what would come, not what had passed. She said this out loud as well, liking the way it sounded—like a poem. "All things are in His hands," she added, knowing this was also true.

Netty had loaned her two satchels in which to pack her belongings. Her fine clothes had no place in the woods, and so she brought only her boots, work dresses, and winter things—hat, scarf, coat—heavy and thick. The rest would stay behind in a trunk Netty would later collect. At the trunk's bottom was a brush she did not wish to forget. Before Judith had learned to walk, she had grasped and gnawed its handle. Fine imprints from her small milk teeth still marked both sides. It had always stopped her tears. Ruth hoped that it would do the same for her in the coming weeks. She lifted it and put it into the sack in the middle of everything to keep it protected.

Satisfied that she had everything she needed and nothing she did not, Ruth carried her things to the lobby. She gave instructions to the bellman regarding the trunk's retrieval and was relieved to see that the carriage was there just as Ms. Wendell had promised. Because it was the last time she would ride in it, she noticed the tears in the velvet upholstery and the places in the leather walls that were thin and white. Surely countless women had ridden in these seats, clutched the handles to steady themselves, perhaps cried onto the dirty floor. Ruth put on the veil as the horses' shod hooves clanked on the hard ground. She imagined the puffs of dust they must be kicking up, the clouds that hung around their wooly feet.

Watching the moonlit Helena streets, everything and everyone in the city seemed still. In the fields not far away, the farmers and ranchers were awake. They were dressed and bent over their work, but here, she and the driver were the only people in motion. As was their custom, no pleasantries were exchanged. The metallic jangle of the carriage and its wheels turning spoke for them both.

When they pulled into Barrett's driveway, Ruth did not wait for the driver to help her with her bag. Netty had arranged for the horses to be tied nearby, and Ruth trusted that they were there without checking. It was long before the girls would wake, and the sky that touched the roof and walls of the house had not yet begun to yellow. She walked around the home to the back door the matron had left open and stepped softly inside.

The house smelled of breath and wood polish. Ruth passed a vase of tea roses, their pleasant fragrance masking the scent of women sleeping. With one foot on the bottom stair, she looked up to find Judith waiting at the top. She was poised and ready, holding her own soft satchel over her shoulder. When their eyes met, they smiled like two little sisters causing trouble. Ruth waved her down, and Judith descended eagerly, taking each step lightly. Ruth heard only her dress slipping over each step's carpeted edge.

She took Judith's hand as she stepped onto the main floor and kissed her cheek. As they passed it, Ms. Wendell's office door latched shut, causing both women to jump and scurry towards the exit. Ruth could not help but look over both her shoulders before she led Judith back out the door. They walked quickly until they were almost running. Once they were past the driveway, they did not care about the noise they made. Ruth glanced back and saw that Judith was holding her belly, as though it might drop without the support, and that she was giggling. Ruth laughed, too, because they had done it. They had escaped! And it had been so easy, like taking off clothes or swimming on a hot day.

Judith did not bother Ruth with questions. She trusted that she knew the way and had everything in order. As they came into view of the horses, the animals whinnied and snorted at their approach. The one Ruth had ridden before angled its ears towards her and sniffed the air carefully. She whinnied again and stamped her foot. Ruth took Judith's bag from her and dropped it inside her horse's saddlebag. Then she knelt down to help her climb into the saddle. Judith was heavier than Ruth expected, and she nearly toppled over from her full weight on her shoulder.

Once Judith had settled on her horse, Ruth climbed easily onto her own seat. She clucked once with her tongue and then squeezed her mare's ribcage with her heels, lunging forward. They were on their way.

Ruth looked back at Judith over her shoulder and nodded to her for reassurance. Judith looked strong on horseback, like a warrior, and Ruth was proud of her for her bravery. They did not dare to speak as they rode. Judith smiled with her mouth closed, staring straight ahead at the flanks of Ruth's horse.

As the sun prepared to glow across the prairie, they watched smoke spirals rise into the graying sky. Ruth could not see the chimneys, but she knew that someone had lit each one and now stood before it, warming his hands and face. She breathed and could see her breath. There were clouds of steam around the horses' mouths, too. The end of the year was eating up the warm air completely—a hungry man licking his plate.

They climbed the hill easily, and Ruth spotted a single robin on a branch above her head. It did not fly away as they passed but cocked its head stiffly and chirped. The robin would surely tell its robin friends of the strange sight he'd witnessed.

At the top of the hill, before they walked along the ridge and descended along the back of Helena, they paused to take in a last glimpse of the city. It had been months since Judith had been beyond the Barrett walls, and the shock of the world hit her full in her chest. Frozen parts of her spirit thawed at the sight, at the warmth of the lives below just barely touching her own. Her face showed her hunger for contact, for conversation and society. Her eyes were sad for the first time that morning, but Ruth let her think of those things she missed without interruption.

When she had seen enough, Judith turned her horse from the view. Ruth lead the way along the ridge until there was a dense patch of trees. This was where they would dare to enter Helena, under the cover of the forest and the dim morning. They would not be long in the position, only a quarter of an hour.

Once they were on the hillside between the trees, the horses relaxed. Their ears did not point so far forward, and they ceased their vigilant rotations. There was no evidence of man other than a few leftover strands of barbed wire, so brittle and orange that Ruth's horse stepped on one and it snapped. The rusty metal was the color of the clay and sank into it, surrendering to its fate, she thought how everything that falls, the earth eventually consumes—leaves, bones, flesh, regrets and dreams, blood and tears.

Ruth considered the men who once lived on the mountain, those who struck it rich and those who lost everything. Backs hunched, tunneling like moles—digging, digging, sifting. Looking in the earth for treasure seemed to come naturally. It was something a body knew how to do, eyes knew how, and fingers, too. Ruth imagined herself as a miner, hat on, wading in the river, chipping away at ugly rocks.

"Ruth," said Judith from behind her, interrupting her thoughts. She realized Judith must have said her name many times before she'd finally heard. "Why did you never marry and have children?" she asked without warning. There was an ache in Ruth's lower back and then it knotted. She was glad Judith could not see her face. Had she guessed? Had she heard gossip of her past? Had she always known and been too polite to say?

"I was not made for motherhood," Ruth finally said.

"Nonsense! Look at how you've always taken such good care of me!"

"You have only known me in my later years," she said. She turned around in her saddle, grasping it with her left hand to twist. "I wanted a child, but it was not God's will." Ruth spoke these words slowly and with a low voice so that Judith would not press further. Ruth did not want Judith to know that she had been given a son, and that she'd lost him as though he were a pair of stockings. Judith should not know that such things happened every day.

Judith frowned, and Ruth saw sympathy in her eyes. She was sorry for her that she'd never had a family, but she did not say it out loud. Judith knew that pity would only embarrass her. Instead, she looked to the side and then down at her horse's mane. She leaned forward, rubbed it high on its cheek, and said something Ruth couldn't hear. In the breeze, her voice was thin and sounded like a bird's whistle.

The rising sun entered the trees behind them. The hair of Judith's horse suddenly turned orange, and her own dark tresses, rose and gold. Ruth sucked in her breath, savoring the moment in the quiet morning when Judith was with child—safe, smiling, radiant.

The sun warmed the pine needles, and their scent strengthened and wafted. The invigorating smell revived the band of travelers. Judith hummed a hymn Ruth had taught her as a child, and Ruth sang out the words whenever she remembered their place in the melody. Her horse whinnied, wanting to praise the Lord, too. And then, before she thought they should be, they were there.

CHAPTER 15

Standing before the cabin door, Judith noticed there was no knob, only a simple wooden latch. She let Ruth unload the horses and did not offer to help. She wanted to see inside alone. For Netty and Ruth's sake, she wanted to like it.

She lifted the latch and pushed open the door. It was dark inside, and the only light that entered the room came from the doorway and the little cracks between the logs. Judith took a step back outside and found the shutters she hoped were there. Quickly, she opened them, and squares of light replaced the tiny flames.

The blue of the bedspread hit her vision first. With a single sweep of the room, she saw immediately that it was tidy, functional, and warm. The few metal objects—a teakettle on the stove, the handle on a kitchen utensil, a tin next to the fireplace—spangled sunlight.

"It is *perfect*!" she said, swinging round to face Ruth, who stood behind her now. Judith's exuberance flapped like a flag. She turned back around and darted further inside the cottage, plopping heavily on the corner of the bed and kicking her feet up until she fell backwards.

Ruth saw that the stack of firewood outside was modest; a late fall afternoon like this would be perfect for chopping wood. Leaving Judith to explore on her own, she dragged the fallen trees small enough to carry across the soft loam of the forest floor. Propping the first on the stump kept in the ground for this purpose, she dislodged the axe buried in its rings. It had been over fifteen years since Ruth had last chopped wood, but her arms knew the motion and rhythm still. The blood flowed to her hands that were so often cold, and her heart pumped vigorously. She raised the axe high and brought it down across the body of the tree, severing it into small logs. After having sat for so long in the saddle, the strain and stretch in her shoulders and back was a relief.

By the time the wood was gathered and chopped, the moon had risen half way in its course. Judith went inside when the sun set and worked on starting a fire. It was her first, and she struggled to make it catch. When Ruth joined her, she had succeeded only in creating a plume of thick smoke. She looked up at Ruth with exasperation, her cheek streaked with soot and her hands filthy. A pile of discarded matches was stacked on the floor beside her. "It won't light! This God-forsaken wood won't catch!" she complained. Ruth removed her gloves.

"Watch your tongue, young lady! Step away; it's bad for you to breathe all that smoke. Do you want me to do it?" Ruth pulled her back by her shoulder.

"No, just tell me how," she said with determination. Ruth knelt by her side and arranged the logs in the shape of a teepee.

"Like this—you need the space below or you will smother the flames," she explained. "There's no kindling. You need smaller pieces to light first."

Ruth stood up and disappeared outside for a moment, returning with a handful of needles and twigs. She handed them to Judith, who spread them around the base of the logs.

"Try now." She leaned back to allow Judith the room to maneuver. She struck the match against the cobblestone and placed it gently into the nest of kindling. The needles caught immediately and glowed red, followed next by the wood. Ruth showed her how to blow gently at the right moment to fan the flame. Within a few minutes, the logs had caught and filled the hearth with a snapping fire. With pride and satisfaction, Judith sat back on her heels and held her stomach. She watched the fire contentedly and smiled at Ruth before reaching to find her hand. She squeezed it once, gently, and then released it.

The evening passed in silence. Ruth prepared a stew from the ingredients in their small pantry, and they sipped it on the floor near the fire. Ruth saw her own contentment reflected in Judith's rosy cheeks. The baby kicked and Judith swallowed her soup.

"She likes it here, Ruth. She likes it very much." Judith hummed while she ate and rocked herself from side to side. Neither Ruth nor Judith changed out of their traveling clothes. They fell asleep on top of the covers smelling of horses, the air warmed by the fire and their own close breath.

CHAPTER 16

There in the woods, the Lord was with them strongly. His Spirit filled the cabin, choosing Ruth's words for her, comforting Judith whenever she was afraid. Ruth did not see Him, but He was there, as surely as she was, and He was at work. There was much to do; both He and Ruth knew it. She prayed aloud continuously for a safe delivery, for a healthy child, for their survival through the winter. She prayed for Judith's soul. Sometimes, Ruth talked to Alex, but never out loud. She spoke to him in her heart, like God spoke to her.

The Lord had made everything she saw through their small window. He'd made the snow and the trees, the mountains and winter. The Lord delighted in His creation, but sometimes Ruth did not. They often heard wolves howling, and one morning, the backside of a brown bear loped over the ridge. She was thankful that they had packed the rifle.

She picked up the weapon and checked to make sure the round was still in the chamber, setting it back against the wall when she saw that it was. Her mind drifted ahead to Christmas, which would be here in only a week. It was the only Christmas they would all have together, the only one Judith would spend with her daughter, and so she wanted it to be memorable. Judith was accustomed to lavish gifts and to eggnog, to feasts and parties, but this year would be different. They had no expensive presents, no goose, no crystal glasses, galas or waltzes. But Netty would arrive the next day, bringing with her a few special things Ruth had asked her to buy.

While Judith napped after supper, Ruth snuck outside and chopped down a young tree she'd spotted a few days before. It was nearly dark, and the cold made her fingers stiff. She blew hot air into her fists to keep the blood moving and used some of the firewood to make a stand. She set the tree in the corner of the cabin and waited for Judith to wake.

Now that winter had taken hold, they kept the stove burning throughout the days and evenings. Ruth fed it a few more logs and sat on the hearth so that her front became hot to the touch. Judy lay on her right side, and Ruth could see the hump of her hip, shoulder, and cheek. The blanket was wrapped tightly around her body, and her breath was steady. The boots she'd forgotten to remove peaked out from the blanket and hung a foot off the end of the bed.

When Ruth went for walks on the mountainside, there was history in her legs. It came up through the ground, through the bottom of her boots. She'd sewn fur to them, wrapping them in the pelts Netty had brought to help insulate their feet from the cold. Ruth had never felt so much like a Blackfoot. With her furry boots strapped into snowshoes, she walked on top of the snow and thought of Jesus walking on water, of how Peter had dared to join him there. Her miracle boots sat now in front of the stove to dry.

Judith stirred and then opened her eyes without Ruth noticing. The small Christmas tree she'd chopped came into focus. "Ruth," she exclaimed, "it's perfect! We must think of a way to decorate it." Ruth did not want to spoil the surprise, so she just smiled. Judith crawled to the foot of the bed to touch Ruth's shoulder. "Thank you!" she said, kissing her friend's cheek and rising slowly from the bed.

The following morning, Ruth collected snow to melt and prepared a breakfast of oats and tea. Judy was too busy thinking of ways to decorate the tree to suspect anything.

"We have wool," she suggested, "we could tie different colored bows on each branch."

"We don't want to waste the yarn," Ruth replied, delaying. The unmistakable jangle of a horse's tackle and hooves sounded beyond the cabin walls. Ruth sat in her chair and pretended not to notice, but before long, they both heard Netty's voice, loud and high on the other side of the door.

"Open up," she yelled, "It's Mrs. Claus!" Judy laughed and threw open the door and jumped on Netty before she could even put down what was in her arms. Her large belly hit before the rest of her, and Netty smiled. "You are gettin' as round as the moon, my girl!" she said, laying her palm on Judith's stomach.

"I know," she said. "I'm fatter than I ever thought possible!" She laughed. Ruth stood up and greeted Netty with a smile. They did not hug, but she was happy to see her.

"Ruth," she said, "you look well. It seems you are both takin' good care of the other."

"—What do you have there, Netty? What did you bring?" Judith interjected, unable to contain her curiosity.

"Help me with the rest, Miss Ruth, and I'll show you. Judith, promise you won't peek while we're outside," she teased. Judith promised reluctantly, and Ruth went with Netty to unload the last two satchels from her horse. The day proved warmer than the previous, and the light was so bright she had to squint to see. The snow crunched beneath their feet and fell in great clumps from the thawing trees.

"The cabin is warm enough?" she asked. "Everythin' is holdin' up?"

"Yes," Ruth said, "everything is just fine."

'The snow ain't gettin' to you? It's a heapin' lot of snow early this year, but at least it's not as cold as it might be. You've been lucky with the weather."

"Did you bring the things I asked?"

"Of course! They're in this one here," she sniffed, lifting up the bag in her right hand. "And I have everythin' else as well. Don't you worry, Ms. Ruth. I have a mind like a vice. And I wrote it all down, too," she winked, "in case the vice snaps."

"Well, you two, what is all this?" Judith was impatient and excited. She looked like she had on Christmas Eve when she was five. Netty handed the sack to Ruth who opened it up and peered inside so that Judith couldn't see its contents. She pulled out a plain paper bag. Judith looked confused.

'It's corn kernels! We're going to pop corn and string the tree with it! And it looks as though there is enough here to have some to eat after."

"—There's butter, too, and ham," Netty interrupted, "and I brought some of my famous applesauce. You can't have Christmas without ham and applesauce!" Judith's eyes were glassy she was so happy. She rubbed her belly and smiled incandescently.

The friends spent the next few hours popping the corn, decorating the tree, and listening to Netty's stories of town. Most of her tales involved people they did not know, but she told them everything as though they did. Things at Barrett were the same. The matron still did not know Netty had played any part in their leaving. Her youngest had come down with a bad cough. She couldn't stay too long because she had to get back to him and didn't want to travel after dark.

"There's one thing more," she said, "a surprise for you both for that wee little tree there." She fetched one of the satchels, pulled something out, and put it behind her back. "My girls made it, and I thought it might bring some cheer." They were both eager to see what it was. She passed it around to her front and set it in Ruth's hands. It was a star for the top of the tree. "Well, do you like it?" she asked.

"Oh, Netty, it's beautiful!" said Judith. She immediately stood up and hugged Netty.

Ruth wanted Netty to know she also liked it, but she wasn't sure what to say. "Yes, thank you," was all she managed. Netty laughed loudly, and Ruth didn't know why. Judith came closer and leaned over to better see the star.

"It's paper maché, real delicate," Netty explained. It was gold-colored and sparkled with glitter. "There is a hole cut in the top—for the candle flame," she said. "I could only get one candle, but it should last the next few days if you're careful." Netty knew her gift had been well received, and she beamed with delight.

"Well, then," she said suddenly. "I wish I could stay longer, but I must be off." She hit the skirt of her dress to shake out any dust and kissed Judy on the cheek, holding her hands tightly. "Listen to Miss Ruth. She can be a bossy one, but she knows what's best. Most of the time." Netty winked as Ruth turned her head away and pretended not to hear.

She walked out with Netty to her horse while Judith stayed inside. "I don't think I can make another trip before she delivers. I won't be back until it's time," said Netty.

"That may be for the best," Ruth told her. Judith wasn't due until early February, and Netty certainly couldn't stay weeks with them on the mountain, waiting. Unless Ruth went into town herself, there would be no way to get a message to her. She couldn't leave Judith alone, and so she'd been praying about the arrangements. "I think you should return the tenth of February," she said. "Judith may have already gone into labor, but if not, then it will be soon. Will you be able to stay then?"

"Can't say for sure, but I'll do my best. But whether or not I'm here, she shouldn't have too much time with the baby after she's born." Netty looked Ruth in the eye, and she nodded in agreement.

"Thank you, Netty," she said. "We could not have done this without you." She looked at the ground and then at her horse.

"Ah, it ain't much of a thing," she said awkwardly, caught off guard. She quickly changed the subject. "In the one bag we didn't open are a few things for the labor, in case anythin' should be hard. I would'a shown you, but I didn't want to worry Judith. There's a book in there, too. A science book nurses use." She leaned in close to Ruth. "I stole it from the library at Barrett. Don't tell anyone." She winked again and Ruth stared. "Well, goodbye then. I'll see you February tenth," said Netty, mounting her horse.

Although she was short and small, she lifted herself easily onto the animal's back. It stepped forward and shuffled until she pulled firmly on the reigns. "One more thing," she said, "I might have found a mother." Netty kicked the horse and turned around without saying more, leaving Ruth with a thousand questions.

A mother. Another mother for Judy's baby. The mare walked slowly back the way it came until she could no longer hear its heavy hooves in the snow. She would be the only mother Judith's daughter ever knew.

Perhaps this was the answer to her prayers. She heard an owl's sad hoot and found it remarkable than any of God's creation could survive such a winter. Walking back through her own tracks, she stomped her feet on the planks in front of the door. She could hear Judith singing as she arranged things in the kitchen.

CHAPTER 17

The ham and applesauce on Christmas were so sweet. Ruth and Judith ate everything Netty had brought, saving only a thin rectangle of butter for later. Judy put the star on top of the tree and managed to hold the candle in place with wire. There was a star shadow on the floor that reached across to the tips of their feet, and a star on the ceiling, too. Ruth told her about signs from God, the star of Bethlehem and the three magi, about Jesus being born into the world to save them all. Judith nodded, the familiar story having lost its impact long ago. Ruth didn't understand how it was possible or why God would even bother. When she looked at most people or her own reflection, she did not see much worth saving.

When the moment seemed right, Ruth retrieved her gift from its hiding place and put the package on the table in front of Judith. It was wrapped in a scarf, and Judith thought this was the present. "No, there's more," Ruth explained. "Open it." She sat up straight and unwrapped the surprise. When the scarf was free, she wound it around her throat.

"So warm!" Judith said, smiling, staring down at the wooden box that Ruth had carved in secret.

"Slide open the top," Ruth told her, demonstrating how with her hands. Judith pushed down and slid it back. The tracks were smooth but tight, and it did not open easily. Ruth watched her carefully for her honest reaction. She did not reach for the brush at first, but tentatively, she lifted her arm and touched it gingerly with her fingertips, like Ruth had touched the picture of Andrew she'd found hidden in her trunk. Judith knew exactly what it was and what it meant. It was one of Ruth's finest creations—made from basswood, the handle carved with two intertwining birds. The bristles were boar's hair and stiff. She remembered it well.

60

Judith loosened her hair and handed Ruth the brush.

"Will you, please?" she asked. When she was a little girl, Ruth had brushed Judith's hair before bed each night. Judith would tell her everything that had happened that day, what scared her, what new thing she'd seen and didn't understand. Judith's hair had become so thick with the pregnancy, so shiny. Ruth brushed it gently and hummed Silent Night. Just as when she was small, Judith began to talk.

At first, her words were about Andrew. She still didn't use his name, but she confessed that she missed him, that she regretted he would never know they had a child.

"Ruth," she said, "I think he would be happy to know it." Her voice and lips quivered, and then everything fell out. She was how Ruth had been with the priest, saying all that had been in her heart the past months. Ruth kept brushing and listened. "I don't want to do this!" Judith cried. "I don't want to do this!" she yelled louder, shaking her head vigorously. "I will never forgive my mother for this. I hate her. I know it's terrible to say, but I do. I hate her. After I abandon my daughter, I will die. I will die!" she wept. "And I will see him there. At some point, I will see him. How will I pretend? For the rest of my life, I will be pretending. And I will always wonder about my little girl." Ruth put down the brush and turned Judith's face to her, cupping it with her hands, making Judith look her in the eye.

"Hush," she whispered. "Judy, Shhhh. It is too much, I know. Far too much. Shhhh." Ruth folded her inside her arms as best she could. She rocked her back and forth as her wailing subsided, her own body absorbing and muffling Judith's cries, until she was quiet. Ruth lead her over to her bed and tucked her in. Judith did not protest.

"Thank you for the brush, Ruth," she whispered. Her voice was hoarse. "It is the most precious thing. I will keep it always. Thank you." Ruth kissed her on the forehead and told her to rest. She cleaned up their supper and prayed while she washed the dishes. There were tears in her eyes, too, but the Lord reminded her of all the women in the Bible who had given up their children, how sometimes He called people to hard things. "I know, Father, I know. Nothing is impossible with You. She needs You, Lord," she told Him over and over, as if He didn't know.

CHAPTER 18

Winter took a firmer hold in January, and the new year arrived bashfully without note. The snow fell more often and with greater fury. The dark was longer than the light, and day after day, a layer of gray obscured the sun. Ruth read for hours at a time. Sometimes Judith looked over her shoulder and read a few sentences as well.

Judith developed several games to pass the time. Most involved counting—sounds outside the door, Ruth's coughs, the number of cracks in the wood of the cabin, or how many times the baby kicked in an hour. When this became tiresome, Judith worked on a letter to Andrew or ventured outside for a brief walk. The weather, though comparatively temperate for a January in the Rocky Mountains, was still bitter.

It had not snowed for three days, and Judith decided to take the opportunity for some fresh air and exercise. The last time she had been out for a walk, she'd noticed the beginning of a new path Ruth had shoveled leading up the hill behind the cabin. She bundled herself with as many layers as she had, fastened her snowshoes, and threw a wool blanket over her shoulders. She would be visible from their doorstep in almost every direction, and so Ruth didn't worry. Despite the harsh conditions, the exertion was good for the girl.

When Judith first stepped outside, she recoiled from the cold. It was difficult to catch her breath. She trained herself to inhale only through her nostrils so that the air entering her lungs was warmed. Drifts hugged the trunks of the trees, making them appear shorter than they were. Had it not been for Ruth's diligence, their home would have been pressed from all sides with snow as high as the windows.

Staying close to the cabin, she walked around the side to the back. Keeping one hand on the building for balance and one hand on the blanket around her shoulders, she took careful and small steps. Despite the snowshoes, she periodically sank. The beginning of the path was soon beneath her feet, and she waddled up it with gladness, happy for the easier route. She found the frosty air that kissed an exposed sliver of her neck vivifying rather than nettlesome. Judith's spirits were high. She shuffled her way up the gradually sloping hillside and watched for any signs of life. Every few feet, she stopped to listen and survey the white landscape reposing in all directions. There was nothing—only the occasional movement of branches and twice a falling pinecone.

Ahead she saw a line of square pegs and studied it until determining it was the top of a buried fence. Netty had mentioned there were cattle in the area. The fence skirted the top of the low ridge, and although the path ended abruptly where she now stood, she wished to see the view beyond it. She glanced back to the cabin below, which was still visible and large. Judith forged on towards the fence.

Close enough now to reach for the bits of post that showed above the snow line, Judith put out her hand to pull herself up the rest of the way when a loud crack exploded behind her. Startled, she turned abruptly and lost her balance. Flailing her arms, she twisted and threw herself towards the fence to prevent a fall down the hillside, landing face-first in the snow.

Judith rolled to her side and lay there, stunned. Luckily, the snow was soft and deep and had cushioned her fall. The noise had sounded like a gunshot. It must have been fired miles away, the blast carried far by the hollow valley and mountain peaks. Her heart beat rapidly; she'd had a start. She put her feet beneath her and stood up slowly, using her arms as counterweights. When she was fully upright, she reached down to pick up the blanket that had fallen, shook it out once, and put it back around her shoulders. The fright of the gunshot and her fall eroded her bravery, and she decided it was best to head home. She did not turn around, and so she did not see the red drops of blood that trailed behind her on the snow.

The moment Judith fell, Ruth was not near the window. She was making their beds and did not know that anything had happened until Judith returned, her front still caked with clumps of white. They clung to the wool threads with determination and would not be deterred by her forceful shakes.

"I fell!" Judith blurted out, laughing as she said it, lifting her hands in a gesture of confusion.

"Are you all right?" asked Ruth, moving towards her quickly, concerned. She stripped the blanket from the girl's shoulders, dropped it on the floor next to the door, and unfastened her snowshoes. "Is the baby all right?"

"Yes, we're both fine. I made quite the spectacle up there in my furry boots and snowshoes, as pregnant as the moon! It was that gunshot that startled me. Did you hear it?"

"Yes. Here, take off your things." Judith obeyed, insisting all the while that she was fine.

"I told you, it was only a little spill into soft powder!" Ruth removed her coat and her scarf and then her three sweaters, leaving her in her dress, stockings, and boots. Judith could not reach her own feet to untie the laces, and so she sat down on the chair and allowed Ruth to undo them.

Ruth sat back suddenly on her heels. "There is blood on the floor, and on your dress!" she said, pointing to a dense, red circle on her left thigh. "And all over the blanket!" Judith grasped her stomach in panic. There on the dress where she had touched was more blood. "It's your hand!" said Ruth, grabbing it with both relief and alarm. Judith looked down and saw a hole in the palm of her mitten. It was black, and the blood did not show much against the fabric. Upon closer inspection, the red of her wound was vivid.

"What in heaven's name?" she asked, bewildered. They both stared at her hand, which continued to bleed into the mitten and down her arm.

"We need to remove it," said Ruth. She stood quickly and went to the kitchen to fetch the shears. "Keep your hand up, like this," she said, showing Judith. Ruth put the blades at the base of the mitten and snipped along the back of the hand, away from the cut. When she had split it completely in half, the wool clung to the front of Judith's palm, the blood acting like glue. Without warning, Ruth ripped it off, tugging at the wound and making Judith cry out.

"Come with me," she said, taking Judith by the arm and leading her into the kitchen. "We must rinse it clean." They went to the basin, and Ruth poured water from the pitcher on the wound, wiping away the debris and blood. Judith winced from the pain, and Ruth assessed the harm. "It's not large. Hands bleed more than they should." Relieved, they both smiled. Ruth kissed Judith on the forehead. "I will get some cloth to wrap it. Stay here."

Judith looked down at the wound and became lightheaded. She had never seen so much blood, and with her attention, her hand now throbbed fiercely. She did not want to complain, and so she did not speak of the soreness.

"Once," said Ruth, "I stepped on a piece of glass and didn't see the gash until I tracked red footprints across the carpet. And the cold, the cold numbs the pain." Judith wanted to sit down, but she stood where Ruth told her to, using her right hand to grasp the forearm of her left and keep it above her heart.

"Here, this will have to do," she said, bringing over a rag she used for dusting. It was thin and worn, and she tore it easily with her teeth into three strips. She folded one into a small square and left the other two long. Ruth rinsed the cut once more with the water and then dried it with her apron, covering the wound with the first strip, and using the other two to hold the first in place.

"It must have been the fence," explained Judith, thinking back to her fall. It was the only explanation.

"Which fence?"

"Up at the top of the hill behind the cabin. When I fell, I reached for it. There must have been a nail or some wire."

"Come here and lie down. Your hand will heal, but you've had a shock. Why don't you rest until lunch?" Ruth led her now over to the bed and removed her dress. "I'll wash these," she said, gathering them into a tidy bundle. She lifted the covers so that it was easier for Judith to get into bed. She closed her eyes and tried to ignore the pain.

"It is so soon, Ruth. The baby will be here so soon. If she comes early, maybe even tomorrow, or the next day!" she whispered with her eyes still closed. It was the end of January, and Judith was right; her labor could begin at any time.

"Rest now, Judith. Don't think about it. The baby will come when God decides. Go to sleep."

CHAPTER 19

J udith's hand scabbed over and the pain dwindled, but it remained red and swollen. She no longer ventured outside except to walk in small circles at the base of the stairs. They waited expectantly for the tenth of February, but the day came and went, and neither labor nor Netty arrived. Judith was too tired, too swollen and achy to worry, but Ruth paced in front of the fire, stepping towards the door at every sound.

When Netty did not arrive on the eleventh or the twelfth, Ruth became worried. "Where could she be?" she asked out loud, throwing up her hands in frustration. She had come to trust the woman but had begun to doubt the merit of her faith.

"Do you think her husband found out, or the matron? Do you think something is wrong?" asked Judith from her seat in front of the fire. She clumsily knitted a hat for the baby and tried not to think ahead to the next day.

"I, I don't know." Ruth stood in front of the kitchen window and looked out at the familiar view. She knew every tree, every branch. "We should pray for her." Ruth went to Judith's side and knelt down on the ground, bowing her head. Judith bowed her head as well. "Heavenly Father, please protect Netty. She was supposed to be here two days ago, and we are worried. Clear her path and bring her to us." Ruth stood, calmed. "There's nothing we can do. It's in the Lord's hands."

"—That's what you said about my baby." Ruth glanced down crossly at Judith.

"It's true in both cases. Finish your hat."

Neither woman was hungry, and so they did not sit down to supper until well after the sun had set. Judith's stomach turned, and Ruth had simply lost her appetite. Netty's failure to adhere to their plan had revealed just how dependent upon her they truly were. Ruth lay the plates on the table, deep in thought. She had delivered Alex without assistance, but there had been no complications. What if something went wrong? She'd studied the book Netty had left, but reading and doing were different things.

A knock at the door interrupted her thoughts. Both Ruth and Judith saw that it was already dark. Netty would not be traveling at such an hour. Ruth reached for the rifle, but before she could raise the barrel, the door swung open. A leather hat and long brown coat flew inside.

Confused and alarmed, Ruth held tightly to the rifle butt, raising it to her shoulder and squinting her eyes in the dim light of the stove.

"Netty!" cried Judith with tremendous relief. Their intruder shut the door, shaking off her coat and hanging it on one of the pegs.

"I didn't recognize you. I could have shot you!" said Ruth. Netty's antics did not amuse her, and she awaited an explanation for her tardiness.

"They're Edgar's. They're warm. In case you didn't notice, it's dark and awfully cold out there." Netty plucked her gloves from her small hands and stepped out of her boots. "Let me near that fire," she said, moving closer to it and rubbing her hands in its warmth. She leaned down to kiss Judith on the cheek. "So I'm not too late!" she said, pleased.

"Where have you been?" Ruth asked. "And why are you out at this hour?"

"—Did something happen? Did someone find out?" added Judith. Netty looked down at her hands and turned once more to face the fire.

"No, but my husband had to go to Butte suddenly, and I couldn't find anyone to watch the children. It's a mercy he left. He won't be back for a week, and my sister is at the house now."

Judith leaned back in her chair and listened to the fire. She tried not to let her pain show. An hour before, she'd begun to feel a strong tightening across her back and sides. There had been five more, and now a sixth, building and subsiding, painful yet manageable. She closed her eyes and concentrated on keeping her face still. She was not ready. Judith wanted to keep her child inside her, safe and close. There was another deep clenching; it could be nothing other than a contraction, but she dare not name it aloud. The pain reached its pinnacle and receded.

"Netty," began Ruth, "what of the mother? The woman you'd mentioned before?" Netty eyed Judith before answering Ruth, surprised that she would ask the question in front of the girl.

Judith felt suddenly nauseous. She closed her eyes.

"What is she like?" Judith asked hoarsely, in a whisper. "Tell me about her." Netty did not answer immediately. She sought Ruth's permission, who gave it with a nod.

"She's French but married a German. She has one child already, a boy. She sometimes helps at Barrett, lookin' after the girls when they've had their bairns. She's a good worker. I like her very much. I think you would, too. Her name is Marie."

"Why does Marie want my daughter?" Judith asked, the question making them uneasy.

"I don't rightfully know. She wants another child. She must not be able to have any more of her own," said Netty, shrugging her shoulders. There was another contraction, and Judith winced perceptibly, sucking in air. "What is it?" asked Netty, leaning over to touch her belly. Judith batted her hand away.

"Nothing, the baby is kicking." She exhaled and then turned her head to vomit. Netty put her hands on her hips and glared.

"My girl, I do this for a livin', and I've had six of my own! If that was the baby kickin', I'm the governor of Montana!" She glanced at Ruth, searching for solidarity. Ruth stepped quickly to Judith's side.

"Judy?" She put her hand on the girl's shoulder. Judith crossed her arms and frowned.

"She's in labor, for Pete's sake!" cried Netty, throwing up her arms. "When did the pains start?" Judith sighed and brushed the hair from her face.

"A little before you arrived," she answered, defeated and exasperated. "I didn't know what they were at first, but they're getting worse now." Netty clapped her hands with excitement, forgetting her irritation and the circumstance's sadness. A baby was soon to be born, and she would help it take its first breath. She needed to focus and to prepare.

"Ruth, we should boil water and make up the bed. Where is the bag I brought before? We'll need it." Recognizing Netty's expertise, Ruth fetched her the bag and set to boiling the water. Ruth knew that it would most likely be a long while before the baby would be born, but she sought confirmation.

"There is still time?"

"—Still time for what?"

"—For us to get ready?"

"Yes, if everythin' goes well, we may meet this little one by mornin'. But Judy's young, and this is her first. It could go on for a long while. We have plenty of time."

In her element, Netty took charge and whistled as she prepared, shouting words of encouragement whenever another contraction seized Judith. Ruth walked with her, holding her hand, praying.

CHAPTER 20

When Netty declared that Judith was in labor, Ruth helped as best she could. She followed Netty's orders closely; she had helped to deliver dozens of babies, and Ruth had only delivered Alex. She had thought before that she could manage the labor on her own, but she saw quickly that the Lord had sent Netty for a reason. It was a miracle that Judith had not gone into labor until she'd arrived.

Ruth made the bed with the five sheets as she'd been instructed and then got on her knees and prayed. Judith walked back and forth, and when the contractions came, she stopped to lean against the wall or squeeze their arms. She asked breathlessly for the door to be opened for fresh air. Ruth did not know why she had boiled water. There had been no boiled water when Alex was born.

In the early morning, the contractions came more often and lasted longer. Judith yelped and moaned. Netty pressed hard on her back, and water ran from between Judith's legs onto the ground, seeping into the cracks in the floorboards. Netty told her to rest when she could, but she could not bear to lie down. She had to move, and so Ruth walked with her. Netty felt her belly to see if the baby was in the right position. Judy fell to her hand and knees, crying out, and Ruth wiped up the water to be useful.

Soon, Judith soaked through her clothes with her sweat and yelled when the contractions came. Ruth held her hand and stroked her hair. She remembered so well when Alex had arrived. She'd thought she would split in half, that there was no way to survive such pain. She could see that Judith was scared, just as she had been. Ruth told her she was doing well, that the baby was nearly there. She did not know if either were true.

After Netty checked her cervix and Judy screamed that she needed to push, Ruth watched their cabin fill with pink light as Judy bore down. As the sun rose, Netty caught Judith's baby girl after only three pushes. She cleaned out the baby's mouth and slapped her bottom. She obliged, letting out a blessed cry. Netty tied a string around the umbilical cord and put the baby in one of the blankets, laying her across Judith's chest,.

Judy was so tired, but she could not help but smile. She was in awe. She looked at her daughter and at Ruth and did not know what to say. She kissed her soft head. 'I knew she was a girl,' she said, stumbling over her tears. Ruth smiled and found that she was crying as well. She thanked the Lord silently for protecting them both. Soon, Judith delivered the placenta, and Netty and Ruth cleaned up the mess from the labor. Ruth took the baby from her for a moment so that they could change her nightgown and bedding.

Her granddaughter was the most beautiful baby she had ever seen. She was shell-pink and small, with a pelt of wavy hair. It was dark and thick, and Ruth smoothed it gently with her lips. She wiped her off and put her in another blanket and handed her back to Judith. There was no milk in her breasts, but Netty told her she could put the baby near to suckle. And so she did.

"Being born is hard work," Ruth teased, holding the baby's hand with her finger. She did not want to stop touching her. She rubbed her back as she nursed in Judith's arms, the mother and daughter soon falling asleep together.

"It's best if Judith's milk doesn't come in. That'll only make things harder. I'll do my part," Netty whispered sadly, lifting the baby gently and putting her to her own breast. When she was done, she set her back on the bed with Judith, and Ruth and Netty went outside to burn the linens. They had been up all night, and their eyes hurt. Like two warriors after battle, Judith's blood was smeared across their faces and hands. They watched the fire consume the soiled sheets.

"Thank you, Netty," Ruth said. "Thank you for everything."

"You're welcome." They both thought strong, heavy thoughts that kept them quiet.

"One day with her daughter. She should have one day," Ruth finally said. "Can you stay until tomorrow morning?" Netty nodded silently that she could.

When they went back inside, Netty rested her head on the table, and Ruth fell asleep upright in the chair. It was past noon when she awoke, and she was hungry with a painful crick in her neck. Netty was still sleeping, but Judith was awake. Ruth saw a pile of dirty diapers and bloodied cloths on the floor. She brought her water, and Judith drank until the cup was empty.

"Will you brush my hair again, Ruth?" Ruth got the brush and sat beside her on the bed while the baby tried once more to nurse. Judith closed her eyes. "She is perfect. I've never seen such a perfect baby." Ruth laughed.

"All mothers think their babies are beautiful, but in your case, it's true. She's pretty, very pretty. Like her mother," she said.

"I want to give her a name," Judith said. She took Ruth's arm and then her hand. Ruth turned it over and looked at the wound there. It was dark. "It still hurts a little," said Judith. Ruth kissed it and turned her hand back over. She knew Judith wanted to name her daughter to claim her, to mark her as her own. It would only make it that much harder in the morning, but she did not argue.

"What will you call her?" Ruth looked at the baby to see what her name should be.

"I was thinking Margaret," she said.

"Margaret is your mother's name!" Ruth said in surprise.

"Yes, I know!" she laughed, "but it is a family name, too, and it is lovely and strong. And whether she will ever know it or not, she is a Frisk."

"Hello, Margaret," Ruth whispered. She made a small noise and fidgeted as though she approved. Judith stared lovingly at Margaret, lost in her sweet face and tiny fingers.

Ruth cut a piece of cornbread for Judy and used the remaining butter Netty had brought for Christmas. She made three cups of tea and thought ahead to the following morning when Netty would travel with the baby. Ruth sat down at the table and wrote the letter Netty would give to Ms. Wendell. When she was done, she woke Netty to show her. She was groggy and the grain of the table and the seam of her blouse were imprinted on her right cheek. Netty sat up, her neck also stiff. She massaged it with one hand and reached for the teacup with the other, taking a sip and looking over to see how Judith and the baby were faring.

"Tomorrow's Sunday," she said, taking another sip as she gained her bearings. "The girls have chapel Sunday mornin'. The matron'll be there, too. That's when I should arrive." Ruth nodded in understanding.

"When must you leave?" she asked.

"Before dawn. Service is at ten and lasts an hour." Concerned, Ruth sat up tall in her chair, her back straight.

"It will be very cold then, Netty. I don't know if it's safe."

"We'll be fine, don't you worry. I'll strap her to me. She'll be toasty warm."

"How will you get Margaret to the German woman?" Ruth asked.

"Margaret, is it?" she asked solemnly. "I'm still workin' that out," she added. "Leave it to me," she said. "She'll take her."

"Here's the note," Ruth said, "the note for Ms. Wendell." She read it out loud to make sure she hadn't forgotten anything.

"*Dear Ms. Wendell, This child is the daughter of Judith Frisk. Her name, according to her mother's wishes, is Margaret Hall. Judith is safe and returning home to Great Falls. Our agreement is complete. No one will ever know. Thank you for your cooperation."*

"—I did not sign the letter, but she will know it's from me."

"Good," said Netty. "Shouldn't you seal it?" They did not have an envelope, so Ruth folded the letter inside another piece of paper and lit a candle. She waited for the candle to melt the wax as she stared at Netty.

"I will be praying for you," said Ruth, reaching to cover Netty's hand with hers. "I will pray for your safety, and that nothing happens to your job. I will pray for your family. I will pray that God will bless you for everything you've done." Netty's face softened. Ruth took away her hand and dropped the hot wax in a circle on the fold of the paper. The matron would know it had not been opened and that Barrett was safe.

They sat with Judith and Margaret, and Netty told stories of her children, periodically massaging Judith's stomach and teaching her how to do it herself. They laughed and smiled as though grief and devastation did not lurk beyond the door. Judith kissed Margaret's head every few minutes, memorizing her—her smell, her button nose and sleeping eyes, her helplessness.

Netty and Ruth took turns putting logs on the fire, its crackling and glow comforting to them all. Netty waited until Judith and the baby fell asleep, and then she began to gather her belongings. Ruth knew she should also pack. It would not be good for them to stay at the cabin long after Margaret was gone. She decided that they would leave as soon as Judith was able and begin their return journey to Great Falls.

Netty came back inside after checking on her horse. "I made a reservation for you tonight at your old hotel. I told them to save it for you 'til Friday, and I paid them upfront with what you'd given me." She searched through her jacket pocket and pulled out a small slip. "Your receipt," she said, handing it to Ruth. Netty reached into a different pocket and took out two more pieces of paper. "These are your tickets on the Great Northern. They're good until the twentieth." Ruth took them and tucked them safely into her dress.

"Thank you," she said. They had not gone over these arrangements beforehand, and Ruth was impressed that Netty had organized so much so well.

Ruth woke Judith and gave her bread and tea to give her strength. When she left her side, Judith reached for her hand and squeezed it hard, crushing her bones. She did not look at Ruth but took a small bite of the food.

Everyone except Ruth fell asleep again and slept through the night. Every few hours, Netty woke to feed Margaret, climbing out of Ruth's bed and carefully lifting Margaret from her mother's arms. Ruth packed their clothes and swept the floor. There was not much food left, and they would not need what they did have after Tuesday. She put the brush she'd given Judith in her bag on top and folded the baby clothes they'd knitted through the winter, setting them softly with Netty's things. Netty had brought a gown and pair of wool stockings for Margaret that they would dress her in come morning.

Ruth kept watch through the night over the slumbering women, and so she was awake to see the sun rise once more. It was too gentle and too peaceful of a morning. Just as they'd agreed, Ruth woke Netty first. Margaret's limbs jerked as Netty stepped onto the floor, rousing Judith, who knew at once that the black hour had at last arrived.

Margaret suckled her mother while Netty took the saddlebags outside and loaded the horses. Ruth closed her eyes, praying silently as her lips mouthed desperate words. Waiting until Netty was back inside, she took a step toward the bed where Margaret and Judith lay. Judith winced, and Ruth thought that she would not be able to do it, or that she might then and there be taken up to heaven as had Enoch. She wanted nothing more than to *be not*, in that moment, to not exist. Her ears rang as Netty looked at her with concern. "Lord," Ruth pleaded, "help me. Father, help me." Without thinking, then, Ruth reached for Margaret, and Judith inexplicably gave her into her outstretched arms.

Ruth stared at Judith, her own head spinning, as Margaret squealed obliviously. She did not like the sudden cold, and she knew that Ruth was not her mother. Ruth handed her gently to Netty, who changed her diaper once more and then rocked her. She sang a lullaby Ruth had never heard, soft and sad as she fashioned a sling to carry Margaret. Judith sat up in bed and did not take her eyes off her daughter. She was pale, and she shook. She covered her mouth tightly with her hands.

Ruth slid the sling over Netty's head and back. She could hear her own heartbeat and every small noise that Margaret made. Quickly, they dressed her and then swaddled her and put on her hat, placing her inside the sling. The little one did not fuss.

"Do you have the letter?" Ruth asked.

"Yes, here," said Netty, patting her pocket. "Leave the horses tied at the hotel. They'll need to be fed. Don't forget." Judith tried to hear what was being discussed, but their voices were too soft. Ruth looked Netty in the eye, both women sharing the same somber expression on their tired faces. Staring at each other, they were quiet for a moment, uncertain how to proceed. Ruth reached inside the sling, and Margaret grabbed her finger tightly. For Judith's sake, she did not lean down to kiss her goodbye. Silently, Ruth blessed her and asked the Lord to protect her.

Ruth's finger pulled from Margaret's grasp, and then Netty was gone.

Stunned, Ruth moved as quickly as she could to shut the open door behind her, leaning all of her weight against it. Netty was on her horse and riding away before Judith could get out of bed. She tried but was too dizzy and sore and nearly fell. Ruth heard her struggle as she watched Netty disappear through the window.

And then her wailing began. Ruth had not heard such a cry since she had lost Alex. Judith screamed out Margaret's name again and again and pulled at her hair. Ruth went to her and covered her grieving frame with her own. There was nothing she could do to comfort her, and so she allowed her heartbreak to merge with Judith's. Ruth let Judith rage and mourn, cradling her tightly, crying out herself when the sadness was too great for a single voice to carry. The girl did not try to get outside; she did not try to follow. Ruth knew this was God's grace.

Judith wore herself out and collapsed motionless on the hearth, leaving a trail of blood from her desolate womb on the stones. Ruth lifted her and set her in the bed, put fresh cloth between her legs, and pulled the covers up over her. She crawled in next to her and again held her in her arms.

"Shhhh. Shhhh, Judy," said Ruth, telling her what she knew. "You will never forget her, Judy. You will always be her mother. Margaret will be loved, and the Lord will protect her," she whispered, willing her words to be true. Ruth did not know if she heard. Judith was restless and tossed her head into the pillow. She reached out for nothing, muttering and writhing so that Ruth put her hand between Judith's head and the wall to protect her. She kissed her cheek, tasting the saltiness of her tears. With Judith's wet grief still on her lips and her blood on her dress, Ruth succumbed to her exhaustion and sorrow. Just as she closed her eyes, Alex came into focus at the side of the bed. Ruth watched as he kissed Judith's forehead and climbed beneath the covers with them. It was God's mercy that they all slept.

CHAPTER 21

When they took the train back to Great Falls, when they left the cabin and Helena and Margaret, Judith did not speak. She did not speak because all her words were given to her lost baby. Her body was so sore from labor and from sadness. Ruth didn't realize, she didn't know. She'd thought back on that train ride a thousand times since, searching for the signs she had missed, what she should have seen. Judith's face had been so tense. Ruth had thought she was angry, that it was bitterness making her clench her fists and jaw as she did.

Mrs. Frisk greeted them with a kiss on the cheek and kind, chirping words, as though they had actually been in Italy. She did not ask Judith a single question. She saved them for Ruth when they were alone.

"The baby?" she asked.

"A girl," Ruth answered, uncertain what she meant.

"No," she said. She was cross that Ruth had divulged this detail. "It is gone?" she asked again. Ruth stared at her.

"The baby is in Helena. She will be adopted by a good woman." Mrs. Frisk nodded.

"And Judith," she asked, "is she well?" Ruth wanted to tell her that no, her daughter was not well. She had taken it hard. She was broken, and Ruth did not know if she would ever be whole. Instead, she told her that Judith was recovering, because it was as close to the truth as she could come. Mrs. Frisk did not want to know anything else. The crisis had been avoided, the threat to their reputation removed. The matter was closed.

"I do not want to hear of this again," she said. "If you ever tell a soul, I will learn of it, and you will wish you'd died that day with your bastard son. Do you understand me?"

"Yes," said Ruth, too shocked to be angry, even though she did not understand Mrs. Frisk at all.

It had been difficult for Judith to walk from the train to the carriage and into the house. Ruth had thought it was hard because of her ruined heart and tired body. It had happened so quickly. Ruth put her to bed that night, and when she went to wake her in the morning, Judith's left side was like stone. She did not cry once. When Judith seized and thrashed, even when she vomited, she never cried. The doctor came, and he tried to help. He did what he could, but he did not do much more than name the problem.

"Lockjaw," he said, "Tetanus. The case is advanced." He removed his spectacles and wiped his face with a handkerchief. He came to the house for five days, and on the sixth, she died. "Suffocation," the doctor said. "It is common with lockjaw." Judith, her darling, her second born, surrendered as her muscles tightened in on themselves and she could no longer breathe. It was too painful a death for Judy, for her sweet, sweet girl.

As she lay dying, Ruth told her over and over how much she and Jesus loved her. After the second day, Judith couldn't talk. The muscles in her face were too tight, but there were tears in her eyes. Ruth held her hand, although both her hands were turned in on themselves, and she sang every song she could remember.

She did not leave her side. Ruth prayed for her night and day, on her knees, on the floor, but Judy did not survive. David had prayed for his son, too, his first child by Bathsheba. He cried out from the ground and did not eat. While his son died, he only prayed and mourned. But the Lord took the child anyway, and the Lord had taken Judith, too. Ruth was confused, but she knew God's thoughts were not her thoughts, and that His ways were not her ways. Sometimes, this helped her sorrow. Others, it made it worse.

She didn't know whether Judith had gone to heaven or to hell when she died. This, among so many other things, was her fault. Ruth would only know when she went herself to be with the Lord. She saw now how a person got good at devastation. The weight of her anguish was titanic, and yet she still got up each morning, dressed herself, looked after Jack and Phillip, read her Bible and prayed.

Mr. and Mrs. Frisk were in shock. When Judith passed, Mrs. Frisk wanted to know more about their time at Barrett. Ruth could not tell her about the cabin, about the matron giving them permission to leave, about Judith puncturing her hand when she fell. Mrs. Frisk did not understand how it could have happened. Ruth learned later, after she'd left, that the Frisks had withdrawn their money from Barrett. Ruth knew that Mrs. Frisk blamed the home for her daughter's death, but she should have blamed her.

Ruth considered staying to help the family, but she did not. She could not bear to be there without Judith. She cried only in her room at night, knowing that Mr. and Mrs. Frisk would not want her tears mixing with theirs.

Ruth sent a telegram to Helena and let Netty know she would be returning. When she told the Frisks she was leaving, Mr. Frisk was furious. "What will we do? Who will look after the boys?" He'd tried to make her feel ashamed and guilty, but she felt nothing but grief. She thanked him for the years of employment and told him that they had treated her very well. But she still left.

There was never any question that Ruth should be near Margaret, that she should watch over her. How could she do anything or be anywhere else? It was what Judith would have wanted. And so she followed Margaret back to Helena, and she watched. She made a life, and she watched and waited for the Lord to move.

Marguerithe

Helena, Montana
1913-1925

CHAPTER 1

Marie knelt on the ground before a pile of wood shavings and leaves, a square tin open at her feet. Her husband sat on the back steps carefully whittling a small figurine he intended to give his daughter. He did not look up from his work other than to yell, "Be careful!" when Marie lit the match. The summer wind that had kicked up early that morning blew it out. Marie caught her breath, and her hands shook as she tried another.

She cupped the small flame with her right hand before it, too, could be extinguished and lit the crumpled papers from the tin. They ignited quickly, and she tossed the makeshift kindling onto the pile. Leonard glanced up once more to see if the fire had caught and noticed his wife's head was bowed. The sides of her blue dress rippled from the heat, her entire body waving. Marie said a silent prayer and opened her eyes in time to watch the young man's face in the photograph glow orange and then black. The return address in Medicine Hat disappeared. Finally, the picture curled and turned entirely to ash.

He was gone now, the man with the sad eyes. She'd already kept his letter for far too long. No one would know. It had taken three years to get Joseph back, to walk down the street and look the people she passed in the eye, and it had been Leonard who'd made it possible. She would not risk losing her daughter or her husband's esteem. He'd wanted her when no one else had, when she was cast-off and penniless. He'd married her despite her shame. Leonard had already overlooked so much and forgiven such deep flaws of character. Their family was safe now.

Marie wiped her cheek with the back of her hand, leaving streaks of soot. She grabbed the stoker she'd brought outside and poked at the leaves. Her own mother had burned to death, her hair catching fire over the hearth. She'd set the fields surrounding her home aflame as she'd run through the dead crops, a conflagration of screams and prayers, until the smoke stole her last breath. Marie was already married and living in Helena when she'd gotten the telegram, but she recalled the scene as though she, too, had been singed. Without turning, she yelled to Leonard to ask what he would like for lunch. "I'm not much hungry yet," was his reply. His blade continued to methodically carve half-moon splinters from the wood block. He ran his thumb over the smooth progress.

"—Well in a little bit when you are?"

"Whatever you're having, Marie, would be fine." He watched her back once more, admiring her strong, lean figure. He had done very well marrying her. Marie was smart, faithful, and as hardworking as himself. "Come on over here, sweetheart. Come see what I'm making for Maggy."

Marie made sure the fire was burning hotly before coming to his side. She carried the iron tool over her left shoulder, indifferent to the mess it left on her apron. As she came close, the smell of her lilac soap filled his nostrils. Leonard smiled and lifted the wood in his hand so his wife could see. "What do you think, Marigold?"

"What is it?" She squinted and bent her head without kneeling.

"Nothing much now, but it will be a clown, holding balloons." He gestured above his head as though he were holding balloons himself. The brim of his hat cast a dark shadow across his light green eyes.

"Maggy will love that. She loves clowns." Marie tried not to think of what she had just done. Her guilt, however, would not be so easily assuaged. "Should you make something for Joseph, too?"

"I suppose you're right. You're always right with the kids." Marie tried not to wince, but her jaw clenched momentarily. She hoped that she truly had done what was best. Leonard's eyes shot upwards and opened widely. "How about a train car? Yes, that is a mighty fine idea." He didn't wait for Marie's encouragement, but she gave it anyway, placing her cleaner hand on his shoulder.

"I'm going inside to wash up and make lunch. Will you call Joseph and Maggy home when it's time?"

Leonard nodded. "I'll stay out here, watch the fire." Marie set the stoker down at his feet and went inside.

Later, when she had finished carefully setting the table, she heard Leonard's booming voice echo the name of their children across the neighborhood. She could tell from the sound that his hands were cupped on either side of his mouth as he called.

"Lord, forgive me," she whispered as she washed her hands in the sink and began to chop the carrots.

CHAPTER 2

"Helen, stop!" Maggy yelled through laughter, hiking up her dress. The hem of Helen's pleated navy skirt was tucked into her waistband. She kicked through the shallow water of Prickly Pear Creek, splashing Maggy as she waded.

"I'm a knight and you're a princess!" cried Helen. She lowered her head and ran into Maggy's stomach, nearly knocking her into the water. "Honestly, Mags, I give you the best part and you won't take it. Now curtsy!" she demanded, holding her imaginary sword high.

"No, I want to be the knight!" whined Maggy, crossing her arms across her chest.

"Fine, you be the knight and I'll be the princess. Here, take my sword." They exchanged make-believe costumes, giggling all the while.

"Kneel so that I may knight you!" ordered Maggy, speaking loudly with her chin high.

"—But I'm a princess, not a knight!" protested Helen with exasperation. "Remember?"

"Oh just do it! I promise it'll be fun." Helen knelt in the creek obediently but stuck her tongue out at her friend. "Kneel Princess Helen. Rise *Sir* Princess Helen." Helen rolled her eyes as Maggy tapped each of her shoulders with her sword and then stood up.

"You two are the stupidest girls I've ever seen!" interrupted a taunting voice from the bank. Maggy and Helen turned to spy the intruder.

"Joseph, leave us alone! Oh, hi, Georgy," Maggy added when she saw her cousin at her brother's side.

"Didn't anybody ever tell you that girls can't be knights?" he asked mockingly, picking up a large stone and throwing it just short of his sister and her friend, dousing them with a great splash. Helen shrieked while Maggy glared, wiping the water from her face.

"I'll tell Dad if you don't leave us alone," she yelled threateningly.

"Go ahead, and I'll tell him how you're down here at the creek showing off your legs for all the world to see!" Helen blushed and quickly untucked her skirt from her waistband.

"Just leave us alone!" screamed Maggy, bending forward with the force of her yell and squeezing her fists at her sides.

"Come on, George. Let's get out of here," said Joseph with a grin. Unlike his cousin, George did not delight in tormenting the girls, and he especially regretted being an accessory to any cruelty toward Helen. The entire school knew that George loved her, as did Helen, which made for a very difficult test of loyalty at the present moment. Just as George thought he might very well mutiny in favor of his crush, Maggy grabbed her friend's hand and ran up the opposite bank, snatching their stockings and boots before disappearing into the woods. He exhaled sharply in relief, thankful not to have been forced to cross Joseph.

"I hate him!" said Maggy through clenched teeth. "Why does he always have to ruin everything?"

"Because he's a boy, silly, and that's what boys do!" Helen slipped her hand free from Maggy's and sat down on a nearby stone. She wiped the bottom of her feet with her stockings and rolled them back on.

"You're so lucky you don't have a brother, Helen." Helen focused on lacing her boots and said nothing. There were drops of water on her dark hair from the creek that glued a few loose strands to her forehead. Her complexion was fresh and vibrant.

"I'm keeping my shoes off for now," decided Maggy. Helen looked up at the sun.

"I have to go home. It must be nearly supper time."

"Already? Let's just stay a few more minutes, Helen. Please?" Helen extended her hands to Maggy, who grabbed them and lifted her to her feet. Helen looked in the direction of home and then back at Maggy's pleading face.

"It's so hot," she mumbled, fanning herself and stalling. "Oh all right. But if I get in trouble, it's your fault!" she said, shaking her finger. Maggy grinned, slapped Helen on the arm, and ran further upstream.

"You're it!" she yelled over her shoulder, running as fast as she could. Before Helen could think about whether or not she actually wanted to join in the game of tag, she was dodging roots and stones, chasing madly after her friend.

CHAPTER 3

W hen school began, the afternoons were still muggy and languid. The church basement that served as the Lutheran School's classroom was windowless and dank, the darkness compounding the children's misery as they once again squirmed beneath the oppressive Mr. Parsons and his circuitous lessons—given mostly in German but occasionally in thickly-accented English.

"Franklin!" snapped Mr. Parsons. Frankie immediately sat up with drool still on his chin and looked around the room, bewildered. "Come here this instant!" Still dazed, Frankie darted in the opposite direction towards the stairs in a futile attempt to evade punishment. All the students watched with sympathy as Frankie shook his head and refused to come any closer. His large brown eyes grew even larger as they fixated on the paddle. The tip of his right boot caught the leg of Maggy's table, and he tripped forward, upsetting another student's desk. Maggy held her breath and waited for the inevitable.

"Stop it, Frankie! He'll only hit you harder if you run!" whispered Maggy as the boy flew past her again. Either he didn't hear, or he didn't care; the instinct for self-preservation was too great.

Mr. Parsons lunged forward with accuracy and speed, snatching up the escapee by the back of his collar like a naughty cat. He immediately bent Frankie over his knee and raised the worn paddle high above his head. Four loud cracks proceeded before the boy was relegated to the corner for the remainder of the lesson.

"There will be no sleeping in my classroom and no, no…cowardice," said Mr. Parsons, tugging at his vest and putting the paddle back on his desk. He was winded from the chase and took a moment to collect himself. None of the other children dared make a sound. Frankie sniffled and tried to muffle his crying. Every now and then, he reached behind to lightly touch his tender rear end.

Although Maggy watched Mr. Parsons as he resumed the lesson, she found Frankie's whimpering distracting, and her mind drifted back to the past spring when she had walked the wide, sunlit hallways of Helena Elementary with Helen at her side. Those brief and blessed, English-saturated days were now but a bittersweet memory. Maggy sighed audibly.

Pastor Lemke had arrived early at their home one June morning last summer and knocked with obnoxious self-assurance on the front door. Maggy anxiously peeked from behind her bedroom curtains, knowing full well that his arrival could mean nothing but misfortune. In hopes that her mother had not yet heard him, Maggy rushed downstairs and burst into song, skipping and jumping in a flurry she prayed would mask the knocking. He persisted, however, and Marie shooed her strange daughter out of the way and banished her to her room as she moved to answer the door.

Although Pastor Lemke's booming voice normally made her wince each Sunday, his present tone was intentionally hushed and indecipherable. Exasperated, Maggy removed her ear from the floor and paced the length of her room. Meddlesome, irritating man!

The muffled voices below her ceased, and Maggy waited with trepidation. The door shut, announcing the Pastor's departure, and she turned to the window to see him walk towards the street. She ran downstairs and nearly collided with her mother. When she saw her stern face, Maggy burst into tears.

"Enough, Marguerithe! Turn off the waterworks," she scolded. "Pastor Lemke is right. As you get older, good, moral teaching is more important, much more important than geography or math. I've gotten along just fine for thirty years without schooling, but I wouldn't last a day without Christian morals, and you're not going to get that *or* German at the public school. I said we could give the public school a try, and we did." Maggy's tears warmed and bubbled over like a hot spring. Marie was unmoved. She crossed her arms across her chest, unwilling to negotiate. "Run along now and play."

"—But I,"

"—That's enough! The decision is not yours to make." Marie's voice was flinty, and Maggy knew better than to argue. She ran past her mother and out the back door, seeking the solace of her best friend and fleeing the unfairness that haunts the life of children.

The recess bell brought Maggy back to the suffocating classroom and futility of her current predicament. Dejected, she was the last student to exit the basement and break free into the daylight.

CHAPTER 4

"**Y**ou should have seen him, Helen. He kept running and shaking his head 'No', like this." Maggy mimicked Frankie's fearful expression, and Helen covered her mouth to stifle her laughter. The girls met where they had last parted ways earlier that morning and wasted no time in swapping stories from their first days. "Poor Frankie," said Maggy. "And on the first day of school! At least it wasn't me. But I would have had enough sense not to run," she added seriously.

"Poor Frankie," Helen commiserated before quickly moving on to her own story. "Well, Robert kept pulling my hair in the hallway and calling me 'Helly' until I kicked him in the shin. That showed him! He won't bother me again." Helen nodded her head sharply in punctuation, grinning.

"He did it because he likes you, Helen. That's why all the boys bother you." Helen dismissed her explanation with a wave of her hand, rolling her eyes.

"Oh, that's enough of that," she said uncomfortably. "Say!" she exclaimed, her countenance lifting, "I got my allowance today. Want to go to Ralph's?" she asked, grabbing Maggy's hand. The girls linked arms and hurried towards the general store. "Patricia told me they have a new candy. The outside is hard and tastes like strawberries, but the inside is soft and tastes like grapes!" Maggy's eye widened with wonderment.

Ralph's General Store was on the corner of Howard St. and Last Chance Gulch, adjacent to one of the city's more modest hotels and The Helena Independent Newspaper. The girls ran the entire way, pushing the door open with their momentum and nearly falling inside. Mr. Ralph

Wyman eyed them disapprovingly but confined his reproach to a sharp glare. Maggy smoothed the front of her dress and cleared her throat, stifling her laughter. Helen, oblivious to Mr. Wyman's displeasure, searched the delectable shelves and pointed finally to the glass jar containing the new candy she'd earlier described. "That's it, Mags," she said loudly with excitement.

"Shhh, Helen," said Maggy, stepping closer to her friend. Light reflected off the canister at which Helen had pointed and they moved towards it simultaneously. Helen reached into her dress pocket and counted the money. "I don't know how much we can buy with this, but let's use it all, ok?" Maggy nodded enthusiastically as the candy's gold wrappers glinted enticingly.

"How are you today, young ladies?" asked Mr. Wyman, walking around to the other side of the counter.

"Good, Mr. Wyman," they replied in unison.

"Let me guess; you'd like some candy?"

"Yes, that one there, with the gold wrappers," chirped Helen, pointing to clarify her choice.

"And how much would you like?" he asked, taking down the jar and setting it on the countertop.

"All of it!" said Maggy, answering his question honestly.

"Maggy, we don't have enough money! Mr. Wyman, as much as this will pay for," said Helen, dropping the coins into his palm. He looked at the two girls, pushing his spectacles further down along the bridge of his nose, amused. Helen and Maggy fidgeted.

"Alright then." Mr. Wyman scooped the treat onto the scale until it measured half a pound. "That should be about right." He poured the sweet treasure into a cellophane bag and passed it to Helen. "Now, don't eat all of it before supper, girls. You'll spoil your appetite." Something drew Mr. Wyman's attention, and the friends wasted no time unwrapping their first candies and popping them into their greedy mouths. The old, dry wooden boards beneath their feet creaked as their weight shifted. The scent of the lemon oil Mr. Wyman had undoubtedly used to polish the countertops mixed with the flavors of strawberry and grape. Maggy closed her eyes to better appreciate the taste.

"Don't bite it, suck on it, like this!" Helen demonstrated, making a face like a fish. Maggy's eyes sprung open and she laughed, nearly choking on the strawberry treat. Helen hit her friend's back, and the offending candy shot forward onto the floor.

A male voice called from across the store, and the girls turned. "Ralph, can you please help me over here with one more thing?" Maggy saw the face of the man Mr. Wyman had been assisting.

"Pastor Lemke! It's not bad enough that he has to ruin school? He has to ruin Ralph's, too?" Maggy whispered vehemently, still watery-eyed from almost choking. Helen glowered as she watched the man responsible for the girls' separation ask Mr. Wyman a question about shampoo.

"Doesn't he realize he doesn't have any hair?" Helen teased. Maggy snorted at her brazenness and stood upright.

"This much candy must be sinful! Let's go, before he sees me!" she said urgently, pushing Helen toward the door. In her effort to make a swift and undetected exit, Maggy's hip knocked one of Ralph Wyman's displays. She stumbled, avoiding an outright fall, but the same could not be said for the display bottles. The wood stand collapsed altogether, and the bottles flew across the store, as though they, too, were trying to escape. Some thudded heavily on the ground, intact, while others shattered upon impact. Both girls froze. The shards of blue and green would have been pretty had they not signaled disaster. Maggy's heartbeat pounded in her ears as she awaited the consequences of her clumsiness.

"For Pete's sake!" cried Mr. Wyman, hurrying over to assess the damage and nearly turning his ankle on one of the unbroken bottles. Maggy wanted to apologize, but too many emotions strangled her voice. She looked at Mr. Wyman with wide eyes and a guilty countenance.

"We're sorry, Mr. Wyman," said Helen, rescuing her friend. "It was an accident. I don't know what happened." Mr. Wyman's face was momentarily furrowed before he sighed and picked up a shard of glass. His frown turned to pursed lips that finally settled into a wry grin of acceptance. Had the pastor not been witness to the entire scene, Ralph Wyman perhaps would not have been so quick to forgive. Maggy wanted to warn Mr. Wyman that he had drastically misjudged the pastor; it was punishment and not mercy that would impress him.

"You really should be more careful, girls. There wasn't anything in these, luckily for you, or I'd have to charge you for all this. As it is, they're just empty bottles. You aren't cut, are you?" He added the last question out of genuine concern, although he also hoped it would sound generous to the pastor's ears.

"No, we're fine," said Maggy with relief, at last able to speak. "I'm sorry, Mr. Wyman. It was me. I hit the corner of your display. I'm sorry." Maggy looked down at the mess helplessly.

"Ralph," said Pastor Lemke, joining the three now in the middle of the wreckage. "You are too easy on these girls. Marguerithe, you ought to be more careful." Ralph looked at the pastor nervously, uncertain what to do. He gazed steadily at the storeowner until he was forced to speak.

"Pastor, they aren't my children, I—"

"—I'm not suggesting you discipline them, Ralph, but you ought to let their parents know the trouble they've caused." Ralph nodded gravely. He swallowed audibly, and Helen could not help but turn her head to watch his Adam's apple convulse.

"Yes, of course," said Mr. Wyman. He had intended to drop the matter and let the girls leave without any further recourse. Irritated, he shooed them out of the store. "Run along, now. You've caused enough mischief for the day."

Maggy and Helen reached for each other's hands and fled. They ran a full block before they dared to slow down. "You didn't mean to, Mags. It's not your fault. It was an accident!"

"—But now Mr. Wyman hates us, and I've gotten you into trouble, too!"

"The candy!" interjected Helen, realizing that she had left the bag on the counter inside the store. "All that bother, and we left the candy!" Maggy, wanting to make things right with Helen, felt a surge of courage.

"I'll go back and get it."

"No, Mags, it's not worth it. You saw the pastor's face." Maggy gulped in a similar fashion to Mr. Wyman but shook her head, her courage swelling.

"Wait here, I'll be right back." Maggy hurried to the store to retrieve the bag. Ralph Wyman had propped open the door, and Maggy stood silently in the entryway, unnoticed. The two men were still conversing. She took a single step forward, opening her mouth to apologize once again and explain her return, but Pastor Lemke's voice prevented her.

"—I'm afraid it's what we can expect from such a girl, from such a background. I've interceded as much as I can in getting her mother to send her to our school at the church, but there's a limit to what I can accomplish. The Lord will have to do the real work there, in her soul," he said, tapping on his chest. Pausing, he shook his head and sighed. "With a mother like hers, it's a tall order, even for Him. Poor bastard child, left on a doorstep. I'm afraid she'll never amount to very much. Still, 'the things which are impossible with men are possible with God,'" he quoted, pointing upwards with his index finger.

Ralph swept up the broken glass and only half listened to the pastor's words. The scratching of the straw broom and the glass against the floor allowed Maggy to step backwards and away from the front window without detection. She stared at the ground for a moment and tried to control her rapid breathing. She looked up and saw Helen waving at her from the corner. Maggy walked slowly to rejoin her.

"Where's the candy, Mags? What happened?" Helen added quickly, seeing her friend's pallid face. Maggy shook her head.

"Noth—nothing." She stared at Helen, stunned and mute. An automobile went by, which momentarily distracted Helen. She watched it rumble past them with wonder. Maggy was still looking straight ahead when Helen once again turned to her. She grabbed Maggy by the shoulders and shook her.

"Mags! Are you okay?"

"I'm, I'm fine. Let's go home." Helen wanted to probe further but sensed Maggy would not be forthcoming.

"That jerk! Even if he is a man of God, he shouldn't be so mean!" She did not know what had transpired between her friend and the pastor, but she knew it could not have been pleasant. Maggy said nothing. A few seconds passed. Under her breath, Helen mumbled, "The candy wasn't that good anyway."

Maggy held Helen's hand tightly, squeezing it the rest of the walk home. Even though her friend's palm became sweaty and uncomfortable, Helen did not let go.

CHAPTER 5

It was a slow week at work for Leonard. He'd finished painting the DeWitt's home ahead of schedule, and so he found himself uncharacteristically without much to do on a Saturday. Marie was attending a Helena Women's Club meeting and would not be back until the late afternoon. He rose early, despite having nowhere to go, and drank his morning coffee while reading the newspaper, as was customary.

Prominent photographs highlighted the War in Europe and the Montana State Fair on the front page of the Helena Independent:. He grunted, fingering his mustache and shaking his head. Leonard found the editor's decision to include these incongruous topics together distasteful. He scanned both articles and turned the page.

Leonard was a fine paperhanger. He loved his family and took pride in his work, in the perfect seams he created, the smooth paint strokes, all the things he made with his hands. But the conflict in Europe often distracted and unsettled him. Undoubtedly, war was an issue left to greater minds than his. He was not opposed to serving, to dying to protect his family and freedom, but Leonard, who always walked steadily towards action and responsibility, was not entirely at ease with his adopted country's wavering. If the conflict required American intervention, and he was not entirely certain that it did, then America should face the challenge boldly. Doing nothing when something should be done was wrong.

Maggy opened the back door and shut it quietly behind her. She knew not to disturb her father when he was reading his paper, but this morning, Leonard welcomed the interruption.

"Where were you?" he asked, folding the newspaper in quarters and setting it on the table.

"Nowhere," she answered, shrugging her shoulders. This explanation would not have satisfied her mother, but it did him.

"And your brother?"

"He's with George. They're playing baseball at the park." Leonard thumbed his suspenders, pulling them out so they were taut and releasing them with a snap. He picked up his empty cup of coffee and looked down at the dark stains ringing its bottom. Maggy came closer and leaned on his chair.

"Let's go fishing," he said suddenly, slapping the tabletop.

"But you normally take Joseph."

"Well today I want to go fishing with my daughter." Maggy smiled, deeply pleased. "You haven't forgotten what I taught you, now, have you?" Maggy shook her head adamantly.

"Nope, I remember all of it," she said confidently. "Whenever Joseph goes, I watch him and make him let me have a turn." Leonard smiled, his large white teeth conspicuous beneath his dark mustache.

"That's my girl. Well, go get changed. I'll get everything together. Be outside in ten." Maggy kissed her father on the cheek and ran out of the kitchen and up the stairs to her bedroom.

Leonard hummed a song he'd heard on the radio as he gathered their equipment.

"I read in the paper this morning that the State Fair is coming next month, Maggy. Would you like to go?" Leonard held back a branch so that Maggy could pass by safely.

"Oh yes!" she cried without hesitation, skipping once in excitement. Leonard chuckled. "Can Helen come, too?"

"Well, you two are joined at the hip. I didn't think it would be possible to separate you long enough to take you on the Ferris wheel. I hear they're having one there this year, you know." Maggy smiled wildly. She had never heard of a Ferris wheel, but it sounded marvelous.

They took their time walking down to the river, pushing aside thorn bushes and picking blackberries whenever a plump one came into sight. By the time they reached the water, Maggy's hands were stained dark purple. She wiped them thoughtlessly on her pants.

Leonard's fishing rod had been a wedding gift from his three sisters. It was made of split bamboo and was the finest thing he owned. His father had not been much of a fisherman, so Leonard was mostly self-taught. He stepped boldly into the Missouri, holding out his hand to his young daughter.

"You're not going to catch any fish from there, sweetheart. You have to get in the river, softly, so the fish don't know you're coming." Maggy took her father's hand and put one foot in the water, making sure there was shore below. "There you go. Come on now." She stepped the rest of the way in and did not let go of Leonard's hand. Although Maggy regularly spent hours in Prickly Pear Creek, the water here was far bigger, wider, the current stronger. She clutched Joseph's rod in her free hand and shivered at the cold.

"Steady now, *spatzi*." Leonard withdrew his hand from hers. He spent the next few minutes watching the surface of the water. When a fish rose, his eyes narrowed and his mouth twitched. He unhooked a fly from his shirt pocket and placed it carefully between his lips.

"We're going to catch ourselves a Big Brown, my dear. Just you wait." He tied the same fly onto the end of both their lines.

"Now, you have everything you need. You remember how you hold it?" Maggy nodded, wanting to please her father but feeling self-conscious and nervous. "Good girl. I'm going to go upstream just a little so we're not fishing the same hole." Leonard stepped slowly towards the bend in the river, the water rushing against his legs. He turned once to look over his shoulder. Elated that her father was allowing her such autonomy, she tried to imagine what her mother would think. She was sure she would not approve of his leaving her side, which made the moment all the more thrilling.

"Those fish are quaking in their boots!" he called to Maggy in a hushed voice. She beamed and watched her father slowly move further away. Maggy tried casting a few times, but the line fell slack in a useless ribbon on the water. She cast once more, and it became hopelessly tangled. This was why Joseph only let her try at the end of the day when he'd already caught his share. She decided to sit on a large boulder in the river and watch her father cast instead. Whereas her movements were awkward and jumpy, his were smooth and precise. It was comforting to watch him fish, to see him so steady and adept.

For the past month, Maggy had tried to forget what she'd overheard at Ralph's, but doing so had proven difficult. Although she did not know what it all meant, she did know that she had stumbled upon a terrible secret, something shameful. It was the pastor's tone, the expression on his face, the way he shook his head. She'd had to look up the word he'd used in the dictionary. *Bastard*. The knowledge was disorienting.

She had not played with Helen for a week afterwards. Her mother had let her stay home from school for three days before proclaiming her illness imaginary. There was never any question of asking her parents about what she'd overheard. She was responsible for the utterance of those words; it was her misbehavior that had led the pastor to pronounce his judgment, not just on her, but on her mother as well. Why had she gone back for the candy? Why had she been so clumsy! Thinking of the incident made her dizzy. But now, here on the damp, mossy boulder in the Missouri, the sounds of the river and the nearness of her father buried

Pastor Lemke's condemnation.

Leonard cast his line far across the water, deftly dropping his fly into a promising seam against the opposite bank. The fish struck immediately, and he set the hook. Maggy saw the tip of his rod bow strongly towards the surface of the water, and she clambered down from the rock, running to him as fast as she could.

"Come here, Mags! I'm going to need your help with this one! Hurry!" When she reached his side, he laughed loudly. "It's a big one! Unclip my net. When I tell you, scoop her up." Leonard clenched his jaw and let out more line as the fish made a run downstream. Maggy's heart beat loudly. She squinted to see the creature struggling for its life below the surface. It broke through the river into the air and bowed in half, its silver scales momentarily glinting blue and pink before smashing back into the water. Maggy gasped in awe. "She's a beauty!" declared Leonard, and Maggy nodded in agreement. She held out the net with both hands, bracing for the critical moment when she would be called into action. Leonard patiently worked the fish, letting him run and then stripping him back in. He spoke just above a whisper, "Now!" The fish was so weary from the struggle that the final moment of victory was anticlimactic. Maggy easily trapped it in the net and waited for her father to take over.

"There we are now. Well done, *spatzi!*" he proclaimed, squeezing her shoulder and taking the net handle into his own hands. The fish floundered hopelessly against the webbing, and Maggy could see its gills billow as it strained to breathe. They waded carefully back to the bank where Leonard turned the fish out onto the dirt to take its measurement. Closing one eye and placing his hands at either end of the fish's body, he whistled. "I'd say that's nineteen inches, Mags. That is one of the biggest rainbows I've ever caught, sweetheart!" Maggy stood faithfully at her father's side, appraising the prize, feeling a rising sense of pride. She crouched down to see it better. As the creature lay dying, its skin was shiny and pretty, even though its mouth was a strange, angry shape. Maggy touched the scales with her finger.

"I bet Joseph never caught a fish this big!" she said suddenly, turning to look up at her father with glee.

"No, Ma'am," he said, folding his arms across his chest, holding back his laughter. "I meant to catch a brown, but this rainbow will do just fine." Leonard lifted open the lid of his fishing basket hanging from his side. "Will you do the honors?" Maggy carefully slid her small hands beneath the motionless fish and lifted it towards her father. He bent his knees, and she placed it gingerly inside the wicker container. Maggy leaned down and wiped her hands on the grass. Leonard watched the river momentarily, and then he fixed his gaze on his daughter as he began to tie another fly onto the end of his line. Her hair was darker than

Marie's, and her eyes a lighter, brighter blue. She was thin and tall, and she had a particular way of walking that belonged entirely to herself. Maggy smiled at him from beneath her hat, displaying two missing teeth.

"I like wearing pants," she declared, patting her pockets. "It's a lot easier to run!" Preparing to tighten his knot, Leonard had one end of the filament in his teeth. Before doing so, however, he spit out the line, wrapped it around his hand instead, and hooked the fly onto his shirtfront.

"I have a better idea. I'd say we've caught ourselves a 'plentiful sufficiency' already, don't you think, Mags?" Although uncertain what he meant, Maggy nodded, wanting to be agreeable. "I want to show you something. It's on the way back." He tucked the loop of line back into his pocket and unstrung his rod, reeling the leader and the line all the way back in.

"Do you have everything?" Maggy looked around and nodded. They set out on the path they had taken to reach the river, slipping unnoticed into the trees.

Leonard hummed as they walked, a sense of peace settling in his gut. Maggy recognized the tune and joined in. Neither sang the words, only the melody. Leonard carried both their rods now and shortened his stride so that Maggy could walk more comfortably. When they reached a fork in the trail, he turned down the path they had not previously taken, and Maggy followed curiously behind him. "The Missouri River is the longest river in America. Imagine that, right here in Helena, something so grand." Maggy tried to see around her father to the trail ahead, enjoying the surprise and anxious to arrive at their secret destination.

Suddenly, Leonard stopped walking and turned around to face his daughter. He knelt down and pushed his hat up so that he could see into her eyes. "I know something has been bothering you, Maggy. For a while now. Did something happen? At school, maybe?" She lowered her gaze to the ground. "And I know you're a lot like me, which means you don't want anyone to know, and you don't want to talk about it." He held her by both shoulders and pulled her into his arms. He hugged her tightly, his palm pressing against the thick braid that hung halfway down her back.

He had witnessed the disdainful looks she sometimes received from townspeople, the women who gave perfunctory greetings to him while glancing at her askance. It was only a matter of time before Maggy was old enough to notice these things, to sense the difference in her treatment. Perhaps it had already begun. Leonard pulled back from the hug. He gave her the chance to speak, in case there was anything she wished to say, but she remained silent, her heart beating rapidly. Leonard stood up and set his hand atop her head, mussing her hair playfully. She smiled.

"That's fine, *spatzi*. You don't have to tell me."

They walked a little further to the edge of the trees and stepped into a clearing. "We're here," Leonard said. "This orchard used to belong to the Davis family, but they've all gone now. Now it grows wild and doesn't belong to anybody. He looked down at Maggy to see if she understood. "They're plum trees, Mags. The weather here isn't any good for a reliable crop. But every few summers, if you hit it right, these trees give up everything they have and yield the biggest, juiciest plums I've ever tasted. The funny thing is they grow better wild than they ever did when John Davis tended them." Leonard put down their fishing equipment and took his daughter's hand, running to the base of one of the trees. An old rotting ladder rested against the trunk, and Leonard kicked it away. With a single heave, he lifted her up onto his shoulders. Maggy laughed and held tightly to his head.

"Alright, go ahead. Pick some. Pick as many as you want and drop them in here," he said, unclipping the fishing net from his belt and lifting it up to her. "We'll bring them home to Mom." Maggy plucked the plum closest to her face. "Go on, taste it." Maggy took a bite and the juice sprayed onto her father's hat. The flesh was warm from the sun. She put the whole plum into her mouth and ate around the pit, spitting it out when she was done.

"Hand me one of those!" said Leonard, holding tight to Maggy's legs with one arm and reaching for a plum with his free hand. Maggy gave him one and continued to collect the fruit.

"I hope mother makes pie!" she said.

"I hope she makes jam," said Leonard with a mouth full of the sweet fruit.

"Move a little to the left, Dad." Leonard stepped left so that Maggy could reach another batch of plums. She paused in her collecting, thinking.

"Does Joseph know about this place?" she asked.

"Nope, I haven't told anyone about it. Not Joseph, not even your mother." Maggy smiled with satisfaction.

"I won't tell anyone. I promise." A moment passed before she added, "Not even Helen."

"Good girl, Mags. We wouldn't want word to get out." Maggy nodded, solemnly. They collected fruit, eating and harvesting, until the net was full. Leonard lifted Maggy from his shoulders and set her down. Cradling their spoils in his arms, he showed her the fruits of their labor.

"There must be thousands!" whispered Maggy with awe and excitement. All traces of whatever had been ailing his daughter had vanished. Her expression bore nothing but delight. Leonard sat down on the ground and leaned against the tree, shutting his eyes. Maggy watched him and then sat down beside him, careful to lean her head back in the same manner.

"You're a smart girl, Mags," he said with his eyes closed, enjoying the shade the tree provided and the coolness of its bark. "You have horse sense. That's something you can't teach. But you like school, too, don't you?"

Maggy shrugged her shoulders. "I like *public* school." Leonard opened his eyes and tilted his head. He chuckled and then sighed. "You like being with Helen," he said wisely. "Your mother thinks it's best if you go to the Lutheran school. She's right. At least for now." Maggy sat up and crossed her legs, leaning forward to pick at the grass.

"I hate math," she said bluntly, ripping a big clump of grass from the ground.

"But you like reading. You're always reading—always your nose is in a book," he teased, tapping her nose with his index finger.

"I like the stories. I see them in my head." Maggy collected daisies to make a daisy chain. When she grew bored with this, she slit a blade of grass with her fingernail and placed it between her thumbs, blowing into the makeshift reed. Twice, a low screech sounded. An hour passed this way before Leonard sat up and cleared his throat.

"I'm thirsty," he said, swallowing and then wincing. "Let's go home."

Helena, Montana
1923

CHAPTER 6

The shop girl at The Helena Mercantile measured a generous scoop of butterscotch candy for her elderly customer. Her plain dress and apron hung loosely on her angular frame, and her dark hair was pulled back tidily at the nape of her neck. She weighed the portion and smiled.

"Exactly a quarter of a pound, Mrs. Wallace. Is there anything else I can get for you today?" The white-haired patron took a moment to decide, her spectacles magnifying her foggy blue eyes. The head of her cane shook under the weight of her body, wobbling her hand and arm.

"No, that's everything, dear. The doctor says I shouldn't have too many sweets."

"That will be ten cents, please." Mrs. Wallace slowly opened her handbag and searched inside for her coin purse. She smacked her lips when her hand at last found it.

"Would you be a dear and fish out the dime for me?" she asked, giving the purse to the young woman, who happily obliged.

"Thank you very much, Mrs. Wallace," she said, placing the money in the register and then handing the candy to the customer. "Let me help you to the door."

"Oh no, no. I don't want to be a bother. There's some strength left in these old legs yet!" Concerned, the girl carefully watched Mrs. Wallace make her way to the door and out onto the street.

"Good day!" she called out after her. The door swung closed.

"Maggy," interjected a voice from the back room, "Have you seen my notepad, the small one I was using earlier?" She glanced quickly around the store but did not find it.

"No, I'm afraid not, Mam. It's not out front. Here, I'll come help you look," Maggy said, rubbing her neck as she walked.

"Ah, here it is!" the disembodied voice exclaimed. Notepad in hand, Mam appeared triumphantly from the back room, eyeing Maggy with humor.

"I would lose my head if it weren't attached to my neck," she said, smiling. "There now, we're running low on flour. I hope the order arrives on time this week. You can never tell in such weather!" she said, looking through the large front windows to the wintry scene beyond. "Winter is not a kind season," she stated, staring. Blinking twice, she remembered her current task and studied the items once more.

"Let me read the list to you, and you can let me know what needs to be restocked," Maggy said, reaching for the notepad. Mam handed it to her reluctantly.

"Very well. I suppose that's why I hired you." Maggy smiled. She had been working at the Helena Mercantile since just after Ralph's General Store had closed its doors and changed ownership. The new owner, Mam, had no surname or at least did not give it. It was clear to all that she was a foreigner or a mulatto, and wild stories circulated for the first few months after she became the sole proprietor and changed the store's longstanding name. As curiosity drove the city's population through her door, business was initially very good. Once the novelty had faded, however, many of Helena's citizens took their patronage elsewhere.

It was around this same time that Maggy had begun to dream of attending the State University of Montana. At first, fearing ridicule—she was failing out of Latin, after all—she'd told no one of her secret aspiration. But as her desire solidified and her grades improved, she confided in Helen and ultimately in her parents, who were initially skeptical but gave their blessing with one stipulation—she would have to get a job.

Having seen a notice in the window for help, Helen dragged Maggy to Ralph's to apply for the position. She'd not set foot inside the shop since overhearing those jarring words seven years before. Maggy held Helen's arm tightly for courage and slowed her steps as they approached. Helen pulled her friend towards the door.

"Come on! We didn't come all this way for you to stand outside like a ninny. You want to go off to university, don't you? Well, it's not free. You need to go inside and ask about the job," Helen said with exasperation.

"Okay, okay. Just give me a moment." Maggy smoothed the front of her dress and hair. "Do I look okay?" she asked.

"Yes, very competent," said Helen, reassuringly. They peered through the large front window as they approached, but all they could see were their own reflections and the street behind them. Maggy took a deep breath and pushed open the door, half-expecting to collide with Pastor Lemke. The store was greatly changed, and both girls stood in the doorway gawking at the new interior. The gray walls had been painted a buttercream yellow, the old light fixtures replaced with new brass ones, and lace curtains now hung ornamentally over the tall windows. A woman popped up like a jack-in-the-box from behind the counter, startling them both.

"Oh, hello," said Maggy, unprepared. "I mean, good afternoon, Ma'am. I was hoping to speak with the owner about the sign," she'd said, stumbling over her words as she pointed to the window. The woman wiped her hands with the rag she held and dropped it on the counter. She stared at Maggy, flustered, before regaining her composure.

"I, I am the owner," she said, "How, how may I help you?" Helen and Maggy looked at one another, speechless. The woman's black hair was worn in a large bun on the top of her head, and her brown face was decorated with a maze of wrinkles. There was a small gold cross around her neck and a gold band on her left hand. "I can see I'm not quite what you expected, but I can assure you that I *am* the owner. My name is on the deed. Would you like to see it?" she'd added teasingly. Helen elbowed Maggy and nudged her forward.

"Ask her," she'd whispered.

"My name is Marguerithe Gerhardt, Ma'am. I came to ask if you are looking for help, for a cashier," she fumbled, her face growing hot. Unexpectedly, the woman clasped her hands together and smiled.

"The Lord answers prayers, girls! I do, in fact, have the need for a cashier, Miss Margaret." The woman extended her hand. Maggy hesitated before reaching to shake it, deciding not to correct the owner's pronunciation of her name. "You may call me Mam," she said, offering no further explanation. "It is good to make your acquaintance. And who is your friend?" she asked, facing Helen.

"Helen Carlisle, Mam," replied Helen, awkwardly.

"Miss Margaret and Miss Helen," she'd repeated, concentrating on Maggy. The large brown eyes studying her were astute yet kind, and Maggy's tension subsided. "Miss Margaret, have you ever worked as a cashier before?"

"No, I have not."

"Can you count money, add and subtract numbers?"

"Yes. I worked as an English tutor before, but never in a store." Watching Mam's reaction, Maggy swallowed, wishing desperately that she'd lied rather than admit her inexperience.

"Well, I suppose beggars can't be choosers. You may have the job on a trial basis. If you do well, then you may stay on after the first month. How does that sound?"

Maggy had not expected the meeting to go so well or her fate to be decided so quickly. She thought a moment before answering. "Yes, I am pleased," she'd said, subduing her enthusiasm with what she thought passed for a professional reply. It was a phrase she had heard her mother use many times.

"I am pleased that you are pleased, Miss Margaret," said Mam with amusement. "Will you begin tomorrow, then?"

"I…yes, yes, I will begin tomorrow," she'd said, again struggling to keep up with the unfolding events. "I have school until three for the next month, but then it's summer break, and I can work all day."

"School?" Mam said, frowning momentarily. "I'd forgotten. Very well, then, be here tomorrow by three-thirty." She'd picked up the rag she had previously dropped and rubbed the wooden countertop in swift circles. "And do not be late, Miss Margaret," she'd added.

"No, I won't, Mam. Thank you, thank you very much. It was very nice to meet you, Mam," said Maggy, stepping backwards.

"Good day Miss Margaret, Miss Helen," she said, nodding her head goodbye. Mam watched the glass door shut behind them. Both girls immediately turned to each other, grinning, as they hurried down the street and out of view.

CHAPTER 7

T he store was unexpectedly busy the remainder of the afternoon, and so Mam and Maggy did not finish the inventory until the following day. When they had, Mam was weary. "I'm going to go upstairs now for a rest, Margaret. I'll be down shortly," she said, untying her apron and hanging it on its nail. When she'd purchased the store from Ralph Wyman, the deed had included the entire building, making her the owner of a two-bedroom apartment above The Helena Mercantile. The flat allowed for the convenience of an afternoon nap, which she took every day shortly after Maggy arrived for work.

As Maggy tidied up one of the displays, she saw Helen approach and then pause outside the store. She wore a red plaid coat with matching hat and a fur muff to keep her hands warm. The choice of color set off her complexion and eyes beautifully, and Maggy noticed a man on the street tip his hat at Helen as he passed by. Maggy could see by the eager expression on Helen's face that she had some piece of good news to share. She stepped inside, pulled her hands from her muff, and brushed a few snowflakes onto the floor.

"Mags, you're not going to believe it!" she began with breathless excitement. "They posted the winners of the Lewis and Clark Girls Sewing Contest, and I won! I won the blue ribbon! They're going to hang my work at the library, for everyone to see!" Her arms both outstretched, she waved them in jubilation.

"That's wonderful, Helen!" Maggy said sincerely, grabbing her friend's cold hands. She did not have Helen's gift for needlework, nor did she much enjoy sewing. Nonetheless, she was proud. Beaming, Helen laughed in astonishment at her own success.

"It's for the pillow cover I made, with the lace and tiny blue and gold flowers. Remember?" Her joy was uncontainable, and she continued before Maggy could respond. "Well I didn't think very much of it when I entered it into the contest. I never expected to win, and now I've gotten the blue ribbon!" Maggy smiled enthusiastically.

"When will they put it up at the library?"

"Next week, and then I'll have my picture in the paper, too!" Noticing the clock on the wall, Helen squeezed Maggy's hand. "I just came by to tell you. I couldn't wait. I have to get home to help mother with dinner. We're having somebody-or-other over to the house tonight, and she's in a panic." Helen rolled her eyes and smiled.

"I'll see you tomorrow, then. Say hello to the family for me. Bye!" called Maggy as Helen left the store, waving. Maggy picked up the pencil she'd set down and tapped the bottom of it against the wood, a smile still on her lips.

The bell rang, sounding the arrival of another customer. It was so soon after Helen's departure, Maggy thought her friend must have forgotten something and returned to fetch it, but a tall, unfamiliar man entered the store in her place. He removed his hat and tan leather gloves and looked around.

"Can I help you, sir?" asked Maggy, tucking a strand of hair behind her ear. He stared at her a few seconds, and Maggy averted her eyes. "This is your first time here, I believe. I know all the regulars. Is there something you need help finding?" She cleared her throat and waited for his response.

"I'm just killing time and getting out of the cold. I'm waiting to meet a friend. Do you mind?" he smiled politely and studied Maggy's face.

"Yes of course. We have hot cider if you'd like some." Maggy gestured in the direction of the pot.

"Thank you, you're very kind. Yes, I would love a cup." An item drew the man's attention, and he walked towards the nearby shelf. As Maggy poured his drink, she glanced and saw he was holding a brush in his hand.

"The owner of the store makes them herself. Aren't they fine?" she asked with esteem, handing him his drink. He stared at the brush and nodded, setting it tentatively back on the shelf as though he'd like to buy it but could not afford to. His well-tailored suit and refined deportment, however, told another story. He took a sip of the cider and smiled.

"This is very good. Thank you. There's nothing so good as a hot drink on a cold day." Maggy smiled. "Don't let me keep you from your work," he said hurriedly, fearing he was doing just that. She headed back behind the counter and pretended to busy herself with dusting. The man drank his cider and walked the length of the room, admiring various objects for sale, glancing at Maggy occasionally. Maggy was curious about the newcomer but did not want to be impolite.

"Are you from out of town, sir?" she asked, finally. He thought a moment and then quietly answered.

"Yes, I'm actually down from Alberta, but I'm originally from Montana," he added, clearing his throat. "I took the train."

"On business?" The man nervously looked into his drink. "I'm sorry. It's really none of my concern," said Maggy quickly, sensing his discomfort and regretting her persistence.

"No, it's a personal matter," he answered.

"I'm Marguerithe," she offered in consolation, reaching out her hand and hoping to put the man more at ease. He smiled.

"It's good to meet you, Marguerithe." He set his empty cup down on the counter and reached into his coat pocket to remove his wallet but did not offer his name. "How much do I owe you for the cider?" he asked.

"Oh, nothing. It's complimentary. Mam, the owner, she thinks it's a nice thing to offer customers in the winter." He raised his eyebrows in surprise and put away his wallet.

"Is this magnanimous owner here?"

"She is, but she's on her break," Maggy answered. He appeared disappointed.

"Have you worked here a long time?"

"A few months," she replied. "I'm earning money for university next spring," she added, feeling rather boastful and foolish as she said it.

"Really! Well that *is* something," he said. Encouraged, Maggy continued.

"The State University of Montana in Missoula."

"You must be a very smart young woman then," he said, charitably. "A lot of people think education is wasted on women, but I disagree." Maggy blushed. The man smiled again and then glanced out the window. "I think I see my friend," he said, putting on his hat. "Thank you again for the cider and the conversation. It was very nice to meet you, Marguerithe."

"Yes, it was nice to meet you, too, sir. Enjoy your stay in Helena." He pulled on his gloves in the doorway and looked once more at Maggy as he pushed his way out onto the sidewalk. Disappointed he had to leave, she watched him cross the street and disappear from view.

Maggy turned on the radio softly and began to sweep the floor. She was filling the dustpan when she heard Mam's footsteps on the stairs.

"Did we have any customers while I was napping?" she asked, walking towards Maggy as she fastened her necklace around her neck once more.

"Just one. But he didn't buy anything. He was waiting for a friend."

"I see. I prefer the paying kind, but maybe he will remember us in the future." There was only one more patron the rest of the evening, and so Mam decided to close early. After Maggy had counted the money in the till and deposited it in the safe, she pulled on her coat and hat. Standing in the doorway a moment to wrap her scarf around her neck, she saw that Mam was watching her strangely.

"What? What is it? Do I have something on my face?"

"Oh, don't mind me. You just looked so grown up—so much like...," her voice trailed off into silence. Maggy smiled, by now accustomed to Mam's eccentricities.

"Goodnight, Mam. See you tomorrow."

"Goodnight, Margaret."

CHAPTER 8

Two days later, Maggy stopped by the post office after school on her way to work. To her delight, there was an envelope awaiting her.

"And who do you know in Missoula?" asked Mrs. Sandstrom, handing her the letter.

"I'm not sure," replied Maggy, the woman's nosiness irritating. When she saw the return address, her heart beat rapidly. Anxious to be alone, she quickly left the post office and turned into the alley, tearing open the envelope. With initial trepidation, she read the acceptance letter from the State University of Montana three times before truly believing that Mr. Gene H. Clapp was pleased to offer her acceptance for the following spring quarter. It was the greatest moment of her young life, and Maggy looked about her on the street, hoping to find a familiar face to share in the good news. She ran all the way to work but was forced to delay her outburst when she saw that Mam was currently helping a customer.

Maggy slipped into the back of the store and tied on her apron, tucking the letter in its front pocket. When she stepped back out onto the floor, she recognized the man as the kind gentleman from the other day. He looked nervous, but when he spotted Maggy, his demeanor changed.

"Good afternoon," said Maggy smiling, happy to see him again. "I see that you're still in town."

"Yes, you look very well today, Miss Marguerithe," he noted. The excitement of her acceptance and the dash from the post office had brought color to Maggy's cheeks and vibrancy to her eyes.

"Thank you."

"—Yes, yes she does," said Mam. Turning in Maggy's direction, she continued. "This gentleman was inquiring after you, and I was just telling him that you would be in for work at any moment. And there, you see, I was true to my word." Mam smiled and the man turned his hat in his hands.

"I was walking by and thought I would come in and leave some money for the cider. I know you said it was free, but I didn't feel right about it," he explained. Pulling a nickel from his pocket, he held it out for Maggy to take. Tentatively, she took it and dropped it in her apron. Mam studied the man.

"Sir, have we met before?" she asked, as though it were a foolhardy thing to ask.

"I'm from out of town, so it's unlikely," he replied, averting his eyes and putting his hat back on his head. "Well, I should be going." He lingered a moment near the doorway. "Good luck with university, Marguerithe. I am sure they would be lucky to have you."

"I, well, I actually learned just now that I have been accepted for the spring quarter!" Maggy blurted out, waving the written proof in her hand, too excited to question the propriety of sharing her news with a stranger.

"My heavens!" exclaimed Mam. Simultaneously, the man walked toward her and offered his hand for Maggy to shake.

"Congratulations! What a wonderful announcement," he said.

"Is it true, Margaret? Is it official now?" asked Mam, squeezing Maggy's arm.

"Yes, it is! I can't believe it. They must be awfully desperate for money," she joked. The man watched Maggy warmly.

"I am sure your family must be very proud of you," he said. He did not wait for her reply. "It was good to meet you. Thank you again for your kindness. I hope we will cross paths again," he said earnestly, opening the door. "Good day, Ma'am."

Mam followed him with her gaze, "Sir, I didn't catch your name."

"Hall, Andrew Hall," he replied, letting the door close behind him.

Mam's arm shot up and reached out, as though to call him back, but she did not speak. She took the acceptance letter from Maggy, who saw that the paper rustled with the shaking of her hand.

"Are you feeling all right?"

"I'm a bit light-headed," Mam said. Maggy took her arm.

"Let me help you upstairs. When you're feeling better, you can read the letter." Maggy helped her up the stairs into her apartment and draped the blanket across her lap.

"Try to get some rest," she said kindly, latching the door closed and walking back downstairs to the store.

Mam's hands continued to tremble as she sat on the sofa. She looked at the gold band on her finger she had bought for herself many years before and slid it painfully over her enlarged knuckle, setting it in a glass dish on the coffee table. It was a small lie that afforded her less scrutiny.

She pinched the bridge of her nose and furrowed her brow, trying to steady her breath. Andrew. He had found them. In the sixteen years that had passed since they'd last met, he had become a man. She'd sent him a letter years before explaining all that had happened with Judith, revealing the existence and location of his daughter, and enclosing the creased note Judith had written him on the mountain. But he had never replied, and she'd been uncertain he ever received it. When he'd stepped across the threshold of Helena Mercantile, she had not placed him.

Ruth knew she had changed. She had withered into a middle-aged woman with a husky voice who appeared a decade older than she was. Despite the grief that would always live at the base of her heart, she had grown happier with time, less serious and more inclined to laughter. Her complexion, her stature, her words, her thoughts, her name—all had softened. Even her flint-black hair had faded almost entirely to grey. She had become more and more like the people around her, adopting their gesticulations and turns of phrase. Judith would not have known her; perhaps even Alex would have been fooled. But Andrew had somehow recognized her. She'd seen it in his expression. It was his familiarity that had given her pause.

"Oh, Andrew!" she whispered aloud, covering her face with her hands as tears overcame her.

CHAPTER 9

Maggy peeked out through the frosted window at her father and brother, both men surrounded by their own frozen breath as they cranked the car engine. Snow still blanketed the town and surrounding mountains so that the crystal encrusted grasses and rocks glittered as the sun rose. The months since receiving her acceptance to the university had passed swiftly, and Maggy stood now in the foyer of her home with her trunk at her feet, waiting to embark upon her first great adventure.

Leonard and Joseph carried Maggy's things outside and loaded them into the Ford, while Helen cried and repeatedly made her dearest friend promise to keep in touch. At seven, everyone climbed into the car, muttering of the cold, cramped seating, and early hour. All talk soon died away, leaving nothing but the melody of the sputtering car and crunching snow. Helen took Maggy's arm and smiled through tears. Leonard held his wife's hand and watched the road while Marie stared out the window at the lonesome scenery. Joseph whistled an inappropriately jovial tune.

They made good time and arrived at the Union Depot a quarter hour early. Leonard arranged for his daughter's belongings to be loaded onto the train, and they all took a seat at The Beanery. Leonard and Joseph ordered coffee, while the ladies took tea. Leonard observed his daughter over the rim of his cup and noted with satisfaction that she was a fine young woman, attractive and smart in her new fur-trimmed coat and with a sensible air about her. He tried to read the newspaper but found it difficult to concentrate, folding and unfolding it instead. Marie picked a few pieces of lint from Maggy's sleeve and patted her hand. Helen rested her forehead pitifully against her other shoulder.

When the station agent announced it was time for passengers to board the Overland Express, Marie jumped in her seat, and they all rose simultaneously. Maggy's parents had surprised her with a new carpetbag she now held through its handle on her forearm. The green wool scarf wrapped warmly around her neck was a gift from Helen, who'd knitted it especially for the occasion. Joseph gave his sister a black umbrella with an ivory handle that was packed away in her trunk.

"Goodbye, Helen," began Maggy.

"I can't believe you're actually leaving Helena and *your* Helen," Helen whispered in her ear as she hugged her friend roughly. "Don't forget me!" Joseph put his arm around Maggy's shoulders and pulled her to him.

"Be careful out there, sis," he said. When Maggy saw her father's thick mustache began to quiver, she quickly embraced him and buried her face in his chest. He stroked her hair momentarily and kissed the top of her head.

"Work hard, Mags, and have fun," he said. "You must know how proud of you we are." Maggy could no longer fight back her tears and turned now to her mother with a flushed face and runny nose.

"Marguerithe, you look a fright," she quipped, wiping her daughter's cheeks with her handkerchief. "I traveled across the Atlantic when I was half your age and across the country at seventeen. You mustn't be afraid," she said, holding Maggy by both arms. "Once you're settled, write to let us know how you are." Marie's stomach clenched with anxiety, but her voice remained steady. "There now. That's my girl. No more tears. This is a *happy* day. It will be an adventure!" she said.

Leonard stared at his wife in disbelief and felt a tremendous love for her. He knew how difficult this was for Marie. She took something from her pocket and handed it to Maggy. "This was my mother's. It is the only thing I have from her," she said, giving her a small velvet box. "It was my communion present. Don't look inside until you're onboard. You'll be in my prayers, Marguerithe. Find a good Lutheran church. Hurry on now—you'll miss your train," she said, motioning for her daughter to go. Maggy kissed her mother and put the gift in her coat pocket.

"I love you. I will write—promise," she said. Maggy turned and walked up the steps to the train and handed her ticket to the man who greeted her. She clutched her bag to her body and tried not to cry. All she had wanted was to leave Helena, and now that she was on her way, it seemed an impetuous decision. Panic seized her throat, and she found that she struggled to speak when meeting her cabin mates. They were a young couple on their way to Clinton, a small town near Missoula where the husband was to take a teaching position at the local high school.

As their polite conversation dwindled and Maggy heard the final call for passengers, she positioned herself to see her family on the platform. She waved to them as the train lurched into motion, pressing her hand against the window. They were all still, except for Helen, who waved vigorously and blew her kisses. "Goodbye," she whispered through the glass, heavy with fear and doubts. The glass clouded from her emotion. She felt conspicuous and fumbling and never so alone.

"—Where is it you said you were going?" asked the husband as the train pulled away from the station. Maggy dabbed at the corners of her eyes and tried not to turn her head to see those she loved most one final time.

"The State University of Montana," she answered. "I'll be a freshman." He raised his eyebrows in surprise.

"Really now? It is a fine school, yes a fine school indeed," he said reassuringly. The wife unfolded her hands from her lap and touched Maggy's arm.

"We'll give you our address, and you can look us up if you get lonely. It's only one stop away on the train." Maggy sniffled and exhaled, touched by their kindness. She waited until she could no longer see the station to open the small box her mother had given her. Inside was a gold cross necklace, thin and darkened with age. It was similar to the one Ruth wore. Maggy removed it from the box and fastened it around her neck, feeling immediately anchored to home. She held the pendant with the tips of her fingers, turning it over in her hand as she listened to the train's wheels screech along the tracks.

The railroad took them through the Rocky Mountains for the duration of their journey, and the rugged scenery rose and fell in jagged peaks and titanic boulders as they sped by. With each station name announced, Maggy grew less apprehensive. The dense forest just beyond the clearing of the tracks gave way to towns that she had never before seen, and her initial desire to leave Helena, to travel and go somewhere new, was refreshed.

Just before Bearmouth, her companions went to the dining car and left Maggy alone for the first time since boarding the train. She opened her bag and searched for her book, but instead her fingers touched the bristles of the brush that Mam had given her. She took it out from the bag and studied it. It was so kind of her to have given her anything.

On Marguerithe's last day at The Helena Mercantile, Mam had gone upstairs for her daily nap but quickly returned below with a rectangular box.

"This is for you, Margaret. It's not one we sell here—it's from my own personal collection. It's always been my favorite, and I'd like for you to have it." She handed the box to Maggy, who lifted the lid with curiosity. Maggy stroked the brush with admiration.

"It's beautiful," she said.

"It's old, but it's special, in many ways." Maggy held the gift and looked at it more closely. The carving on the handle was intricate—two swallows in flight. When she turned it over in her hands, she saw the initials, "JF." Little indentations peppered its length.

"Thank you, Mam. I've never seen anything like it. You really didn't have to get me anything. Thank you," she said with genuine appreciation.

"I'm glad you like it. You can use it at school and think of us back here in Helena." The thought saddened them both, and Mam took the brush from Maggy, setting it back inside its box and securing the lid. "Don't forget it when you leave tonight," she said, quickly kissing Maggy on the cheek and walking back up the stairs.

When Maggy had finished sweeping the store and counting the money, she went to say her final goodbye but found the apartment door uncharacteristically locked. She knocked lightly but did not persist when there was no response. Maggy went downstairs and left a brief note for Mam to find in the morning, thanking her once more for hiring her and for the gift. She would be home for summer and would come and visit then.

Maggy put the brush away and found her book. Opening its pages, the motion of the locomotive and the clanking of the cabin interrupted her concentration and soothed her to the point of sleep. Her eyelids lowered, and she struggled to pay attention to the story. Unable to resist the fatigue that overtook her, her book fell to the side and rested between her hip and the wall.

When the couple returned from their breakfast, they found the unusual young woman asleep, her head pressed into the corner and her novel on the floor. The wife kindly picked it up to preserve its spine and set it down on the seat beside her. They spoke in whispers for the remainder of the way to Clinton, certain that the girl needed the rest for all that lay ahead. When she showed no signs of stirring, the couple quietly gathered their things and left the compartment without waking her, leaving behind a note with their names and address tucked inside her book.

It was the voice of the ticket agent that finally roused Maggy from her deep sleep.

"This is your stop, Miss. *Missoula*," he said politely. Startled and disoriented, Maggy looked at the empty cabin for a trace of her companions.

"They got off at the last stop, Miss," he explained. Maggy nodded, still befuddled with sleep and unable to grasp his meaning.

"Oh, we're here!" she said, suddenly understanding. She scrambled to collect her belongings, almost forgetting her book and hat. The ticket agent handed these to her kindly and smiled.

"Your trunk is already on the platform," he said, standing aside to let her pass.

"Thank you, sir," she said. He tipped his hat. Maggy stepped down and walked toward the men unloading the train's luggage. Someone from the university was supposed to meet her, and she glanced tentatively at the countless passing faces, uncertain which one among the crowd might be his. While she waited, she picked out her trunk and dragged it to the side.

She stood and scanned the station once more. It was then that she saw a young woman her own age holding a sign with Maggy's name written on it. She had dark hair, fair skin, and a slender figure. When their gazes at last met, Maggy waived at the girl, who smiled and quickly walked to join her.

"Miss Gerhardt, so good to meet you," the woman said, vigorously shaking Maggy's hand. "My name is Stephanie Fenn. I'm a sophomore at the State University of Montana studying Biology," she explained rapidly. "Did you have a good trip?" she asked, her green eyes glinting as she took Maggy's arm and gestured to a young man to collect the trunk. "I do so enjoy taking the train!" she stated with enthusiasm.

"Why, yes, I did have a fine trip. It's nice to meet you, Miss Fenn," she said, catching up with the conversation. "Does the college send people to greet all of its new students?"

"Well not the college, but the Young Woman's Christian League does, and please call me Steph. We try to arrange this sort of thing for everyone we can, though some ladies slip through the cracks or don't want our help," she said, grinning. Maggy smiled back, deciding definitively in that moment that she liked Stephanie Fenn very much. They climbed inside the car that awaited them, and the man who loaded her trunk took the driver's seat.

"Miss Gerhardt, this is Mr. Billy Walton," she said, gesturing first at Maggy and then at the driver.

"Pleased to meet you, Miss," he said.

"Likewise," replied Maggy, sitting back in the seat.

"We'll take you to the main building so you can check in, and from there we'll go to your boarding house," said Stephanie with excitement.

"Do you like it at the University?" asked Maggy. "I wasn't sure if there'd be any other girls," she stated.

"I *adore* it here, and don't worry, there are plenty of other girls. Not too many, though," she said winking, "if you know what I mean." Maggy, in fact, did not know what she meant, but she smiled as though she did. Steph lifted a clipboard from the seat, which appeared to hold several pages of important information. She ran her finger along the paper until she found what she needed. "Ah yes, you're boarding at Mrs. Toomey's. I think you'll like it there very much. Mrs. Toomey is strict, but she takes *good* care of her residents—this is Higgins Avenue here that we're on now," she interjected. Remembering again the strain of conversation, Steph patted Maggy's knee gently. "Mrs. Toomey has helped many students make their adjustment."

"Their adjustment?" asked Maggy.

"To the life of a coed, of course! I will tell you right now that it's *nothing* like home and probably nothing like what you've imagined." Seeing the concern that appeared on Maggy's guileless face, she quickly added, "It's far better! I'm from Butte, and this place knocked my socks off! You'll probably want to join one of the sororities next quarter. I'm a member of Delta Sigma, and it's a great way to make friends and have something to do other than study. Oh, I didn't ask you what you'll be studying! How rude of me!" cried Stephanie.

"Education. I plan on becoming a teacher," explained Maggy, feeling provincial.

"—There it is!" cried Steph, pointing straight ahead through the glass of the windshield. "Main Hall," she said with satisfaction. The car had turned left onto a long stretch of road that ended in the distance at the base of a hill. In front stood a scholarly brick edifice with a lofty clock tower. Soon they approached the entrance of the campus, and the path curved in a large circle in front of the main building. The land in front had been entirely cleared, creating an expansive lawn for student activities in the warmer months. She could see from their position that the clock read precisely three fifteen.

"That's the Women's Hall there, and Science Hall. The one to the left is the library—you'll be spending the rest of your life in there," she teased, rolling her eyes. "The President's house is there, and that's the gym and field behind it. Of course, the outside facilities are closed for the winter." Maggy tried to remember all the designations but could recall nothing but Main Hall. It was in front of this grand building that they finally parked.

"If you'll excuse me for a moment, I'll run inside. I need to speak with the registrar to clear something up. Do you mind seeing yourself in and reporting to the front desk? They'll give you instructions." Steph ran up the stairs, not waiting for permission.

Maggy looked at Mr. Billy Walton, who rested his arm along the front seat and pulled a cigarette from his pocket. "I'll wait here," he said, casually. She stepped from the car and tilted her head back to take in the tower's full height.

There were buildings much taller in Helena, perhaps with more history and greater importance, but none held as much meaning to Maggy. It seemed to her that her dreams would either come true or be shattered in the next few moments, and she hesitated to know which.

Wrapping her coat around her, she walked up the stairs slowly, pausing to gawk at the archway as she passed beneath it. She opened the heavy front door only wide enough to allow her thin body passage. The door shut, and Maggy stood in a shining entryway. The floors, the furniture, the soaring ceiling all gleamed with care and stateliness. She stepped further into the room and turned in a circle. She could not help but smile. Maggy's previous fears dissolved in an instant.

A woman wearing a green cardigan looked up from her desk with darting eyes. In a loud voice, brimming with pride, Maggy did not wait to be addressed.

"My name is Marguerithe Catherine Gerhardt, and I am checking in for my first quarter." As Maggy signed her name to the bottom of several forms and received an orientation packet, Stephanie appeared at her side.

"Is she giving you any trouble, Mrs. Schneider?" teased Steph.

"Not at all, Ms. Fenn. Ms. Gerhardt has been polite and efficient," she explained, believing she paid Maggy a large compliment in saying so. "Everything is in order with her accounts, and she may begin classes on Wednesday."

"Wonderful! Then we're off!" said Stephanie, linking her arm with Maggy's as though they had been friends for years. As they approached the car at the base of the steps, Maggy spoke under her breath.

"Not bad for a girl left on a doorstep!"

"Pardon me?" said Stephanie, not making out Maggy's words.

"Oh nothing. I just think that I'm going to like it here very much," she responded, grinning and hopping energetically into the back seat. "Billy, could I have one of those cigarettes?" she asked. She'd never before smoked, but now seemed the perfect moment to try. Billy raised his eyebrows but tilted the pack toward her. She slid one out and waited for him to light it. Stephanie feigned indignation.

"Peggy Gerhardt! I'll see that your mother hears about this!" Maggy smiled as the embers at the end of the cigarette turned orange. *Peggy Gerhardt*. She inhaled deeply and her head spun. The smoke filled her lungs, and she coughed loudly and spasmodically. Her eyes watered as Steph slapped her back. They all smiled, and Peggy handed the cigarette back to Billy.

"Thank you," she said. Billy laughed and flicked the butt outside into the snow, starting the car and driving them wildly toward Ms. Toomey's.

CHAPTER 10

Peggy wrote home faithfully each week, even if the letter's composition meant staying up an hour later than she should. Her room at Mrs. Toomey's boarding house was on the second floor, affording her a view of the street and Main Hall in the far distance. It was spacious yet sparse, with a dresser, single bed, braided rug, and small wooden desk.

Stephanie encouraged her to join the Young Women's Christian Association and introduced her to her circle of friends, including Virginia Pratt, a quiet and kind sophomore who shared Peg's love of books. Upon her mother's continued promptings, she did seek out the German Lutheran Church in Missoula, where Mrs. Toomey, among others, attended.

Sitting in the worn and scratched pew, pangs of homesickness struck her, and she thought often of her parents, especially her father. It was for this small taste of home that she was drawn to wake early Sunday mornings. But as she missed Helena less and less, and as her homework and other social obligations increased, her motivation and desire to do so diminished. By the second month, she sought reasons not to go and avoided Mrs. Toomey's inevitable Saturday evening invitation to accompany her the next morning. She found such a reason in Hugh Pratt.

The first time Peggy had seen Hugh, he'd been resting on the porch of his fraternity drinking a glass of water, half of his football uniform discarded, the other half around his waist. His hair was sweaty and disheveled, and he'd effused confidence and ease. Peggy was walking by herself, and Hugh had politely wished her a good afternoon from the balcony. Startled, Peggy stared at the handsome man and searched her mind for the proper response. All she had managed was a nod and the faintest trace of a smile before scurrying on her way.

When he'd appeared the following Sunday with Virginia, and she'd introduced the good-looking man as her brother, Peggy had just as much trouble thinking of anything to say.

"How do you do? I'm Marguerithe, but everyone calls me Peggy," she'd said, shaking his hand, "Or Peg, whichever you like," she'd added.

"It's good to meet you, Peggy. I'm Hugh." He looked her squarely in the eye and then squinted. "I think I saw you the other day, walking?" Of course, Peggy had immediately recognized him as the football player on the front porch, but she'd pretended to have difficulty placing him.

"So you're the girl my sister won't stop talking about." Virginia hit him on the shoulder, embarrassed, and Peggy smiled. "Well it *is* good to finally make your acquaintance." He bowed then in such a way as to mock the antiquated gesture. Peggy giggled and returned the bow, a regal expression on her face.

Sundays were the only day Hugh did not have football practice, and so this is when he most often accompanied Virginia. The friends sat in the parlor and talked, or Virginia played the piano and Hugh sang. Peggy discovered that among Hugh's many gifts, his honey-toned tenor was paramount. Due to a lifetime of family entertaining, the brother and sister harmonized effortlessly, and it was a treat for Peggy to sit and listen.

Occasionally, the trio went for a walk through town or down to the river. Peggy found Hugh handsome, strong and charming. She liked how one corner of his mouth lifted higher than the other when he smiled. He had a sharp wit, which surprised her, as she had assumed before speaking with him that his athleticism precluded any real intellect.

Soon, whenever she was not actively engaged in some activity or conversation, she found that her mind drifted inevitably to Hugh's handsome face. The crush was a nuisance, as Peggy knew her infatuation was preposterous, but it was also lovely. Never before had she been romantically interested in anyone; the new sensation was intoxicating—foolish, perhaps—but sweetly addictive. She told no one of her feelings, especially not Virginia.

"You and Ginny are something else, you know," Peggy said, a few weeks after she had first met Hugh. "My brother, well we're not at all like you two. I don't think he's missed me a day since I left," she explained without self-pity. "He's much older—I'm sure that's part of it. We never had very much in common." Looking down at her hands, she had an idea. "Wait here, I'll be right back." Peggy disappeared and came back down the stairs with the black umbrella Joseph had given her before she'd boarded the train to Missoula.

"Here, look. This was his gift to me when I left for school," she said, handing the umbrella to Hugh so he could inspect it.

"It's a fine umbrella. Very practical, I'd say," he laughed. "Just look at that ivory handle. Impressive. Not the most exciting gift, but it will come in handy."

"Oh I've already used it a dozen times, and it is a good umbrella, I'm sure. I don't mean to sound ungrateful. It was nice of him to get me anything. It's just of all things to give your sister who's going off to university—an umbrella?" Peggy grinned. "I love Joseph, but I pity his wife on anniversaries. He doesn't have a romantic bone in him." She set the umbrella down and uncomfortably searched for something else to say. Hugh took a step closer, a flirtatious smile forming.

"That's something that Joseph and I do not share," he said, charmingly, looking intently at Peggy. Virginia and Steph came back into the room from the kitchen, interrupting their conversation.

"Hugh, do you want to show them Dad's shop?" He ran his fingers through his hair and smiled with irritation at his sister.

"Yes, I'd be happy to show them if you think they'd like that sort of thing. It's just a store," he said, shrugging his shoulders. Hugh and Virginia had been born in Missoula, and their father ran a successful bakery known throughout the city for its blue-ribbon cinnamon rolls.

"Sure, sounds fun," said Peggy, thankful for the distraction.

Hugh and Virginia walked ahead of Stephanie and Peggy, allowing Steph a chance to say what was on her mind.

"Peggy, I'm certain that Hugh likes you," she said in a hushed voice, linking arms with her friend. Peggy looked at her with alarm, questioningly. "Oh don't give me that look. I've seen how he acts around you, how he stares at you. He's never so well behaved as when you're around. It's like two different men!" Stephanie paused and waited for Peggy to respond. The girls noticed that Hugh had taken an unsuspected turn onto a street that did not lead into town, and that he was pulling his sister after him. Curious, they followed.

"Well, what do you think? Do you like him, too?" Peggy blushed, unwilling to admit her infatuation. "Oh, you don't even have to say it. I know you do! Marguerithe Gerhardt, you like him very much!" she said, squeezing Peggy's arm and grinning. "You should know he's planning on asking you to be his date for the upcoming formal." Peggy stopped and turned to face her friend.

"What? What formal?"

"It's for the fraternities, but you don't have to belong to a sorority to go. Will you say yes if he asks?" Peggy reeled from the revelation.

"If he asked me, I'd go," she finally stated. "But I don't think he will." Peggy looked down at her feet and smiled as she imagined attending the dance.

"I knew it!" said Steph, laughing. "And don't be silly! He'll be the luckiest man on campus to have you as his date," she added kindly.

The group ended up at the Clark Fork River instead of the bakery and spent the afternoon on its banks, laughing as they skipped stones and told stories. As Virginia impersonated their rhetoric professor, Hugh smiled, but his mind was clearly elsewhere. He stared across the river to the fields beyond and then to the hills at their base. It was a wide yet uninteresting expanse of land they had all looked upon many times.

"There used to be teepees here," he said unexpectedly. The girls' laughter subsided and they wiped the tears from the corners of their eyes.

"What?" they said in unison.

"It's true. I've seen photographs. Right here, in this spot, a tribe lived here, at least for a while."

"What happened to them?" asked Peggy, intrigued.

"Moved to a reservation or into town or died," he said casually. He faced his friends and grinned. "I bet it's haunted," he said mischievously, lifting his arms above his head and groaning like a ghost, wobbling towards them. Peggy jumped back and skipped to the side, avoiding his grasp.

"Don't be daft, Hugh," said Virginia, ripping up a patch of grass and throwing it in his face as he came near. The tuft landed in his wide-open mouth, and they all laughed as he tried to spit it out.

"I could use one of Dad's cinnamon rolls," said Hugh, wiping his mouth with his sleeve. Hunger gnawing at their stomachs and the promise of a fresh-baked treat luring them away, they all concurred and at last made their way to town.

CHAPTER 11

Mrs. Toomey answered the knock at the door with flour in her hair and on the front of her apron. "Oh, Mr. Pratt, please excuse my appearance! I was just in the middle of baking bread. How can I help you?" she asked glancing toward the kitchen, distracted and embarrassed.

"Good afternoon, Ma'am. Apologies for my timing. Is Peggy home?"

"Come in, come in," she said, pulling him hurriedly through the doorway. Mrs. Toomey stood at the foot of the stairs. "Peggy! There's a Mr. Pratt to see you!" she called.

Absorbed in her studies, Peg only heard Mrs. Toomey call her name. She walked in a fog to the top of the stairs before staring down to see Hugh, smiling up at her meekly.

Mrs. Toomey led Hugh into the parlor as Peggy descended the stairs and joined them. "Don't mind me, now. I'll just catch up on my needlepoint. You two pretend I'm not even here," said Mrs. Toomey. It was the first time Hugh had come to the house without Virginia, and her absence was conspicuous.

"Is Ginny okay?" she asked, concerned.

"What?—Yes, Ginny's fine, I'm sure," he answered, confused. He removed his hat and held it by its brim, turning it over in his hands. "You look pretty today," he said awkwardly, blurting it out more loudly than he'd intended.

"Thank you," said Peggy, positive that she did not look pretty. She had spent the past several hours bent over her desk reading John Donne, and she still wore her spectacles and thick, shapeless cardigan. She suddenly became very aware of her dowdy appearance and wished she'd had the foresight to change before coming downstairs. There were a few moments of silence as Peggy waited for Hugh to speak.

"Yes, well I've come to ask if you'd like to be my date for the spring formal my fraternity is throwing. Nothing rowdy or inappropriate," he added for Mrs. Toomey's benefit, who despite her busy hands, hung on every word. Peggy could not believe that Stephanie had been right. She stared at him blankly, imagining what she would tell her friend, so that he cleared his throat and shifted his weight.

"Yes!" she said, suddenly realizing that he awaited her reply. She leaned forward and touched his arm without thinking. Hugh smiled with relief. "When is it?" she asked.

"A week from Saturday, at six. You can make it then?"

"Yes, I think so," she said, smiling broadly and nodding. "What should I wear?" she asked, worried that she might not have the proper dress for such an event. Perhaps Stephanie had something she could borrow.

"Oh, well I'm not sure. All the fellows will be dressed in tuxedos, so whatever the lady's equivalent is, I guess," said Hugh. Mrs. Toomey snorted audibly from her seat in the corner.

"Don't worry, dear. I can show you what you'll need," she said, looking down her nose at Hugh from her seated position. Hugh put his hat back on.

"I have to get to practice. Marguerithe, I'm so glad you said yes. I would have felt awfully dumb if I'd come here and you'd turned me away," he said with sincerity. His lack of confidence flummoxed her. Peggy could not believe that Hugh had any doubt that she would agree. "I'll see you on Sunday, at our normal time?" Peggy nodded happily.

"See you then!" Hugh let himself out, and Peggy turned to face Mrs. Toomey, who eyed her with restrained amusement.

"My dear, you look as though you've swallowed a rainbow," she chuckled. Although she had been hard on Hugh, the truth was that she did like the boy. He was a fine enough young man, his only faults being that he was neither German nor Lutheran. Peggy's countenance darkened.

"What is it now, Marguerithe?" asked Mrs. Toomey.

"You don't suppose he asked me because he felt sorry for me, do you? Or because Ginny made him?" she asked, the pernicious thought seeping into her mind.

"Marguerithe Catherine Gerhardt, that is the most ludicrous thing I have *ever* heard," she proclaimed, thrusting her needlework aside and rising with authority from her chair. "To be sure, Mr. Pratt is fortunate to have such a fine young lady accompany him to his fraternity event. You could do far better than him, my dear. If anyone is the object of condescension, it is he, not you!" She shook her finger with vigor and did not avert her gaze. "I promised my sister that I would look after you, and she will no doubt report to your mother everything I tell her. I hold myself personally accountable to Marie, and you *will* be the most charming girl there, even if I have to sew your dress myself." She took Peggy's hand and kissed her brusquely on the cheek.

"Now, I was in the middle of a loaf, and shouldn't you get back to your studies?" she reminded Peggy.

"Yes, but there's no point now. I won't get anywhere until I tell Stephanie what's happened." She walked to the door and put on her coat. "I'll be home in an hour!" she said as she shut the door and ran all the way to Women's Hall to find her friend. Mrs. Toomey shook her head and walked back slowly into the kitchen.

"Youth!" she exhaled with nostalgia, kneading the dough she'd abandoned as the grandfather clock struck one.

CHAPTER 12

On her way home from a visit with Mrs. Gloege, Marie stopped in town at the butcher's to buy a large roast for Leonard's birthday dinner the following evening. With much sneaking and plotting, she'd put together a small group of family and friends to join them. She knew that Leonard, who was normally so modest and shied from attention, would secretly delight in such bother being made over his birthday.

As Marie left the butcher, she spotted Helen walking towards her on the street. A tall, unfamiliar man accompanied her, and the two were clearly delighted to be in each other's company. Helen did not yet see her, and so Marie took the opportunity to observe the pair. The man was surely much older, perhaps in his thirties, with broad shoulders and a strong frame. His skin tanned and his frame muscular, Marie guessed that he labored to earn his pay. She wondered if Helen's parents knew how he took their daughter's arm with such familiarity. The man whispered something in her ear, and her cheeks flushed. Marie's eyes narrowed as she waited to be seen.

"Good day, Helen," she said tersely, shifting the parcel of meat to her other arm. Helen smiled broadly at Marie, and it was with some relief that Marie immediately saw the girl was neither embarrassed nor secretive.

"Hello, Mrs. Gerhardt. Let me introduce you to my friend, Paul Summers." The man removed his hat and bowed his head.

"Good day, Mrs. Gerhardt. It *is* a fine day," he affirmed, looking again at Helen as he spoke.

"It is, Mr. Summers, and it's also good to meet you."

"Here, let me carry that for you," he offered, relieving Marie of her roast.

"Paul is walking me home, so we're going the same way," explained Helen. "I've told him all about Mags and her family."

"It's true, Mrs. Gerhardt. If you don't mind my saying, I feel like I know you already." Marie looked at Paul and immediately assessed that he was an honest man, not given to frivolity or flattery; he meant what he said. With closer proximity, Marie saw that her earlier guess at his age was likely correct.

"A special occasion?" he asked, raising the meat into view.

"Ah, yes," said Marie. "It's my husband's birthday tomorrow. He'll be fifty-five years old. It's something to mark, I think. Helen," she continued, "You'll come to the party, won't you? You know that Leonard thinks of you as a second daughter. It would make him very happy to have you there. Your parents are coming." Marie thought a moment and then added, "Mr. Summers, if you are free and would like to come, too, you'd be most welcome." Without Marie seeing, Helen raised her eyebrows and pinched Paul's arm, encouraging him to accept.

"Yes, thank you. I would like that." An acquaintance they passed and momentarily greeted briefly interrupted their conversation.

"What were we saying?" asked Marie once they'd continued on. "Oh yes, what do you do, Mr. Summers?" she asked. Helen stifled her laughter, certain that the topic had not before been broached.

"I'm a rancher, Mrs. Gerhardt, born and raised," he said plainly.

"And you're from Helena?" she asked, gleaning as much information as possible before they would part ways. She would report both to Leonard and to Marguerithe everything she'd learned. Although she wished to discover his age, as this was presently her greatest objection to the man, Marie was unwilling to be so bold.

"No, I came to Helena a few years ago now. I'm originally from up north—Havre." She nodded her head.

"Mrs. Gerhardt," interrupted Helen, "Have you had any word from Maggy?" Reluctant to give up her line of questioning, Marie succumbed to the desire to speak of her daughter.

"I had a letter two days ago. I'm sure she tells you more than she does me, but she says that she's doing well in her classes, and that she doesn't have much time for anything other than studying. She seems to love it. Marguerithe always did like to read." Trying to determine whether or not Maggy had confided in her mother, Helen waited for any mention of Hugh Pratt. She wished she had so the two could discuss it, but it seemed Maggy had chosen to withhold her beau's existence.

"I'm so glad she's happy there. I don't know what possessed her to leave Helena and go to Missoula, of all places, but it was good of you and Mr. Gerhardt to let her go."

"Well I don't know about all that," said Marie, uncomfortable with the praise and reaching for the roast. Paul handed it to her and smiled.

"Here we are," she said. "I'll be counting on you both for tomorrow evening. Be over by five."

"Good day, Mrs. Gerhardt. It was a pleasure."

"Likewise, Mr. Summers, Helen."

Marie walked the distance from the sidewalk to the front door and looked for signs of her husband. From the stoop, she watched Paul say goodbye to Helen and observed him kiss her hand. Despite her reservations about his age, Marie smiled.

She opened and shut the front door quietly, the memories of her and Leonard's first years together playing in her mind. She slipped into the kitchen and hid the roast in the icebox. Once it was safely tucked away, she looked for her husband around the house but did not find him; he must still be at work. How she wished he did not have to keep such long hours!

Marie found the last letter Marguerithe had written and sat down in the rocking chair to read it once more. She was saddened to find no mention of any romantic interest amidst the scrawled lines of her daughter's hand. Seeing Helen with Paul, the way in which her great beauty was magnified to an even larger extent by his attentions, Marie could not help but feel that it was time for Marguerithe to make her own match. To her amazement, her little girl had reached the age when most women would begin to marry. Marie was certain she would soon hear news of Helen and Paul's own engagement. She took out a fresh piece of paper and began her report to Marguerithe, informing her daughter that her best friend would likely soon wed.

CHAPTER 13

The night of the dance, Hugh arrived promptly at seven, his crisp tuxedo accentuating his athletic frame. He carried a corsage of lilies and respectfully allowed Mrs. Toomey to pin it onto the bust of Peggy's dress. She'd borrowed the white, floor length gown from Ginny, who'd worn it the year before. It had a sequined, formfitting bodice held up only by her curves that made her feel exposed. She'd been reluctant to wear it, but when she came down the stairs, Hugh grinned as though he'd just won the state championship.

"Marguerithe!" he said, holding his breath. She joined him and took his arm, and they quickly said goodnight to Mrs. Toomey, who handed Peggy her stole and exhibited all the self-control she possessed in not reminding them to be back at a reasonable hour.

Hugh had borrowed a friend's automobile for the occasion, and he politely held open the door for her as she stepped carefully inside. The evening was frigid, and she was eager to get out of the cold. Her heels gave her pause, but she did not slip on the ice. Wrapping the fur tightly around her shoulders, she tapped her feet quickly on the floor to warm her bare legs.

"Are you ready?" he asked, playfully. Peggy nodded, smiling, grasping the door handle as the car leapt forward towards the fraternity.

The pathway to the front door was lit with lanterns that cast a warm glow on the cobblestones. There were several other couples there when they arrived, but none that Peggy recognized. "Don't worry, Peg. I won't leave your side," Hugh said, rightly assessing her panic. She took his outstretched hand, and he ushered her from person to person, making introductions. After the initial chitchat, she nibbled on the shrimp cocktails and observed the party's décor, allowing Hugh to steer the conversation without interruption. Someone had taken great lengths to turn the fraternity into a regal ballroom, and all had come in their finest attire. Although her dress was secondhand, she fit right in. She was so thankful to Ginny she could have kissed her had she been present, which she desperately wished she were.

As the night progressed and she'd finished her second glass of wine, Peg grew less self-conscious and more at ease until, at last, she was honestly enjoying herself. Thankfully, Hugh was not much of a dancer and only lead her onto the floor during slow numbers. They talked about their friends and the school, about football and plans after college. Neither could stop smiling.

As the last song ended, Hugh spotted the president of his fraternity, and excused himself to go say a brief hello. "I know I promised I wouldn't leave you alone, but it will only be a moment," he said, squeezing her hand.

Her throat dry from all the talking, Peggy approached the punch bowl just as another couple stood chatting with their backs to her, their own cups in hand. She did not mean to eavesdrop, but their words were lifted and carried towards her ears without her consent.

"Can you believe who Hugh brought?" the girl asked her date. "I suppose he is getting more involved in charity work," she joked nastily. The young man at her side snorted and shook his head.

"I don't understand what he sees in her. Hugh could have any girl he wanted!" he declared with subdued disgust. Peggy finished filling her cup with punch and tried to sip at it casually. The tears came to her eyes despite her best efforts, and she blinked rapidly, struggling to keep them from falling onto her cheeks. When she sensed she was about to lose the battle, she set down her cup and fled to the ladies' room.

Hugh looked up from his conversation to see his date slip away. He watched her with no clue of her distress, only with admiration. The back of her neck was slim and delicate, set off by a single strand of pearls. She had worn her hair elegantly, and her small waist was accented perfectly by the cut of her gown. To Hugh, she was refined and mysterious, unlike any of the other girls at school. She was thoughtful and soft spoken, and yet her intelligence and lurking humor were undeniable. He answered the question the president had posed and waited for Peggy to emerge.

Peggy sat on the toilet in a private stall and tried to compose herself. She had to agree with the young couple's assessment. What *did* Hugh see in her? The borrowed dress and pearls of which she had been so proud now seemed old-fashioned and second rate. She fingered the corsage Hugh had given her. It did not matter if he were fooled; no one else was. She should not have come.

Peg opened the door of the stall and stared at her reflection in the mirror. Regrettably, she had no powder with her to mask the redness of her eyes and cheeks. She dabbed her lips with the lipstick she'd brought in her purse and touched up her hair. No matter how much she wished she could, she couldn't stay in the ladies' room forever.

Peg put on a brave and convincing show for the rest of the evening, smiling warmly and with only a trace of sadness as Hugh took her hand and led her back onto the dance floor. Fortunately, the festivities ended shortly after, and Hugh and Peggy were blessedly alone once more as they drove home and parked. On the doorstep, he took her hand.

"Peggy, I had a wonderful time tonight. I hope you did too," he said eagerly, looking her in the eye.

"Yes, it was very nice." Had it not been for the couple's biting words, she would have declared it the best of her life.

"None of those girls held a candle to you, Marguerithe." Peggy blushed and felt silly, his words kind yet false. As much as she was enamored of Hugh, she could think of nothing to say and wanted desperately to go inside. She did not realize at first that he was leaning to kiss her until his lips were but inches from her own. Unprepared and shy, she turned her head so that the kiss landed tenderly on her cheek.

"Goodnight, Peggy," he said softly, cupping her face with his right hand. Peggy waited with looming horror for him to try again. To her relief, he did not. He walked down the steps and then waited for her to open the door and step inside. As she closed it, he called to her from the street.

"Would you see me again this week, Peggy? Wednesday evening? We could go to the movies."

"I'll have to see, but that sounds nice," she said, unable to refuse him outright. Hugh grinned and took a deep bow.

She shut the door and leaned against it, closing her eyes. Thankfully, Mrs. Toomey had not waited up. Peggy removed her heels so as not to wake anyone and tiptoed up to her room, carrying them in her hand. She hurriedly got undressed and draped her clothes over the chair, climbing into bed and wrapping the blankets snugly around her body.

CHAPTER 14

Although it was past noon, Leonard lay asleep in bed, the curtains drawn. Occasionally, he stirred and could hear his wife's steps below in the kitchen. He'd risen at half-past five as always and upon standing, grown lightheaded. Thinking perhaps it had been something he'd eaten the night before at his party and that the sickness would soon pass, Leonard tried again to dress for work. He was hot and flushed and thirsty, and so he called for Marie. She hurried up the stairs and appeared with flour in her hair.

"What is it, Leonard?" she'd begun to ask, irritated. When she saw his face, she hurried to his side and helped him back into bed. He'd grumbled and protested, throwing aside the blankets Marie pulled over him.

"No, I don't care how much Mr. Brookes wants the room completed by the end of the week. You are not getting out of this bed until the doctor sees you." Leonard's eyes were heavy, his vision, blurred. He wanted to fight with Marie more, to get to the Brooke's place before he was fired, but he found that his body would not cooperate. His head sank into the pillow as though made of iron. Marie disappeared and then materialized once more.

"The doctor will be here in a few hours. He has some other calls to make first, but then he will see you. He's given you direct orders to stay in bed until he comes," said Marie, standing at the side of the bed, her hand on Leonard's arm and a glass of water in her hand.

"Fine, fine," he grumbled. "Will you call over to George and tell him for me?" he asked while reaching for the water and drinking it all at once. He handed the empty glass back to her before rolling over on his side and falling asleep.

After she did as he'd asked, Marie stood by the bed, studying her husband. She put her head close to his chest to listen to his heartbeat. Marie put her hand to his forehead, frowned, and then sat in the chair until worry drove her downstairs to finish the doughnuts she'd begun earlier that morning.

The oil sputtered as it reached frying temperature, and Marie threw the raw pastries into the pan. She was anxious for the doctor's arrival, turning at every sound outside while listening for his knock.

Leonard did not get sick. For the entire duration of their twenty-year marriage, he had not once missed work due to illness. He'd had mild colds and a few bouts with the flu, but nothing so serious as to confine him to bed. Lost in thought, Marie left the doughnuts to fry far longer than they should have. It was the noxious smell of burning oil that roused her.

"Oh for Pete's Sake!" she swore under her breath, pulling the brown, unappetizing mess from the pan. She threw them directly into the trash and left the pan where it was. Marie sat down at the kitchen table and stared at her hands helplessly. The night before had been so lovely, and now this! All his friends had shown, even Helen and her suitor, and Leonard had been utterly surprised to find everyone awaiting his arrival. She'd baked a banana cake, his favorite, and sang boisterously along with all the guests as they sang him a happy birthday. At the table where she now sat, Leonard had put his arm around her waist and pulled her onto his knee, kissing her cheek and whispering in her ear, "Thank you."

The small signs she'd noticed over the past few months stacked into a menacing pile of symptoms—the lethargy, the thirst. Marie bowed her head to pray when she heard a loud knock at the front door. Jumping to her feet and hurrying into the front room, she opened the door widely.

"Good morning, Mrs. Gerhardt," said her visitor, "I hope I'm not disturbing you?" Mam asked, sensing that perhaps her visit was poorly timed. The woman stood with both hands on her cane, waiting patiently for Marie to answer.

"No, not at all. Please, come in. I was expecting the doctor, that's all." Marie had not immediately recognized Marguerithe's former employer, having only spoken with her once before. Mam carefully stepped over the slight lip of the doorway, and Marie took her arm.

"The doctor?" she asked with concern. "Is someone ill?"

"Yes, I'm afraid it's my husband. He's upstairs now resting. It's nothing catching, I don't think—don't worry," explained Marie. "Please, have a seat," she said as she helped Mam down onto the sofa. "Would you like some tea?" she asked once her guest was settled.

"If there's some already made, yes please. Otherwise, water is fine." Marie went into the kitchen and returned with a saucer and cup of tea.

"I added cream," she said as she handed Mam the drink.

"Thank you." Mam lifted the cup to her lips, and Marie noticed that her hands shook. She must have stared, as Mam raised her eyebrows and offered an explanation.

"I'm to have had a stroke, they tell me," she said without self-pity, "but I didn't come here to share my burdens with you, my dear. I can see that you clearly have plenty of your own." She smiled with compassion, the left side of her mouth frozen in place, so that the impression was more of a grimace.

"How is Margaret?" she asked with anticipation, arriving at the point of her visit. Puzzled, Marie took a seat opposite the woman.

"Marguerithe? She's good, I'm happy to say. College agrees with her. She writes that she loves it." Mam sat back on the sofa and smiled with satisfaction. It gave her great peace to know that the girl was happy. Marie heard footsteps overhead and the sound of the bathroom door closing.

"Excuse me for a moment," she said, hurrying up the stairs. When Leonard did not emerge from the bathroom after a few moments, she opened the door and found him sitting on the toilet with his head in his arms.

"Leonard!" she said with alarm, bending down and lifting him up.

"I had to go again," he mumbled. Marie wetted a towel and washed his face, soaking it once more and draping it around his neck. He swatted away her hand only once, the cool water refreshing. She helped him as best she could back into the other room and made sure he was comfortably in bed before going back downstairs. Mam had risen from her seat and stood admiring a small oil painting on the wall.

"I'm afraid he's not doing any better," said Marie, dismayed.

"Would you like me to go, Mrs. Gerhardt? I am happy to stay if you think the company might do you good as you wait. I'm afraid I'm not very much help, but I do still have the use of my tongue." The woman's presence was surprisingly comforting to Marie, and she found herself wanting Mam to stay.

"That would be very good of you, at least until I can get hold of my son," she said, picking up the telephone. As Marie spoke with the operator and attempted to reach Joseph, Mam observed the woman who had raised Margaret, noting her blue eyes and strong hands. There was a foundation of vigor beneath her presently rattled façade that Mam instantly liked.

She had not been entirely honest with Marie. It was not only her growing preoccupation with Margaret's collegiate success that had prompted her visit. Since her stroke, Mam found herself wondering more and more about this woman who had taken Judith's place. It was equal parts curiosity and concern that had led her to call on Marie that day, and she was determined to establish some kind of relationship with her. She saw now that it was the Lord's doing, as most good things were. He'd found a way to use her, even in her crippled state. She could be some consolation to Mrs. Gerhardt, if only as a distraction. Mam averted her gaze so as not to unnerve Marie with her strange smile.

"Joseph is coming right over," said Marie after hanging up the phone, visibly relieved.

"Joseph is your son?"

"Yes, he's a postman," she said, interlacing her fingers and folding her hands.

"Margaret is a fine young woman, Mrs. Gerhardt. She was an excellent worker—always on time and good with the customers. So kind. Good with money, too. I relied on her greatly and feel her absence at the store," she said. "I'll need to hire someone new. If you know anyone reliable, please send them my way."

"Yes, of course."

"—Don't let me keep you, Mrs. Gerhardt. If you need to check on your husband, please go ahead."

"If you don't mind, I'll just make sure he doesn't need anything." Marie went into the kitchen and took down a large basin from the shelf. She brought it up to Leonard's room and put it by his bed. He was asleep, breathing heavily. Marie left the door open so as to better hear him and went back downstairs. She took the stairs slowly, sucking in her breath and holding her stomach.

"How is he?"

"Asleep for now." Marie sat back in her chair. Clearing her throat, she touched the back of her hair and brushed invisible crumbs from her dress.

"Are you from Helena?" she asked, trying to make normal conversation.

"No, outside of Great Falls, but I've been in Helena a long time now —eighteen years."

"And you, Mrs. Gerhardt?"

"I'm from France, but I came here as a little girl. My English isn't what it should be," she said, self-conscious of her accent.

"Neither is mine," said Mam, smiling. "None of us are ever what we should be, are we?" she asked, sighing. "And yet the Good Lord is so faithful, so kind to forgive us our countless shortcomings."

Marie nodded in agreement. "I told Marguerithe to find a good German Lutheran Church near the school, but Mrs. Toomey, her landlady, tells me she's stopped going," she shared with dissatisfaction. "I don't think it's good for her to go without the church's influence for long."

"She's been in my prayers, Mrs. Gerhardt, and will continue to be." The front door opened, and a dark-haired man entered, his face pale with concern.

"Joseph!" said Marie, rising and meeting her son. She kissed him on the cheek. "You know Mam from Helena Mercantile? She's been sitting with me and keeping my mind off your father."

"Hello, Mrs.—?"

"Mam, please just call me Mam. It's good to meet you, Joseph," she said from the sofa. She observed the young man, noting that his complexion was far darker than his mother's. "I'll leave you two, now, as I'll only be in the way," she said, putting her weight on her cane as she stood. Joseph rushed to her side and took one of her arms to help her balance.

"Can I drive you home?" he asked, thoughtfully.

"No, that's very kind. I am happy for the walk. It's how I got here, and it's how I'll leave. Your mother needs you here, my boy," she said, patting his hand. She stared into his face and spoke without thinking. "Your skin is dark, like mine!" she said, immediately embarrassed by her outburst. This was something else entirely foreign since the stroke. Mam, who had always been so close and careful with her words, found that there were times she could no longer censor herself; she often said things out loud that should have remained unspoken. Joseph stared at her with confusion and then averted his eyes.

"Yes, I've been outside a lot recently," he explained. "It's one of the best things about my line of work." Marie walked behind the two thinking of Leonard. She had not heard the comment to her son.

"Thank you for staying, Mam. It was a great help," said Marie as the woman turned to face her.

"I'm glad we finally have spoken, Mrs. Gerhardt. Please do not be a stranger. Come by the store anytime and just say hello. I'm always happy to have a visitor." Since Margaret had left for Missoula, Mam's days consisted mostly of silence. Although she did not like to admit it, she was lonely. The loneliness caught her by surprise, as she had always preferred solitude. Even in the midst of tragedy, during the hardest parts of her young life, she had chosen her privacy and freedom over company. But in recent years, her isolation began to grow uncomfortable and take on the appearance of decay. She was too capable of spending an entire day doing nothing but sitting and thinking. Thankfully, she had the store to keep her mind sharp and give her purpose. Without it, she would have become a sluggard.

"I have a small flat above the store. It's very modest, but you are welcome any time for tea," she said now to Marie, turning to face her at the bottom of the front stairs. Joseph went back inside to check on Leonard while Marie said farewell to her guest.

"I think I will do that," said Marie, feeling warmly towards the old woman.

"Your husband will be in my prayers, Mrs. Gerhardt."

"Please call me Marie," she said. Before she could stop herself, Mam returned the gesture.

"And I'm Ruth." Marie watched her walk away, making her way slowly down the street before going back into the house. Mam did not realize until well into her long journey home that she had spoken her forgotten name to Margaret's mother. She had not used it in decades, and it sounded unfamiliar and untrue as she considered it. She did not feel like a woman with that name, nor did she wish to recall all the sadness of Ruth's life. The stroke had made the division between Ruth and Mam so complete that she thought of her years before Helena as belonging to another woman. Ruth's losses and opinions, her habits and gestures, were not Mam's. But Judith and Margaret transcended both epochs. She prayed silently as she leaned heavily on her cane and shuffled home.

CHAPTER 15

Bringing with him a bouquet of daisies, Hugh called on Peggy a few days after the formal. His mouth was cottony as he waited for the door to open. When Mrs. Toomey appeared, he swallowed and cleared his throat before being able to speak.

"Hello, Mrs. Toomey. A fine day, isn't it?" he asked politely, gesturing at the sun and trees around them. Mrs. Toomey took a moment to feel the air and look beyond his shoulder before agreeing.

"Good afternoon, Mr. Pratt. Please come in."

"I've come to give these to Peggy," he said, holding the flowers forward.

"Yes, of course, well I'm afraid she's not feeling very well. I don't think she should be disturbed. But I'm happy to put those flowers in some water and bring them up to her. They might help her to make a speedy recovery," she added generously, unable to withstand the pitiful, worried look on the young man's face.

"It's not serious, is it?" he asked with concern, handing the bouquet to Mrs. Toomey.

"I don't think so. Most likely just a cold, but she's resting now." Hugh was visibly disappointed, having brought the flowers with great expectation of spending time with Peggy.

"Please tell her I hope she gets better soon," he said, placing his hand on the doorframe.

"Of course, Mr. Pratt. Now if you'll excuse me, I have a soufflé in the oven that needs my attention." Hugh stepped backwards and nodded that he understood.

"Good day, Mrs. Toomey."

"Good day."

Pushing aside the lace curtains, Mrs. Toomey watched from the parlor window as Hugh walked slowly down the street. He put his hands in his pockets and seemed only to watch his feet.

Mrs. Toomey went to the kitchen and pulled out her favorite cut crystal vase, filling it with water and arranging the daisies so they fell evenly. She carried the gift carefully up the stairs to Peggy's room and knocked quietly before turning the knob and entering. Peggy sat at her desk reading what could only be a letter. Mrs. Toomey saw immediately that the girl had been crying, and she did not wish to intrude. She set the flowers down on the table beside her bed.

"These are from Mr. Pratt. I told him just as you asked me to, although I didn't like it, Marguerithe. It is wrong to tell lies, regardless of their size. I won't do it again. If you do not wish to see Mr. Pratt, you will have to tell him so yourself," she said firmly.

"Yes, of course, Mrs. Toomey. Thank you so much. Thank you for bringing them up and putting them in water." She admired the pretty bouquet from her desk chair. It was the first time she'd been given flowers.

"Daisies. They're perfect," she said simply.

Mrs. Toomey took her leave, stepping lightly down the stairs and back into the kitchen so as not to disturb her soufflé.

Peggy rose from her seat and walked over to the arrangement, lightly touching the petals with her fingertips. The romance and kindness of Hugh's gesture brought fresh tears to Peggy's eyes and made her ashamed of the lie she'd spoken through Mrs. Toomey. It was true that she did not feel well, but it was no malady of the body that kept her confined to her room. She could see no way of telling Hugh the truth without undergoing further ridicule and humiliation, and Peggy was already far too bruised to withstand such an assault. She'd watched his arrival from her bedroom window and had desperately wanted to see him, to hold his hand as they walked into town. What had occurred at the formal, however, would prevent any such lovely scene from ever unfolding.

That morning, she'd chosen to stay in bed and nurse her sorrow, skipping class. The letter that had arrived from her mother did nothing to help her spirits. The news of Helen's impending engagement was ill-timed and only added to the misfortune of her own situation. Of course, Helen had previously written to Peggy to tell her about Paul Summers, hinting that they did plan to marry, but seeing the words in her mother's hand somehow made it truer. It did not help matters that she had also suggested, almost cruelly, that Marguerithe give more attention to social engagements and attempt to meet someone herself. Peggy wept, the irony too sharp.

Sitting hunched over the bed and staring miserably at the flowers, she wiped her face and looked around the room blankly. Finals were approaching, and Peggy could not afford to do poorly. She stood up in annoyance, disgusted with herself for falling apart so completely. Walking back over to her desk, she sat down and pushed her books aside. Instead she took out a few sheets of paper and decided to return her mother's letter.

She touched upon Hugh only to say that she'd accompanied him to a dance, satisfying her mother's desire to hear of her social life but leaving her to speculate on the nature of their relationship. She contemplated mentioning that they were only friends, but she did not know if even this would be true by the end of the week

By the time she finished the letter, she felt much more settled. Her cheeks were dry and her puffy eyelids less swollen. She decided to take a walk and mail it that very moment.

CHAPTER 16

The remainder of the quarter passed in a blur, Peg's finals and end-of-year events keeping her blessedly preoccupied. As she packed up her room, she had to admit that other than the fall-out with Hugh, who now refused to speak to her, her first quarter at the State University of Montana had been an overwhelming success.

Steph and Billy drove her to the depot earlier that morning. Knowing they would be reunited shortly in the fall, the friends exchanged only a brief goodbye. Finding her seat quickly, Peg chatted casually with the older woman next to her, closing her eyes and daydreaming when their conversation dwindled. It was an uneventful and pleasant ride.

After a few hours, the train pulled slowly into Helena, and Marguerithe eagerly watched the platform for her family, half expecting them to be wearing the same heavy winter jackets and hats in which she had last seem them. Through the window, Peg saw with delight that both her mother and Helen wore floral dresses and open-toed shoes. They looked pretty and fresh, their hair done loosely beneath straw hats.

The train had not fully come to a stop when Peggy ran to the front of the car with her bag and stood on the stairs. As soon as she could risk it, she leapt onto the platform. Immediately, she noticed that Helen's sparkling eyes were offset by a glittering engagement ring. Peggy dropped her bag, and the reunited friends embraced warmly. She went directly from Helen's arms to her mother's. When Marie at last let go of her daughter, she stepped back and smiled with satisfaction.

"You *do* look well, Marguerithe." Marie could see with one glance that her once timid daughter had matured in the months away. She moved with greater grace and confidence. Marie rubbed her shoulders and kissed her again on the cheek.

Maggy looked up at her father, who laughed and pulled her to him, squeezing her and rocking her back and forth.

"Mags, we're so happy you're home!" he said gruffly into her hair. As they embraced, the prominent bones of her father's arms and ribs pushed into her own. He had grown thinner, and his skin was sallow. She looked at her mother with alarm, who indicated with a heavy gaze that Peggy was not to say a word. Marguerithe obeyed, taking the arm her father offered and walking towards her luggage.

"I'm sorry that Joseph isn't here, but he couldn't make it with work. He'll be by tonight for supper," said Leonard, apologetically. "You are glowing. I've never seen you so very pretty," he smiled, making her blush.

"I think you're a bit biased, Dad," she said, dismissing his compliment. "I'm the same as before." As she spoke the words, both Peggy and her father knew that that they were unequivocally untrue. She was not the same. Although Leonard knew that the change was positive, Peggy was uncertain. She felt disoriented standing once again in Helena at her father's side. The scene was so familiar, and yet it was as though she had slipped into an old set of clothes that did not quite fit. Helen came alongside the pair and took Marguerithe's other arm.

"So Maggy, what do you want to do first? I mean, after we get your things put away? Are you tired?" Without waiting for her friend's response, she continued. "Will you come over to the house? Paul's dying to meet you!" she gushed, leaning towards her friend. No one had called her Maggy in months, and it took her a moment to associate herself with the name. She turned to look at her mother.

"That's fine, Marguerithe. Supper will be ready by five. Just be back by then."

Helen peppered Marguerithe with questions as they drove home. The two had kept up a lively and consistent correspondence, but this did nothing to satiate Helen's thirst for even more detail of Peg's time in Missoula. Marie interjected her own questions during the moments that Helen, forced to draw breath, paused in her volley. Leonard smiled at the frenzied joy of their reunited family, remaining mostly silent while relishing the sound of his daughter's voice.

When they pulled in front of the house, everyone helped to unload the car. Peggy lingered before going inside, studying the home in which she had grown up and lived all her life. She had feared that all things and people in Helena might pale in comparison to Missoula and her life there, but the opposite was true. As stirring as Main Hall had first been to Peggy's imagination, the impression her old, white house now made was in no way inferior. Its two brick fireplaces and single gable, pointing humbly upward, were a welcome and familiar sight. How many times had she turned the bend in the road to see those simple features showing her the way home? A bicycle was propped on the porch, and the rough, short grass that covered the yard was already yellowing.

As Peggy took a step onto the veranda, the boards creaked as they always had. She rested her hand on the colonnade her father himself had smoothed on his lathe. Peggy had not expected her homecoming to provide such solace. The last month at school, with the strain of exams and the unraveling of her romance with Hugh, had taken more of a toll than she'd realized. Unexpectedly, she felt heavy with fatigue. She wanted nothing more than to go up to her room and sleep until supper.

Helen went next door to prepare Paul for Peggy's imminent visit, and Marie and Leonard walked with their daughter up to her room.

"We left it the same for you," said Leonard. "We didn't touch anything." Peggy could see that everything was indeed as she had left it, but the shine of her dresser and lack of dust indicated that there had been special care taken in preparing the room for her arrival. Peggy turned and hugged her mother tightly, which caught Marie off guard.

"Oh my!" she exhaled, at which both her husband and daughter smiled.

"It *is* good to have you back, *spatzi*," said Leonard, looking at his daughter fondly. "I hope you don't mind my still calling you that, now that you're a woman of the world," he teased. Marie took her husband's arm, leading him out into the hallway.

"Why don't you freshen up before you go to Helen's," suggested Marie, which Peggy knew meant that her fatigue showed. "We're having pork chops tonight," she added. "We can catch up once Joseph's here." Marie and Leonard walked downstairs, Leonard leaning on his wife's arm for balance. Peggy tucked the unruly strands of hair back into their bobby pins and splashed her face with water. She traded the wrinkled dress she'd worn on the train for one less tailored and put on her cross.

When she came into the kitchen to let her parents know she was leaving, the smile on her mother's face indicated her appearance had greatly improved.

"There now, you look very nice," said Marie. Remembering she had something she wanted Peggy to take to the Carlisle's, she searched through the pantry until she found it.

"Here, give this to Henrietta. I just finished the batch yesterday afternoon," she said, handing her daughter a jar of her tomato jam. "It's especially good this year, if I do say so myself. The tomatoes are sweet, even though it's so early in the season." Marie turned back to her task, which Peggy saw was the washing and snapping of green beans.

"I can stay and help if you like," said Peggy, remembering the hours she had spent as a girl aiding her mother in this very task. Although it was tedious, she now felt a longing to stand at her side and hear the crisp break as the ends were discarded. She lingered a moment until Marie looked over her shoulder.

"No, no, there's no need. I'm almost finished here. Go meet Paul and say hello to everyone for us. There are plums on the table if you'd like a snack," she added. Marie turned back around, dismissing Peggy, who smiled at her father. She snatched one from its bowl and took a small bite, testing its ripeness.

"Not as good as the Davis plums, Dad," she said.

"No, of course not. None ever are," he said, winking. Peggy held the jar of tomato jam in her hand and left out the back door.

CHAPTER 17

W hen Peggy returned from the Carlisle's, Joseph had arrived. "Hey, sis," he said, giving her shoulders a quick squeeze. He stepped back and squinted at her. "Say, you've gotten taller!" he said.

"I have not, Joseph. I'm the same height as when I left," she replied with irritation.

"You look taller to me," he repeated, shrugging.

"So what did you think of Paul?" interrupted Marie, setting the table for dinner.

"I like him. He sure is head-over-heels for Helen. But the wedding won't be until the fall after next. That's an awfully long time to wait. She asked me to be the maid of honor!" said Peggy, pleased.

"Did you give Henrietta the jam?"

"Yes, and she says, 'thank you.'"

"—I like him, too," said Leonard, who was seated at the head of the table, his ankle crossed on his knee. "He's a good man, solid, no frills. Helen needs a man like that," he declared, stroking his mustache, "to keep her on an even keel."

"He is a good deal older," said Marie with a disapproving tone. Placing the meat on the table, Marie removed her apron and brushed her hands together. "There," she said looking over the meal, "Dinner is served." Peggy took her usual seat, and Leonard said grace.

"And what about you, Marguerithe? Did you meet anyone special at the university? Did anything ever come of that Hugh fellow you mentioned?" Peggy's eyes darted as she dished the meat onto her plate.

"Well, no, I didn't. I think romance might be better left to people like Helen," she replied. "I don't much have the stomach for it, I don't think." Marie frowned at her daughter and swatted the air with her hand, dismissing the statement as ridiculous.

"Leave her be, Marie. She'll meet the right man at the right time. There's no rush," interjected Leonard. Marie playfully glared at her husband before changing the subject.

"Fine, fine. You'll never believe who I've become friends with, Marguerithe," she said, skipping Leonard and passing Joseph the potatoes. "Mam, that's who!" she said as though the news startled her. "She's a good woman, Marguerithe, though a little strange. She told me to call her Ruth. You should have invited her over long ago! She has a special place for you in her heart, I'd say. She's always asking about you and prays for you every day. You should be sure to see her while you're home." Peggy nodded and listened with interest, their relationship surprising.

"I've gone a few times over to her apartment, and she's come here twice now for tea. It's so much easier for me to get around than for her. Did you know she had a stroke?" asked Marie.

"No!" said Peggy with alarm, "I didn't. When did it happen? Is she okay?"

"A few weeks after you'd gone. Yes, I'd say so. She walks slowly and uses a cane, but her mind is still sharp. Of course the stroke caused some paralysis, but you get used to it."

"—Paralysis?"

"To the side of her face. You really only notice it when she smiles."

"How did you become friends?" asked Peggy with genuine curiosity.

"Well, she paid us a visit one day. She walked all that way just to ask how you liked school. Can you imagine?" Marie looked at Leonard before continuing.

"And she was very good to me. She stayed with me when I was worried sick about your father." Peggy looked at her dad with alarm. He set down his silverware and wiped his mouth with his napkin. Clearing his throat, he looked his daughter in the eye.

"Might as well come out with it—I see how you're looking at me. The doctor says I'm sick," he said.

"—He has diabetes, dear," explained Marie. Peggy had heard of the disease but did not know what the diagnosis meant. "There are new treatments, Marguerithe. Very promising treatments," she said encouragingly.

"—But they're all very expensive," added Joseph, drumming his fingers on the table. His expression was sour and his tone sharp.

"Joseph," scolded Marie. Peggy looked at the faces of each of her family members, trying to fit the pieces of the puzzle together.

"I can't really work anymore, sweetheart," said Leonard, getting to what was for him, the hardest piece of news to break. "We won't be able to afford to send you back to school." Peggy's heart beat rapidly. If her father could not work, then his illness was indeed serious.

"Dad, I don't care about school. Are you going to be okay?" Marie looked at her husband anxiously, searching for the right words. Leonard pushed his large portion of green beans around the plate with his fork.

"He may live for a long time yet, Marguerithe, but there's also the chance that he will not. Diabetes is hard on the body." Peggy stared at her father, and her eyes filled with tears. She couldn't speak. She took a sip of water and tried to compose herself.

"All these vegetables will kill me before the diabetes, Mags. I'd give my left kidney for a potato," he joked, hoping to change the mood of the conversation and lift his daughter's spirits.

"Maggy," he said now in a somber tone. "I'm not a young man. I'm fifty-five. That's already more years than I have a right to expect. *Something's* going to kill me. It might as well be this," he said shrugging his shoulders. Overcome by the revelation of her father's illness, Peggy sobbed loudly once before she covered her mouth and cried silently. Joseph shifted uncomfortably in his seat and tried not to look at his mother, whom he knew would also be fighting back tears.

"We've all had some time with this, Marguerithe," said Marie, her voice shaky. After the doctor had delivered his diagnosis the day of Mam's first visit, Marie had sat in the chair at Leonard's side until the sun set. She did not cry. She'd stared at the wall, biting her fingernails and thinking. In truth, the doctor had stated that Leonard most likely only had a few months to live. He would be surprised if he lasted the year. Marie could not bear to say these words aloud to her daughter now. She preferred to give her a small ledge of hope on which to grasp, even if that ledge would inevitably give way.

"I've taken on more shifts at work," said Joseph.

"And I've gotten two new mothers in the past few weeks," said Marie. Peggy's mind raced.

"I'll get a teaching position," she offered. Peggy felt selfish and foolish for going away to school. If they had not been forced to pay for her tuition, they would have more now to see them through Leonard's illness.

"There's something else," said Marie with a strange smile on her face. Peggy could not imagine what else her mother might have to share. She braced herself for the worst.

"We're moving to California!" she cried with excitement.

"What? Why?" asked Peggy, the cascade of events bewildering.

"The doctor said a change of weather might help your father, and we've always wanted to see the Pacific Ocean."

"Yes, we have," said Leonard, smiling at his wife. "And if these really are my last days, I'd like to spend them somewhere nice." Peggy stared at her parents and tried to understand their decision. "Joseph will be staying here, of course. He'll be a married man soon." Leonard paused, "But we assumed you'd come with us." Marie cleared her throat. Peggy stared straight ahead as her eyes darted back and forth in thought.

"Of course I'll come with you," she said with practicality. "When are we moving? Where in California?" Her own willingness to leave behind everything she had grown to love over the past six months surprised Peggy, but she could not be away from her father during what might very well be his last days. Her mother would need help, surely. Her imagination leapt forward to the journey, to the seaside, to sand and warm weather and film stars. If the impetus behind the move further west had not been so dire, Peggy would have brimmed with enthusiasm.

"At the end of this summer, we'll fit what we can in the Ford, and the rest we'll ship or sell. We don't know yet where, maybe San Francisco or Los Angeles, but we won't be coming back to Helena," said Leonard with certainty. Happy for the distraction, Peggy cleared their plates from the table.

"There's pie in the oven," said Marie, rising to join her daughter. She held Peggy's hand and then opened the oven door. "Be a dear and hand me that towel," she said, pointing. Peggy did as she was told, and Marie brought the steaming pie out onto the cooling rack. "Cherry," she said, smiling. Leonard watched his wife and was filled with gratitude. When she passed Leonard on her way to serve Joseph his slice, he took her hand. His thick mustache brushed her skin, and the sensation of its bristles remained long after he had let go.

CHAPTER 18

L aced with picnics and languid mornings, the summer passed uneventfully. Peg tutored languishing students in Math and History but did not take on full-time employment. Instead, she helped her mother with the housework and stopped in to say hello to Mam once a week. She'd hired on a new girl to replace Peg, or she might have asked for a summer job. Mam wanted to hear all about The State University of Montana and what Peg had been learning, listening attentively without interruption to stories of Ginny and Steph, her eccentric education professor, and Mrs. Toomey. Peggy did not mention Hugh. Each time she left The Helena Mercantile, Mam kissed her on the cheek and told her how proud of her she was.

The Gerhardts packed their belongings slowly through the summer until only the necessities remained. Before long, Leonard and Marie stood inside an empty home. Everything had been sold, given to family, packed into the car, or shipped ahead to Marie's brother in California. Without the weight of their bodies, their furniture, or memories, it seemed that the house might, at any minute, float heavenwards.

He and Marie had lived the majority of their life together between its walls, raising two children and earning just enough money to survive. It had given him such satisfaction the day he'd moved his young wife and child under its roof, and now they would leave it behind, turn it over to another family that would build its own routines and habits, filling it with different sounds, strange voices and aromas, erasing all evidence of the Gerhardts.

Marie turned in a circle in front of the fireplace. Each step sounded with startling resonance. Leonard gently pressed his hand against his wife's lower back and drew nearer to her.

"Marigold, it's time to leave," he said softly.

"It has been a good home, Leonard, a fine home," she said decidedly. "It's the only real one I've known." She pulled on her white gloves and hugged her purse against her side. Leonard leaned his face towards hers, and she cupped it with her right hand before kissing him softly. "I love you," she said spontaneously, looking him in the eye, her mouth quivering. He kissed her once more.

"Let's go, sweetheart. California won't wait," he said, leading her outside and shutting the door. Marie walked directly to the car where Peggy was waiting and climbed into the back seat, staring straight ahead.

Having convinced her father that she was capable of getting them at least as far as the interstate, Marguerithe took the driver's seat and changed from her mittens into leather gloves. Leonard primed the engine with the choke and crank, reached inside to turn the key and set the throttle lever, and then gave the crank a mighty yank forward. The engine roared into motion, and he took his seat next to his daughter.

"Take us to California, Mags!" he said, patting her leg and smiling. Marguerithe glanced once at their house before pulling out into the street. Passing Helen's home, she saw the familiar face of her best friend peeking out from behind the living room's lace curtains. Helen had come by earlier that day, sobs choking back her words, and kept her farewell emotional but brief. Peg blew her a kiss as they drove by, certain that the move would do nothing to diminish their friendship.

As they came to the interstate, Peggy grasped the wheel loosely and grinned at her father who hummed a cheerful tune. She pulled the throttle down further, taking her foot off the pedal and sending them chugging rapidly down the road. Marie held onto her hat and yelled against the breeze.

"Slow down, Marguerithe! We want to arrive in one piece!" Leonard grinned at his daughter and hummed louder.

They made their way westward without urgency, stopping at the various roadside attractions and backing the Tin Lizzie up steep hills when their fuel level was low. Leonard could not drive the long distances he could have managed before his illness. His fatigue had grown difficult to manage, and he fell asleep momentarily at the wheel more than once. Wanting to preserve his dignity, Peg watched him closely and only offered to spell him when she could see his eyelids droop and close against his will.

It was a week before they reached Boise and another had passed when they cut across the southeast corner of Oregon and first entered California. Although it was not the most direct route, they headed for the coast and drove south along the precipitous cliffs, marveling at the expanse of dark blue and booming waves. As they approached the

Golden Gate, they entered a thick fog embankment that obscured everything but the tops of the bridge's spires. Marie frowned and shivered in the backseat, forcing them to stop and pull sweaters from their luggage.

They stayed four days in San Francisco, camping just outside the city each night beneath soft, salty redwoods. Although it was exciting and beautiful, all three frowned at the unusually damp, cool weather in late August. Decades of subzero, Helena winters created a strong distaste for unseemly temperatures, and all the dampness was likely to harm rather than help Leonard's condition. Unanimously, they continued south, the sun shining more brightly and warming their chilled bones the longer they drove.

With enough daylight left for several more hours of driving, they reached Bakersfield on a Tuesday afternoon and pressed on. Dusk eventually settled across the surrounding orange groves and alfalfa fields, saturating the landscape with pink and vermillion. The smell of freshly laid fertilizer rose thickly from the earth. Leonard grew drowsy, and they stopped so that he could switch seats with Marie. He reclined in the back and fell asleep quickly, leaving mother and daughter to sporadic observations interrupted by long stretches of silence. Peggy kindly slowed her speed so that her mother would be more at ease. Marie sang softly, the wind snatching away the words so that they were only audible in brief clips of consonants and fleeting melody. Peggy did not recognize the tune but kept the rhythm with her fingertips on the steering wheel. The clattering of the Ford's loose joints jangled as they hit uneven stretches of road.

An hour passed and the blue shadows turned to black, obscuring their faces and engulfing the back seat, so that only Leonard's occasional moans gave away his presence. It was a sense of invisibility and protection the early night afforded that led Peggy to ask her mother a simple question.

"Why did you take me in?" From her tone and how she stared straight ahead, Marie knew that Peggy alluded to those many years ago when, for a few days, she had been another woman's daughter. Marie looked at Peggy's profile, but only the sheen of her hair was visible. She felt her mouth become immediately dry.

"I've often wondered why you never asked. You were always the most curious girl. I couldn't understand it," Marie explained, shaking her head. "For a while, I was sure you didn't know, but then it seemed you did. I was amazed. Every morning, I thought that this might be the day, the day you wanted to know. But it never was." Marie ordered her memories and feelings, arranging them chronologically, instinctively suppressing those that she must never divulge. Once the events were safely recollected, she answered her daughter's original question.

"Your father and I had tried for years to have a baby. Eight years. We both desperately wanted a little girl, and then you appeared. You were that baby, an answered prayer. You needed a family, and we needed a child," she said, alternately rubbing her kneecaps and spine, which ached from the many hours of sitting.

Peggy's heart fortified itself, preparing for an assault of emotion, which came swiftly with pounding in her ears.

"Did you know my—the woman who gave birth to me?" she asked, clearing her throat.

"No. No, I did not," answered Marie truthfully. She thought a moment before continuing, anticipating Peggy's train of thought. "I don't know why she gave you up, only that she did. A wet nurse kept you at first—a Mrs. Nearbonne." Marie looked to her right at the dark hills and could smell much more than she could see. "A few months later, we adopted you, and you came to live with us. You were such a quiet baby." She turned her head to look again at her daughter. "Leonard said once that it was almost as though you were afraid to disturb us, that you were grateful," she said with a tone that dismissed the likelihood of his statement. "Still, you *were* the sweetest thing, never wanted to put anyone out," she said fondly, remembering with tenderness those precious, early days.

Marie waited for Peggy's next question, but none came. Marie could have said more. She could have told her of the letter Marguerithe's father had written when she was a toddler, the photograph he'd sent. She could have remarked that Marguerithe had his eyes. She briefly considered the possibility before dismissing it with distaste. It was not the time for confession; after all, she'd burned his letter and picture for a reason. The smaller truth she had just shared with her daughter was undoubtedly large enough for the moment. She hoped it would satisfy her.

Although Marie could not see, Peggy's cheeks were wet with tears. She cried silently, without any movement. In her imagination, her mother was tall and graceful. She had wanted to keep her baby girl, but for some tragic reason, she could not. Although Peggy had her own features and appearance with which to start, she could never clearly picture her mother's face. She thought her hair must be dark and her eyes blue, but other than this, the woman remained ethereal.

"You've always been *our* daughter, Marguerithe. There was never any difference in how we loved you or treated you," she said. "I hope that, at least, was clear." Peggy did not dare to wipe her cheeks for fear of her sadness being discovered. Instead, she nodded and tried not to sniffle. Leonard snorted once and changed positions, rolling over as best he could in the confined space. Marie reached into the back seat and pulled the fallen blanket back up over his chest.

"Does Joseph know who *his* father is?" asked Peggy. Marie stared with alarm at her daughter.

"You are full of surprises!" she exclaimed, unnerved. Although she had always guessed that Marguerithe knew the truth of her birth, there had never been any indication that she had known anything about Joseph.

"Leonard *is* Joseph's father—the only father he has ever known, and the only father that ever wanted anything to do with him," she said, defensively. "Joseph's father did nothing when I had to place my baby in an orphanage, when I couldn't even feed myself—when I had nothing," she said bitterly.

"—I'm sorry," said Peggy. "I didn't mean—" she began, letting her voice trail off without completing her thought. Feeling a compulsion to explain, Marie continued.

"I was sixteen, Marguerithe. I'd worked since I was twelve," she said with regret. "It's no excuse, mind you—sin is sin—whatever the reason for it. And I did pay. Dearly." Marie rubbed her palm with her thumb and looked down at her hands. "He was Jewish, the son of my employer—a cantor. When his father found out, I was fired. When mother found out, she told me I was no longer welcome under her roof," she said grimly. Peggy listened alertly, astonished. Marie's melancholy displaced her own, and Peggy felt the urge to comfort her. How hard it must have been! She was overcome with a sense of guilt for having pressed her. What did any of it matter? She had been so fortunate to find the family she had.

"Leonard was never bothered by any of it," said Marie. Peggy marveled at him and his goodness. What her mother had said earlier was true. Peggy had always been grateful for her parents, but grasping their true faithfulness and love more clearly now, her gratitude billowed. She had many more questions, but the woman sitting beside her could not answer them. Only the faceless lady who had left her behind could complete the story.

"I'm going to close my eyes now for a bit, Marguerithe. I suddenly feel *very* tired," sighed Marie, leaning her head back against the seat.

"That's fine," whispered Peggy, increasing the throttle and placing both hands on the steering wheel. She sat upright and concentrated on the winding road, the evening's revelations keeping her company late into the night.

CHAPTER 19

T he sun had not yet risen when they at last reached the outskirts of Los Angeles. Leonard sat now in the driver's seat, his daughter to his right and his wife sleeping heavily in the back. Peggy had welcomed her father's offer to drive and quickly fallen asleep in the passenger's seat.

Leonard pulled over on the side of the road at a particularly pretty stretch of beach. The ocean here was much lighter and softer than the ocean up north, fading from dark green to a pale blue, and he found it hard to believe that they were both part of the same vast Pacific waters. As though careful not to scare away the travelers, the breeze came sporadically and never did more than lightly touch the hair exposed beneath his hat.

Marie and Peggy woke as the sun rose. He wanted the initial glimpse of their new home to be memorable. Before Peggy saw the sea, she smelled it. It was her father's back that first came into view, framed by a coral sky. His shoulders were bony and frail against such a large backdrop. Concern for his wellbeing brought her to sitting. The blanket fell into her lap, and she found that the morning air did not chill. Leonard, leaning against the hood of the car, turned his head and smiled at his daughter.

"Not too shabby, Mags. Not too shabby," he said, turning back to the noteworthy vista and stretching out his arm, as though presenting it to Marguerithe as a handmade gift, another of his carvings. Marie awoke when she heard her husband's voice.

"Marigold," he said sweetly, moving to the side of the car and opening the door. He gave his wife his hand and helped her down onto the sand, her stiff joints cracking loudly. "I give to you...Los Angeles!" Marie held tightly to the hand he had offered and squinted, the shimmering ocean bright with silver.

"I'm sure that Los Angeles is behind us and not out there on the water, Leonard," she teased. "But it *is* pretty, I must say."

Peggy stayed in her seat, draping her arms over the door edge and resting her chin on her arms. "I'm hungry," she said, yawning widely. Leonard chuckled and squeezed his wife's hand.

"Let's get some breakfast and call your brother."

When they arrived at the address Jess had provided, a tall, burly man stood in the driveway, his arms folded across his chest. Marie had not seen her brother for twenty years and would not have known him had the number on the mailbox not matched the one on the slip of paper in her hand. As their eyes met, he slapped his thigh and let out a loud "Ha!" that Marie immediately recognized from her childhood.

They had kept in contact over the years solely through infrequent letters, keeping one another apprised of only the most important of life's events. Jess knew she had a son who was a postman, a daughter who had gone to university, and a husband whose health was failing. Marie, in turn, knew that his wife had passed away five years before, that he had not served in the War, and that he was the proprietor of a small market near his house.

With great energy and familiarity, Jess shook Leonard's hand, hugged his sister and niece, and began to unload their belongings. "This way," he said in nearly perfect English, walking to the left of the house into the backyard, a suitcase in each hand and one under each arm. "I figured you'd like your privacy, so I went ahead and fixed it up. It's no Buckingham Palace, but it'll do." He referred to the neatly maintained cottage before them, painted cheerily in light yellow. There seemed to be more windows than walls, and Peggy immediately loved it. In Helena, they would have frozen in such a building, but here, she knew that the weather would play no significant role in their daily lives. It was something to be enjoyed, not planned around and cursed under her breath.

Footsteps sounded behind them, and they all turned to see to whom they belonged. Peggy half expected to see Clark Gable appear and offer to give them a walking tour of the city. Instead, a lanky young man with a thin mustache and thick glasses stood before them.

"Ah, Charles. This is my family, the Gerhardts, come all the way from Montana," Jess explained, proudly.

"I figured as much. I saw the car out front and thought I'd come say hello. I live two doors down," he said. Charles stepped closer and shook everyone's hand, repeating his name for each introduction. "Charles Keane. Nice to meet you." He was unassuming and charming in his politeness. Peggy took note of his deep-set blue eyes. "Peggy," she said at the proper time. "Nice to meet you, too."

"I'm from Illinois myself, so I know a thing or two about weather. I've never seen any better than out here." With amusement, Marie watched the young man pretend not to notice her daughter.

"And what do you do, Mr. Keane," she asked, "in this perfect California weather?"

"I'm studying to become an optometrist, Mrs. Gerhardt," he said seriously, sensing he was being evaluated for some position to which he had not knowingly applied. He could not tell from her reaction whether he had failed or passed the test.

"Marguerithe is studying English," she countered, causing her daughter to blush. His eyebrows raised in surprise, lifting his spectacles a centimeter higher on the bridge of his prominent nose. Peggy smiled apologetically at the stranger, excusing her mother's behavior.

"Education, actually," she corrected. He cleared his throat.

"Well, let me help you with your things," he said, taking the bags from Marie and Peggy and carrying them inside the cottage. Peggy elbowed her mother and frowned, placing her hands on her hips as their new neighbor leaned over in the entryway. "Please," she whispered insistently to Marie, who ignored her daughter's embarrassment and followed Charles into the house.

Leonard, Jess, and Charles unloaded the remainder of their belongings while Marie and Peg walked through the unfamiliar rooms and found homes for them all.

"He is a nice young man," Marie stated as she hung one of her dresses up in the closet. "Serious, with a good future ahead of him."

"Mom," sighed Peggy, helping her mother unpack her things, "I'm sure he *is* a nice young man." She left her protest at this, deciding it would do no good to try and persuade her mother that as serious and promising as Charles surely was, she had no interest in him. As soulful as his eyes may have been, he was simply not the sort of man she would ever date, let alone marry. Peggy changed the subject.

"Uncle Jess couldn't look more like you," she commented.

"Really? I always thought he looked so much more like Father," she said absentmindedly. No image of the man Marie referred to as her father appeared in Peggy's mind.

"Did I ever tell you how Papa wore a top hat and tails around New York when we first came to America?" she asked with a smile in her eyes. Peg shook her head. "Yes, it was quite the sight. Orchard Park didn't know what to think! If you've ever wondered where your mother gets her flair for the dramatic, you can blame your grandfather," she teased.

"Well, I like Uncle Jess. I'm glad he's my uncle," she stated.

"Are you now?" said her mother with humor. "You make judgments about a person very quickly, don't you Marguerithe?" Peggy blushed once more.

"Shouldn't I like him? After all, he is your brother." Marie stopped what she was doing for a moment and looked out the bedroom window at the three men burdened with luggage, walking single file into the house.

"Yes, of course you should," she said somberly, remembering how Jess had failed to stand up to their mother or come to her aid when she'd been unable to care for Joseph.

"He's given us a home now," she added. "He *is* a good man now." She turned her back on Peggy and leaned over to unlatch her trunk. "Marguerithe, why don't you go see about the kitchen? I'm fine here." Peggy obeyed and left the room, walking directly into Charles.

"Pardon me," he said, stepping aside to let her pass. She felt his eyes on her as she turned the corner.

CHAPTER 20

The first meal Marie prepared in their new kitchen was steak, which Jess had generously discounted from his store. Leonard protested, feeling that his wife's brother had already been too generous, but Jess would not allow Leonard to refuse his kindness. "We're family," he stated, this being the only explanation required. Leonard conceded after offering to repair the shutters on the front of the house as payment.

Everything that had loaded down the Ford had already been brought inside and put away, creating an immediate sense of permanence. Marie had decorated with the few pieces of artwork and family photographs she had not sold before the move so that any visiting stranger would think the family around the table had lived in the cottage for years.

They stood for grace, and all three heads bowed simultaneously. Leonard leaned heavily on the back of the chair for balance and closed his eyes. "Holy Lord," he began. A long pause followed, and Marie opened her right eye to see why her husband had stopped. There was a sheen of sweat on his forehead, and his skin was pale.

"I'd like to, if you don't mind, Leonard," interrupted Marie, coming to his aid. Relieved, Leonard conceded. Peggy did not listen to the words of her mother's prayer but instead focused upon the heavenly smell wafting upwards from the steak. "Amen," she heard her parents both whisper. Peggy was too eager to take her first bite of the meal to notice her father slide heavily into his chair. Marie patted his knee beneath the table, offering him her strength.

"Serve me a piece of that delicious meat, Marigold!" he managed to say, his voice trembling only slightly. He grabbed his fork and knife clumsily, holding them too tightly. Marie placed two slices of meat on his plate as Peggy scooped a mountain of mashed potatoes onto her own. She waited impatiently for her turn. Marie handed the platter to her daughter. "I forgot the rolls!" she exclaimed, jumping up from her seat and disappearing momentarily into the kitchen.

Marie did not see her husband collapse. She heard the table clatter and then a sickening thud on the wood floor as his head collided with the unforgiving planks. Peggy's panicked shout followed. Marie threw the rolls onto the counter, half of them falling into the sink, and ran back into the dining room.

In the seconds that passed between the heavy sound of dead weight hitting the floor and Marie's reappearance in the dining room, she had already accepted the fact that she would most likely never speak with her husband again. She braced herself for the sight of him, but she still found herself unable to breathe as she rushed to his side.

Peggy knelt with his head lifted in her lap, frantically calling to her father to wake up. She looked with terror at her mother as she entered the room, her eyes flashing wildly. "Get your uncle and tell him what's happened. He'll know what to do." Marie took her daughter's place, cradling Leonard in her arms and curling over his still body. Peggy ran from the room, grateful for the assignment, too scared to consider that this might be the last time she would ever see her father alive. Marie kissed Leonard's damp forehead and cried silently into his chest, rocking him back and forth. She held him as tightly against her own body as she could. His skin smelled of her lilac soap. "I love you," she whispered again and again into his ear. "Not yet. Not yet. Please, Leonard. I love you."

Peg

British Hong Kong
1931-1932

CHAPTER 1

"Isn't it *spectacular?*" whispered Helen excitedly, pinching Peg's side with astonishment. As Sue's aunt checked them in at the front desk, Helen and Peg stood arm and arm in the lobby of the Peninsula Hotel, gawking at the marvelous interior. The great room was resplendent with white marble floors and glittering chandeliers that dangled loftily overhead. Peg's gaze was naturally drawn upwards to the cathedral ceiling tastefully adorned with golden filigree. The restaurant to her right brimmed with men and women sipping tea, their disparate voices creating an exhilarating hum.

"It's all so very, very, *British,* isn't it?" Helen remarked, encompassing the hotel with a gesture of her hand. Peg inadvertently made eye contact with one of the bellmen, who scuttled to her side before she could motion for him to stay where he was.

"Oh no, I'm sorry. I don't need anything. Thank you," she said uncomfortably. Nodding, he stepped back to his empty cart near the elevators and awaited his next orders.

The brawny ocean liner that had been their home for the past six weeks dominated the lobby's view of Victoria Harbor.

"As much as I loved the *Asama*, it will be *so* nice to be off the ship and back on land again, especially *here*." Peg smiled broadly now, the hotel's allure irresistible. "Where's Sue?" she asked, noting that they were missing one of their party.

"She went to the restroom. There she is now with Agatha." Agatha and Sue turned, and Helen waved her arm to draw their attention. A different bellman followed behind them, key in hand.

"This gentleman will show us to our rooms. They said our luggage should be up within the hour," declared Agatha as she removed her gloves one finger at a time, speaking in the concise, formal manner to which Peg had grown accustomed. Agatha was kind to those she knew well but generally unfriendly to the rest of the world. Despite being Sue's aunt, she was only five years older than her niece and fellow traveling companions. As her nature dictated, she had quickly adopted the role of chaperone—a part, in Helen's opinion, that she took rather too seriously.

Overcome by their surroundings, Sue grinned at Helen and Peg and scrunched up her nose before releasing an awkward, boisterous laugh. It was this same laugh that had first endeared her to Peg during their early weeks of classes at the University of California, Southern Branch and had made them fast friends. Sue had the mottled and fair complexion of a redhead, and her bluish green eyes—lined with white-blonde eyelashes —were small, bright, and closely set.

"Can you believe this dump?" she joked. "I wish we could have found something a little more, well more *grande.*" Agatha exhaled sharply in annoyance. Helen giggled while Peg smiled and again looked through the windows across the bustling harbor.

"Wonderful, isn't it?" Peg exhaled. "I could get used to this." Smitten, all the women made gestures and sounds of agreement. As the elevator doors closed, the operator took his instructions from the bellhop, and the exuberant friends began their smooth ascent to the fifth floor.

Susan and Agatha shared an adjoining, identical room to Peg and Helen. Both quarters had views of the bay, two double beds made up with luxurious white linens, Oriental dressers, and boldly patterned rugs.

"This tub is the size of my kitchen!" came a muffled voice from the other bedroom. Peg and Helen immediately moved to their own bathroom and simultaneously gasped.

"Do they expect us to host a party in here?" joked Helen. "What else are you supposed to do with a bath this size? I'll drown!" Peg began to unbutton her blouse, reaching for the thick robe hanging on the back of the door.

"I'll let you know," she smiled, shooing Helen out and shutting the door behind her. Truly, the bathroom itself was as large as her bedroom back home. She turned on the hot water, finished undressing, and wrapped herself in the robe as she waited for the tub to fill.

"Hey! That's not fair. Don't you take all the hot water!" yelled Helen through the door. "I'm next!"

"Keep your britches on," muttered Peg under her breath as she shed her robe and slipped into the steaming, slick water. She leaned her head back and closed her eyes. Her thoughts soon drifted across the ocean to her cottage in Los Angeles and the pain that had compelled her to embark upon this singular trip. Her body relaxing in the deep tub, she supposed she should really thank Charles for his betrayal.

"I, I, I'll have to tell my mother. See what she says. Marguerithe, why didn't you tell me sooner?" The sudden wariness in his voice, the pinched look in his eyes, the way that he leaned away from her, as though to gain distance and see her more clearly through his bifocals.

Peg hadn't planned on telling him, but he had inconveniently forced the issue by proposing. He'd caught her completely off guard. They had dated off and on for three years, and while she had of course entertained the thought of marrying him, the truth was that she was not at all certain he was the man with whom she wished to spend the rest of her life. Surely, it was not enough to only respect and admire her future husband, to enjoy his company as she did any friend. A single glance in the mirror and the reminder there that she was neither getting any younger nor a great beauty easily silenced her doubts.

She'd spilled her secret partly to bide her time, to allow herself a few moments to consider a life with Charles Keane before furnishing her answer. Peg had rehearsed this conversation many times in her mind. For as long as she had been aware that marriage was something women did, she had practiced how she would tell her betrothed the news of her unsavory entrance into this world. As much as she had dreaded rejection and condemnation, she now knew that there had been a part of her that assumed any man who loved her enough to propose would overlook her past.

She had thought Charles meek and kind, and even in his hesitation, he had been neither angry nor deliberately cruel. But she had miscalculated the importance of breeding to this man whose forefathers had farmed the land since their arrival from England. Charles had been taught to pay attention to bloodline, to purity of stock. He could not help but question her worth, her health, her fitness as a potential wife and mother.

When Peg finally did utter the words, it was the first time in her life that she had spoken them aloud. They caught in her throat as the room began to spin. Tightly grasping the edge of the table, she steadied herself.

"You should know something, Charles." She wetted her lips and bit them. He could see her struggle and put his hand over hers. "I was born out of wedlock and adopted by Mom and Dad, by Marie and Leonard. I don't know who my real parents are or where they came from." She tried to look him in the eye but found the weight of her confession and all the years of shame forcing her gaze to the ground.

Momentarily, his hand remained over hers, but slowly, discreetly, it slid to the table and then into his lap. She dared not raise her eyes to meet his but closed them instead, knowing in that instant that he did not love her as a man should love his wife, that he did not love her the way she had always hoped to be loved. It made no difference that she wasn't entirely sure she loved him, either. She thought of protesting his withdrawal, defending herself against his judgment. If anyone should pay the price for this sin, surely it was her mother and father, whomever and wherever they were.

Before she could protest, however, he'd broken the upsetting silence.

"I, I, I'll have to tell my mother. See what she says. Marguerithe, why didn't you tell me sooner?" Peg had felt sorry for him as she'd looked into his face, drawn and pained, the color gone and his eyes hardened. She should have told him from the beginning. What if he knew about Joseph, about the whole sordid family history? No, she saw now that her family would never meet the standards of his own. The Keanes had once been Irish kings, after all. Keane infants were always born at least ten months after marriage, and if they were not, the involved parties at least had the decency to keep the truth hidden.

She had been so foolish; she saw that now. Although he would never admit it, Peg knew that her confession had inexorably changed their relationship. They could never marry.

Peggy cleared her throat, steadied herself, and prepared to give him a way out.

"Yes, yes of course." And then she'd remembered Sue's foolhardy invitation to accompany her across the ocean to Asia. She'd dismissed the possibility and laughed at her friend, but now she knew that she would, in fact, go with her. "I'll be in China this summer, Charles. It's probably better if we take some time apart," she said decisively. Charles managed only mild surprise at her announcement, the previous revelation too disturbing for him to much care that his intended would soon embark on a journey halfway around the world. Before he could say anything further, she'd risen from the table and walked briskly to her own home, shutting the door firmly behind her.

An hour passed, and her breath gradually steadied; the tears dried, leaving thin trails of dried sheen. She wiped her face with her fingers and looked at her pink, puffy reflection in the mirror. Glancing at the empty room, her gaze landed on the clock. Her mother would be home soon and demand an explanation for her dishevelment. She moved to the bathroom and splashed cold water on her face until the redness subsided. Well, Sue would certainly be surprised to learn she'd changed her mind! Peg dried her hands on the cheerful yellow towel just as she heard the front door open and her mother's unmistakable footsteps head for the kitchen.

"Marguerithe! Where are you? Are you home?" Marie called out as she passed through the front door.

"Here, Mom. I was just using the restroom." Peg joined her mother in the kitchen and only halfheartedly listened to Marie's complaints of soaring food prices as she helped her unpack the groceries. Despite her best efforts to conceal her emotions, the slowness of her movements and occasional pain in her smile gave her mother pause.

"Is something the matter?" she asked. "You're a hundred miles away."

"No," answered Peg, opening the pantry to put the bag of oatmeal on the top shelf. She stared up at the red and blue label and tried to think of what to say next. It should have been an effortless and cathartic thing for Peg to tell her mother that her only prospect of marriage had just vanished, but Marie adored Charles. Peg could not stand to see her image of him sullied nor to repeat aloud those terrible words he had spoken.

"Actually," she said as she turned to look her mother in the eye, "I have news." Marie raised her right eyebrow, awaiting the pronunciation.

"I've found a good use for some of the money Mam left me in her will. I'll be spending the summer in China," she smiled, shifting her wait onto her right hip and warily gauging her mother's reaction. Marie's only response was to fold the cloth grocery sacks and put them away in the entryway closet. Peg watched her leave the kitchen to do so and then return. Marie grasped the chair back and shook her head.

"China," she said as though testing the word aloud for any portents of disaster. "And you think Ruth would approve? Somehow I don't think a trip to China is what she had in mind when she left you the money." Corresponding monthly, Marie and Ruth had continued their friendship even after the family moved to California. Through a transcribed sharing of their daily lives, they had grown even closer than when they'd both lived in Helena. A second stroke had suddenly claimed Ruth's life, and it was the executor of her estate that had contacted Marie. If Ruth hadn't astonishingly bequeathed five thousand dollars to her daughter, Marie might never have known what had befallen her friend.

"Well, she didn't say. She didn't put any stipulations on the money, and Sue and her aunt are going, too." She'd been flabbergasted that Mam had left her anything, let alone such a large sum. It didn't make sense, and as was fitting her former employer, there'd been no explanation in her will.

"Are they now? Times certainly have changed, haven't they?" Releasing the chair, Marie fixed her hair and moved to the sink to wash her hands. "I have to get supper started. Will you hand me the bowl over there and the eggs," she said, pointing to a large metal bowl stored on top of the refrigerator.

Peg did as instructed and let the matter drop. She stared fondly at the back of her mother's head as she cracked six eggs into the bowl. Peg knew Marie was afraid for her daughter and could not understand why any sane person would board a ship traveling away from the United States. Still, Marie kept her concerns to herself and let her daughter be the slightly peculiar creature she knew her to be.

Marie and Peg prepared the soufflé in silence. Only as Marie set the casserole dish gingerly into the oven did she revisit Peg's summer plans.

"I suppose you'll need a few new things, then, won't you? We should go shopping this weekend for a dress." Peg grinned and hugged her mother.

"That sounds perfect."

CHAPTER 2

B y the time the sun had set and the green waters of Kowloon Bay turned black, the initial giddiness of their arrival and the thrill of their opulent accommodations had still not faded. Peg and her friends at last gave way to their fatigue and went to bed early. Helen opened the window in their shared room before they retired.

"So we can be soothed to sleep by the sounds of Hong Kong," she said romantically, falling onto her bed and sighing. Peg, normally a light sleeper, was too tired to argue. The clanking of the wooden boats in the harbor was occasionally perceptible beneath the roar of cars in the street. "I'm so glad you talked me into coming, Mags. I needed to get away from everything."

To everyone's astonishment, Helen had not, in fact, married Paul. She'd ended her love affair with Mr. Summers two weeks before the wedding and uncharacteristically refused to tell Peg why. Nonetheless, Peg was almost certain it had been at Mr. Carlisle's insistence. Knowing him, she was sure that his plans for his daughter and their family included far more than her marrying a rancher.

While there had been other men in Helen's life since the broken engagement, none were able to capture her full attention, let alone her heart. It was not from lack of trying and sincerity that her suitors failed. She had turned the heads of many prominent businessmen who'd lavished her with attention and gifts, all of whom Mr. Carlisle would have happily welcomed into the family. Despite her insistence to the contrary, Peg could clearly see that Helen was still very much in love with Paul. No man stood a chance until he was excised from her affections. The regularity with which she ran into her old beau did nothing to improve Helen's plight, especially as he, too, had remained single. Really, it was Shakespearean in its tragedy, and Peg hoped this trip around the world might give the star-crossed lovers the distance and perspective they needed to at last move forward.

Peg slipped beneath the crisp, luxurious covers of her bed and sighed, closing her eyes and remembering with sadness how happy Paul and Helen had been together. She drifted off her first night in Hong Kong to the deep call of a steamship entering the port and the loud ticking of the hotel clock as she wished silently that Helen might find someone new to love.

Peg awoke at sunrise and slipped into the robe the maid had lain across the foot of her bed. Helen snored softly, her arms thrown above her head. Climbing into the stuffed chair, Peg turned it to face the window. The tourists were absent, but the natives were already hard at work. A sea of pointed, woven hats bobbed along the streets, breaking off along separate channels as they flowed down the narrow tributaries of the store-lined alleyways. They carried their items inventively—strapped to their backs, balanced on poles across their shoulders, or pulled behind them in large-wheeled carts. Even the finely dressed women carried paper parasols.

Looking past the roads to Kowloon Bay, Peg watched as a young man dove from the edge of his small wooden vessel into the deep water and did not emerge. She leaned forward in alarm and put her fingers to the glass when a few moments later, his shimmering wet head emerged. "How odd," she noted in a whisper. The other boats in the bay, many nearly perfect replicas of his own, seemed to be somewhere in the process of casting, letting down, or pulling in their nets. The early sun glinted silver off the scales of the fish trapped between the rope fibers.

A blur of white entered her periphery, and Peg refocused her attention on a blonde European woman, dressed from head to toe in spotless linen, who stepped confidently from the dock onto one of these precarious boats. She held a thick object between her waist and elbow, and the family she greeted responded with warmth and familiarity. Peg feared the woman would dirty her dress if she was not careful and wished she would step back onto the dock.

Helen stirred and Peg ran to her bed, jumping playfully atop her sleepy friend. Helen groaned and swatted blindly in the air.

"Get up, lazy bones! We have so much to see!" cried Peg, the urge to uncover whatever the East was hiding burgeoning with the rising sun.

When it was clear that her exuberance would persist until she opened her eyes, Helen turned towards Peg and scowled.

"Good morning," laughed Peg, rudely pulling the covers back and throwing them onto the floor. Helen grabbed the pillow next to her and swung it as hard as she could from her reclined position, hitting Peg squarely in the face. Despite herself, Helen laughed and pulled up to sitting. She rubbed her eyes, yawned, and looked at Peg.

"I'm not agreeing to anything until I have a bath and some breakfast. Then we can talk." She stumbled sleepily into the bathroom and shut the door. Peg wasted no time in selecting a white blouse with navy buttons and a matching skirt. She unrolled the curlers in the front of her hair, brushed it all through, and left it loose. From her purse she took a tube of pink lipstick and applied it sparingly, blotting her lips and checking her teeth.

Phoning their friends' room, she tried twice with no answer. Knowing Agatha's propensity for early rising, Peg concluded they must both already be downstairs enjoying breakfast.

"I'll see you at the restaurant, Helen. I'm going to have a look around," Peg called through the bathroom door. She hurried out into the hall without waiting for a response and took the stairs to stretch her legs. When she reached the ground floor and swung open the door into the lobby, its fineness once again startled her into self-consciousness. She touched her hair softly and scanned the room for Sue and Agatha.

Although it was no later than seven-thirty, the restaurant was nearly full with travelers and businessmen. A shock of orange hair caught her eye, and Peg moved quickly to join her friends. Sue glanced about in boredom, desperate for someone, anyone, to interrupt.

"Hi," said Peg as she approached and sat down in the empty chair. "What did I miss?"

"Good morning, Marguerithe," said Agatha, nodding formally.

"Hi yourself," replied Sue in her usual manner. "Nothing, I'm afraid. Helen's still asleep?" she asked with amusement.

"She's getting ready. Have you already eaten?"

"No, we're waiting for our food now." Peg perused the short, pretty menu and decided on scones and coffee. She was too excited for anything more. The waiter came with Sue and Agatha's meals, took Peg's order, and poured her beverage.

"We *are* in China, Peggy. You should probably order tea," teased Sue, knowing how much her friend enjoyed her morning cup. Peg lowered her drink with concern.

"You're right! I don't want to miss *anything*," she said.

"It's a beverage, Peg, not the Great Wall," joked Sue. Peg swatted the air in the direction of her friend's arm. When the waiter shortly after brought her scones, Peg asked for a cup of tea as well, which he delivered immediately. She sipped the drink and frowned at its grassy flavor.

Sue leaned forward eagerly. "I was chatting with the concierge earlier and asked for recommendations. Victoria Peak is a must, as is Recluse Bay. He said the markets all around town can be interesting but to be careful and not go alone. If it's the whole gang, I'm sure we'd be fine. There's a list of restaurants and theaters we can get from him as well. Oh, and there's a ferry to Macao we apparently *must* catch at some point."

"Great!" said Peg, taking her final bite of scone and washing it down with coffee. In a hurry, she pushed her seat back strongly and knocked into the chair behind her. She turned to offer her apologies.

"Oh, excuse me. I'm so sorry." A sandy-haired man turned in agitation, his coffee having spilled onto his plate. When he saw the sincerity of her expression, his consternation dissolved. He noticed Sue across the table, stood, cleared his throat and smiled, leaning forward on the back of his chair.

"No harm done. May I introduce myself? Fred Warner," he stated with swagger, addressing his introduction to the entire table. Peg glanced at the two other men seated at Fred's table and quickly determined the only possible recourse was to return the greeting.

She nodded and smiled cordially. "Hello," was all she said.

"Good morning, I'm James and this is Cop," the other man offered in a British accent, gesturing towards the older looking fellow with a cap of tight blond curls to his right. Peg was uncertain she had heard him correctly, her puzzlement showing on her face. The blond man appeared irritated at the compulsion to explain.

"That's my last name—Cop. Well, Copley. Willem is my Christian name."

"I see," said Peg, uncertain how to respond. "I'm Marguerithe and this is Sue and Agatha." All members of both parties now introduced, the conversation came to a halt. Peg noticed that Cop looked impatiently at James, as though eager to return to their discussion.

"We were just on our way to get our friend. It was nice to meet you. We should be going if we want to see all the sites," said Peg graciously, noting the stark contrast in reaction between Cop and Fred. The latter did not understand or ignored Peg's efforts to disengage, whereas Cop was noticeably relieved.

"What do you have planned?" asked Fred, trying not to appear too interested. Peg stifled her amusement. She saw Agatha, none to secretively, roll her eyes before interjecting.

"We haven't yet decided. Have you any recommendations?" she asked, turning the conversation to good use. The men all looked at each other and Fred spoke.

"Yes, I recommend that you meet us back here with your friend in ten minutes, and I will be your personal tour guide through the wild, exotic streets of Hong Kong."

"Wild and exotic?" teased Sue. "Yes, then you had better be our guide." Fred stood up straighter and slapped James' back, as though they had both just won a prize.

"Fred here has been in Hong Kong all of a week, but what he lacks in knowledge, he'll make up for in imagination, I promise you," quipped James. Peg laughed and Cop stared, which immediately silenced her. He was none too happy about the turn of events and spoke up to remind them that he had an appointment to keep in half an hour.

"Mr. Copley," said Agatha, "You are here on business and not on vacation?"

"No, I'm on holiday, but there are a few things I need to take care of this afternoon."

"*Mr.* Copley," jabbed Fred, "I was offering my services, not yours. You are free to go any time you like." Cop stood and carelessly tossed his napkin onto the table.

"It was nice to meet you all. Enjoy your day," he said, nodding at each woman in turn before weaving his way through the restaurant's round tables and stepping with purpose through the front door.

"You'll have to excuse Cop. He's a very single-minded sort of fellow. He has his plans and likes to stick to them, even when something better arises." Peg watched in disbelief as Sue blushed. It was the first time that Peg had ever witnessed her friend at a loss for words.

"James, what about you. Want to tag along?" Just as James was beginning to excuse himself as well, Helen appeared behind Peg with a rousing smile.

"What have I missed? Nothing fun or important, I hope!" she said charmingly.

"James, Fred, this is Helen, the last of our gang." Helen offered her hand as none of the other women had, and while Fred grasped it briefly, James kissed it. Everyone averted their eyes uncomfortably before Fred interjected.

"—He's British," he offered, shrugging his shoulders. James seemed not to notice the impression that he had made on the other women. He looked only at Helen.

"I was just telling Fred how I would greatly enjoy accompanying you all on your sightseeing trip."

"Wonderful!" proclaimed Fred, slapping him once again on the back. "Are you ladies ready now, or do you need to go upstairs and get your things?"

"I'm ready," said Helen, pleased by the response her arrival had garnered. Sue and Agatha agreed.

"I'll be right back. I left my pocket book," said Peg. She hurried away from the table and the fawning men, irritated that she would have to humor two love-struck gentlemen during their first day in Hong Kong. That the older man had left rather than be her partner was not lost on her. Peg felt her plainness keenly and avoided looking in the hotel's many mirrors as she grabbed her purse and quickly headed back downstairs.

CHAPTER 3

A lthough James had been raised in Hong Kong as a young boy, Fred insisted upon leading their little tour group. All three men, the women soon learned, worked for Saucony-Vacuum Oil Company in Singapore and were on vacation for the summer. They'd decided upon Hong Kong when James had been able to secure free accommodations with family who still lived in the city. They had been in town for a week and treated themselves to daily breakfast and compatriot conversation at the Peninsula Hotel.

"It finally paid off," Fred flirted. Agatha eyed Fred condemningly. She had quickly assessed that he was harmless but still found his incessant romancing grating. She did not understand Sue's evident attraction to the man and wished, without drawing too much attention, she could advise her niece to not be so easily wooed. If Fred ever left Sue's side, she would say something.

James was equally as enamored but guarded his interest more carefully. While pointing out various buildings and sites, giving them thorough history lessons on each, he made polite conversation with Helen. Were it not for his handsomeness, Helen would quickly have grown weary of his pedantic and stuffy air. Her mind drifted as he explained Britain's long relationship with Hong Kong, but when he mentioned opium, her glazed expression vanished.

"Opium? How scandalous!" she said gleefully. Peg frowned. She did not think it appropriate to delight in such a ruinous thing but kept her disproval quiet, soon growing annoyed with her own solemnity.

As they made their way to Queen's Road, the people clamoring to her left and right vied for her attention. While many wore loosely woven and rough garments, well-suited to manual labor and the heat, others chose brightly colored silks, fastened high on the neck with a distinctive row of buttons. Some of the Chinese they passed were barefoot, while others wore flimsy sandals. The exception were the businessmen in their crisp British suits and the women they paraded on their arms with high-heeled shoes far more fashionable than Peg's. When their path crossed that of a fellow European, the men tipped their hats, and the ladies smiled demurely.

A man selling vegetables peered at Peg through the crowd and motioned for her to come closer, yelling something she could not understand. Peg smiled back uncomfortably but stayed with the group until he made such a commotion that the street turned in unison to investigate the noise. Wishing to avoid a scene, Peg strode swiftly to his stall.

"I don't speak Cantonese, or Mandarin, for that matter. I can't understand what you're saying," she stated plainly with growing agitation as the man continued to talk loudly. The rest of her group waited at a distance, and she raised her hand at them to stay where they were, embarrassed enough without any additional attention. In order to silence the peddler, she was going to have to buy something. As she reluctantly opened her pocket book, he encouraged her with a nod.

Rubbing his chin with his fingers, the man closed one of his eyes and stared at Peg with his head cocked. His finger shot into the air, and he picked up a basket at his feet. There were a dozen or so delightful coin purses brightly decorated with dragons and cherry blossoms. He raised his eyebrows with expectation, seeing immediately that he had read his customer well. Peg smiled and chose a blue and red one.

"How much?" She emptied a few coins onto her palm and held it towards the vendor who took the correct amount, careful not to touch her.

"Peggy! Hurry up!" cried Sue. Just as Peg was turning to join her friends, a clearing in the crowd at the busy intersection to their left revealed two figures, a man and woman standing beside the heavy glass doors of a stately, pillared building. The woman's white dress and blonde hair made her look uncannily like the adventurous lady Peg had watched through her hotel window that morning, and her companion was, unmistakably, Willem Copley. She and then he laughed casually before he took her elbow and guided her across the street in Peg's direction. So this was the important business to which he had to attend. She moved quietly to rejoin her friends. Before she could announce that Cop was coming their way, Fred spotted him.

"Hey!" he yelled, waving his arms to get Cop's attention. When Cop saw, he said something to the woman before steering them over to the group.

As she came closer, Peg saw that his companion was striking, with clear blue eyes and hair a soft shade of young wheat. Although petite, Peg sensed that the woman was vigorous rather than fragile. The remnants of a smile still clung to Cop's lips. Clearly, the woman's company agreed with him. Peg took a step backwards so that Helen and Sue both stood ahead of her in greeting.

Cop shook hands with Fred and James and ignored their questioning expressions. Fred stared repeatedly at the nameless blond woman until she was forced to introduce herself.

"Hello. It's nice to meet you. I'm Claire, Claire Wards." She seemed comfortable and genuinely pleased to meet Cop's friends. Helen, Sue, Agatha and Peg all gave their names, and Helen whispered in Peg's ear.

"Who are these people?"

"It's their friend who left before you came downstairs this morning," she whispered back. "Now we all know why." Glancing at Cop, Helen's eyes twinkled, and Peg held her breath.

"Hello. I'm Helen. I understand you met the rest of the gang earlier this morning. What was your name?" she asked.

"Cop," he answered plainly.

"No, I asked your name, not your profession," she replied. Peg covered her mouth to suppress her laughter as Cop looked at Helen with greater attention.

"That *is* my name, Willem Copley, but most everyone calls me Cop."

"Oh, how rude of me! I'm so sorry!" said Helen. Cop's brow tensed but his mouth smiled, as though he could not decide whether Helen's boorishness had been intentional or an honest blunder. Fred blurted out the question on Peg's mind.

"What are you two up to?" he asked plainly, as only a close friend would dare. Cop glanced at Ms. Wards and tried to formulate an answer. Claire interrupted, saving him the explanation. She held up the book she was carrying as she spoke.

"Cop had a few questions that I was attempting to answer," she said. When she saw that no one understood her explanation, she tried again.

"We were reading the Bible together." Ms. Ward was genuinely perplexed by the group's bewilderment. She eyed Cop disapprovingly.

"Ms. Wards is a missionary here in Hong Kong," explained Cop. "She is the daughter of close family friends back home, and I promised her folks I would check in on her when I was in town. Claire and I grew up together. She's rather an expert on the scriptures, and I thought I would pick her brain on a few passages."

Fred and James blinked and stared at Cop with confusion. The subject matter of the conversation left Fred without room for jest, and he chose instead to avert his eyes and watch the busy street. While it was certainly not the explanation Peg had expected to hear, she did not understand the group's reticence. Although she could scarcely remember more than one or two passages, she spoke to break the uncomfortable silence.

"Which verses were you studying?" she asked kindly. Ms. Wards turned to her with pleasure and gratitude, taking Peg's hand in an act of familiarity that dissolved any aversion she may have felt toward the woman. Peg liked Claire Wards, despite herself.

"Romans eight. It's one of my favorites, of course. Cop thought I had some sort of expertise that honestly, I don't possess." She spoke without pretense and smiled at Cop.

"Are you here by yourself, Ms. Wards?" asked Helen. "I mean, would you and your husband like to join us on our tour of Hong Kong?" Peg would have punched her friend in the shoulder if they had been alone.

"Oh, no. I have no husband. I am 'married to the Lord,' as they say." Perplexed, Helen puckered her lips in thought.

"You don't look like any nun I've ever seen," she finally said.

"Heavens no! I'm not a nun, nor am I Catholic, for that matter."

Cop nervously watched the groups' baffled expressions, attempting to gauge the impact of everything Claire candidly declared. Standing with her now, he acutely felt the juxtaposition of her faith with his friends' skepticism. He looked at Marguerithe, her apparent familiarity with the Bible pleasing.

He had been preparing for some time to tell Fred and James of his new faith but had neither found the appropriate time nor the right words to explain. The internal transformation had been so profound, and yet neither Fred nor James had noticed anything out of the ordinary, a fact that disturbed him. Shouldn't there have been a marked difference, the sort of change that provoked questions? This was one of the matters about which he'd wanted to speak with Claire. Now, she had exposed him, and the perplexed look on Fred's face spoke volumes.

"Oh, well, then would you like to join us?" asked Helen, recovering from the woman's eccentric announcement.

"Thank you, but no. There is a family I promised I would visit shortly. I really should be going. They live across town." She kissed Cop familiarly on the cheek.

"It was lovely to meet you all. You are in good hands. Enjoy your sightseeing, and I hope to run into everyone again before you leave. God bless." Claire Wards nodded her head farewell and walked smartly from the group, her wiry frame stepping nimbly between the rickshaw drivers and pedestrians before disappearing in the crowd. Their unusual conversation had left Peg befuddled, and she realized as soon as Claire left that she'd not mentioned seeing her earlier that morning.

"You keep peculiar company, Cop," teased Fred. "*Pretty*, but *peculiar* company." He grinned broadly, knowing better than to press his friend further.

Although Cop joined the party, he said not a word the remainder of the afternoon. He did not notice his surroundings, and if it had not been for James' swift reflexes, might have been run over more than once. With

Helen and James paired off and Fred and Sue shamelessly flirting, Peg felt it her duty to at least attempt conversation with the distracted gentleman.

"Ms. Wards is certainly...*charming*, isn't she?" When Cop frowned, she feared he mistook her choice of words for a veiled criticism. "I like her very much," she added hurriedly.

"Yes, she *is* very likable, as you say." A few more efforts without more than one-word replies, Peg turned her attentions to Agatha and then to her own thoughts. Claire had been sincere and poised, and although she had no husband, her singleness was not a problem that required a remedy. Despite having introduced her as nothing more than an old family friend, it seemed impossible that Cop would *not* be interested in the woman. Had she been open to courting, surely he would have jumped at the chance. She and Cop may not have been an item, but that did not mean that his heart did not wish they were.

The group parted ways at the hotel and promised to meet the following morning for breakfast. To Peg's surprise, Cop allowed himself to be included in their plans. She was pleased he would be joining them, even if he were secretly in love with Ms. Wards.

With the energy of racehorses, Helen and Sue dressed for dinner and remained downstairs in the lobby until late in the evening. Peg and Agatha retired early—Agatha from exhaustion and blistered feet, and Peg to have the opportunity to let her mind wander in the dimming room, at last alone with only the subdued score of the peninsula and the hotel pianist to accompany her pregnant thoughts. Despite the bright, loud day, all the new sights and aromas, Peg's mind hovered longest over the enigmatic Claire Wards and her curious devotion.

CHAPTER 4

Although no alarm had been set, Peg again awoke at the first wash of daylight. She slipped on her robe and once more went to the window, pushing aside the curtain. When she did not see a white figure among the boats in the harbor, she knew she had hoped to see Ms. Wards once again visiting the fishermen. She exhaled and let the curtain fall back into place. Helen did not stir as Peg quickly dressed, throwing on one of her more casual outfits and running her brush through her hair before heading downstairs.

When she stepped out into the lobby, there were only three others present, and she was thankful for the stillness. She slipped into the nearest seat at the restaurant and ordered toast, eggs and coffee, which she consumed in too few bites. The soft light warming the tablecloth grew brighter as the sun rose higher, and Peg's body ached for fresh air and movement. As she finished the coffee, she decided she would walk down to the docks.

The distinct aroma of Hong Kong greeted her—its blend of spices, fish, exhaust, and salt water. Peg tried not to stare as a woman with wrists like a sparrow passed carrying a heavy pot filled with steaming liquid. Strapped to her back was a newborn baby. Despite the unnatural angle at which his heavy head hung down, the boy was in a deep sleep, not to be roused by his mother's perpetual industriousness.

Once she arrived at the water, Peg confronted dozens of smaller docks that shot out like spindles from the main hub. Stepping onto the widely spaced wooden planks, the structure bobbed, and she nearly tipped into the bay. Alarmed, she heard laughter and turned to find its source. A girl no more than twelve stood on a boat twenty yards away, her mouth covered by her own hands as she giggled at the foreign woman's clumsiness. Feeling conspicuous, Peg smiled and raised her hand to wave at the observer. The little girl's laughter was abruptly silenced as a pair of arms yanked her around her waist and swatted her on her bottom. Peg's hand remained in the air as the woman she assumed was the girl's mother glared at her and did not return her greeting. She dropped her hand and looked away, confused and a little offended.

Smoke rose from several of the boats, spiraling effortlessly into the lemony morning sky. She took a deep breath and decided to venture down the precarious planks to her left. With her first step, a man on the boat directly in front of her began yelling and gesticulating violently. Despite the language barrier, there was no mistaking that she was not to come any closer. Blushing, Peg felt naive and sorely out of place. What had she been thinking? Just as she had given up on the whole endeavor and was turning to run back towards the hotel, a hand touched her upper arm.

Startled and spinning to confront her attacker, Peg nearly fell once again into the bay. She cocked her leg back to kick whomever it was that wished her harm.

"Ms. Wards!" cried Peg in relief. "I am *so* happy to see you!" she said breathlessly, clutching the woman's forearms to steady herself.

"Ms....?" Peg could see Ms. Wards struggle to remember her name or recall exactly how it was that this disheveled, panicked American knew her.

"Gerhardt. Um, Marguerithe. But please, call me Peg."

"Peg, oh yes. We met yesterday. You are one of Cop's friends. What on earth are you doing here?" she inquired with plain astonishment.

The absurdity of her presence struck Peg squarely in her gut, and she feared there was no way to explain herself without appearing either insane or idiotic.

"I went for a walk," was all she said. Claire looked her in the eye skeptically. "I've never seen anything like this," Peg offered, gesturing to the hundreds of wooden boats surrounding them, hoping the additional explanation would satisfy her rescuer.

"Well, this isn't really a place for tourists, Peg. Especially women."

"Yes, I gathered that by all the yelling," she joked. Ms. Wards watched Peg closely, still uncertain as to her motives. Peg released her grip and smoothed her hair nervously, noticing that Claire held her Bible in the crook of her arm as she had yesterday.

"Do you always carry it with you?" she asked, pointing at the book and hoping to redirect their conversation. A smiled formed on Claire's lips.

"Yes, that's why *I'm* here. I visit a few families on a daily basis and read God's word with them. Last week, an entire family accepted Jesus as their Lord and Savior!" she exclaimed with delight. Forgetting the strangeness of their meeting, Claire relaxed as she began to tell Peg of her ministry.

"I've been coming down here for nearly a year and had almost given up hope that any of the Tanka—the boat people—would come to the Lord, but God did a mighty work last month and grabbed hold of the heart of one of the teenage boys. He told the rest of his family about Jesus, and now they've all been grafted into God's family tree. Praise the Lord!" she cried at the end, unable to subdue her enthusiasm. "I'm going to read with them now. None of them have Bibles, so the time I spend with the family in the scriptures is of the utmost importance," she said, clutching the book and tapping its cover.

Peg struggled to follow Claire's explanation and to demonstrate the enthusiasm she knew the woman expected. She tried to smile warmly, but her eyes revealed her insincerity. She understood very little of what she'd said. A few moments of silenced passed as Claire looked at her and then out at the bay and back at Peg. Fiddling with the pendant around her neck, Claire's gaze became dreamy and her shoulders relaxed.

"It's beautiful in its own way, don't you think?" she said quietly.

"The water, you mean?"

"Yes, the water and the mountains." Claire turned her back to Peg and folded her arms across her Bible so that it was pinned to her chest.

"*And for all this, nature is never spent. There lives the dearest freshness deep down things. And though the last lights off the black West went, Oh morning, at the brown brink eastward, springs – because the Holy Ghost over the bent World broods with warm breast and with ah! bright wings.*'" Claire spoke just loudly enough to be heard. "It's a poem —a silly thing, really, but lovely. I think, sometimes, it perfectly describes...*everything*." Claire turned back to Peg. "The Lord uses even language to reveal His glory. Jesus *is* the Word. He loves words." Claire's mouth spread into a wide grin. "That's what I tell myself when I talk a person's ear off." She laughed aloud and extended her hand to Peg.

"I have a wonderful idea! Would you like to come with me to meet the family?" Claire's eyes suddenly and perfectly reflected the expansive water spread smoothly before them, and although Peg felt both drawn and repelled by the notion, she took her hand.

"I knew I would like you, Peg. I knew it when we met yesterday. And please, call me Claire. You've, after all, just endured my poetry recital. I say that puts us on a first name basis. And, I am praying, from this moment, that the Lord will make us sisters in Christ."

Bewildered, Peg shrugged her shoulders, and Claire laughed again.

"I'm speaking gibberish, aren't I? She did not wait for a response, the answer evident. "Let's go see the Pangs."

They walked further down the main dock, Claire with confidence and a sure foot and Peg, with care. Claire spoke over her shoulder as they proceeded, and the jumbled mass of boats began to separate and sharpen into distinct vessels. Some were like row-boats, others long and narrow with a barrel secured to the top; some were large with many masts, or small and plain; and still others were decorated with lush fabrics and bright paper lanterns.

"They are outcasts, you know. The British and the Chinese both look down on the Tanka. They aren't allowed to set foot on land, and they aren't permitted to marry the 'real' Chinese. They've lived this way for centuries. It's incredible, really. Many of the women are prostitutes, and at least half of these vessels you see are floating brothels. They are the only native women who will cater to the British and foreigners. The Hong Kong and mainland Chinese won't go anywhere near white men."

Claire spoke plainly and without embarrassment, and the information seemed to shock Peg more than the missionary. Claire noted Peg's surprise.

"Yes, I was once rather taken-aback as well. But you see, I've been coming here for quite some time now, and I know most of the women by name. If I had been born into these circumstances, I might also have resorted to prostitution. They have a different language, customs, personalities, but we all have *the* most important thing in common." She paused for effect and waited for Peg to ask.

"—And what is that?" she played along, not imagining she had *anything* in common with a Tankan prostitute.

"God made us all in His image. Well, there are really two things we have in common. We are made in His image, and we all need Jesus to save us from our sin." Claire turned her head, and Peg caught the glint of tears in the woman's eyes. She was far stranger than Peg had realized.

Unable to think of an appropriate response, Peg let the dramatic statement hang in the air between them. She thought on Claire's words but could do nothing with them other than to detachedly admire their conviction.

Peg had always assumed she believed in God, as did most people she knew, but faced now with a faith that surpassed hers as a hurricane does a breeze, Peg saw that her belief was not the same animal as that which her escort possessed. Her own faith was a pretty trinket she took off and on. She wished she could believe as completely as did Claire, but she feared that she could not. A voice from years before filled her ears—Pastor Lemke who had broken her heart with his contemptuous exclamation. Was his God the same as Claire's? It was impossible. Claire's God seemed worth knowing; the minister's a deity from whom one must hide.

They took a path to their right and came almost to its end when a woman with a remarkably wrinkled face and bright black eyes popped her head out from the boat nearest them, letting out an exclamation Peg did not understand.

To her amazement, Claire spoke to the woman in her own language.

"I've just introduced you and asked if Mrs. Pang would mind your joining us."

Peg couldn't think of what else to do, so she bowed and smiled. The woman laughed and pointed at Peg, addressing Claire with a joke of some kind that made Mrs. Pang laugh even louder.

"What? What did she say?" Claire blushed. "Mrs. Pang is just teasing you. It's a good thing. She only jokes with people she likes." Mrs. Pang said something else and gestured for them to come aboard.

The two women stepped onto the narrow boat, and the musky, intoxicating scent of sandalwood filled the air like smoke. Peg had never smelled anything like it and tried not to cough as the cloying aroma caught in her throat.

"Mrs. Pang's family trades sandalwood. They are well off, as far as Tankas go." Peg tried not to stare at the humble accommodations in which they now sat. Mrs. Pang had rolled back one of the walls so that fresh air blew Peg's hair and relieved the suffocating smell of her livelihood. The bay was visible, as were the boats and inhabitants next to theirs. There was a teapot with two cups resting on a mat on the floor, a discrepancy that Mrs. Pang quickly remedied by pulling another cup from its home on the shelf. Claire handed a small, wrapped package to their hostess as she poured them all tea. Peg sat on the floor of the boat next to Claire and hesitantly took a sip. To her delight, the tea was far milder and sweeter than at the Peninsula.

Mrs. Pang said something else, to which Claire quickly responded and smiled. "She's eager to get to our reading." Mrs. Pang spread her hands towards Peg and bobbed her head. The woman clearly wanted Peg to do something, but she had no idea what.

"She's offering to let you pray," said Claire, who quickly came to Peg's rescue by closing her eyes, bowing her head, and beginning herself to pray instead. Peg bowed her head thankfully but kept her eyes open, gazing at the hand-woven mat made of some kind of grass. She tried to focus on the sound of Claire's words but found her mind drifting as the unfamiliar clanging of Mrs. Pang's language tumbled. A man yelled outside the boat angrily, but Peg did not dare look to see why.

"In Jesus' holy and precious name we pray, Amen." Claire ended in English on Peg's behalf and immediately began to read aloud the passage of scripture to which she had earlier flipped. Turning aside to Peg, she instructed her to read over her shoulder so that she would be able to understand. Peg did as she was told but, once again, had difficulty concentrating. Peg read it three times before making any sense of it.

As Mrs. Pang and Claire conversed, Peg watched the enthusiasm in Mrs. Pang's face and listened to the intensity of her voice. Reading and discussing the Bible was invigorating to this old woman. Peg watched as she came more and more alive. At one point, she leapt up from her seat and began to pace, wobbling the narrow vessel with her lively questions. She listened intently to Claire's answers.

Peg read the passage once again and let the sentiment sift itself into a single, concise thought. *Nothing can separate us from the love of God.* She considered the statement before passing judgment. Peg did not feel loved by God, nor, if she were honest, did she love him. She loved her mother and her father, Helen and Joseph. She had thought she had loved Charles. No, she did not love God. She did not know him well enough to love him. How was a person to love someone she never sees and cannot touch, someone who allows mothers to abandon their infants and children's spirits to shatter? The words in the passage rang false. She cleared her throat at the realization and tried to decide whether or not to mention her findings to Claire.

Mrs. Pang suddenly stopped her pacing and grew very quiet. Claire took the opportunity to turn to Peg.

"Well, what do you think?" Peg frowned, not wishing to hurt her friend's feelings.

"Go on, you can say it," said Claire.

"Well, I don't think it's true. God doesn't love me and, frankly, I don't love him either," she said quietly, her face hot from her bold declaration. Peg expected a rebuttal but received none. A minute passed in silence before Claire finally spoke.

"Marguerithe, God *does* love you. Hear me when I say it. God *loves* you. He isn't like us. He doesn't ever love without showing it. He demonstrates his love in the very beauty of the ocean, in allowing you to awake this morning and find yourself, here, reading His Word, and most of all in sending His Son to die for you. Imagine your mother giving *your* life so that another could live! No mother I know would ever make such a sacrifice. There is no greater love than this. But I believe you when you say you don't love God. That is *entirely* true, and that, my dear, is the problem." Peg blushed a second time.

Her initial admiration of Claire waned as she grew weary of so much religious talk. Surely, all things in moderation. She was beginning to see that her new acquaintance was not just passionate but a zealot.

Claire grew quiet, and Peg felt badly for wanting to escape. The woman was only answering her questions.

"Were your parents missionaries?" asked Peg.

Claire threw her head back and laughed.

"Papa, a missionary! Not in a million years, I'm afraid."

"They, they don't share your convictions?" asked Peg, bewildered.

"No." Claire's expression darkened and her voice fell. "I have prayed for them without ceasing, but neither of them have come to know Christ." Peg could not help but think that Claire must not be a very good missionary if she had been unable to convert even her own family.

"I wish it were up to me, that I could say *just* the right thing, that I could make the perfect persuasive argument that Papa and Mummy would be unable to refute. But, it's not. God softens the heart, God saves, not *me*." Peg watched Mrs. Pang as she eyed the two Westerners observantly.

"The Lord is the only one who will never betray us, who will love us perfectly and completely, even when we are the most unlovable. People are inherently disappointing, Marguerithe, including yours truly. It's our nature, our sin. If you're trying to find a person to fill what only God can fill, well, you will be hurt every time. There's a word for it, you know—idolatry. God desires that He would be the first in our hearts, above anyone or anything else."

Mrs. Pang interrupted, and Claire nodded in response.

"It's time for us to finish up. Mrs. Pang has to get back to work. She'll pray for us, and then we'll go."

Mrs. Pang rejoined them on the floor and took the hands of both women, closing her eyes and bowing her head. There was something about her urgency that forced Peg's eyes downward. She could not understand what the devout old woman said, but her voice grew in intensity and then subsided in a solemn whisper. Peg wished she knew how to pray. Her mind reached out to God with a wordless cry, saturated with emotion but devoid of form.

"Amen," Claire whispered.

She squeezed Peg's hand and then gave Mrs. Pang a kiss on the cheek, arranging her subsequent visit with a brief exchange. As the two visitors stepped back onto the dock, Mrs. Pang called out for them to wait, disappeared momentarily and reappeared with something in her hand. She shuffled over to Peg and flung a tiny wooden cross strung on a thin brown thread around her neck, saying something gently to her as she tied it in a knot.

"Mrs. Pang says she will be praying for you," said Claire as Mrs. Pang smiled knowingly at her blonde friend. "She also says that you should come with me again next time." Peg laughed nervously. She glanced at the watch on her wrist and gasped.

"I had no idea how late it had gotten! I have to get back to the hotel. All my friends are probably awake and wondering what's become of me. Helen will be worried sick!" They walked quickly back to the shore, at which point Peg invited Claire to return with her and spend the day with them. When Claire politely declined the invitation, Peg was relieved. As much as she admired the missionary, she did not think she could bear any more talk of sin and salvation. Claire kissed her lightly on the cheek, and the two parted company.

Peg could feel Claire's gaze upon her but did not turn to wave a final goodbye. She slipped into the hotel lobby and, with her head down, ran straight into another guest. She and her victim looked at one another momentarily, stunned. Cop held her by the elbows.

"Are you alright?" he asked with amusement.

"Yes, I'm so sorry. I wasn't watching where I was going." Peg became acutely aware of her appearance—her lipstick that had surely worn off, her hair messed by the sea breeze, her casual attire. Why did it have to be him? Couldn't she have run into Agatha or even Fred?

"You must have been up early," he said, leading her to offer an explanation. His attempt at conversation surprised her.

"Yes, I can't seem to sleep past sunrise." She glanced over to the restaurant and saw Fred and James seated at a large table by the window. James put his hand up in a gesture of greeting and gave her a faint smile. She returned the smile, turned her attention again to Cop, and noticed his gaze fall upon her new piece of jewelry. His eyes flickered, but he said nothing.

"I should go upstairs and get ready. I'm sure everyone is wondering where on earth I could be!" Cop nodded and took a step towards his friends.

"We'll be waiting in the restaurant," he called over his shoulder.

CHAPTER 5

When Peg entered her room, Sue and Agatha were sitting in the high-back stuffed chairs. Helen stood with her hands clasped behind her back, pacing.

"I'm sorry, I'm sorry!" Peg said with both hands in the air, surrendering. "I'll only be a moment!" She slipped into the bathroom and shut the door before anyone could question or reprimand her. Their voices carried through the wood, laced with agitation.

"Next time you go off alone, would you please at least leave a note?" asked Helen, who was demonstrably the angriest of the group.

"Yes, I'm sorry if you were worried. I didn't think I would be so long or I would have. But next time, even if I'm just going for a quick walk, I'll leave a note. Helen?"

"What?" she responded, tersely.

"Would you be a peach and grab me my white dress? The one with the embroidered flowers on the hem?"

Exasperated, Helen stomped to the closet, yanked the dress off its hanger, and banged heavily on the bathroom door. Peg opened it a crack and met her best friend's narrowed eyes.

"Here!" she said, thrusting it through the small space. Peg opened the door just wide enough to give Helen a peck on the cheek.

"You're not off the hook!"

Peg shut the door again and reappeared a few minutes later, her hair fixed and a fresh coat of lipstick applied.

"There! Good as new," she said, giving everyone a broad smile. "Shall we go down now? The men are there waiting. I ran into them as I was coming up."

"Well why didn't you say so in the first place?" said Sue, irritated that she had been robbed of a few precious moments with Fred. "And don't think you're going to get off not telling us where you went this morning!" said Sue, shaking her finger in Peg's direction. "Say, is that new?" she asked, pointing at the cross Mrs. Pang had tied around her neck. Peg fumbled with the knot. It would not budge, and so without much thought, she reached for the fingernail scissors in her toiletry kit and snipped the thread. She swapped it for a small string of pearls her mother had given her when she'd graduated college.

"It was a gift."

"A gift? From whom?" asked Helen, bewildered. Her eyes suddenly brightened, and one eyebrow arched. "From an admirer?" she asked.

"No, no. From a woman I met on my walk. I'll tell you more later," she said quietly into Helen's ear as she grabbed her friend's arm and ushered her towards the door. She was not sure why, but she dreaded having to recount her time with Claire. It was not so much that she feared ridicule, although she was certain Agatha would chide her for coming within a few feet of such notorious harlots, but that she did not at all know how to explain what had transpired on that small boat.

"I'm famished!" declared Agatha as they walked down the hall towards the elevator.

"Amen!" said Sue jokingly. Peg glanced at Sue, struck by the difference in conversation from only moments before on the wooden dock. Peg grinned. She was far more comfortable here than she had been sitting on Mrs. Pang's mat, pretending to pray with her head bowed. She shook her head slightly, trying to toss the last vestiges of holiness from her mind.

As the elevator rang out with each floor they passed, Peg felt more and more like her old self. When they reached the lobby, she snuck a brief glance at her reflection in the mirror. Her cheeks pink, her eyes bright, her figure flattered by her breezy dress—she was surprised to see that she looked rather lovely.

Once in the restaurant, everyone exchanged warm greetings, and the men stood to pull the chairs out for the women. Peg could not be sure, but she thought she felt Cop's eyes on her as he pushed Agatha's chair in. When she raised her gaze to meet his, his quickly looked away and returned to his own seat.

"I thought we'd spend the day in Victoria City," began James. "Take the ferry across the bay and ride the gondola up to Victoria Peak. There's a wonderful view from there of Hong Kong. It's the highest point on the island, and then we can spend the rest of our time along Queen's road. I'm sure you ladies have not gotten anywhere near your fill of shopping," he said, smiling knowingly.

Everyone agreed that it was the perfect plan, and they ate their meals quickly, eager to begin their adventure.

The group stepped outside together, and Agatha immediately raised her parasol. Helen snorted at the old-fashioned accessory but was noticeably humbled when several stylish Chinese women passed by carrying the same.

"It simply makes good sense!" chortled Agatha, smiling as she turned and stepping onto the street. Helen suddenly clapped her hands together.

"Let's take rickshaws to the ferry!" she cried effervescently. Although it was only a short walk down to the water, James acquiesced.

"Yes, we'll be on our feet all day. We might as well take it a bit easy at the start." He led them towards the rickshaw stand where dozens of young Chinese men leaned heavily against their resting carriages, awaiting customers. James walked confidently up to the first driver, took Helen's hand, and helped her into the contraption. He hopped in beside her, and Fred and Sue took the second rickshaw. Unprepared for the prospect of such intimacy, panic seized Peg as she thought she would have to share with Cop.

"You two go ahead," he said, gesturing for Agatha and Peg to take the next car. "There's not enough room for three. I'll ride alone," he offered gallantly. Peg stepped thankfully into the rickshaw and smiled at Agatha, who was struggling to close her parasol.

"Blasted thing!" she muttered, finally managing to fold and tuck it in beneath her legs. James told the drivers they were all headed to the ferry, and they lurched forward in a line. Agatha yelped and grasped the edge of the rickshaw with one hand and her hat with the other. Peg laughed and turned to see how Cop was getting on. He sat soberly and comfortably, as though awaiting a shoeshine, his foot resting atop his opposite knee and the brim of his hat pulled down to shade his face.

Peg faced forward and laughed once more as Agatha shrieked.

"Slow down!" she yelled.

"Agatha, he's not even running!" said Peg, tears coming to her eyes at the ridiculous situation. "You have to calm down!"

Within two minutes, they arrived at the bay, paid their drivers, and walked towards the ferry sign written in English and Chinese.

"It's called a *sampan*," explained James. "This type of boat, that is." He instructed them to pay their fare aboard the ferry, and everyone stepped carefully onboard. The sampan and the bench that ran its perimeter were both wooden, and there was a crude fabric awning secured to rusted cleats by a single frayed rope. Peg glanced at all these details and tried not to think too much about the vessel's sea-worthiness.

There were three men talking amongst themselves, and she watched as an elderly British couple joined them on board. The man's glasses reminded her of Charles and his passion for optometry. Sitting in Victoria Harbor aboard the sampan ferry, Peg did not actually miss him. She missed the comfort of having someone, but she did not miss him, specifically. The thought was unnerving. A pang of loneliness pinched her gut. If he had not done so already, he would forget her by the time she returned.

A hand touched her shoulder, and Peg jumped. She had not noticed Helen sit down beside her. Peg was filled with gratitude for her best friend's presence and gave her a heartfelt hug. Helen returned the embrace warmly. When she pulled back, she looked her in the eye and detected unrest.

"What is it?" she asked in a whisper, not wanting the others to hear. Peg looked away momentarily and then lowered her gaze.

"No-nothing."

"Maggy, I've known you since you were a blond, chubby-kneed three-year-old. You can't fool me."

"I was only thinking of Charles." Her jaw clenched and the corner of her mouth twitched. "If you ever catch me thinking of him again, you have my permission to throw me overboard."

Helen laughed. "You miss him?" she inquired gently.

"No, that's not it, exactly. I just can't believe after all this time with him, that *poof*, it's all over." Peg stared at the water blankly and then regained her focus. "Anyhow, I suppose it's better it happened now." For once, Helen said nothing. Her eyes brightened, and she leaned towards her friend.

"There happens to be a handsome man within a stone's throw who keeps sneaking glances at you. There is no better medicine for a broken heart than another man."

"Oh, don't be ridiculous, Helen. I don't think Cop would 'sneak glances' at Greta Garbo. Every time I try to talk to him, he can't be bothered. I'm not going to make a fool out of myself chasing after a man whose heart is already taken. Frankly, I can't compete with a saint, especially a *pretty* saint." Peg re-crossed her legs as the ferry driver cast off and simultaneously started the engine.

At the precise moment Peg was turning to give Helen a final reason Cop was disinterested, her eyes inadvertently caught his. She did not look away. He stared at her uncomfortably and then slowly smiled. It was not a polite smile; she had seen that cursory expression several times since they first met. If she'd had to name it, it was both pained and appreciative, as though he watched something beautiful disappearing from view.

She felt her face grow warm. Peg turned back toward the water and then watched her hands.

"Don't be a buffoon, Maggy!" said Helen, swatting Peg on the arm. "Mr. Policeman is not in love with that odd nun, I guarantee it." Helen leaned back on the bench and put her head on Peg's shoulder. For the first time, Peg allowed herself to entertain the possibility that her friend might be right.

"Now, you have to help me with my problem. How do I get rid of this silly British fellow? He's such a bore!" said Helen, rolling her eyes and yawning. Peg laughed and leaned into her friend, saying nothing. The water was close enough that she could have reached down and dipped her fingers in it. The froth the bow threw upwards as it moved through the low waves sprayed periodically on the back of her neck.

"Do you ever miss Paul?" Peg asked.

"No. Well, yes. Sometimes. We would have so much fun here together. I know we would," she said wistfully, lost in thought, "if I could ever convince him to leave Montana, that is. Say, how long until we're there?" she asked loudly to all who could hear.

"Twenty, thirty minutes tops," answered Fred, the motor and waves clipping his words.

Helen repositioned herself so that her head rested on Peg's shoulder.

"Wake me, will you, when we've arrived. I hardly slept a wink last night." She yawned once and closed her eyes, her breathing quickly deepening so that Peg knew without looking that she had quickly fallen asleep. Sue walked towards her friends and folded her arms, wrapping her blue cardigan tighter around her thin frame. Squinting, she leaned forward, grinned and shook her head.

"How does she do that?" asked Sue.

"She falls asleep on the toilet, you know. And, once, she fell asleep in the shower," offered Peg in a whisper, trying to stifle her laughter while keeping her body still. Sue's eyebrows arched and she covered her mouth as she laughed.

"A rare gift for a rare beauty," said Sue, smiling fondly at Helen as her mouth dropped open and a string of drool dribbled from the corner. Peg's body shook as her laughter intensified, and yet Helen did not wake. "I'd better get back to Fred before they notice sleeping beauty here. She'd kill me if she knew I'd allowed the men to see her like this."

CHAPTER 6

Peg spent the remainder of the ferry ride looking out across the bay as their impending destination grew clearer and larger. Purposefully, she did not turn her head or her eyes. Although she could not see him, Peg felt Cop's presence as though he were a fire. She knew precisely where he stood at all times.

As they drew nearer to the port, the sampan driver called out in heavily-accented English, "Hong Kong Island! Victoria City!" Helen jumped and sat up wearily, dabbing the corner of her mouth with her sleeve and readjusting her hat.

"No need to yell," she said with disgust, bracing herself against the side of the boat as she stood. As she saw the approaching city, her lips parted and she sucked in her breath. Their seats offered the best view, and so the entire group joined Peg and Helen. "It looks like Venice!" declared Peg under her breath. Turning to the group, she qualified her assessment. "Not that I've been to Venice, but in pictures, it's kind of the same." A few heads nodded in awed agreement.

The European stone buildings with colonnades and ornate balconies rose from the water, belying their heavy foundations magically anchored below the waves. Like all cities built on the sea, Victoria watched the bay and open waters beyond with alert expectation, carefully observing the weather and the size of the ocean swells for threat of storm or tsunami. Sloping steeply upward behind the waterfront were hundreds more structures, until an abrupt break in stone gave way to the dark green backdrop of the mountain. What looked to be private homes peppered the verdant hillsides, and Peg's gaze rose upwards until she found what must be the mountain's peak.

"There! That's our building. Vacuum Oil Company," shouted Fred, grandly annunciating the word *Vacuum* and pointing enthusiastically to a large building that stretched along the entire block.

The men had made this approach a dozen times now, and Cop's reaction was always the same—admiration. Each time he rode the sampan and came upon the superlative city, he was reminded of what men with vision and skill could accomplish. This was the sort of man he strove to be—one who made things, things that would help others, that would last. He had left college for the war his sophomore year and been funneled into construction engineering. The work suited him well, but just as every woman and child touched by the Great War, he still sometimes wondered in quiet moments how different a course his life might have taken had Archduke Franz Ferdinand avoided that bullet.

The ferry threaded its way between the junks and other boats to its assigned slip. Helen took Peg's hand in sincere excitement as they disembarked, but also as a sign to James that she did not presently wish to be bothered. As considerate as James naturally was, he either did not read Helen's cues or chose to ignore them, taking her other arm and placing it in his. Helen rolled her eyes so that only Peg could see and released her hand, setting her own atop James' as he narrated the specific history of several of the closest buildings. Peg smiled at her friend's meager efforts to appear interested.

As they moved in the direction of the Peak Cable Tram, Peg could not walk in a straight line for the excess of bodies. There were those with studied decorum and others with no regard for decency. White faces, brown faces, powdered faces, black hair, braids, men with hair longer than women, Parisian attire and traditional Oriental garb. Bamboo flutes harmonized with metallic gongs and a warbling voice fleetingly pierced the clamor before the roaring beast of the city swallowed it whole. It was no wonder the people here worshipped dragons. They lived within the creature's fiery breath, slept within its belly, walked along its hardened scales in the serpentine streets.

The pace was frenetic, the wares diverse, scintillating, and occasionally repulsive. Peg looked to her left and saw something silver and gleaming, fine and valuable. She turned to her right to find a table displaying severed snakeheads. Gasping and looking away, she tried to regain her composure. Irritated, she pursed her lips and dodged the sedan chair that plowed through her path with no concern for her safety. Cop reached out to remove her from harm's way, but she reacted before his help became necessary. Peg did not notice the gesture.

The street on which they had turned was narrow and the buildings on either side towering, creating the illusion that they leaned inward and might, at any moment, collapse on the oblivious pedestrians below. Tall banners decorated with indecipherable and elegant characters were stretched between stories, and splashes of red spattered the entire scene as though evidence of some recent bloody massacre. A man with dark skin and a well-manicured beard wore a navy-blue uniform, a turban, and a rifle strapped across his chest. He stood stoically at the corner, back pulled straight, observing passersby. Peg stared.

"Nothing like it, is there?" commented Fred, noting Peg's fascination with the Sikh policeman and her general astonishment. "Hong Kong takes some getting used to."

"I think it's glorious," gushed Sue, her cheeks flushed and eyes bright with pleasure. Peg suddenly felt absurd for her fixedness, for her condemnation of the poor snake vendor, for being taken aback by all the movement and sound, by all the people—British, Oriental and unidentifiable.

They passed a woman preparing a meal in a large pot over an open flame, her children lined up behind her, watching the group of tourists with wide eyes as though they were the spectacle. Without malice, the mother ceased stirring the cauldron and sloshed the contents of a bucket into the street at Cop's feet, soaking his shoes and the lower half of his trousers with what, upon later olfactory inspection, was some sort of fish broth. He stopped abruptly and stared at the ground in shock, then up at the woman, who gave him no more than a cursory glance before resuming her chores. The flock behind her burst into laughter and was immediately silenced by their mother's sharp glare. Cop gave the boys and girls a wry smile, shook off his legs one at a time, and resumed his walking.

"The dangers of Hong Kong promenading," James chuckled. He shook his head and watched his friend, surprised that Cop had not lost his temper. The women said nothing, but Peg felt sympathy for the man. His feet must be awfully soggy, and they still had the entire day before them.

Fred quickened his pace to catch up with Cop and gave him a slap on the back. He said something no one else was able to hear, and Cop threw his head back in an uncharacteristic laugh. Peg smiled and could understand for the first time since meeting the men why they were all friends. Cop stepped into a rectangle of light, and the edges of his body melted, his blonde hair made white. The loud voices of two men jutted forcefully into the scene as he stepped back into shadow.

"There, that's where we catch the Peak Cable Tram," remarked James as they turned the corner and spied the lower terminus. A hundred yards ahead was a group of thirty or more tourists waiting in line against the wall of the terminal building. A giant clock boldly proclaimed the time for all to see, which had the effect of making everyone either anxious or ambivalent to its announcement. They took their place at the back of the line just as the red tram showed its nose through the first of several stone arches planted periodically along the tracks. Fred attended to their tickets at the counter, purchasing third class for all.

"I'm afraid first and second class are reserved for residents of the

Peak, British officials, military and police force," he said in a high voice, passing each his ticket as he mimicked the agent.

The tram pulled into the station, screeching and releasing a loud hiss as it came to rest. Passengers disembarked with purpose, and those waiting in line climbed on. Their group shuffled now beneath the shade of the tiled roof, thankful to be momentarily out of the sun. As Helen and James stepped aboard, it became clear that there would not be room for them all. Sue, Agatha and Fred slipped into the last three spaces before the operator informed those still in line that they would have to catch the next tram.

Flustered, Peg clutched her small purse with both hands and swallowed. Helen waived at her with an impish grin, leaning forward in her seat.

"We'll wait for you at the top!" she yelled. "Be good!"

Peg turned halfway around towards Cop and smiled nervously as she watched the tram pull out of the station and rise up the mountainside. She cleared her throat and glanced back at the other people in line. Most were European with Fedoras and heavy jewelry. They all seemed to shift their weight impatiently in unison, so that the crowd tilted left and then right. When the silence between her and Cop became insufferable, she blurted out the first thing that came to her mind.

"I ran into Ms. Wards this morning," she announced, regretting the confession immediately. He would want to know the circumstances of their meeting and what they had discussed, and Peg had no desire to explain.

"Small world," he commented, putting his hands in his pants' pockets. Surprised by his lack of curiosity, Peg could think of nothing more to say.

"This morning, you were wearing a small wooden cross around your neck," ventured Cop. Peg automatically reached up to the necklace she now wore and pressed it with her fingertips.

"Yes. It was a gift," she explained, seeing from his expression that he wanted more detail. Unwilling to tell him of the old Tanka woman who had tied it on earlier that morning, she glanced down at her shoes before speaking. "I didn't think it went with my outfit," she said, instantly bemoaning the frivolous explanation.

"Claire actually has one similar," he added. Peg desperately wished they could both think of something other to discuss than the compelling Claire Wards.

"You said your first name is actually Willem?" she asked inartfully, the inept jump in topic jarring.

"That's right."

"That was my grandfather's name on my father's side. You're German?"

"Yes, my family was from Stuttgart originally. They came over in the late 1800s. My grandfather didn't want any of his sons serving in the king's army, so they emigrated during the Franco-Prussian War."

"Have you ever been? To Germany, I mean?"

"Yes, as a small boy. I remember the thick forest surrounding the family home and my great-grandmother's marzipan," he grinned. Peg returned his smile.

"My grandfather, Willem, had the most preposterous mustache. He waxed it every day and twirled the corners upright," she gestured with her fingers, rubbing them together at the edges of her mouth and pursing her lips. Cop laughed, a genuine and robust sound that pleased her ears. "Or that's at least how my father described him. I haven't ever been to Germany. My mother was from Arras, my father from Bremen. He called me *spatzi* as a little girl. Sparrow. *'Ich liebe dich mit ganzem Herzen, mein spatzi,'* he'd say. He always told me he loved me in German. *Mein spatzi,*" she said again in a lower, wistful tone. The old, familiar words tasted wonderful in her mouth, a favorite candy from childhood to be relished.

"He is no longer with us?" asked Cop, gently.

"No, he passed away when we first moved to California." Cop watched Peg carefully and sensed her sadness.

"I'm sorry," he offered, simply. The conversation died momentarily.

"I was my mother's *bärli*," Cop finally said. "Still am, as a matter of fact," he added with humor.

"Bear?" she asked, grateful for the change in theme. "No, I don't think that's right. Perhaps a lion or a coyote," she teased. They held each other's eyes more comfortably and for longer moments. Peg had been terrified as she'd watched the first cable car with all her friends ride up the hill and out of reach. Now, she was glad.

"A coyote? I can't imagine why!" he said with a sly smile. Peg watched him and saw that her judgment was accurate. His eyes conveyed that same sense a coyote's imparts—alert and knowing, startling.

A bell rang announcing the arrival of the next tram. The routine unloading and loading resumed, with Peg and Cop the first to board. As Peg reached for the gleaming brass pole to pull herself onto the first step, Cop took the back of her arm without asking, helping her to her seat. There were no boundaries between the seats, no separate seats at all. Instead, she sat next to him on a slick, highly polished wooden bench that quickly became full. As each new body slid onto the end of the row, she found herself pushed closer and closer to his side until her right leg and arm pressed tightly against his own. She smiled self-consciously, trying to pretend as though she had not noticed the contact, as though every part of her did not want to stand up and leap from the trolley. The car lurched forward and began its steep ascent of the Peak.

Their nearness did not appear to affect Cop, who calmly took in the view of the city as the tram rose steadily up the mountain. Peg tried to do the same but found herself unable to focus on anything other than the small movements of Cop's left hand or left foot, the change in his breathing, the scratching of his head. It was unbearable. They passed beneath the first stone archway, and the bay opened before them like a gift.

"That's not something you see every day," he said, letting out an appreciative whistle.

"No, it certainly isn't." Peg tried to lean away from Cop but found herself pressed against another man who made no effort to mask his admiration of her legs. She quickly readjusted herself and rested against the lesser evil.

"Let's count the boats in the harbor," he suggested playfully. He raised his left arm and began pointing at each boat as he counted it aloud. As Peg could not be certain which one he was counting at any given time, she ceased her efforts.

"Oh come on now. Be a sport." He took her hand in his and used it rather than his own to count the remaining vessels. Peg was certain that her face was the same shade of red as the tram's bright trim, but she did not pull her hand away. She was too shocked to say anything. To her horror, a giggle escaped her lips instead.

"Eighteen, nineteen, twenty…"

"Twenty-one, twenty-two, twenty-three…"

"Say, so what are you? Twenty-eight? Thirty?" Her countenance fell and her bright eyes dimmed. Cop immediately sensed her reticence.

"Forgive me, that was strange *and* rude. It's just that you seem much more, well, mature than your friends." Peg slid her hand from his and placed it firmly in her lap, scrunching the fabric of her skirt tightly between her fingers. She knew she seemed older than Helen and Sue, that she gave off an air of seriousness. Cop's observance of this trait made her stiffen with self-consciousness.

"Twenty-eight," she said quietly, seriously. Cop frowned at her voice and tried to deduce how he might redirect the unfortunate turn in conversation. He leaned forward from his waist and placed one hand on his knee so that he was able to turn his torso to face her.

"I didn't mean anything by it. Maturity is something I admire," he said carefully. "I'm not a young man myself, you see." Peg's expression must have indicated even greater annoyance, for Cop leaned back in his seat and exhaled loudly. He was trying to be respectful but had offended her further. Frustrated now and flummoxed, Cop grew quiet as well.

When they at last reached the end of their ride, Helen noticed with displeasure that the two had not managed to break through their previous awkwardness. One look at Peg's rigid face, and she knew that something unpleasant had transpired. She glared at Cop with open disdain and quickly walked to Peg's side, linking her arm and dragging her onward.

"For some absurd reason, the tram doesn't go all the way to the top. We have to walk the rest of the way," she said in between heavy breaths. "My own walking, talking guide book told me as much on the way up," she joked.

The white, sprawling Peak Hotel sat perched on the edge of Victoria Gap, overlooking the harbor. Peg noticed it with disinterest. She felt immensely foolish; had she really thought a man like Cop would be interested in someone as plain and uninteresting as herself? He was simply being kind, making the best of an awkward circumstance. *Mature!* And for a moment, she had thought he might have fancied her. Claire's words from earlier that morning came to mind. The missionary was right; people were disappointing.

"What did he do?" Helen finally asked.

"Commended me for my maturity, told me it was a characteristic he greatly admires. I think it was his way of politely rebuffing me." Helen brooded, considering her friend's report.

"Are you *sure* that was his intention?"

Peg shrugged, and Helen looked at her a moment longer before sighing loudly.

"Well good riddance to bad rubbish. He's a boob," shouted Helen over her shoulder so that Cop knew exactly to whom she was referring. Fred gave him a look to ask what he had done, but Cop just shook his head. He took the hat he had been carrying in his hands and placed it firmly on his head, tilting the brim downward.

There was a multileveled pavilion at the peak's zenith, and several areas opened out onto the view with no wall or guardrail. A peasant man wearing a tattered shirt and shorts and a conical hat stood at one corner surveying the expanse as though it were his kingdom. Peg doubted he had enough money for the tram; he would have taken a rickshaw or walked. She then noticed the empty rickshaw on the other side of the platform and concluded he must be its driver. Had he hoped to pick up a fair or ascended the peak merely to enjoy the vista, the sky, the refreshing breeze? The man turned and stared directly at Peg, who promptly stepped forward in the opposite direction, giving him the faintest of smiles.

Helen, Agatha and Sue came to her side, and everyone was quiet as they admired the beauty of the sea and mountains, the silent city below. It was delightfully cooler. To their left, the number of houses spattering the hills gradually thinned, culminating in a few grand estates with swimming pools and private roads. Beyond the last remnants of human habitation were green mounds descending in size towards the shoreline. All of Kowloon and Hong Kong lay at their feet, with Mainland China in the distance.

"The area only recently opened up to Chinese. It used to be a

European and non-Chinese-only residential area, but they repealed the law in twenty-nine. Not much has changed, though. It won't until the locals become wealthier and can afford the real-estate prices." James' eye glinted. "Up until a few years ago, people were still dying of the plague. It wasn't as bad as earlier in the century, but thousands and thousands died of it. Filthy, terrible disease." He shook his head and grew quiet.

"Back behind us on the other side of the island is Repulse Bay. It has the best beaches around. Say, we should all head over there later in the week," Fred enthusiastically suggested, changing the topic. The thought made Peg sick to her stomach, donning her swimsuit in public perhaps being the thing she wished to do the very least in life. Everyone else, however, was thrilled with the idea, even Agatha. Peg resigned herself to future humiliation.

"Another spot you really have to see is Aberdeen Harbor. It's a floating city. Hundreds, even thousands of people—the Tanka—live in these small boats," added James. "We could do both the same day. Stop at Aberdeen first and then head on to Repulse Bay."

"Perfect!" said Sue and Helen in unison. Peg eyed Helen with annoyance. Agatha moved away from the group to read a nearby plaque, and Peg joined her as an excuse to put some distance between herself and the others. She glanced at the engraved words but did not read them. Instead, she wandered further away towards a break in the surrounding wall that faced the more remote portions of Hong Kong Island. She looked out across the impressive view.

What had she hoped to find? Why had she traveled thousands of miles across the Pacific? Was it simply to see things as beautiful as this? New beautiful things rather than the same old ones? She had been born in beauty, cradled in the rough arms of the Rocky Mountains, the winters cruel, the springtime glorious, the rivers wide and bulging with water and trout. Although everyone had known her name, her past, there had been freedom there she had not, at the time, appreciated. It was the sort of freedom and contentment found only in open spaces, tall grasses, the proximity of wildness—families of moose and bear, eagles and owls—in daily routine punctuated by luxurious moments of inactivity and rest.

She'd been all too eager to leave behind Montana's frontier and trade it in for the sprawling cement sidewalks and highways of Los Angeles. And, of course, her father had been so ill. It was his dying wish, but she'd enjoyed the anonymity, the opportunity, and the quickened pulse of a real city. Still, Peg had never found there what she had thought she would, the treasure that would trump all others—success, peace? She could not name it.

Peg knew she was not the only one who suffered from this malady. This specific breed of insect—the immortal, resistant, persistent bug of discontentment—inundated the city, perhaps even the whole country. It was untrue that money could not buy happiness. Peg learned that people who said such things had never been poor. It could and had provided a certain kind of pleasure, gladness born from stability and possession, from a full stomach and paid utility bills. It was true, however, that this sort of comfort was incomplete. The delight of money was small in comparison to the happiness of which she dreamed. *Great joy.* Great joy was possible; it *had* to be possible. Was it buried in marriage, in children, in status or adventure? Was this why she was in Hong Kong—to discover if her Great Joy lay in odyssey, if it might be unearthed more readily on foreign shores?

She'd fled from Charles' rejection, and here, at the Peak, with her dearest friends and three handsome men, the loneliness had not subsided. It should have been enough. How disappointing! How tragic! Was there no end, no cure to be taken? Moments distracted her—the snakeheads and Cop's encounter with the fish pot—but when all the fuss ceased, her dissatisfaction remained.

Could it be as simple as love? Was she like every silly girl in novels and films, completed by the one man tailor-made just for her? The love of her father and mother had warmed her but never permanently kept out the cold. Familial love was necessary, but it was not enough. She had known the love of true friendship in Helen and Sue, but this, too, had left her wanting. Romantic love was the only sort she had not known, and it was this that drove men and women across the face of the earth, that gave people a reason to keep living.

Vanity, vanity. It is all vanity. The phrase whispered through her mind, but she could not name its source.

When Cop had taken her hand on the tram, her spirit had leapt inside her. *"At last!"* it had cried. And then the bitter waters of refusal had once more engulfed her. It was the same here on the other side of the world as it was in Los Angeles, as it had been in Helena. She was not, nor would she ever be, any man's desire. The truth rang in a doleful tone that resounded across the warm, cloudless sky. She would not marry.

Momentarily, Peg held her breath. With the possibility of marriage discounted, perhaps she could find other more meaningful ways to spend her life. Surely, she was not the only spinster in the country? What *did* a husbandless woman do, a childless woman? *Anything she wanted.* The answer should have made her smile, but it did not. Instead, it felt as though her organs and bones had been eviscerated, leaving only hollow skin hovering precariously over the cliff. She exhaled. Such vastness stood before her despairingly, too large to manage. The breeze intensified, threatening to cast her exuvia like ash across the faces of her friends. Peg tucked the strings of hair behind her ears the wind had blown free and steadied herself.

Turning to face the group, she smiled weakly at Sue and Helen and stepped toward them.

CHAPTER 7

They dined at one of the Peak restaurants, and Peg was once more forced into proximity with Cop. They sat beside each other, the only mercy being she did not have to look directly at him as they ate. He spoke to James on his left and across the table to Agatha. Peg appreciated the woman's humility and willingness to be the fifth wheel. Given her own recent vow of spinsterhood, Peg looked at her with a new affection.

Really, Agatha was not without her appeal. She was smart, thoughtful, neat, unselfish, and her hair was thick and lustrous. Yes, her glasses were unflattering and her dress ten years out of fashion, but with the right clothing, at one time, she could surely have attracted a husband. Peg wished to ask Agatha why she had not married but did not dare. Now a decade past the typical nuptial age, there was no hope. The woman was not quick to smile, and she held her body impossibly rigid, but she also did not complain and seemed to honestly enjoy their trip. Perhaps the secret was to expect less—from life, from people.

It was on his third repetition that Peg finally realized Cop was addressing her. She turned to stare at him.

"Would you *please* pass the salt?" he asked impatiently. She blinked, reached for the salt, and placed it before him on the table, picking her fork up once more and cutting her piece of fish into a tidy, manageable piece. In her periphery, she could see his agitation and the quick glance he gave her despite his best efforts to appear unaffected. He calmed himself and tried again.

"Was your family German Lutheran?" Peg raised an eyebrow and answered coolly.

"Yes," she answered.

"So was mine," he offered, hoping she might say something further.

When it became clear that she would not, he wiped his mouth with his napkin and laid his hand on the table.

"Listen, this is really very foolish. My intention was not to offend, but clearly, I have. If it helps, I retract my earlier statement about your maturity. You have proved me thoroughly wrong in my estimation, and I beg your pardon." Peg found his terseness impossibly irritating. His voice was nearly a whisper, and she doubted that, with all the noise of conversation, anyone else at the table could hear his words. "The thing is, I'm an old man. Thirty-six, you see. And I, well, I just wanted to be forthcoming." He cleared his throat and took a sip of water, stumbling over his words while readjusting the napkin on his lap. Peg's pride and stubbornness reared, and before she could stop herself, she spoke spitefully.

"Why on earth would you think your age would matter to me in the least?" It was an arrow fired with precision. Cop angrily cut his food and took a bite, chewing furiously. His humiliation was palpable, and Peg was pleased.

Helen noticed something unpleasant transpiring between Cop and Peg and interceded.

"Maggy, do you know what you're going to get your mother as a souvenir?" She had meant to ease the tension and provide a distraction, but the question's implication made Peg feel pathetic.

"No, not yet. Something silk. She'd like that, I think." Helen waited a moment, assessing the situation before speaking again. She gave her friend a pleading look, begging her for her understanding.

"And what about Charles? I know he must miss you terribly. You two have been together so long, and this is your first long separation. He must have already written you a dozen letters by now. He's so mad for her, it's almost embarrassing. Poor fellow," she said nonchalantly to the entire table. The rest of their companions looked up from their plates. The clinking of silverware ceased as they broke away from their conversations to focus on Helen and Peg's exchange. Fred looked at Cop and back at his food, blushing empathetically.

Helen's line of questioning and assertion of Charles's undying love caught Peg completely off guard. She took a sip of water to stall. Thankfully, the waiter appeared to ask if there was anything more he could get them, giving her a few extra moments to consider her options. When he'd gone, Peg decided the best course of action was simply a coy smile. Let everyone interpret as they wished.

Cop did not attempt to speak to her for the remainder of their lunch or the afternoon. Twice humiliated, he retreated. Peg stewed over her perceived slight and spent the rest of the day at Helen's side.

"Once he's done nursing his wounded pride, he'll come around," Helen finally whispered as they stepped onto the tram that would take them back down into the city. "There's nothing like a little jealousy to make a man attentive."

"Well, it makes no difference to me. I've given up on men altogether. I *will not* marry, and I *will not* have any children, and I *will* find a way to live a good life nonetheless." Helen stared with amusement at her best friend and rested her hand on Peg's forearm.

"It's not as desperate as all that, Maggy. There's hope," she said reassuringly. Infuriatingly, tears came to Peg's eyes, and she blinked them away in annoyance.

"No, there is not. Hope is cruel and stupid when it's a lie. I have had only one real possibility my entire adult life, Charles Keane, and it has fizzled into thin air. Look at Ms. Wards! She is unattached and *completely* happy. I'm already too old to find a husband; I'm tired of looking. I surrender," she said, throwing her hands up above her head.

"First, Claire is boring and satisfied with intolerably little. And second, we're the same age! Are you telling me that I, too, am a lost cause?"

"Helen, you are a dear, but you know that your situation is hardly the same." Peg looked away. Her temper sparked, Helen removed her hand from Peg's arm.

"I don't care what you say, Maggy. This nonsense will all pass as soon as the next man courts you. And there *will* be a next man. If not Cop, then another, better man. And if there is not, then you and I will be old maids together, buy a big house, and raise horses."

Peg could not help but laugh. She shook her head.

"No, it won't pass," she said gently, "and I'd prefer chickens. Horses are too much work." Peg's humor reassured Helen that her friend was not past saving, and she smiled broadly. Peg folded her hands around her purse and watched the view from earlier in the day appear in reverse. She looked only straight ahead and did not once feel that inexplicable sense of being watched. Her little chess game had worked, but the victory provided precious little satisfaction. Now Cop would surely leave her be.

CHAPTER 8

F or the rest of the week, Fred and James accompanied the women. James arranged for their participation in a tea ceremony, to attend the opera and the ballet—European *and* Chinese—as well as to meet the governor at his home on the Peak. Each time they gathered at The Peninsula, James offered a brief excuse for Cop's absence. It was more embarrassing for Peg than if they had simply ignored his disinterest. On the fourth day without him, James' apologies thankfully ceased.

Without the pressure of romance, Peg was able to breath more easily, to immerse herself more completely in their explorations, to appreciate Fred and James' nearly opposite personalities, and to come to count the fine men as true friends. She enjoyed witnessing their easy rapport— brotherly and kind—partaking of James' encyclopedic knowledge and Fred's sharp wit. Their friendship grew intimate and comfortable at a speed attributable only to a shared experience of foreignness and knowledge that their time together would soon come to an end.

Rising at dawn Tuesday morning and packing totes for the beach, the group finally made a plan to spend the day at Aberdeen Harbor, followed by a leisurely sunbathe at Repulse Bay. The day before, Peg had purchased a prodigious straw hat that provided dense shade, not only for her face but for her entire body as well. It was far more dramatic a thing than she typically wore, and when she put it on, she felt immediately like a Hollywood starlet. The dark sunglasses completed the impression, and she grinned shamelessly at Sue and Helen beneath its enormous brim.

Fred and James stood waiting at the dock dressed in breezy, casual attire. The easygoing fashion suited Fred, whose sandy hair unavoidably reminded one of the beach. James, however, appeared uncomfortable and exposed without his signature tailored suit. Helen could not help but giggle at his awkwardness before taking his arm in sympathy and commenting on his changed appearance.

"Jimmy, you look like you're from California!" she teased. She'd never before called him Jimmy, but the name perfectly fit the persona of this new man who stood before her.

"It was Fred's idea. 'You can't wear a suit to the beach,' he said. 'I most certainly can,' I told him, but he'd sent all my suits to be laundered, the clever chap," he explained with irritation. "They don't fit properly!" he hissed through his teeth as he grabbed some of the shirt fabric between his fingers and attempted to make it sit respectably upon his shoulders.

"You should listen to Fred more often. You look downright handsome," said Helen, unable to resist the discomfort she knew she would cause him with such a direct compliment. Instead, James surprised her. He smiled and gazed at Helen as though finally certain of her interest. Alarmed, she turned away but kept his arm.

"Well, what's the hold up? That's the sampan there, isn't it?" asked Helen, deflecting attention from herself and pointing at the boat already taking on passengers. James nodded, his grin only growing. He handed Helen her ticket and passed another to Agatha, while Fred gave one to Sue and Peg. Peg noted how the men had divided the women amongst themselves so as to share the financial burden of the two extra tagalongs. It was a kind but unnecessary gesture. She had enough money with her to pay her own way and decided then that she would not allow Fred to front another penny on her behalf.

The ride across Victoria Harbor was uneventful. Platoons of junks sailed on their starboard and port, the ferry's driver waving familiarly at the owners of passing vessels. As it came in to view, the capital city was no less impressive to behold this third time, and they paused briefly there to let off and take on passengers before setting out once more.

The boat hugged the coastline, passing a few unpopulated, leafy coves and inlets, the island's native foliage impressively lush. Most of the inhabitable seaboard was home to thatched huts, tourist bungalows, hotels and restaurants. The beaches at which they did not stop appeared pristine and lovely, and Peg wondered what made Repulse Bay so special as to warrant the additional journey. The wind blew beneath Peg's dress and cooled the skin of her legs, the constant breeze cutting the intolerable humidity. She breathed easier and periodically closed her eyes in the sunlight.

She turned to observe Sue with Fred and Helen with James. Her dearest and oldest friend smiled flirtatiously with the revived Britain, while Sue and Fred shared a quieter and more authentic moment, holding hands, gazing out over the sea. Peg searched Sue's face and saw there that she loved the man at her side. The truth startled Peg initially, and she wondered if it were truly possible to love a person after only knowing him for such a short time. But as Sue leaned her head on Fred's shoulder, his own expression revealed equally deep emotion. What would they do? While the end of their trip seemed years away, it would come sooner than they liked. Would Sue bring herself to board the *Asama Maru* once more and set sail for Los Angeles? Was there any other choice? Concerned, Peg thought on the options until, unable to solve the riddle, she turned back to watch the island.

The sampan turned towards the shore, and they veered smoothly into the wide mouth of Aberdeen Harbor. While the floating homes near their hotel could have aptly been described as a small village, Aberdeen's formed a vast city. From a quarter of a mile out, boat after boat touched tangentially, converging in messy honeycombs. As they drew nearer, the larger patterns divided into individual cells of activity and color. The impressive sight greeted them flamboyantly—an old gypsy woman festooned in bright scarves winking merrily with mischievousness. Peg smiled back.

Stacked high with goods to barter or sell, the boats were packed tightly with families and fishermen. The amphibious city floated between two worlds, adolescence and adulthood, terra firma and pervious ocean. It clung for safety to its mother's skirt, while ever longing to sever the ties that kept it safe but moored, one day to set sail and never return. Larger, taller junks stood at attention—sentinels in a distinct line—their fishing nets hung to dry over the ships' furled booms. The more modest vessels were like muddied saltwater pearls strung across the dark green water.

Their ferry motored ahead steadily towards the city, and the unmistakable aroma of sandalwood assaulted their nostrils. Peg immediately recognized it as the same intoxicating smell that emanated from Mrs. Pang's home. Helen scrunched up her face and held her nose. The unique chorus of the Tanka preparing breakfast replaced the sounds to which Peg had grown accustomed. Wood clanked against wood, iron sizzled with popping oil and rice, children slurped the unknown contents of crude bowls, and thousands of shrimp cascaded from nets onto decks below.

Peg watched with fascination as a young boy on a narrow raft used a long pole to leverage himself beside a delicate black bird in the water. He grabbed it by the neck, yanked it onto the raft, and stole the scaly contents of the bird's mouth with his tiny hand. The feathered victim gave the fish up without protest, and Peg saw there was something tied around the fowl's throat. James noticed the scene and Peg's reaction.

"He's just doing it for the tourists. They normally use cormorants for river fishing. If we went far up the Pearl River, we'd see them there."

"Does the bird starve?"

James chuckled at her concern. "No, it can swallow the smaller fish. The cuff only prevents it from eating the large ones." Their boat came to rest against the pier, the engine cutting off, but no one loaded or disembarked.

"I haven't seen *that* before. They just built it this year, I believe. A seminary, of all things. A Catholic Seminary. *Holy Spirit something-or-other*," remarked James, pointing at a green-tiled roof on the flattened hill. Peg looked up at the grand stone seminary and then below to the fishing village made entirely of wood and fabric. One stood still and thoughtful; the other pulsed and waved. What did the Tanka think of this unyielding, sail-less structure, unable to catch the wind or maneuver towards a better catch? Would any ever enter through its carved doors? She did not think it likely.

The sampan's motor whirred to life and propelled them onward so that they exited the harbor at the eastern end. Peg's thoughts rushed ahead to the inevitable conclusion of their trip. Fred sat down beside her.

"When do you return to Singapore, Fred?" she asked.

"We all have until the beginning of August, the third to be exact, and then Cinderella turns back into a pumpkin. We're all under contract, you see. Three years," he said, holding up the corresponding number of fingers. I'm a year in already." He dropped one of his fingers. "And James and Cop have just begun." Helen heard but dismissed the information, unconcerned. Sue rummaged through her purse indifferently, her lack of concern a flimsy charade. Watching Sue, Fred suddenly blurted out, "But I can bring a wife! I...I can marry." He did not look at her but down at his hands, which he then ran nervously through his hair. He slapped his thigh.

"I never was one to beat around the bush!" he finally said, laughing at himself. Her mouth agape, Sue covered it with her fingers and began to laugh, a chortle that began tight and forced but ballooned riotously. At first, Fred looked at her with a flash of annoyance, fearful she had judged him absurd. When he detected no malice, he began to chuckle too and, soon enough, joined her in her raucous laughter. The two made a ludicrous sight, and Peg watched them both with amused affection. Fred took Sue's hand and squeezed it while they both bent over to try and regain their breath. She slapped him on the back and then rubbed it gently, her nails tracing swirls along his shirt.

"You know what I like most about you, Fred?" she said. He raised his eyebrows.

"How hard you are to read. I never know what you're thinking." This got them both worked back into a frenzy that subsided and reignited several times before they at last pulled into Repulse Bay. Peg knew then that their romance would not end with the summer.

As the sampan pulled into its slip, she saw with amazement that a familiar figure awaited them at the dock. Cop stood with his arms folded across his chest, his hat cocked to one side, the sun almost directly overhead casting him in a stark contrast of shadow and light. Leaning back on his heels, he raised one hand calmly to his friends in greeting, a faint smile on his lips.

Something in her gut grew wings and fluttered up into her chest, hovering above the waves, unsettling all that had only recently been so tidily arranged.

CHAPTER 9

Peg wasn't sure when they'd left the ferry and made their way to the matsheds on the beach. She understood that she was to go inside and change into her swimwear, and that the men were doing the same. She could hear only a thudding heartbeat where her thoughts should have been and, every now and then, the sea surging. An explanation for his presence filtered through her disorientation. "I caught an earlier ferry. Couldn't miss a day at the beach." Deaf and reeling as though a grenade had detonated nearby, she opened the woven door of the straw shack and stepped inside.

It was dim yet hotter, and beads of sunlight poked through each crack in the thatching. Hadn't she resigned herself to a life of singlehood, to freedom and travel? Hadn't she decided he was not worth another moment's consideration? Then why had her knees buckled and her heart raced when she saw him there on the dock? Didn't her heart know that the object of its affection would only harm her?

Removing her hat and opening her tote, she undressed and dressed mechanically, pulling the swimsuit straps up over her shoulders, fluffing out the suit's skirt so that it covered her rear and thighs and hid the shorts beneath. She put her hat back on, bunched her towel under her arm, and emerged into the seaside's startling brightness.

Before she could escape back into the hut with any kind of grace, Peg made eye contact with Cop, the only other person in the group who had finished dressing. She froze, her hand still on the door, quickly assessing her options. Trapped, she shut the door and walked down the two steps into the sand, looking straight ahead and finding a nice spot closer to the water to lay her towel. It was warm and soft beneath her feet, soothing her from below. Cop did not immediately follow but respectfully waited for Fred and James to also appear before coming toward her.

They all arranged their towels in relation to hers, allowing enough room for the remaining ladies who would shortly join them.

"Do you swim, Peggy?" asked Fred in a friendly, light tone.

"Yes. I do. I love the water." She dared a glance in their direction. Cop and Fred wore the same cutaway black suit with white belt, but James, to her astonishment, wore only a pair of shorts, leaving his chest bare. Instinctively, she looked away, her mind whirling. Helen's voice called out from behind her shoulder, giving her the perfect excuse to glance at James once more.

"Whosever idea this was is a genius!" she laughed. Peg caught Helen's reaction to James' nakedness and blushed for her friend who did not look away but strode confidently up to the man and unrolled her towel next to his. Helen's own suit was off-white and more formfitting than Peg's, her lean legs and trim waist difficult to ignore. Agatha wore the previous generation's fashion, far more modest and cumbersome, while Sue donned a flattering deep green suit that matched her eyes. Although unaware of the impression she made, Peg's own light blue choice was lovely on her as well, and her taller frame lent itself well to the garment. Cop escaped into the cool waves with a loud splashing of his legs before diving beneath the surface. Fred and James followed, swimming out farther than Peg would have dared.

"Shall we join them?" asked Sue. Peg stood up from her towel and tossed her hat and sunglasses into the sand.

"Agatha and I will watch our things; you two go ahead," said Helen. Sue took Peg's hand, and they ran youthfully into the surf, forgetting their thorny romances and enjoying instead the ocean's cleanness and candor.

The women floated on their backs, drifting further away from the shore, staring up at the high-domed, watercolor sky. The moment was serene and delicious, and Peg reveled in her weightlessness as the sun warmed the top of her body. Without warning, a pair of strong arms disrupted the tranquil scene, scooping beneath her knees and arms. Based upon Sue's scream, Peg guessed that her friend was also under attack. Before she could figure out precisely what was happening, she was in the air, the salt water streaming from her body in chords of silver as she landed with a loud, indelicate *plop*. Another body twisted and kicked beside her, and Peg made her way to the surface with desperation. Sue's head broke the surface at the same moment, and the two locked eyes. A grin spread across Sue's face, and they both snapped their heads to locate the culprits. Fred and Cop kneeled in the shallow water so that only their shoulders were exposed. Laughing with their heads thrown back, their Adam's apples glistened and bobbed.

Sue wasted no time and swam to Fred's side, throwing all her weight on his shoulders so that he sank beneath the surface. Peg stared at Cop, who smiled at her tentatively. Blinking, she squeezed the ocean from her eyes. His unexpected playfulness had disarmed her entirely. Without thinking, she splashed him with both hands and disappeared below the surface, holding her breath as she fully submerged herself in the sea. She smiled there, where no one could see, in the muffled, swaying waters.

When she resurfaced, he had swum closer.

"Come on," he said, plainly, as though nothing upsetting had ever transpired between them. "Let's go out farther."

With four strokes, she was at his side, and they swam together beyond where the waves crashed.

"This is good," he said, not looking at her but even further out to sea. "You're a good swimmer," he commented with approval.

"My father taught me. There was a lake we used to go to every summer growing up. And when we moved to California, well, I go to the beach as often as I can." When he did not respond, she added, "So are you. Good in the water, I mean." The tops of her arms swished back and forth along the surface as her legs scissored below.

"College," he said. "Before I joined up, I swam for the University of Maryland. It's the only sport I was ever any good at."

Cop looked at her then, steadily. She thought he would say something more, but he did not. Normally, such a protracted gaze would have unsettled her, but she held his eyes and did not turn away.

"I'm glad you're not mad at me anymore," he said, finally.

"Oh, well, I overreacted." Cop raised his eyebrows and frowned slightly in a waggish admittance of truth. She splashed him, and he kicked his heels up and floated on his back. Peg did the same, and the ocean's natural current brought their bodies together and then apart so that they touched lightly, momentarily. Still on their backs, Peg heard Cop's voice through the water that covered her ears.

"We should head back." They pulled their legs down through the waves and lifted their heads, righting themselves, and swam toward shore. When they got into shallow surf, they stood and trudged the rest of the way, knees high and splashing. Cop took a step closer to her and threw his arm behind her back, grasping her waist and pulling her to his side. Before she could think of how to react, he had released her. He strode forward and sat down on his towel.

Helen stood with her hands on her hips, surveying their exchange, looking back and forth between Peg and Cop.

"Well I'm glad to see we're all on speaking terms again!" she said loudly, throwing her hands up in the air with a laugh.

Fred grinned. "Let's head up to the Lido. I'm starving." The women quickly threw on sun dresses over their suits, and the men their shirts.

"We can really go in there like this?" asked Agatha distrustfully, presenting her casual attire with a condemning wave of her hand.

"Not in the dining room, but we can sit out on the veranda and order there," answered James. Now that his chest was covered, Peg found it easier to look at him. She gathered her belongings, picked up her sandals in one hand, and walked towards the undulating white building shaped like a breaking wave. When they reached the pavement, she slipped them on. Helen's arm cradled hers and pulled her close, but she said nothing, only offering a small, familiar smile. Peg was thankful not to have her previous words, spoken with such conviction, thrown back at her.

The Lido host escorted them to a second story balcony and allowed them to choose their own seats around a cramped round table. The chairs faced the ocean, while the overhang shielded them from the sun. Iced tea was ordered all around. They selected a few platters of food to share, and everyone ate greedily, their recent swim and the salt air creating a gnawing hunger. The group was content to enjoy the long pockets of silence and soothing view, the shifting waterscape and fellow beachgoers below.

High above the shore, Peg watched the tops of the trees planted in a neat row at the beach's edge shake with wind. They held fast to their needles, not losing one, even when an especially strong gust ripped through their branches. Satiated and happy, she leaned back in her seat and unwrapped the scarf from her hat, playing absentmindedly with the diaphanous fabric. Her companions' voices clinked like crystal in the background until the loud rubbing of chair legs moving heavily across the floor grabbed her attention.

"Peg, did you hear? We're going to go for a stroll and take a tour of the building," said Sue as she stood. "Want to come?" Peg did want to see the rest of the Lido, but she was too content where she sat to move.

"I think I'll stay here." She noticed Cop, who had risen, sit back down. When they looked in his direction, he shook his head no.

"Suit yourselves. Be back in a few minutes."

Peg and Cop watched their friends disappear one by one as they each turned the corner, their voices trailing behind them until they opened the door and stepped back inside. Peg continued to finger the chiffon and turned to look at her cohort.

"I suddenly just feel so lazy. I could take a nap right here." She yawned, covering her mouth.

"You have a few new freckles here," he noted, pointing to the bridge of his own nose. Peg touched her face self-consciously. "When I was a boy, my family had a beach house where we'd spend the summers. I've never slept so well as in that house. I'd open the windows at night to hear the surf. There's nothing like it," he said.

A stronger breeze swept across the balcony and wrinkled her shift. As it became unexpectedly darker, they both looked up at the sky. A wall of clouds had appeared and blown swiftly across the face of the sun, turning the golden light blue and then back to gold as the sun reappeared. The dance repeated, and a pigeon landed on the ledge, cooing once before strutting along the edge towards a handful of crumbs.

"It won't rain, will it?" she asked.

"Probably. It's monsoon season, after all. But it won't last."

A great peal of thunder shook the building, and Peg jumped upright in her seat, eyes wide. Cop chuckled and she scolded herself for the overreaction. She was not afraid of lightning, but the sound had startled her.

"Don't worry. We're safe." The sunbathers on the beach scrambled back to their towels and bags, hurriedly stuffing items beneath arms and hanging them on wrists as they ran for the large umbrellas. Before the last of those fleeing had found shelter, a torrent of rain drove deafeningly into the sand, ocean and pavement, the variable mediums responding in a broad range of percussive tones. Everything in the storm's path was instantaneously soaked. Never having experienced monsoons, Peg sat forward in her chair, awed. The water fell so thickly that she could only see the objects behind it as though through a fish tank. Everything lost its definition and blended into whatever it touched. The furious rain splashed her feet.

"Thank goodness we're here and not out there," she mused. Cop nodded and his gaze lost focus.

"What is it?" she asked. He snapped back into the present and gave her a small smile, shifting his weight.

"During the War, we were caught in the rain for five days once. It didn't stop for a moment, I mean, not even *one second*. When it finally did, I thought I'd never seen anything better than the sun pushing back those clouds. Half of the men got trench foot, many of those had to have feet and legs amputated. Somehow, I never got it." Cop ran his fingers through his hair and closed his eyes.

"Once the rain had stopped, everyone hung up their socks and boots on their rifles, sticks, trees—whatever was handy. Our entire camp looked like my grandmother's balcony on laundry day." There was humor in his voice, but he did not laugh.

"What did you do in the War?" When Cop did not respond, Peg thought she must have phrased her question incorrectly. She tried again. "I mean, what was your job?"

"Engineer. Mostly I helped build bridges, dug trenches, put up shelters—hospitals sometimes. A lot of repair, helped make sure the men had clean water, got rid of barbed wire." He started to say something more but stopped. Peg watched him but did not press him further. "There were other things, too," he finally said, "but I don't think you'd like to hear about them." He glanced at her out of the corner of his eye and back out at the pounding rain.

"You always hear men talk about faith in the trenches—finding God on the battlefield—but I was too busy to give that much thought. There was too much damn line to repair, too many roads that needed fixing. Too many good men died and bad men lived. I couldn't see any method, any rhyme or reason. There didn't seem to be anything of God I could point to. I escaped with all ten fingers and toes, all my limbs, not even a run-in with shrapnel. But, of course, many were not so lucky." He turned to see how his foray into war and religion had affected her.

"About a year ago, when I lost my sister, I stopped running—from God, I mean. I know that sounds like He was chasing me down, which I guess He was." Cop shrugged his shoulders and suddenly turned his chair so that it was square with Peg's. "You'd think my wife leaving me would have gotten my attention, but it didn't. It wasn't for another decade, watching Cathy suffer like she did and shrivel away, that I started asking questions—that I started to think maybe what I thought about God mattered at all." He searched her face for comprehension. Peg tried not to let her alarm show.

"You were marr...married?" she asked, swallowing and clearing her throat.

"Yes," he said gravely. "It was a rash, stupid thing. We met right before I was to ship out and decided to go ahead and get hitched. The day after, I left for England. I'd only known her for two weeks, and it was another two years before I saw her again. I don't think she was faithful. I can't blame her, really. I guess even then I knew it was a farce, a flirtation taken too far. I wrote her each week but never got a letter back. Not one. That's when I started to guess all was not well on the home-front. Still, after the war was over, I was glad to have someone to come home to, and I thought we'd finally get to know each other then. It was two months later that I woke one morning to find her closet cleaned out and a note on the dresser. The divorce papers came a month after that. Seemed she'd been planning it all for some time. I signed them," he said, shrugging his shoulder. As though tired by the intimate confession, Cop exhaled loudly.

"I'm not sure how you do it, Marguerithe. I don't like talking about myself and yet here I am, spilling my guts." He looked evenly into her eyes. Peg offered a short, forced laugh as she made a few computations in her mind.

"So you couldn't have been more than twenty?"

"Yes, twenty to the day, as a matter of fact. It was my birthday." He thought a moment more. "It was all so long ago, Marguerithe. And things are so different now, *I* am so different now. Now I know marriage is sacred, not something to be entered into lightly." Peg stood and moved to the edge of the balcony, resting her elbows on the high cement wall. He watched her sun-kissed shoulders, her thin neck and the damp curl against it that hung free from the pins, keeping the rest of her hair tamed. He rose and joined her, leaning heavily against the wall so that his torso was parallel to the ground, his full weight supported by his shoulders, his head hanging between his arms.

"Isn't there anything you regret from when you were young and foolish?" he asked teasingly. "Some skeleton to make me feel better about mine?" She smiled genuinely but abruptly stopped when she thought on the one thing that might trump his own tale. Knowing she had to offer him some intimate morsel, she scrambled to find a different, acceptable confession.

"Well, before I came on this trip, I was engaged." He turned his head and looked up at her, his expression falling.

"*Was,* as in *no longer are?*" Peg nodded.

"Not engaged, exactly, but proposed to. Almost-engaged is more accurate."

"What happened?" he probed, his jaw and eyes tense.

"He turned out not to be who I thought he was," she said, realizing as she spoke the words that this had been the heart of Charles's betrayal. "I thought I could trust him, I thought I wanted to trust him. But since I've been away and had time to think, well, I see things more clearly. I don't think he was ever the man I was supposed to marry. I just wanted him to be." Peg turned towards Cop.

"This is the Charles that Helen mentioned?" he asked. Peg nodded, blushing.

"He did me a favor. He showed me who he really was before I gave the rest of my life to him. I suppose I should be thankful." She wanted Cop to know the truth, to give him the gift of knowing why she was here, something personal of herself.

"Well, Marguerithe, don't worry. I won't take advantage of your fragile state," he said flirtatiously, placing his warm hand over hers. Her proximity to Cop made her aware of every bare strip of skin exposed to the ricocheting raindrops, every part of her that was close enough for him to touch. The rain stopped, abruptly and dramatically, her ears struggling to adjust to the sudden silence after the weather's climactic last note.

She covered her mouth with her hands and shook her head before finally throwing it back and laughing. Cop surveyed the spectacle, admiring her joyful eyes and the sweetness of her shyness before his own lower laughter joined hers. As the pretty duet faded, a million thoughts flooded his mind, a dozen different contradictory "shoulds" and "should-nots." He wanted to be respectful, to let her know his intentions were honorable. He touched her mid back and leaned towards her ear, speaking barely above a whisper.

"You can trust me." The hushed words exploded through her heart, and she looked at him alarmed, questioningly. *Was it true?*

Before Peg could respond, Fred's voice called out as the rest of the group returned.

"How was the tour?" asked Cop in a deliberately confident and booming voice, letting the hand that had recently rested against Peg's back fall to his side. She looked at him quickly, at her hands, and then at Helen, who seemed to be in ill humor.

"What's wrong?"

"I took a little tumble, that's all. My pride and I will be fine any moment now," she joked, throwing herself down in the nearest chair and resting her head.

The dark cloud cover that had moments before drenched the earth was whisked away as though some embarrassing mistake. The sky was clear again, the sun brilliant.

"Who'd like to go for another dip?" asked Fred, reaching for Sue's hand and holding it against his chest as he looked eagerly at the group.

"Count me in," said Peg, lustily eyeing the cool water. She needed time to mill over Cop's assertion. Peg grabbed Agatha's arm and pulled her towards the door. "Come on, we didn't come all this way to have a sandwich. You'll regret it if you don't at least wade in Repulse Bay." She grinned at Agatha's stern expression but did not let go. The woman, perhaps weary of always refraining, acquiesced, allowing herself to be dragged down to the wet sand.

Cop watched them leave and feared he had said too much.

CHAPTER 10

Although on vacation, the engineers had to check in at their local office to complete paperwork and receive updates to their respective assignments, and so for the next three days, the women found themselves alone. Without shame or censorship, Sue carried on about Fred's humor and attentiveness. Helen disparaged James whenever possible, while Peg, in turn, privately relished her frequent thoughts of Cop.

She read in the chair in the early morning hours or walked down to the lobby and paced the marble floor. Her conversation with Cop at the Lido replayed relentlessly through her mind. The discreet, brief touches they'd shared, their heady flirtation—they made her stomach flip. But his failed marriage gave her pause, as did the way in which he'd spoken of God. Peg could only decipher the faintest implication of his words and longed to understand more. With the clarity that only early morning hours offer, the solution called loudly in her mind; she needed to speak with Claire Wards.

When the clock read six-thirty, she grabbed her shawl and purse and went to the restaurant. Peg ordered a cup of coffee, too preoccupied to indulge in a protracted meal. From her room, she'd brought a notepad and pencil and distracted herself by listing expenses and purchases from the prior day. With satisfaction, she found herself well within her budget, which meant that she could enjoy the upcoming trip to Macao more than she might have otherwise. The round and discrete numbers on the page settled her busy brain and helped her to clearly formulate a plan. As her options were few, it was simple; she would look for Claire at the docks. It was a foolhardy quest and unlikely to succeed, but there was no one else who could answer her questions, and she coveted the distraction, regardless of its outcome. Dabbing at her mouth and leaving a small tip for the waiter, Peg dropped her napkin on the table and slid out her chair.

To her dismay, despite the early hour and low sun, the young day was already insufferably hot. She grabbed at her shawl and stuffed it into her purse with disgust. Surveying the sky, there was no indication of impending rain. Although she was thankful for the shade her hat cast, the additional heat it produced made it scarcely worth the tradeoff. Within ten steps, her entire body had broken into a sweat.

Engrossed in fantasies of swimming, Peg came quickly to the dock. She looked about to get her bearings and to search for Claire's unmistakable golden hair. At last succumbing to the sweat pooling on her scalp, she removed her hat and used it as a fan as she shaded her eyes with her other hand. Squinting, she scanned the area, hoping to see Claire's face at any moment. With no success, she decided to investigate more closely, walking the length of the wooden planks towards Mrs. Pang's boat. When Peg arrived where she had thought she would find her, there was another much larger vessel in the small sampan's place. Aboard, a teenage boy and a man who must have been his grandfather eyed her with hostile curiosity.

"Are you Peg?" asked a female, heavily accented voice. It rang disembodied from her left, and Peg turned to see to whom it belonged. A young woman in her early twenties stood aboard what looked to be Mrs. Pang's boat, but the girl was entirely unfamiliar. She held a tangle of net in her petite hands.

"Why yes, I am. How do you know my name?" she asked. Peg removed her shawl temporarily from her purse and mopped her face. It had been the right decision that morning not to bother with makeup.

"My mother and Claire told me about you." Peg saw that the girl's almond-shaped eyes were a startling light green.

"Your mother is Mrs. Pang?" Peg asked. The girl nodded with amusement, the answer to Peg's question obvious. "Your English is very good. Where did you learn to speak?"

"Here and there," she answered cryptically, shrugging her shoulders. The mixture of British and Cantonese accents produced a hybrid entirely captivating. Peg wished the woman would speak again.

"You know my name but I don't know yours," led Peg.

"Lily," she said simply, reaching down to her feet and picking something up that Peg could not see. "Why are you here?" she asked plainly.

"I was hoping I might run into Ms. Wards."

"No, she does not come today." Although striking, Lily did not have the same warmth and generosity of spirit that her mother radiated. She seemed heavy-laden with too many cares for her young age. It was a poignant combination in one so pretty.

"My mother is away, too. I will tell her you came to see her when she returns." Lily turned to step inside the boat, dragging the net with her.

"Do you read the Bible with Ms. Wards and your mother?" Peg called out, uncertain why she cared.

Lily looked at her and scowled. "I don't have time to sit and read fairytales or talk to ghosts." She turned completely away from Peg so that her last words were hushed and echoed softly inside the sampan's barrel. The ire of the girl's response made Peg reflect upon her own animosity. Is this how she, herself, sounded to Claire? She vowed then that if she were to find her that day, she would be more gracious.

Standing up straighter and glancing to her left and right before raising her chin and stepping forward, Peg walked to the sampan's rail with determination and rapped it three times with her knuckles.

"Lily, please, I have one more question and then I promise I'll leave you be!" she called. The boat was not large enough for Lily to not have heard her plea, but there was no response. "Please. It's important." A few seconds later, Lily emerged. She looked Peg stonily in the eye and waited.

"I know you must be busy, but do you know where I could find Ms. Wards?" Lily held up a wet dress and moved towards a line that had obviously been hung for laundry. She carefully draped the garment over it, her back turned to Peg.

"There is an orphanage I know she sometimes visits, but she could be anywhere. I do not know if that is where she is." Without turning around, she folded her arms across her chest, her elbows pointing sharply at the deck, and continued. "It is close to Statue Square. If you ask someone near there, they can show you where it is." The lightening sky framed her delicate profile.

"Thank you so much. I'll get out of your hair now." As Peg walked back down the dock toward land, Lily called out after her.

"Tell Sister Magdalene that Wai-Ling says hello." Peg stopped and looked over her shoulder at the girl, who had already disappeared back inside the boat.

Hurrying more quickly than the weather made prudent, Peg headed back to The Peninsula and hailed a rickshaw. From her seat behind the driver, he looked like every other she had encountered—the same hat, the same sinewy arms and calves, the same tanned skin. He carried her at a good clip, and Peg stared at the sweat that dripped down his neck and back. She could not help but feel a sense of indignity for these men who stood in the stead of horses and mules. It was animal, not human work, and she wished they didn't have to do it.

The rickshaw rolled to a stop before a statue of Queen Elizabeth, and Peg stepped out onto the steaming cobblestone, paying the driver and thanking him. As he took on another passenger, Peg eyed her surroundings. Spotting only tourists, she walked past the square towards a restaurant with a pretty patio and intended to inquire there when, to her disbelief, she spotted Ms. Wards seated at one of the wrought-iron tables, resting calmly in the ample shade of its yellow and red striped umbrella. She toyed with the small spoon in her teacup, swirling the contents absentmindedly. Although she was alone, Peg noted that the place-setting opposite hers displayed a plate of crumbs and a half-finished beverage. When she was close enough to cast a shadow at Ms. Wards' feet, she cleared her throat.

Claire glanced upwards casually, as though not expecting the noise to be directed at her. When she recognized Peg, a wide smile spread warmly across her face.

"Why hello! What a lovely surprise," she said with sincerity. "Are you out sightseeing?" she asked.

"Good morning. No, not exactly. I was actually looking for you," she said. Peg glanced over her shoulder to see if Claire's absent companion might return. "Are you here by yourself?"

"No, actually, I'm here with Willem. He's just inside settling the check." As she spoke his name, he stepped out onto the patio, stuffing a few bills into his wallet and then tucking it into the inside pocket of his jacket. Peg froze.

"Oh, I'm so sorry to intrude. Never mind. It's not important. I'll leave you two to your tea." Peg turned to exit quickly without detection, but Claire reached out and grabbed her forearm.

"Don't be silly. We'd love your company." With Peg's wrist caught firmly in Claire's slim fingers, her arm extended and body half-turned towards the street, Cop at last looked up and saw her. He paused, as though making certain he had seen correctly, and then smiled.

"Hello," she said.

"Hello. What—what are you doing here?" he asked, flustered.

"I—I was trying to find Ms. Wards, and, well, here she is." He pulled a chair over from an empty table to their left and motioned for her to have a seat.

"Thank you," she said as she lowered herself onto the cool iron. The waiter appeared and Peg ordered only water. Claire took a sip of her tea and noticed with humor the expression of horror that appeared on Peg's face.

"Yes, I *am* drinking hot tea in this weather. It's how you know you've been too long in Hong Kong." There was a moment of silence as the trio sought an acceptable topic of conversation.

"I met Lily. She's the one who told me to look for you here. Well, not *here*, exactly. She told me to find the orphanage nearby, that you might be there," she said, by way of explanation.

"I haven't yet gone, but I will when we're done here." There must have been a question on Peg's face, for Claire tilted her head.

"What is it?" she asked.

"Oh, well, it's nothing—none of my business," Peg answered, taking a long drink of the water the waiter brought. The cold condensation against her palm was shocking and wonderful. After she had taken her fill, she held the glass to her forehead.

"Lily is unique, a strong girl and a hard case. I've never encountered such a difficult shell to crack, but I've made a vow to the Lord that I won't stop trying as long as he has me here in Hong Kong," Claire explained, guessing at the object of Peg's curiosity. "But why were you looking for me?" Claire asked, pointedly but not without kindness. She glanced at Cop, who alternated his attention between the two women. Peg opened her mouth to speak but shut it without issuing an explanation, his presence preventing her from declaring truthfully why she had spent the morning in search of the pretty missionary.

Adroitly assessing the situation, Cop slid his chair back and stood up, grabbing his hat off the table with one hand.

"I'll leave you two ladies to talk in private. I have a few matters to attend to before we go to Macao, and there are some topics of conversation not fit for male ears," he teased. He went to take Peg's hand, and she thought for a moment that he might kiss it, but as he brought it towards his mouth, he changed his mind and instead squeezed it awkwardly midair. He pushed his hat down on top of his head and turned before the moment became more embarrassing.

"Thank you, Claire, for tea and for agreeing to meet with me at the last minute," he said quickly, remembering his manners before taking long strides across the street away from the women.

They both lingered upon his departure, watching him melt into the crowd.

"Claire, I'm so sorry to have butted in and ruined your morning. I'm mortified. I, I had no idea you would be with someone, with Cop." Peg held either side of her glass as it rested on the table.

"Don't be silly. You haven't ruined anything. We were quite done. And of course you didn't know Cop would be here. You didn't know *I* would be here." She watched Peg. "And he doesn't think you were looking for him either." She grinned. "I may be a missionary, but I'm not blind to all the things of this world, you know—to romance—for example." She cocked her head to the side and waited for Peg to say something.

"Did you two have a good tea?" Peg asked, circumventing the topic.

"Yes, we did." Claire took another sip from her cup and sat back in her seat, closing one eye and aiming at Peg with the other. "And I'll not tell you what we discussed, so I wouldn't bother asking," she said, a teasing smile on her lips. She drummed the table with her fingernails. Peg offered a faint smile, attempting to conceal her embarrassment. "— Other than to say that you *did* come up in our conversation." Claire leaned towards Peg as her playful expression changed, taking a moment to gather her thoughts before speaking again. "I say this as your friend, Marguerithe, but just because two people have certain feelings for each other, it does not mean that they should act on them." She looked Peg in the eye for effect and did not avert her gaze. Peg felt her stomach sink at Claire's sudden turn in tone. Brow furrowed, she did not know how to respond.

"I, I don't understand."

"—Well, I said that I wasn't blind to this sort of thing, not that it was a good idea." Seeing the effect her words had upon Peg, Claire carefully considered what to say next. "May I be honest with you?" she asked, genuinely seeking her consent before continuing. When Peg motioned for her to go on, she took both of her hands in her own.

"I'm sure a lot of what I'm about to say won't make sense, but, you see, the *very spirit* of God dwells inside Cop, and because of this, his life is not his own. Our Heavenly Father explicitly warns believers not to be united with unbelievers." Claire paused to see if Peg understood, but her face was emotionless and alarmingly still. *"'Be ye not unequally yoked together with unbelievers: for what fellowship hath righteousness with unrighteousness? And what communion hath light with darkness?'*

Peg felt light-headed. She pulled her hands away from the woman and smoothed the napkin across her lap. Tears filled her eyes, and the blood returned, rising from her belly up to her neck and flooding her head. Peg fought to control her temper. Taking a drink of water, she swallowed slowly.

"Ms. Wards, while we may have shared a few conversations, you know nothing about me. How can you sit here in judgment, telling me, more or less, that I am not good enough for Cop, that I am, as you put it, 'unrighteous,' that he is 'light' and I am 'darkness?' You say that you are a Christian? I would say that is true; you are like almost every other Christian I've known—condemning, cruel." Her voice rose in volume and her pulse quickened. "How dare—

"—Peg, please. You misunderstand. I am *not* judging you. I do not know you well enough to say, but you may, in fact, be a *far* kinder person than Cop. You may be far *too* good for him for all I know. I wish you could understand. It's like an elephant marrying a giraffe—unnatural." Brooding, Peg glared hotly at Claire and held her tongue.

"I say these things out of love, out of protectiveness for you both. I don't want to see either of you hurt, and I'm almost certain that no one has ever explained these matters to you. Cop should have; he should never have flirted or held your hand or anything without first knowing that you, too, loved the Lord!" The implication that Cop must have shared the details of their last encounter made Peg squirm. Was he second-guessing himself?

Bewildered and fuming, Peg resented the woman's intrusion and felt any and all control of her short-lived romance with Cop slipping from her grasp. *Nonsense and stupidity!* Yet watching the Claire's face, Peg saw that she was genuinely concerned. She had not spoken maliciously.

"I know you don't want any advice from me, and I'm not sure that Cop will heed my warnings, but, Peg, you need to sort things out with the Lord." She raised her eyebrows and sighed. "Trust me when I say that *the* most important relationship you will ever have is with God Himself." Relieved of the burden to confront this woman of whom she had grown so fond, Claire sighed, leaned back in her seat, and watched the people on the sidewalk hurry by.

"You know," began Peg, softly, still furious but her breath steadying, "I wasn't sure what I would ask you today if I found you. I didn't really know why I was looking for you, only that I needed to speak with you, that you were the one who could answer my questions about God and Cop. I suppose, in your own way, you've done just that.

Claire turned quickly to look at her and smiled intimately, unwilling to forfeit any chance at a continued friendship.

"—It was the Lord, Marguerithe. He had you seek me out."

Peg's stubbornness bloomed, a streak of willfulness and rebellion sparked. It was her life, and Cop was a grown man. He could make his own decisions, and so could she. Claire had overstepped.

"Ms. Wards, I can look after myself and so can Willem. Please keep your nose out of my affairs, no matter how well-intentioned your concern may be." She stood abruptly so that she knocked the table with the top of her thigh and spilled Claire's tea. Claire stood and reached for her.

"Peg," she pleaded, her eyes bluer from her tears. "I've made a mess of things. Forgive me."

Peg spun around and almost ran from the patio, her heels clicking loudly with the force of each step. Cop would undoubtedly hear of her outburst, but she didn't care. Let him cast her aside. Let him choose a ghost, as Lily put it, over her. Oblivious to her surroundings, she wiped hot tears from her cheeks and walked the rest of the way back to The Peninsula.

CHAPTER 11

U nable to bring herself to face Cop, Peg feigned illness and stayed home the morning her friends were to travel to Macao. Helen offered to stay behind and play nurse, but Peg declined, preferring to be alone.

"What should I tell him?" asked Helen before shutting the hotel room door.

"Tell him I'm unwell but not to worry. I'll be fine by the time everyone's back, I'm sure." Helen shrugged her shoulders, leaving Peg to stare at the walls, the ceiling, the floor and finally, most satisfyingly, out the window at the harbor. She was weary, so tired of the peaks and the valleys of romance, the way things so suddenly went sour. Peg grabbed the straps of her purse and decided to go for a walk.

With no destination in mind, she wandered the maze of streets, stopping to taste dumplings, rice, and fruit along the way. The air was cooler than it had been since they had arrived in Hong Kong, and she enjoyed every moment of its freshness. She strolled until a bench facing the bay caught her attention. It seemed the ideal place to sit and eat the dragon fruit in her hand, and so she rested there, savoring the unusual flavor of the spiked, pink delicacy. She crunched its black seeds between her teeth and touched the green thorn closest to her thumb. It was something found in a fairytale, a fruit to grow one larger or smaller, to put a heroine to sleep or heal a fatal wound. Peg liked it, and she liked sitting there on a wooden bench in Hong Kong, with the aquamarine waters of Victoria Harbor slipping beneath the hulls of countless fishing vessels. She liked the sun on her face, and she liked being alone. Her thoughts were melancholy, and it was wonderful to sit in them without having to pretend she felt otherwise.

When she was young, she had looked up into the drawn faces of adults and wondered what could have caused such scarring, such sadness of spirit and sharpness of tongue. Some seemed scarcely able to stand beneath the weight of their suffering. Disappointment, betrayal, loss— these were the fundamental particles that composed a life. Yes, there were the blessings, the flashes of laughter, but they were brief and erratic, far too irregular to offer any reliable foundation.

Who was the fortunate soul whose days upon this earth did not end in some form of regret? Who found that life was as magical and thrilling as she had thought it to be as a child? Who had thought himself capable of great things, noble things, and discovered with the passing years that, indeed, he was and, ah, even so much more! Peg did not know any such providential people. No, most she knew began in a flurry of motion and promise and, with each heartache and tragedy, with each disappointment, grew more and more still, until, at last, disabled by timidity, the gears slowed and each day was ground down to a dull, dissatisfying routine— not a life but a ritual, entirely devoid of passion. She had thought there would always be so many options, so many avenues down which she could walk, but approaching thirty, there were fewer and fewer to be found. Aspirations had once been like the air—plentiful and unappreciated. Not until they had vanished did she value their preciousness.

After finishing the dragon fruit, Peg lingered until she noticed a mother and daughter eyeing her, clearly hoping she would soon leave and allow them use of the bench. She gathered her things and walked along the water before making her way to the Victoria City Ferry. She rode across the bay with a handful of strangers, and when she stepped off the boat onto the island, she set her course for the Peak. Rather than take the tram again, she flagged down a sedan chair and road like a sultan up through the mountain's cool atmosphere. Although the box in which she sat was high and cramped, the seat within was comfortable, and the rocking motion created by the swift steps of the two men carrying her lulled her to the point of yawning.

She intended to travel to the top, but a building with a green tiled roof and white pillars with red characters caught her attention. An old woman stepped out from its front door with a strange expression on her face as another passed her and disappeared inside. Already near the peak's pinnacle, Peg decided to explore the site and later walk the rest of the way. She approached the entrance tentatively, uncertain whether or not she was permitted to enter. To her right she noticed a plaque and, with gratitude, saw its explanation was translated into English. "Man Mo Temple – Temple Dedicated to the Gods of Literature and of War."

She pushed open the heavy front door and slowly allowed it to shut against the weight of her arm. The room was dim and filled with smoke so that she coughed loudly once before stifling the next with the crease of her elbow. The sound reverberated eerily through the thick air, and a man turned sharply in her direction. Hundreds of red candles burned throughout the room, and as her eyes adjusted to the darkness, she saw there were several people kneeling in prayer. One woman grasped a thin stick in her hand to which she held the flickering flame of a candle, igniting it in a simmering bright orange. The ashes fell away and a plume of smoke floated upwards. Peg followed the white trails with her eyes where it rose to the ceiling and pooled into a manmade sea of cloud. Sandy, conical spirals hung in rows like beehives there, some alight and others not. These, too, produced a strong, sweet aroma that filled Peg's lungs and made her head swim. The woman placed the stick into a pot of sand and cupped her hands above it, collecting the smoke and raising it upwards above her head as an offering.

The room was cavernous, but she could easily view the two large wooden statues she assumed must be Man and Mo – Literature and War. She found a bench nearby and took a seat, folding her hands in her lap and observing the devout as unobtrusively and respectfully as possible.

What would Claire say to these people who prayed so earnestly to other gods, to statues carved by human hands? Were they misguided, naïve? She grew angry again with the missionary, detesting her assuredness and condemnation. Agitated, Peg stared at the statue of Man, hoping to find an answer in his serene face. A bouquet of fresh lilies rested atop his carved hands, and a lantern with red tassels hung within inches of his head. She peered into his wooden eyes. There was nothing there—no peace, no truth. It was merely a statue, an oversized figurine, something her father could have made.

Overcome by the smoke, a wave of nausea turned her stomach, and she rose abruptly in response. Bolting for the door, she upset the corner of one of the incense altars, jolting the top from its base, toppling its contents to the floor and dousing the nearby statue with a layer of ash. The clang of the brass as it hit the floor sang out irreverently. Before anything could be said or done, she ran to the door, flung it open, and lurched outside into the fresh air, taking a deep long gulp and exhaling slowly.

Bent over with her hands on her thighs, she continued to force the smoke from her lungs and take in clean breaths. She did not know if she believed in Jesus, but she did not believe in this—statues and incense, bowls of food left for imaginary gods to consume.

Surrounded through her life by people of faith, Peg saw now that she had mistaken their conviction for her own. She'd been raised Lutheran, and its tenets had shaped her view of the world, of herself, and yet she could see now that she had never really believed her ministers or the Bible they loved to quote. Perhaps she had inherited the faithlessness and doubting of her real mother, the woman who had not believed enough in herself or her family to raise her own daughter. And what of her true father? Had he even known of her existence? Had he not loved her or her mother in the slightest?

Marie and Leonard had loved her well, had wanted her terribly, but this fact somehow paled in comparison to the shock of her abandonment, and it always would. The possibility of a God who actually loved and knew her seemed preposterous and unfounded. Frankly, she was tired of thinking about it all. There would be other, more opportune times to consider the fate of her soul. Good and evil, redemption and punishment —it was all too much for vacation.

Tired and sick to her stomach, Peg rode once more across the harbor waters rather than continue up the Peak. As she walked through The Peninsula's lobby doors, the enormous clock on the lobby's wall read five-thirty. She headed directly for the elevator when she caught, out of the corner of her eye, a familiar face. Helen was seated alone on one of the hotel's sofas, eyeing her accusatorially.

"And where have you been?" she asked loudly, not waiting for Peg to come closer. Peg hurried over to where she sat to avoid yelling across the lobby.

"I was feeling better, so I went out for a walk."

"All day? I've been sitting here since ten o'clock this morning," she said angrily, folding her arms across her chest. "When I told everyone you were sick and wouldn't be coming with us, they all insisted that we postpone the trip to Macao until you were well. I came back to tell you and, to my surprise, found the invalid had escaped her cell." Her eyes narrowed and lips pursed as she bounced her crossed leg up and down.

"I, I don't know what to say. I'm sorry. The truth is that I wasn't sick. I just didn't want to be with anyone today. I wanted you all to go ahead without me, not miss out because of me." She sat down next to Helen and looked down at the floor. "I'm so sorry," she said again, beginning to cry. "I had an unsettling encounter with Ms. Wards yesterday, and it threw me for a loop. I'm better now, though, I promise. The cobwebs are cleared. A day alone wandering did wonders." Peg wiped away her tears and managed a weak smile.

Helen turned abruptly to face her friend. "I suppose it had something to do with Cop, this 'unsettling encounter' with Claire? Really, Maggy, you have to stop being so damn sensitive about these things and second-guessing yourself at every turn. If I stopped to think even half as much as you did, I would turn in circles!" She threw her hands into the air in disgust and shook her head. Peg could not help but smile.

"You're right, you're right, and I'd decided the very same thing just as I walked through those doors."

"Hmm. I'll believe it when I see it," she retorted skeptically.

"What can I do to make it up to you?"

"You'll come with us to Macao tomorrow, of course." Peg nodded in agreement. "And no more fibs, either. If you ever make me worry like this again, I'll have your hide!"

Peg took Helen's hand and smiled.

"Agreed."

CHAPTER 12

The grand steamer was a welcome change from their usual sampan. Peg impatiently waited to board, futilely fanning her face with her ticket. Having arrived early, James and Cop were already on board, while Fred stayed behind to wait for the women.

"Glad to see you're feeling better," he nodded.

"Thank you, yes, I am," replied Peg, embarrassed that her lie to Helen had been believed. "You really didn't have to hold up your visit to Macao for me," she offered. "But, of course, thank you that you did. I wouldn't have wanted to miss it." She smiled warmly now at Fred, appreciative of his thoughtfulness and pleased for Sue that she had unearthed such a kindhearted fellow.

"There, now. It's our turn," said Fred, turning towards the crewman controlling the passengers' entry who signaled with an impatient flick of his wrist that they were to hurry aboard. They followed the line of people along the deck's edge and looked for James and Cop, the former standing directly before them as they turned the corner.

"There you are!" said Helen, scarcely bothering to mask her delight. James reached out both his hands and took hers in them, pulling her into his torso and kissing her on the cheek. Peg could not mask her surprise at their intimate greeting. Helen looked at her as though there was nothing to tell.

"Ladies," he said with a polite nod, "You all look lovely." Agatha frowned and Peg smiled. With a resonate bellow, plumes of black smoke spilled from the ship's two towering stacks. James led them up a wide staircase to the level above. The fresh air flowed freely here amidst the rows of wooden chaise lounges, and at the opposite end of the deck sat Cop, his black-and-white-shod feet propped on his seat, crossed at the ankle. Peg quickly diverted her attention to a middle-aged couple arguing loudly over their apparent lateness as they dropped their belongings onto nearby chairs.

"Thanks for saving us a seat," said Fred to Cop, who now stood.

"Good morning, everyone," he said in a friendly tone.

"Morning," they said in unison.

"I hope this will do. If it gets too breezy, we can always move inside, but I thought it would be nice to be out here, at least for the first leg of the trip." As everyone set down their purses, hats and scarves, Peg felt Cop edge closer in her direction. She busied herself by draping the strap of her purse on the chair's back. By the time she'd secured it, he was at her side, touching her elbow.

"Hello," he said. "You are feeling better?" he asked, looking for her eyes as he bent down.

"Yes, I am. Thank you," she said nervously. Having spent the majority of the previous day imagining the impact Claire's assessment of her soul had made upon the man, she had not expected him to approach her with such affection.

"Are you sure? You look a bit pale." She thought that she probably did.

"No, I'm fine. I promise." She forced herself to meet his eyes and gave him a weak smile. She picked up her hat from the chair and turned it by the brim in her hands.

"It's quite a ferry," she commented innocuously, changing the subject. He reluctantly redirected his attention to the ship and nodded in agreement.

"It is. They serve food and beverages one level down if you get hungry or thirsty. It's about a four-hour trip."

"—Hey, we're going to have a look around," interjected Fred. Capitalizing on her supposed invalidism, Peg reclined in her chair instead.

"I'll go get us something to drink," said Cop, walking with the group until they parted ways at the stairs. She did not bother to protest or to let him know her order.

Once they were gone, Peg rose and walked to the rail, observing the sloshing of the paddle wheel and the hiss of steam. She watched the coast slowly grow smaller and muted. They seemed to be heading south away from the mouth of the great Pearl River she had hoped to see.

Turning around to place her elbows on the rail, Peg watched the passengers with light attention, flitting from one person to the next. She tried not to think of Cop's return and what she would say. Try as she might, she could not predict his behavior. She had thought with certainty that he would avoid her, at least distance himself, but Claire's meddling seemed to have left no lasting scar.

His blonde hair appeared first in the stairwell, his broad forehead and angular jaw following immediately after. He displayed a bottle of Coca-Cola in each hand and a pleased grin on his face.

"A little bit of home," he said, passing her the already opened beverage.

"Oh, perfect!" she said, taking a long drink and savoring the familiar flavor. As she always did, she closed one eye and looked into the bottle.

"You know, I have a confession to make. I wasn't actually sick yesterday." Peg glanced at Cop out of the corner of her eye, but he did not react. "The truth is that I wanted to have some time to myself. I had a...*memorable* conversation with Ms. Wards after you left, and well, it gave me a lot to think over," she said, exhaling. Cop brought the glass bottle to his lips but did not drink.

"You can't take everything Claire says to heart, you know. She can be...what's the word I'm looking for? *Zealous*. Yes, she can be rather *zealous*, and she always speaks her mind, whether or not she should. But she does mean well." When Peg said nothing further, he frowned. "I'm sorry, was I far off? It's really none of my business." He faced the ocean and looked into the distance, his voice trailing.

"No, right on the mark, actually. She told me, she said that..." Peg struggled to find the words.

"—What she said is between the two of you." He looked at her gravely now. "I value Claire's view of things and her wisdom, but her opinion is not gospel." Cop took a sip from the bottle and after a lingering moment of silence, smiled at her broadly.

"Marguerithe," he mused, "Margaretta, Marguerite, Margharita. I like the name. It's a classic." She returned his smile. Although the levity of this new strain of conversation was welcome, Peg could not entirely shake the importance of the last. Her stomach flipped nauseously, from Claire's judgment or from the rocking of the waves, she could not be certain. Swallowing, she felt the blood drain from her face.

"What's wrong? What is it? I take it back. I hate the name," he joked.

"I suddenly don't feel well. Honestly, I think I'm truly going to be sick." He took her arm and led her back to their seats.

"Here, lie down." She reclined and closed her eyes, wishing the sea would, if only for a moment, stop its incessant rolling. He held his sweating Coca Cola bottle to her forehead.

"Does that help?" She licked her lips and sighed, opening her eyes only part way.

"Yes," she whispered, the violent nausea strangling her throat. "I'll just lie here for a few minutes, and hopefully it will pass. I don't understand. I wasn't sea-sick *once* on our Pacific crossing or on any of the other ferries."

When she next opened her eyes, Cop reclined in the seat to her left, reading. She couldn't tell how much time had passed. She took the opportunity to watch him unnoticed and saw, upon closer inspection, that it was a Bible in his lap. Peg's reaction was immediate and visceral. She felt self-conscious and ashamed, as though all her secret thoughts, lusts, and sin would be exposed. Despite her anger, she could not shake the sense that there was some truth to Claire's warning; it was indeed wrong for her to pursue this man, to cause his piety to falter. The conviction was a foreign one. It unsettled her, this thinking someone else's thoughts.

Eventually sensing her attention, he closed the book. "Ah, sleeping beauty wakes. Do you feel better?"

"How long was I out?"

"Not long—thirty minutes or so." He swung his feet to the ground. "The gang came back, but when they saw you were resting, they went to get something to eat below." Dragging herself upright, she put her hand to her forehead.

"Yes, I do feel better. That was so strange! I swear I have never been seasick a day in my life!"

"I took the liberty of getting you a glass of water," he said, passing her the drink. "Take a sip." She dutifully complied and savored the cool liquid in her hot, dry mouth. A young couple strolled by, arms wrapped tightly around each other. They stopped at the railing, and the man leaned down and kissed the woman passionately, holding her face in his hands. Peg blushed. Cop, too, watched the couple a moment before looking away.

"What were you reading?" she ventured, desperately. "I mean, I know you were reading the Bible, but what specifically?" She drank her water nervously.

"The Song of Solomon," he answered, not meeting her eyes.

"What does it say?" she asked, her curiosity getting the better of her. He picked up the well-worn book and held it open with one hand. Pausing a moment to read the beginning of the passage, he glanced at her and back down at the page and then began to recite the verses.

Thy lips are like a thread of scarlet, and thy speech is comely: thy temples are like a piece of pomegranate within thy locks.
Thy neck is like the tower of David builded for an armoury, whereon there hang a thousand bucklers, all shields of mighty men.

His voice grew quieter, and he stumbled over his words. Peg felt her face flush and saw that Cop's cheeks were also pink. He silently scanned a few more lines, dropping further down the page, and then continued.

Thou hast ravished my heart, my sister, my spouse; thou hast ravished my heart with one of thine eyes, with one chain of thy neck.
How fair is thy love, my sister, my spouse! how much better is thy love

than wine!

The sensuous words pulsed through her chest. What kind of book was this? Surely, he was toying with her. Cop put the Bible down on his seat. His eyes focused on the leg of her chair, and he cleared his throat.

"Well, that's one way to end a conversation," he said, the corner of his mouth twitching. He ran his fingers through his hair and let his hand rest on the back of his neck. "I should have warned you, I think, before reading that."

"No, I, I just wasn't expecting anything in the Bible to be so, so…"

"—Provocative?" he interjected. He nodded in agreement. "I know. I was pretty surprised by it myself."

"Is it something new they've just added?" He looked at her with amusement. "It's just that I'm positive nothing like that was in my mother's Bible. She would have thrown it in the trash." Cop laughed, and the sound broke the tension between them. His face relaxed.

"No, it's not new. I think, among other things, that it's a description of the way, uh, *love* is supposed to be between a husband and wife." He cleared his throat once more. "You know, I think that's enough of that. I'm pretty sure that romancing a woman using the Holy Scriptures is immoral," he joked.

"No, that seems…" unable to find the adequate word, the phrase hung in the air, incomplete.

"—Exactly." He stood up and immediately sat back down, not knowing what to say. She watched him in his agitation, his discord visible. Peg found herself on the verge of confronting him about what Claire had said, the desire to know once and for all what he truly believed climbing its way into the light. Swallowing, she forced the urge back down. It was not the right time for such a question. Really, they still barely knew one another.

"Would you excuse me a moment, please?" he asked. He walked to the opposite end of the ship and was soon hidden by their fellow passengers. Peg stared straight ahead, blinking, his departure abrupt and strange. She lifted her heels and lowered her feet to the floor, sitting up slowly to prevent dizziness. The nausea seemed to have passed, and she rose.

Not knowing where Cop might have gone, she decided to go for a brief walk until he returned. She headed in the direction she had seen him go but then cut over once more to the port side of the ship. Hong Kong had shrunk to the size of her fist, and she wondered how the tiny patch of green had ever held not only her but also all the people on board the *Veneza*. Distance condensed the time on the island into a brief moment— a flickering and fading star. She counted the days they'd spent and knew that only a few more weeks remained. The possibilities the short days contained sat in her cupped hands like fine seashells. Marveling at their exquisite design and delicate coloring, she longed to know what shape they might take.

As Peg approached the hull's front, she saw that Cop stood at its narrowest point, both hands gripping the boat. She moved to her left to get a better view and still remain hidden. His tall frame and broad shoulders were bowed, his eyes closed, and she could see that his lips, every now and then, moved slightly. There was no other explanation than that he was praying.

His face was shadowed but his hair lit brightly, and he had removed his jacket and rolled up his shirtsleeves so that the muscles of his forearms pressed against the fabric. Peg sucked in her breath. He was beautiful. Her heart beat loudly. The penitent expression on his lowered face struck her deeply in her spirit, and she wished, for a moment, to have whatever it was that he did, to speak with someone in the way he must be, telling everything and trusting completely. Did God respond to his confession? Right now, as she looked on, was he forgiven and guided?

Cop raised his head but did not turn to leave his place at the bow. He looked out across the water towards Macao, took out a handkerchief from his jacket slung over the railing, and wiped the back of his neck. Peg pushed off from the pillar behind which she hid and hurried back to the chaise lounge.

It was another five minutes before he approached, and his troubled countenance was gone. She smiled up at him innocently.

"Where did you go?" she asked as lightly as she could muster.

"Oh, nowhere," he answered, glancing away. He resumed his position on the chair next to her, facing forward before deliberately turning his head to look at her.

"So, tell me about your life in Los Angeles. What do you do?"

"Oh, well, I teach. I teach young women secretarial skills—shorthand, typing, that sort of thing. Most of my students come from Mexico, actually, and a lot of them don't speak English very well."

"Do you enjoy it?" Peg smiled before replying.

"Well, yes. I do think it's important. What I mean is, at least I am helping these women to further themselves, to become employable.

"What about you? Do you like working for the oil company?"

He paused a moment to gather his thoughts. "It's good, important work. I'm glad to do it. The only thing I strongly dislike is the contract I had to sign. Reminded me of the Army—signing away my right to walk away at any time, to tell my boss to go to hell, to take a job somewhere else." He smiled broadly now. "Excuse my language." Cracking his knuckles, he changed the subject. "But you're from Montana, originally. How did you end up in California?"

"My parents. My father became sick, and he and my mother decided that the weather in California might be just the thing he needed. We drove in our Model T and camped along the way. I loved it. We were maybe going to live in San Francisco, but my word, the fog! Have you seen the fog there? It was the middle of summer and barely sixty degrees, damp and miserable. So we kept going down the coast and settled in Los Angeles."

Cop raised his eyebrows. "My parents would never have done anything as adventurous as all that." Pausing a moment, he took a drink from her water glass without asking permission. "Tell me, what is Montana like? I've always thought of it as wild, filled with grizzlies and bearded men with axes." Peg laughed.

"That's not too far from the truth." Peg smiled freely, losing herself in the memory. "Honestly, I couldn't wait to get out of there. I grew up always dreaming of someplace better, well, someplace larger at least, where I didn't know everyone and everyone didn't know me. I even went to college in Missoula, not because I liked school—actually, I hated it and was never any good at it—but just to get away." She laughed at herself and shook her head. "Silly and expensive, but I don't regret it. Not for a moment. Turns out I loved college. I loved being on my own. I loved Missoula and my professors, but I wasn't there long. I think when we moved out to California, my mother expected me to come to my senses and find a husband. I'm not sure what came over me, but I enrolled in the University of California Southern Branch and finished up my degree there."

"So you have a bachelor's degree? That's impressive."

"Impressive? Cop, you're an engineer, for goodness sakes! I'm just a teacher." She paused. "And I also have my Master's," she playfully added. It was Cop's turn to laugh, and he did so boisterously. It was infectious, and Peg joined in.

"Where *did* you get that charming laugh?" he asked, shaking his head in admiration. His compliment made her suddenly self-conscious, and Peg faltered to find the proper response.

"Oh, well, that's sweet," she finally said, shrugging her shoulders.

"You're not very good with compliments, are you?" he observed, good-naturedly.

"What? Um, well no, I suppose I'm not," she grinned.

"So if I were to tell you that I was praying that God would give us time alone on the tram ride up to the Peak, that would make you uncomfortable? Or that I find it incredibly challenging to put two words together whenever you're around? I suppose if I were to say something like that, you might not know how to respond?" He sat forward now, an earnestness in his eyes that belied the faint, flirtatious smile on his lips. Peg uncrossed and then crossed her legs, nervously tapping her right foot against the chair. He reached out and took her hand, playing with her fingers. "Marguerithe— "

Helen dropped down on the seat next to Peg and grinned mischievously, unconcerned that she might be interrupting their conversation.

"Look what we found?" she said, holding up a deck of playing cards, her eyes sparkling. Peg quickly glanced at Cop and then back at her friend.

"Who's dealing?" Peg asked, happy for the reprieve, as the rest of the group appeared and sat down beside them. Sighing, Cop grabbed the deck and began to shuffle.

The friends spent the remainder of the ferry ride playing five-card draw and drinking gin and tonics. Peg, who still felt a little woozy, nursed an iced tea and watched Helen and Sue grow more raucous and funny with each sip of their cocktails. Having lost her tenth straight hand, Helen stood up and threw her cards on the table.

"Ladies and gentlemen, I can neither play cards nor hold my alcohol!" she announced, giggling and then throwing herself back down on her chair. Cop glanced at Peg, a wry smile on his face. She saw his glass was still full, the ice-cubes melted. He had won the majority of hands, a fact that riled Fred.

"Our friend Cop here is quite the shark, I'll have you all know. You'd be smart to watch out for him. Tell them the story of how you won your General's sidearm in a game of blackjack," he urged, slapping his friend on the back. "Go on, impress the ladies," he said jocularly. Cop shuffled the deck in his hands with nimbleness.

"I don't think anyone wants to hear a poker story," he said, dismissing Fred's prodding.

"Pish!" said Sue. "That's *precisely* what everyone wants to hear. Come on, tell us!" she begged, grabbing Fred's arm and leaning heavily on him. Cop cleared his throat.

"When things were slow, the men would play poker. All the officers would get together, and sometimes the games got pretty high-stakes— and it was a Colonel, not a General—I got into it with Colonel Marks who had a reputation for risky betting. He was out of money but insisted on wagering his Luger. He'd taken it off the body of the first man he'd killed in the war. He wore it like a trophy. I hate to say it, but I *coveted* that pistol. Well, Marks wouldn't take no for an answer, and long story short, I flipped twenty-one and he went bust. Needless to say, once the Colonel sobered up and spent a few lonely days without his Luger, he wasn't too happy with me." Cop grinned and split the deck. "It was worth it," he added. They all laughed, James downing the rest of his drink and Helen whispering something into his ear. Peg jostled the ice in her glass and smiled at the story.

"Ooh! Maggy, tell them *your* poker story!" Helen suddenly proclaimed, leaning forward and squeezing Peg's knee. Cop looked at her with amusement.

"Do tell," he said.

"*You* have a poker story?" asked Fred.

"No— "

"—Oh yes she does," interrupted Helen. "Tell them about that time in college with that boy…" prodded Helen.

"Helen!"—

"—Oh don't be such a spoil sport. If you won't tell them, I will!" Helen turned to the rest of the group and began to narrate animatedly.

"I wasn't there, so this is all second hand, but Peggy ended up in a poker game at a frat house. Don't worry, it was all proper, on the *up and up*," she said the last words in a British accent. "There were other ladies present, and I'm sure Peg conducted herself with perfect decorum. Anywho, none of them had any money, so they played for favors, and Peggy ended up having to write one of the boy's term papers for him!" Helen burst out laughing, tickled with the tale.

"The joke was on him, really. He ended up with a 'C' on that paper," added Peg, joining in the laughter.

"Well aren't you full of surprises, Miss Peggy," teased Fred, relishing the ammunition the story provided. Peg blushed and Cop dealt the cards for the next hand.

"Let's change things up a bit here, make them a little more exciting. Queens wild," he declared, "in honor of our lovely ladies." Peg picked up her cards and carefully arranged them, knowing immediately which she would discard. She glanced at Cop over the fan of cards; he appraised her with an admiring smile. She returned her attention to her hand and thought how much she loved this, sitting here with her dearest friends at the side of a man whose company she never wished to leave.

CHAPTER 13

By the time the *Veneza* docked in Macao, the effects of the mid-day cocktails had dissipated, leaving the partakers lethargic. Agatha, Peg and Cop were energetic and ready to see the sites, but the rest of the group lobbied to first check in at the hotel. It was not nearly as grand as The Peninsula, but at less than half the price, they were all willing to overlook its modesty.

The gang gathered in the small lobby before heading to their rooms.

"So!" said Helen, resting her suitcase on the floor. "What shall we see first? That is, of course, after our nap?"

"Nap? But it's already half-past one! We'll hardly get to see anything if you sleep now," protested Peg.

"There's tomorrow morning, too, and I'm sorry, but I simply cannot take one more step in this horrible heat and these horrible shoes without first having a snooze."

"Sorry, Peg, but I'm with Helen," said Sue. "We could come meet you somewhere once we're up if you want to get going," she suggested.

"How about the ruins of St. Paul's? That's not far from here and is a must-see. We can meet on the steps at three. Sound good?" asked Cop, taking charge of the situation.

"Agatha, are you coming with us or staying?" asked Peg.

"I'll stay here," she said, eyeing Helen and Sue with a motherly, protective air. "Enjoy yourselves."

Peg grabbed her purse. Walking to the door and opening it for her, Cop stood to the side.

As they exited the hotel, the intensity of the midday sun assaulted them. A bench bathed in shade beckoned from across the street, and they hurried to it.

"There's a square not too far from here, I believe—Largo Do Senado.

If you're up for it, we can walk." Peg wilted at the thought of exerting herself in the noon heat, but strolling together through the streets of Macao won out.

"Let's walk," she said, giving him a large, warm smile as the tree's leaves cast lacy shadows across her face and neck. He held out his arm, and she hooked it with her own. "But if I melt, you have to promise to scoop me up off the sidewalk."

"Deal."

The pungent aroma of the nearby canal faded as they headed into the heart of the city, passing apartments and padarias, livrarias and mercados. They pointed and smiled more than they spoke, and both seemed to take as much pleasure in being with one another as they did the city itself. They continued down the Rua do Gamboa and then onto Rua da Alfandega, drawing closer to Senado square. As they passed a three-story building painted mint green, Peg squeezed Cop's arm.

"*I* love how much *they* love pastels," she commented, delighted. "It makes everything cheerier, don't you think?" Cop stopped walking.

"—There's the square!" he said, pointing behind Peg's shoulder. He unhooked her arm and grabbed her hand. "Come on," he urged. "You're going to love this." Her hat nearly fell from her head, and she pressed it back into place with her free hand, laughing.

"I don't think it's going anywhere. We don't have to rush!" she teased. But as they stepped into the landmark's perimeter, she understood his eagerness. Three impressive structures stood out amongst the rest, dramatically marking the square's key borders. One looked older and simpler than the others and was white with green shutters, another tangerine with dozens of ivory colonnades, the last officious and plainer. In the center of it all was a circular fountain with an iron sculpture in its middle. Its water bubbled lazily.

While it was obvious the buildings held some significance, Peg was not, at the moment, interested in learning more. She wanted merely to look at them, to appreciate their lines and color, this taste of the Mediterranean in China.

"What do you say I buy you some ice cream?" he asked. Snatched from her revelry, she stared at him blankly. "You know, that cold, sweet stuff?"

"Oh, that sounds *amazing*. They have ice cream in Macao?" Cop pointed at a small storefront. He took her hand once more, and they strolled to the shop, stepping inside.

"Strawberry," said Peg. Cop looked at her, entertained.

"Strawberry...?"

"I'm getting a strawberry cone."

"Don't you want to see the selection? They might have something better."

"Better than strawberry? No, I always get strawberry. So far, the very best I've ever had was in Helena, but I'm willing to keep an open mind."

A young man stood behind the counter wearing a white paper hat and apron. He nodded at Cop as the couple he had been helping stepped away.

"Good afternoon. The lady will have a strawberry cone, and let's see…I'll have the chocolate swirl." The worker managed to scoop both orders by the time Cop had taken a handful of coins from his pocket and counted out the correct amount. He took the cones as the man silently handed them across the counter and passed Peg hers.

"Thank you, sir." Standing there in the store, watching one another with amusement, they each took several licks of their frozen treat.

"Well, is it better than Helena?" Peg thought a moment.

"No, I can't say that it is. But it's still delicious." They walked towards the glass door, which Cop opened for her, stepping to the side.

"We'll have to eat these fast if we want to avoid ending up covered in goo." They aimlessly walked the perimeter of Senado Square, licking their cones and fingers, foregoing any attempt at comportment. They contentedly watched the children, women, and fellow tourists explore the landmark.

They came to the other end of the square, and she could see the top of some sort of church or cathedral. It appeared two-dimensional, as though part of a theater set.

"Ah, St. Paul's. That's where we're meeting everyone. Say, what time *is* it?" Cop turned in a circle, looking for the clock tower he'd spotted earlier. "It's a quarter to three. Do you want to head over now?"

"Sure." She bit into the last triangle of her ice cream cone and wiped her sticky fingers on the thin, dirty napkin that had come with it. She took his arm once more, switching her purse to her other wrist, and he escorted them in the proper direction.

"Say, I've been wondering something. How did you and Helen become friends?" he asked. Peg grinned.

"Why do you ask? Do we seem so different from one another?"

"Well, yes, as a matter of fact."

"We're not *that* dissimilar, well, personality-wise, I should say. As far as looks, we couldn't be any more different—she's petite and feminine, I'm tall and gangly; she's beautiful, I'm well, *not*—but we've been friends for ages, since we were small, small girls in Helena. She is my oldest and *best* friend. If you got to know her better, you'd understand." Peg paused, silently reminiscing. "You know, we crashed my father's brand new Model-T once!"

"You? Now that is something I would have liked to have seen," said Cop, laughing. "But what you said before is rubbish."

"Excuse me?"

"About your being gangly and plain. You're dead wrong. Sure, Helen may be pretty, but she has *nothing* on you." He spoke seriously now. Peg blushed and grew uncomfortable.

"Hundreds of men would beg to differ with you, Cop, and so would my reflection in the mirror." Peg meant to diffuse the situation, to dismiss his compliment and change the subject, but instead the conversation had taken a serious turn. He peeled her hand from his and unhooked her arm, holding her by the shoulders.

"Marguerithe, I noticed you first, and only you. I may not have said anything to James and Fred, but I chose you the moment I saw you at breakfast, before you'd even sat down and bumped the back of Fred's seat. I saw you walk in, and I thought, 'Now *there* is a woman, a woman a man could really *be* with.'" Peg stood looking into his ardent eyes, stunned into silence, entirely unsure of what to do or say. Every part of her had been trained to distrust such a confession; yet she believed him. One look at his face, and she knew he meant it.

Somehow, they had made their way to the foot of St. Paul's, to the base of the staircase. She had been correct before; all that remained of the cathedral was its spectacular edifice. It was a ruin with no interior. Peg momentarily mused on the site's sad poetry until Cop's hands slid from her shoulders down her arm and then dropped inwards so that he held her waist. And then, before she realized what was happening, he pulled her to him and kissed her, gently, just once. Her lips tingled and so, for some reason, did her hands.

"I hope you don't mind," he said quietly, her body against his chest. She breathed into his linen shirt and smiled to herself but said nothing. "Was it that bad of a kiss?"

She lifted her gaze and met his. "No, it's just so romantic. Standing here with these ruins behind us, kissing. It's like a postcard." He stroked her hair back from her face. Glancing upward, he smiled.

"People are staring. I think someone just took a photograph!"

"No—are you joking?"

"No, actually, the man is walking this way!" Cop released her from his embrace and turned to face the approaching photographer.

"You want picture of kissing pretty lady?" the man asked in broken English, giving them a crooked smile.

"Pardon me?"

"I take photograph of you two smooching. St. Paul's there, too. Great shot. Very romantic. Twenty cents." Peg eyed the man suspiciously, but she could not help but want to see the image. "Write address here," he said, taking a small notepad and pencil from his pocket. "When ready, I mail to you. Yes?" he smiled again, nodding eagerly.

"How do we even know there's any film in that camera?" asked Cop.

"I honest, hard-working," the man said, incredulously, slapping his chest with authority and glaring at Cop.

"Hmm. Sorry, buddy, but that isn't going to cut it. Thanks but no thanks," Cop said skeptically, dismissing him with finality.

A familiar voice boomed from behind them. "Cop!" yelled Fred, waving his arms. "Cop!" They turned and saw James, Helen, Sue and Agatha approaching. Peg heard a camera advance and the opening and shutting of its lens. With Cop distracted, she snatched the photographer's notepad and scribbled down her address in Los Angeles, slipping him a dollar.

"Smart lady," he smiled, hurrying away towards his next unsuspecting customer.

Composing herself, Peg hugged Helen and Sue hello.

"All better now?" she asked her friends.

"We were until we came outside. Does the mercury ever fall below a hundred in this place?" said Helen in exasperation, fanning herself with a small paper fan she'd purchased on their walk.

"What have you two been up to?" she asked coyly.

"Cop took me to see Senado Square. We had ice cream, and that's pretty much it. Somehow, it all took a rather long time," she explained, ignoring Helen's insinuation.

"So this is St. Paul's?" asked Sue, shading her eyes from the sun as she looked up to the top of the broad staircase. "Where's the rest of it?"

"It burned," said James, ever the tour guide, "a long time ago. Jesuits built it and Japanese Christians decorated it. We should get a closer look so you can see the carvings. They're wonderful." As they mounted the shallow stairs, Cop placed his hand on the small of Peg's back, steering her towards the top.

"Have you heard the story of the twenty-six Japanese Martyrs?" asked James as they climbed. No one responded affirmatively, and so he continued. "Well, towards the end of the fifteen-hundreds, Japan decided to make Christianity illegal, and a powerful man, Toyotomi, ordered the execution of twenty-six members of the Third Order of St. Francis. So they crucified the poor chaps and stuck spears in their sides. Three of the martyrs were young boys. It seems that after Japan outlawed Christianity, hundreds of Japanese Christians fled to Macao and brought the remains of the crucified with them." Peg glanced at James, whose neck and face were slick and reflective with sweat. He stopped a moment to take out his handkerchief and wipe it away, dabbing at his mouth before shoving the cotton square back into his pocket. "An outright bloody mess," he commented, "but the survivors did make something magnificent. If anything, they were resourceful."

"And brave," interjected Cop. "Faithful," he said to himself, more quietly.

"Poor souls!" added Agatha, shaking her head.

James' tale cast a somber light on the ruins, and Peg could see from Cop's expression that the cathedral's tragic story had impacted him. Standing at the base of the southern wall, Peg's eyes floated upwards to the top. There were lions and cherry blossoms carved in relief and icons of saints in deep tabernacles. The façade was just like the city itself, a jumble of cultures and beliefs, beautiful yet disorienting. The back of Peg's head nearly rested upon her shoulder blades as she strained to make sense of the ruin's highest tiers. Directly overhead in the center of the wall was a statue of a woman that Peg deduced must be Mary. Above this on the fourth level was a carving of Jesus, with a dove at the pinnacle.

Although the craftsmanship was exquisite, more than anything, Peg found St. Paul's pitiful. All that remained of the cathedral, this house of God, was a single ornamental wall and the crypts below that entombed the Jesuit brothers' corpses. Bones and ruins, and here so many gawking visitors stood and stared, as though only looking at another painting in a museum before moving on quickly to the casinos. If Cop had not been by her side, Peg knew she would have viewed it only as a pretty, peculiar thing, another site to check off as having visited. Somehow, standing next to him and knowing his faith, the site held more meaning.

She observed him now and became nervous. He was agitated and forcefully thrust his hands in his trouser pockets as he kicked a loose stone on the ground. She longed to hear his thoughts, which she knew would surely be dissimilar from her own.

"What is it?" she asked.

"Nothing," he responded grimly. When she continued to watch him, he glanced at her uncomfortably. "It's just all this persecution and, and... *devotion*," he said with a sweeping gesture of his hand. "Honestly, I'm sickened with myself," he said, turning away from her.

"What do you mean? Why?" she asked, alarmed, fearing that his reaction had to do with their recent kiss. Lifting his hat from his head and setting it back down, he looked her squarely in the eye, daring himself to explain.

"Because I can't even manage to be obedient to God for *one* day." She stared at St. Paul's and at the rest of their friends. When she again focused her attention on him, he'd taken a step closer to her and reached out for her hand. "Forget it. It's nothing," he said, feigning a smile.

"I don't think it's nothing," she countered, "or you wouldn't be so upset."

"Upset? This is not me upset. Trust me," he said, smiling reassuringly and pulling her towards him. He stopped just short of kissing her but did not let go of her hand. Peg was not convinced. She briefly buried her face in his chest before pulling away, wishing that Cop's belief did not divide them. Claire's admonition returned to the front of her mind. For the first time, she thought she knew at least a small portion of the cost Cop paid to pursue her. The realization was enervating, and she needed to sit. She lowered herself down onto the top stair.

"Are you okay?" asked Cop.

"Yes, I think it's the heat. It's getting to me," she said, closing her eyes and fanning her face. Despite her own ambiguous faith, Peg did not know if she could bear to stand between a man and his God. Her stomach turned, and she felt panicked. Without protest, she allowed herself to be ushered over to the shade and put into a taxi. Cop offered to ride back to the hotel with her, but she stubbornly insisted he stay and enjoy the city. Reluctantly, he agreed, knowing he would see her later that evening for dinner.

The seat of the taxi felt wonderfully cool against the backs of her legs. She leaned and rested her head against the upholstery, the jostling of the car calming, as the driver's white gloves turned the large black steering wheel with confidence. The dismayed expression on Cop's face as he confronted the ruins of St. Paul filled her mind whether her eyes were open or closed. She thought again and again of their kiss.

CHAPTER 14

The group of friends returned to Hong Kong the following afternoon, saying a reluctant goodbye to Macao. Their time there was brief but memorable, and Peg knew she would never forget St. Paul's. Shortly after their return and before it seemed even possible, the day marking one week until their departure arrived. She awoke with a stomachache and stayed in bed until Helen stirred.

"I can't believe it's almost over!" said Helen. "It's been the best summer of my life, without question. Still, I can't say it won't be good to be home, to wake up in my own bed and have a home-cooked meal. I miss the Rockies. It's a strange thing to miss, don't you think—mountains? But I do. I miss seeing those peaks and furry trees and the cool air. And, blast it, I've missed the best berries for canning and haven't made a single pie. It's a travesty!" she said dramatically, laughing as she stumbled out of bed and reached for her brush on the dressing table. She sat in her nightgown and ran the soft bristles through her hair, turning to face Peg.

Peg tucked the covers beneath her arms but did not sit up. Helen once again faced the dressing mirror and looked at Peg in its reflection as she slipped in her earrings.

"What will you and Cop do?"

"I thought we would all get some lunch together—"

"—No, what will you do when we leave for home?" Helen's tone and eyes were serious, making it difficult for Peg to easily evade her question.

"Oh, well, nothing I suppose. What does a girl do who meets a fellow abroad but think back on their time together fondly?"

"What a bunch of hogwash, Maggy. I don't think that's what Sue and Fred are planning, to simply 'look back on their time together fondly.' In fact, I have a sneaking suspicion that Fred is going to propose!" She hurried to Peg's side now and sat down on her bed.

"What?" asked Peg in alarm. She pulled herself to sitting and threw back the covers. "That's the most irresponsible, silly thing I've ever heard! What does he expect her to do? Just give up her life and friends and family, her country, and stay in Singapore with him?" Peg paced the floor and threw up her arms in disgust. "Well?" she asked with irritation. "Don't you agree?"

"Well, no, I do not, actually. I think it's terribly romantic. And what's so wonderful about Sue's life in California that it would be so awful for her to leave it behind?" Peg stood with her mouth open, staring at Helen, who looked her in the eye without flinching. Her jaw was set, and her dark eyes glowed. "Please, Maggy. Jealousy does not become you."

"Jealousy? Hardly! I'm just concerned for one of my best friends. Yes, Fred seems like a good man, but we've really only known him a few months. Any charlatan or gigolo can keep up appearances for a few months. What does Agatha say?"

"She doesn't know, and don't you dare mention it. I could be wrong. It's not as though Fred told me he plans to propose. It's just a hunch." Helen shrugged her shoulders. She and Peg exchanged one more weighty stare before Helen leaned towards her friend and kissed her gently on the cheek. "I just want you to be happy, darling. And I've never seen you happier than with Cop. Don't throw it away before you've even given it a chance." To her surprise, when Helen pulled away, there were tears in her eyes, which she quickly wiped with the back of her hand. "Now, get washed up and dressed," she said, walking toward the closet. "Should I wear my blue or lavender dress?" she asked over her shoulder.

"Lavender," replied Peg without thought. Her stomach clenched and she wrapped her arms around her middle.

"Come on now!" interrupted Helen with impatience. "Get to it. You can't waste this day when there are so few left." She swatted Peg with the towel in her hand, the sting bringing her back into the hotel room and the soft carpet beneath her bare feet. "We have to find something to wear for the ball on Friday."

"Ball? What ball?"

"Marguerithe Catherine Gerhardt, have you not been paying attention to anything I've said these past few days? The hotel is throwing the extravaganza of the year this Friday, and James has gotten us all tickets. It will be *the* perfect end to our trip!" she said with glee, clapping her hands enthusiastically. "I have *always* wanted to go to a ball, and nothing I packed is even remotely suitable for a black-tie event. I know you are in the same boat, so I've planned a full day of shopping for all us girls. The men won't meet us until supper. So, chop chop!" Helen pulled her lavender dress down over her hips and buttoned the front. "There," she said, turning before the mirror in approval. "You wear that outfit you had on when we arrived in Hong Kong. You look so stylish in it."

Peg did as she was told.

The day of the ball arrived swiftly, the shopping and preparations consuming the week. Peg spent Friday afternoon penning a short letter home and then dressing for the party. After an hour, she stood before the mirror in her gown and jewelry, her hair pinned perfectly, her heeled shoes pinching her toes as they glittered.

"Really, Helen. I don't see how I'll ever dance in these. They look nice but hurt *so* much already," she complained.

"—No whining. Beauty and comfort are irreconcilable," teased Sue. She watched her friend and came to her side, squeezing her arms and then turning so they both faced the mirror.

"I must say, we make a striking pair." Sue's dark blue, sequined gown shimmered and hugged her form like a second skin, her pearled earrings catching the whites of her eyes and teeth.

"Fred will no doubt faint when he sees you, Sue. You are exquisite," said Helen from behind them, stepping into her own gown and motioning for Agatha to fasten the back. Agatha frowned.

"If he likes that sort of thing," she grumbled, embarrassed at how much Sue's dress did not leave to the imagination. "Just promise me you'll wear your stole through dinner. Then, if you wish, you can cast it aside with your morals." Agatha finished fastening Helen's dress and crossed her arms, glaring at Susan. "It's a good thing your mother isn't here, Susan."

Sue snorted and rolled her eyes.

"Well, that's something we can both agree on." Jabbing Peg with her elbow, she refused to allow Agatha's dour mood to ruin the evening.

Peg studied her own reflection. Her gold gown was more ostentatious than any garment she had ever worn, but she could not deny that the color suited her complexion well. Her eyes, too, shone, and her cheeks took on a lovely peach hue. The cream of her décolletage was porcelain smooth, and her shoulders were fine and sculpted, her blue eyes shining.

All three women watched her now, her sudden beauty impressive and unnerving. Helen held her breath and then grinned.

"Maggy. You are *gorgeous*," she said warmly and genuinely. Peg swallowed and smiled with an expression of awe.

"The dress is…flattering," was all she said. She pressed both palms to her cheeks and felt their heat.

"I need to do my makeup," she said to no one in particular.

"I wouldn't do too much. Just a little powder and mascara, a bit of eyeliner and lipstick. Perhaps the faintest dash of eye shadow. You look so beautiful just like this. We wouldn't want to ruin it with a painted face. Somehow, I think that Cop prefers his women *au naturel*," said Helen.

"You do it, won't you? You're so much better at that sort of thing." Helen did not protest but pulled up a chair so that she sat in front of Peg. She opened the dressing table drawer and pulled out her own makeup bag.

"Don't you worry, Maggy. You're in good hands. Now, close your eyes," she ordered, dabbing a brush in powder and bringing it towards Peg's face.

CHAPTER 15

The pain in Peg's feet vanished as she stepped into the elevator. Her dress clung to her body, and she uncomfortably toyed with the straps until Sue swatted away her fingers. Pressing her lips together and switching the small lamé clutch from her left to her right hand, each breath made her head lighter so that she feared she would faint.

When the elevator doors at last opened, all the women froze with unabashed awe at the marvelous scene before them. It was several moments before Helen first broke free from the enthrallment and stepped bravely out onto the gleaming marble floor. It was the click of her heels that broke the spell, and the remaining friends were swept along into the ecstatic lobby. Bright dashes of color punctuated a churning sea of white and black as the female partygoers glittered and strutted. The chandeliers shone brighter, their crystal finer and more reflective than ever before. A string quartet played a festive, lyrical piece.

Peg scanned the crowd for Cop, but he spotted her before her eyes at last found his. He waited patiently until they did, relishing the sight of her, part of him wishing that he could forever watch her in this way, without her knowledge, so that the sight of her was true, unpolluted by effort. She instinctively knew when she did see him that he had been watching her. Try as she might, she could not restrain her smile, and she went to him as though there was no other possible direction she could go.

"Hello," she said, now before him, within reach. He leaned forward and kissed her on the cheek.

"I don't know what to say. I'm speechless." Peg laughed, his silence more flattering than any well-turned compliment. He looked finer in his tuxedo than she could have imagined, and she feared her admiration was far too apparent.

"Ladies, you are stunning. Why, we are clearly the luckiest chaps here," said James, bowing in greeting to each of the women, beaming with pride with beautiful Helen at his side. "Shall we?" he asked, moving towards the congregation of guests lining up to enter the Salisbury Room. He set his empty glass of champagne on the waiter's tray as he passed. Cop led Peg forward, his fingers on her bare back electrifying.

They were seated at their table, and the food arrived promptly. Roasted duck, risotto, grilled asparagus and a few items that Peg could not name were arranged artistically on her plate. Wine, champagne, and other drinks were topped off before the bottoms of glasses became dry. A pervasive air of merriment rose from each table like the steam from the roasted foul they all consumed. Conversation was witty and quick, darts of humor finding their marks, and teeth and eyes sparkled in every direction. It was the finest party that Peg had ever attended, the fraternity gala she'd gone to with Hugh so many years before shabby in comparison.

"I have a confession to make," Cop said, leaning into her. "I haven't danced in years. Don't worry, at one point I was actually quite good, but I'm afraid those days have likely passed. If I'm awful, you just take the lead, won't you?" Peg laughed and took another bite of her meal, washing it down with a sip of wine.

"I, too, have a confession to make," she said cheekily, the wine making her head warm and her tongue loose. "The last dance I went to was in Missoula, Montana when I was a freshman at the university. I wouldn't be able to tell if you were the worst or best dancer on the floor." Cop chuckled, reassured, and looked at her out of the corner of his eye. He was eager to hold her in his arms.

With the guests finishing the main course, an elaborate production of clearing the tables and bringing dessert was artfully orchestrated, all crème brûlées placed at precisely the same moment and South American coffee poured without a splash into their bone China cups. Peg plucked the raspberry from her custard and savored its faint sourness. She cracked the burnt sugar crust with the back of her spoon and then scooped only the smallest dollop of her dessert onto the sterling silver utensil.

"Delicious!" she said aloud, closing her eyes momentarily as she relished the flavor. "What a feast! I knew it would be grand, but I didn't imagine *this*." The women echoed her sentiment, and Fred raised his glass to toast.

"Here's to one last Hong Kong *hoorah*! Cheers!" The crystal stemware clinked musically with its counterparts, a delicate ring sounding. Peg was excavating the last remains of her custard as a low note sounded from behind the red velvet curtain to her right. All eyes turned to find the sound's source as the curtains parted and a tall, thin man stood before a twenty-piece brass band, his black, greased hair reflecting the golden instruments.

"Ladies and gentlemen, let me greet you all and thank you for attending our little soiree. I will be your master of ceremonies tonight, your guide through decades of the world's finest music. I hope you all wore your dancing shoes!" he yelled, raising his right hand and turning to face the band. The room held its breath as his arm swung down like a pendulum, cutting the air so that a familiar song spilled forth, tumbling across the ballroom and nipping at the heels of the men and women anxiously awaiting the chance to dance. Peg saw the first brave couple rise from its chairs and walk gracefully onto the floor, the man parading his date in an arc before masterfully pulling her close to his torso.

"They have to be professionals!" said Fred, intimidated, "Don't you think?" he asked nervously. Before long, another and then another couple rose and stepped onto the floor. Peg felt the table totter and movement to her right. She glanced over to find Cop standing, his hand outstretched.

"Shall we?" he asked. Peg took one last sip of her coffee and placed her hand in his.

"We shall," she said, smiling and allowing him to pull her from her seat toward an opening in the crowd. She turned and motioned desperately over her shoulder for Helen and Sue to come along. With relief, she saw Sue and Fred stand just as she was pulled around to face her partner. As Cop put his hand on the small of her back, and she grasped his other hand and shoulder, he looked down into her eyes. She held his gaze and then turned her head slightly to the side, almost resting it against his collarbone.

He began timidly, leading her only in a small circle, but as his body remembered the steps and relaxed, he broadened their path and his movements. Peg did the best she could to keep up, stepping on his feet more than once and apologizing sheepishly each time that she did. When the music turned to the Charleston, she pleaded for a break, but he insisted they stay, teaching her the steps as the song progressed.

Initially, Peg felt only stiffness and a strong urge to hide beneath one of the tables. She was mortified by her clumsiness and wished that Cop's earlier confession had been truer. It would have been far more comfortable had he been a mediocre dancer at best, but instead, he was clearly one of the most skilled on the floor. Her own gracelessness only highlighted his talent, but as she studied his face for signs of frustration, she saw only joy. His happiness put her at ease, and she began to enjoy the rhythm, the dance itself, and the opportunity to feel Cop's touch with every turn.

By the end of the Charleston, her elbows and heels swung wildly into the air, and she grinned with abandon, clapping and then kissing him on the cheek as the song dissolved into a waltz.

"Madame," he said, bowing formally and assuming the proper frame.

"Sir," she curtsied, once more taking his hand. He lunged forward with zest, and away they went, twirling and spinning in perfect time to the rise and fall of the music.

"Where *did* you learn to dance like this?" she asked with her head leaning back, laughing.

"My mother taught me. Well, she and the Elmsworth Ballroom. I would go with her Friday nights when my father refused. I can tell you with absolute seriousness that I was the hit of the sixty-and-older crowd," he winked, sacrificing correct form to pull Peg closer to him.

A few moments passed before he spoke again. "I hope you know that all of this fancy footwork is just an excuse to hold you," he whispered seriously. Peg pressed her face to his shoulder and closed her eyes.

When the song came to a close, Cop finally led her off the floor. "I'm thirsty," he declared. "You?" Peg nodded, and they headed for the refreshment table. He dipped the ladle into the bowl of punch and poured it into the rose-colored cup without spilling a drop.

"Cop?" she heard a voice from somewhere near ask with uncertainty. Peg turned just as a gentleman moved, and Ms. Wards came into view on the other side of the table. Claire smiled warmly at the lucky meeting, her eyes flinching slightly as she saw Peg at Cop's side.

"Marguerithe," she said fondly, coming around to stand next to them and greet them each with a kiss. She wore a red, floor length gown, more modest in style than the other women present but no less fetching. A single strand of pearls adorned the base of her thin, smooth neck. Her hair, pulled back in a French twist, was simple but lovely. Peg felt suddenly garish and all too fashionable in her gold dress.

Peg glanced at Cop. A tense, forced smile had replaced his carefree expression.

"Claire, how are you?" he asked, still recovering from the shock of their unexpected meeting.

"Quite well, thank you. And yourself."

"Fine, fine," he said, looking down at the ground and taking his first sip of punch. "I have to say, I'm awfully surprised to see you here," he said, patting the back of his head with his free hand.

"And why is that? Because missionaries don't dance or attend decadent parties?" she teased. Leaning towards them in a conspiratorial manner, she looked left and then right before whispering a confession. "The truth is that I'm surprised to see myself here. I was more or less dragged against my will by that gentleman over there," she said, gesturing towards a portly man in his fifties with large round spectacles and gleaming brass buttons on his tenuously stretched tuxedo vest. Peg surveyed him with fascination, certain that, at any moment, one of his buttons would snap free and shoot across the room, likely landing in a beverage or an eye. He was absorbed in conversation with a man his exact opposite—young, thin, handsome.

"The older or the younger gentleman?" asked Cop, diplomatically.

"The elder," she confirmed with a smile. "He is a dear friend of my second cousin, to whom I owe a tremendous favor, and so when she wrote and requested I accompany Mr. Hubbard, I couldn't refuse." She looked at Peg directly now and smiled.

"You look radiant tonight, Marguerithe."

"Oh, well, thank you. So do you," she replied. As Helen and James appeared at her elbow, Peg had never been more pleased to see anyone.

"Ms. Wards!" cried Helen. "Fancy meeting you here. It *is* good to see you," she said enthusiastically. As she saw the pinched expression on Peg's face, her smile faded, and she hooked James' arm, putting distance between Claire and herself.

"Maggy, I need to powder my nose. Would you please come with?" she asked, taking her friend's hand and not waiting for a reply. She pulled her toward the restroom and stopped once they were just inside the door.

"What is it? What's wrong?" asked Helen.

"The last conversation I had with Claire didn't end on a particularly civil note. I'm worried she'll ruin things with Cop," she said anxiously, wringing her hands.

"Nonsense, Peg. Don't worry. Everything will be fine. I'm sure she won't hang around the rest of the evening anyway," said Helen, rubbing Peg's arm reassuringly. "Besides, why on earth would she ruin anything between you? I thought we'd established long ago that she is no threat. I thought you'd grown rather fond of her."

"I had. It's complicated. She doesn't think I'm..." Peg searched for the best word, "—*right* for Cop." Helen eyed her confusedly.

"I don't feel like explaining, but more or less, I'm a heathen and Cop is a saint."

"What?"

"She explained it all much more eloquently than that, but that's what it boils down to. I'm darkness and he's light, and the twain never shall meet!" she said with irritation. "Say, why aren't you dancing?" asked Peg suddenly changing the topic, her brow furrowed.

"It seems that James does everything *except* dance," she said with a frown, "a fact of which he could have made me aware *before* he asked me to be his date to the ball."

"Well, you should dance with someone else then."

"Maggy!" said Helen in feigned shock. "Dance with a man other than my date? My dearest, I have already found my next partner," she added with amusement. "As for Claire, Peg, ignore her! She has nothing to do with you and Cop. Don't allow her to get in the middle." Helen turned now to the mirror and removed her compact from her purse, dabbing at her nose and forehead with its puff.

"Here, borrow some," she said, handing her friend her makeup. Peg stared at her reflection a moment before covering the shiny patches on her face and refreshing her lipstick. When they emerged from the ladies' room ten minutes later, Peg searched the vicinity for Claire and approached Cop tentatively until she was certain the woman had gone. When he saw her, he reached out and took her hand, all traces of tension vanished.

"I was beginning to think you'd been kidnapped," he teased. She smiled back and tried to relax. He seemed the same as he had before Claire's appearance, a fact that reassured her tremendously. "Let's see. Claire says that 'she's sorry she couldn't say goodbye,' that 'it was lovely seeing you again,' and 'to have a safe journey home.'"

The band began another raucous number that Cop immediately recognized. Not willing to waste another moment not dancing, he grasped her hand tightly and pulled Peg once more onto the floor.

CHAPTER 16

Each time Peg glanced at the clock on the wall, she was alarmed to see that the hours were flying with unnatural swiftness. When she was certain that only twenty minutes had passed, an entire hour had been lost. She and Cop continued to dance even as the music grew progressively quieter and the number of couples dwindled, leaving themselves and only a handful of enamored souls on the buffed wooden floor. Sue and Fred had long ago disappeared, and James sat dejectedly at their table by himself, his beautiful date in the arms of another man with more rhythm. Peg eyed Helen as she flirted shamelessly with her new partner.

"Poor fellow," noted Cop, nodding in his friend's direction. "He should just leave," he said. "I'm afraid Helen has found another to lavish her with the attention she requires," he added, not without a tone of disapproval. "If you're going to throw me over for another man, please have the decency to do it quickly and not within my field of vision. Agreed?"

"Helen doesn't— "

"Honestly, I could care less about Helen and James right now," he interrupted, pulling her more firmly against him again. She stopped talking immediately. The scent of his tuxedo warmed by his body and her own was stirring.

"Would you like to go for a walk?" he asked in a low voice, taking a step backward so that air and light shown once again between them.

"Yes," Peg said quietly, not wanting the dancing to end and uncertain what would come next. He let go of her hand, and they walked side by side out of the ballroom onto the balcony where he leaned against the railing and looked up at the dark sky. They were alone. The breeze cooled the sweat on her back and arms, sending a chill through her body.

There was no moon, and the only light came from the interior chandeliers, which had now been dimmed. She watched Cop as he watched the obscured garden and tried to imagine what he might be thinking. There were flowering trees of some kind within arm's reach, and she touched the closest blossom lightly, so as not to bruise the petals.

"I didn't expect to meet someone like you, you know," he said without turning to face her. "I thought I would come on vacation, have a few laughs, and then go back to Singapore at the end of the summer, relaxed and tan." He sighed and stood up straight, slapping the stone banister before looking at her. She saw him search for some confirmation, some understanding in her own demeanor, but she averted her eyes and gave nothing away.

"I keep thinking of my lonely little apartment in Singapore, being there when this is all over—without you. It's going to be pathetic, you know," he said with forced flippancy and a sad smile. She glanced down at her hands.

"The truth is that I don't want this to be goodbye." Peg's stomach fluttered. His voice became serious and lower, his words more rushed. She noticed with affection that it trembled ever so slightly. "Listen. The full truth is that I love you. I love you completely, and I want to marry you. I want you to be my wife." He looked down at her now, resting his hand against her back as he had on the dance floor, the color of his eyes barely discernible in the attenuated light.

She blinked once, twice and heard only her own heartbeat in her ears. She must have heard incorrectly. Up until that moment, she had pretended as well as she could that her relationship with Cop was a summer dalliance, a story to be nostalgically retold in future memoirs. At the most, she had dreamed he might fatalistically declare his love. She had not permitted herself to truly consider that there might be a life together after Hong Kong. As her legs grew weak and her heart raced, she knew her answer would be yes.

"I'm sorry. Say that again?" she asked.

"You heard me. Will you marry me?" Peg saw he was sincere. And then she noticed in his free hand a small open box with a thin gold ring inside. Stunned, she looked back up at him. For how long had he loved her? For how long had he known he would propose? "Stay with me. Come back with me to Singapore. Don't get on that boat. Don't leave me," he commanded passionately. Peg's mind raced, reeling backwards to the moment of Charles' proposal. She had to tell Cop; he deserved to know. She looked again at the ring and his adoring face, knowing that this moment might be the last in which it radiated such unwavering love. Charles' reaction replayed in her mind.

"There's something I need to tell you first. Something you should know about my past." Without meeting his eyes, she continued, taking a step back. "I'm adopted. I was born out of wedlock, abandoned. I don't know who my real parents are." Peg reached for the railing for support. She forced herself to look at him but was only able to keep his gaze for a moment. It was long enough to see confusion in his eyes.

She felt herself withdraw, wanting to kick off her shoes and run. She could not bear to have him turn her away as Charles had. If his rejection had wounded her, Cop's would cripple her for life. He was surely looking for a way out now, a polite, discrete escape.

"And I snore and bite my fingernails and have an aunt who drinks too much!" he said dismissively. "Maggy, what does that have to do with anything? It's a flimsy excuse at best. I understand if I've rushed things, if you think I've lost my mind, but I want to marry you, not your parents, not your family. You. Only you. I'm sorry, but that's the way I feel," he said tenderly. "There's no use pretending otherwise. If you're going to say no, please don't give me excuses. Just tell it to me plainly."

As he spoke, Peg listened with growing hope. When he had finished, she slid down to the ground and sat there, covering her face with her hands. She did not weep, but how she wanted to. She felt both his hands on her knees, and she parted her fingers. He sat before her, kneeling on the ground, watching her with apprehension and concern. She wiped away the tears that had pooled in her eyes.

"Yes. Yes, I will marry you!" she said, throwing her arms around his neck and burying her face in his chest. He removed the ring from its box and slid it on her finger.

"I love you," she said quietly. "I love you so much, Cop." He kissed her once softly and then longer.

"You had me worried there," he said in a hoarse, choked voice. She held his hands, and he pulled her back up to standing. They looked at one another seriously, both wide-eyed, before breaking into laughter.

"We're engaged!" stated Peg, clapping her hands together and bending at the waist. Laughter pealed from her happy throat. Cop watched her and knew, despite Claire's misgivings, that, with time, she would make a good, godly wife. A cloud of guilt blew momentarily across his heart, and Claire's voice as she quoted scripture to him filled him with trepidation. He was being disobedient. This was sin. But he loved Marguerithe too much to be without her. Cop prayed silently, standing there before his betrothed, pleading with the Lord that He would forgive his rebellion and make something beautiful out of it. He knew it was a desperate prayer from a stiff-necked man who knew better, who refused to submit and let her go.

CHAPTER 17

Their goodbye at the port was agonizing, but it was laced with giddiness and anticipation, for Cop and Peg had agreed to be wed within the year. They kissed and held each other's hands, nervous to let the other go.

"I love you," Cop whispered in her ear as she pulled away. "I wish you didn't have to go back. Stay! *Stay with me now*," he implored. "Like Sue with Fred. *Write* your mother to tell her. I'll buy her a ticket to come here," he pleaded. Peg buried her face in his chest and shook her head.

"No, you know I have to tell her in person. I have to give notice at work and collect my things. I have to get my life in order, and then I'll be back. I promise. Nothing could keep me away. I love you!" She kissed him one last time. "I'll write you when I'm home." Cop nodded, holding her hands in his, anxiously turning the ring he'd placed on her finger so recently. She'd never seen him appear so young or helpless. "Goodbye." He kissed her quickly on the mouth and looked down at the ground, and she turned and hurried up the ramp to board the ship. She did not look back to see him again. She knew that if she did, she would never leave.

Cop waited at the pier and watched until the *Asama Maru* disappeared behind Hong Kong island. When the ocean liner was at last gone, he stared off across the bay, ran his hand through his hair, and prayed.

For Peg, the journey across the Pacific was insufferably long. The ports they visited held no further allure; Manilla and Guam were exotic roadblocks and nothing more. She longed to be in Los Angeles, making arrangements for her wedding and permanent move to Singapore. The gold ring on her left hand never failed to thrill her each and every time she saw it. Cop had written on a piece of paper for her a scripture from the Song of Solomon: "*I found him whom my soul loveth: I held him, and would not let him go.*" "Read it," he'd said, "when you're tempted to stay in California." He seemed convinced that a change of heart was inevitable, despite her frequent and sincere reassurance that nothing would or could prevent her from returning.

Fred had indeed proposed to Sue the night of the ball, and to their shock and Agatha's urgent protests, she had stayed behind to marry him later that month. There wasn't anything any of them could say to change her mind. Wishing she could attend their nuptials but knowing it impossible, Peg had kissed her dear friend goodbye on the cheek and found her eyes filling with tears. Her only consolation was that she would see Sue again shortly in Singapore. Sue had slipped a sealed envelope into her hands and asked her to hand deliver it to her parents. "I don't trust Agatha not to read it," she said, winking. "I sent a telegram to Mom and Dad, so they'll know not to meet me, but this will explain more."

The *Asama* arrived in the Los Angeles port four weeks later, and Marie waited calmly on the other side of the rail amidst a sea of eager faces and waving arms. She'd worn her finest hat and polished her shoes and did not smile until she held Marguerithe's hands, pulling her daughter towards her to kiss her warmly on the cheek. Marie smelled of her heavily-applied makeup and the body powder she used after her bath, and Peg smiled into her soft cardigan as they embraced.

"Oh, Marguerithe! Look at you! You're so tan and pretty! My have I missed you, my dear!" Marie kissed her daughter again and squealed like a little girl, wiping away the tears in her eyes. "I can't wait to hear all about your grand adventure!"

Peg had intended to immediately show her mother her engagement ring, but face to face with her now, she lost her nerve. She slipped it off before it could be noticed and tucked it away in her pocket. Marie hugged Helen and Agatha in turn and searched for Sue.

"Is Sue still below?" she asked.

"Um, no. She's still in Hong Kong!" blurted out Helen. Before she could say anything further, Peg interrupted.

"—It's a very long story, Mom. I'll tell you later. Don't worry, she's fine. We're all so tired from the voyage. Let's go home." She was uncertain how she would tell of Sue's engagement without divulging her own, and so she stalled.

Marie eyed them skeptically, but being overjoyed by their reunion, acquiesced without further question. "I suppose as long as you all have all your fingers and toes, it can wait."

The evening of her arrival, Peg unpacked her trunk, setting aside the souvenirs and gifts she had accumulated over the summer. When she came across the coin purse she'd been pressured into buying in Hong

Kong, she held it gently in her hands and smiled. Inside was the wooden cross from Mrs. Pang. She set the precious trinket on her dresser.

With everything put away, Peg surprised her mother with the Spanish shawl and a carnelian pendant, both of which were received with wonderment and gratitude.

"Marguerithe, they're *so* beautiful!" Marie exclaimed, wrapping herself in the embroidered shawl and fastening the pendant around her neck. She studied herself in the mirror and grinned. "I look like an artist!" she laughed. "Thank you." Peg smiled at her mother as her heart sank. She didn't know how she was going to tell her about Cop. Her bright smile darkened, but the jubilant Marie did not see.

CHAPTER 18

A letter arrived from Cop on her fourth day home. Wanting to wait until she'd spoken to her mother, Peg had not yet written him. As she did each afternoon, Marie collected the mail and now held the mysterious envelope high, its return address peaking her interest.

"And who is writing you from China? Sue?" she asked. "You still haven't told me why she stayed behind, by the way." Peg silently opened the envelope and read its contents as Marie watched with curiosity. It was a brief note asking what her mother had said and when she was returning. He missed her and loved her and wanted her back with him. Peg folded the letter and slid it inside the envelope once more. Now was the moment. She cleared her throat and took a deep breath.

"Mom, there's something I have to tell you. Something big. I don't really know how to say it and why I didn't tell you sooner." Marie stared blankly at her and then frowned. Flustered, Peg reached into her pocket and took out the engagement ring, placing it on her finger so that her mother could see it plainly.

"I'm engaged!" she declared. Initially, Marie's countenance lifted and her eyes sparkled.

"You and Charles have finally worked things out!" she proclaimed, grasping her hands together, overjoyed. Peg's chest tightened.

"—No," she said quickly. "I'm engaged to someone else. Cop, his name is Willem Copley. We met in Hong Kong." Marie's eyes dimmed and her mouth fell open. Several moments passed as she tried to make sense of her daughter's announcement. Her pupils darted back and forth.

"Marguerithe? I'm confused," she said. "You're marrying a Chinaman?" Her tone was contemptuous.

"He's an American, and his family is German Lutheran. He works for Saucony-Vacuum Oil. Cop is an engineer," she explained, hoping the information might provide reassurance. "Sue stayed behind to marry his friend, Fred. That's why she didn't come back with us. I know I never mentioned Cop, but we met our very first day in Hong Kong. He is a good man, Mom. You would *love* him." Marie stared, unconvinced and still in shock. "This note is from him. He wants to know when I'm returning."

"—When you're returning?" asked Marie.

"Yes, he is on contract with the oil company for another two years, so we would live in Singapore until then." This was the detail Peg had most dreaded sharing. She did not honestly know how her mother would react. Marie was silent and turned away from her daughter. "I'd want you there for the wedding, Mom. You would come back with me in October. Cop would pay for your ticket. We both want you there."

Peg kept speaking, but Marie did not hear a word. How could her daughter be so foolish, so rash? She'd only known the man for three months!

"—I thought I'd raised you better than this, Marguerithe. I didn't take you for a fool, or Sue for that matter," she finally interjected. Marie's words stung Peg into silence. She stopped mid-sentence, uncertain how to proceed.

"Mom, we're not. I'm not. He's a good man. He loves me. He loves me more than anyone ever has. He loves me far more than Charles ever did." At the mention of her former boyfriend's name, Marie waved her hand in the air dismissively. "It's your life, Marguerithe. Do as you please." She turned and walked slowly into her bedroom, leaving Peg standing alone in the kitchen, her heart racing.

Peg had foreseen concern but not anger. Just as Marie's bedroom door was about to latch, it reopened an inch further. She could only see her mother's lips and nose as she spoke softly through the crack.

"You ought to have the decency to tell Charles. He's been waiting around for you like a lost puppy all summer." And then the door shut with finality, as though she would never leave her room again.

Peg sucked in her breath and tried to compose herself, pulling down her top at its hem so that it lay smoothly across her hips. The tears in her eyes had pooled in the corners, and she dabbed at them with the heel of her palm. Her mother was right; she did have to tell Charles. It was better to confront him now and get it all over with at once. She checked her reflection in the mirror on the way out and headed down the street.

As she approached his home, she tried to push her mother's words from her mind. Still reeling from their exchange, she wasn't sure she could handle any further antagonism. She comforted herself with the possibility that her betrothal would not mean anything to Charles now. They'd made no promises to each other. He hadn't wanted her when he'd learned she was adopted. But another had. A vindictive satisfaction pinched Peg's heart.

She stopped at the bottom of the stairs leading up to his bungalow and took a deep breath. Taking each step slowly, Peg finally used the iron knocker to boldly strike his door. When it opened only seconds later, the earnest eyes behind Charles' bifocals deflated her bravado. She smiled perfunctorily, losing her train of thought, and then remembered what she had planned to say. Peg did not mince words.

"Hello, Charles."

"—Peg," he interrupted, hopefully. "I was hoping you'd stop by. I've been wanting to speak with you. How was your trip?"

"Well, that's actually why I'm here. There's something I thought you should know, or at least something you *might* want to know. I'm not sure." She broke their eye contact and glanced at his window before continuing, bracing herself for his forthcoming enmity. "I met someone in Hong Kong, and we're engaged. I'm leaving to marry him in a few months once all the arrangements are made."

Charles stared at her as though she had stopped by to tell him that it was Wednesday or that the sky was particularly blue. He looked down at her shoes and then past her to the street. "I just thought that, considering how we parted and how long we dated, you should hear it from me." Peg played with her fingers, uncertain how to conclude the conversation.

"Oh. Well, thank you. Congratulations. I wish you both all the best," he said politely, stunned, muttering the last words. "I ought to go. I'll see you later, I'm sure," he said, closing the door without meeting her eyes. Sympathy for the gentle man before her replaced any spiteful glee she might have anticipated. Peg's own heart beat loudly in her ears.

She had done it. There was no one left to tell. The queasiness in her stomach dissipated as her mind turned to happier things—to her impending wedding, to Cop's beaming face when she had accepted his proposal, to leaving America and beginning a new life, the kind she had always dreamed of living. All impediments to her union with Cop had been removed, and nothing now stood in their way; her mother's anger and Charles' pain were but small prices to pay. She knew that once Marie met Cop, he would win her over. Charles would find someone else more respectable, and, in the end, it would all be for the best. She still had to tell the principal at her school that he would need to find a replacement, but he would surely understand. Glancing down at the ring on her finger, she smiled broadly and looked up at the sun.

CHAPTER 19

Marie left her bedroom later in the afternoon, her face puffy from weeping, and made her way to the kitchen where she pretended to prepare supper. Dusk approached on the other side of the open windows as she watched Peg in the living room penning a letter to her fiancé. Her daughter sat with her back straight, her cheeks rosy, and a smile on her lips. The sight struck Marie viscerally, and her breath caught in her chest.

While she normally trusted Peg to make good decisions, she did not trust her daughter's judgment in men. There had been too few in Peg's life for her to distinguish between the good and the bad, and Marie feared above all else that this Mr. Copley was a fraud. Charles, she knew; Charles, she trusted. He was a good man, a reliable man; he had proved himself over the years, and yet Marguerithe was ready to jettison him without thought or remorse. Marie desperately wanted to protect Marguerithe, to shield her from the sort of disappointment that ruins a life, that annihilates a spirit, the sort of heartbreak that one does not ever overcome.

Marie washed her hands in the sink and momentarily focused on the sensation of the warm water. She glanced over her shoulder at Peg once more and then closed her eyes. She could not let her go. Not to marry a man she had never met and one Peg had only known for the summer. Not to move to the other side of the globe! Even though her daughter was a grown woman, it was still her motherly duty to protect her. And there was no one else. Jessie had died suddenly of a heart attack two years' prior, Joseph rarely visited, and Marie had only a few close friends. What would she do if Marguerithe left and never returned? Her own fear and selfishness startled her, but she could not wrestle them back.

Peg rose from her chair, folded her letter in thirds, and slid it inside the envelope. Sealing it and adding several stamps, Marie watched her walk cheerfully outside to the mailbox, set it inside, and raise the box's red flag. Peg did not return to the house to say where she was headed but instead continued down the street, leaving Marie entirely alone. Surprised, she wiped her hands on a towel and then tossed it onto the counter.

When Marie stepped outside, the setting sun was orange and glaring, and she shielded her eyes with her hand. She stared at the mailbox at the end of the drive and looked to her left and right. She was alone. Her pulse quickened.

When Marie reached the mailbox, she did not immediately remove the letter. First, she lowered the flag. And then she waited. For what, exactly, she didn't know. After a few moments, she opened the box's door and bent down to see the envelope resting there innocently, as though it did not threaten to steal away her daughter, as though it did not suspect its own imminent destruction. Before she could reconsider or her daring wane, Marie snatched the letter, slammed the mailbox door shut, and hurried back to the house, her shoes clicking conspicuously on the concrete. She had done it before. For her daughter's sake and the sake of her family, she had done it before. She could do it again, now, and however many more times were necessary, to save Marguerithe from ruin.

In the foyer, she ripped the envelope and its contents to shreds. She did not read it first. When the pieces were small enough, Marie placed them in Leonard's old ashtray, lit a match, and—wretchedly, dreadfully —watched them burn.

Epilogue
Nevada, 1932

T he car ride to Nevada would take five hours—through rocky, then
      sandy, and then orange, painted desert—but all the while through
      arid land. Peg sat heavily in the leather passenger's seat, one leg
bent at the knee and propped against the door, her window cracked so
that she could smell heated cactus and dust. The moonscape on all sides
was disconcerting, and Peg felt exposed. One had only to look to the left
to see her mood—the bareness, the erosion, the untethered Rose of
Jericho that tumbled beneath their tires.

The man driving glanced at her with satisfaction, her thin, tanned legs
pleasant to the eye. He reached over and placed his hand on her knee,
squeezing it once. Peg said nothing but gave him a faint smile, irritated
that what filled her so completely, what seemed so unavoidable, evaded
his detection.

"We should be there by noon. Then we can get a quick bite of lunch
before our *appointment*," he said ironically, winking.

"Yes, sounds good," she replied, taking the hand on her knee and
holding it in her own. Leaning her head back against her seat, she
allowed her eyes to close lightly and her thoughts to cartwheel forward
without censorship. The man's tenor voice occasionally picked up a tune
on the radio and sang a few words before turning to an optimistic hum.

They pulled into the gravel parking lot at three to twelve, and they
both remained in their seats after the engine had gone quiet. Peg was
sweating and silently cursing the Nevada heat as she stared straight

ahead. The sudden silence of the still car was unnerving, and she did not think she could move. The steeple directly in front of them loomed like some kind of sharpened weapon.

Her first mistake had been getting back on the *Asama*; she saw that now. How had she not also considered the impact their separation would have on Cop, that perhaps, with the oceans between them and months apart, his affection might wane? She had been too concerned with her mother and with work. Her actions had been those of a naïve teenager, unfamiliar with the changing tides of relationships, thinking true love, once felt and confessed, was intractable.

"Shall we, my love?" the man asked, removing the key from the ignition. Peg did not respond but placed her hand on the door handle, pushing it down with a thrust so that the door swung open. He stood now outside and reached into the backseat to retrieve his hat. Peg placed one heel and then the other onto the rocky ground and used the side of the car to pull herself upright. She adjusted her dress, pulled on her lace gloves, and patted her hair, breathing deeply as she did so. He came around to her side and offered his arm, which Peg took numbly. She allowed herself to be led to the chapel door and pushed gently through it into the cooler, darker room.

The owner of the establishment met them with large, crooked teeth, grinning obscenely and offering his most salubrious congratulations. She managed to smile and shake his hand before turning away to observe the chapel's décor. He and the man worked out the final details, exchanging paperwork and money. Peg signed something without reading it and then stood where she was told to stand, a bouquet of silk flowers thrust into her hands. Lilies. She hated lilies. The real flower gave her hives.

The familiar, dramatic chord of the wedding march was struck on the organ, and Peg walked down the aisle toward her groom. She tried to mimic the same expression of joy and adoration his face wore, but she feared her attempt was unsuccessful, her smile plastic, her eyes dull. How had it all come unraveled so quickly? With a single pull, the tapestry had been destroyed. She had misjudged Cop more than she had ever misjudged anyone, and her gullibility had cost her everything.

It was not what she really wanted, to marry this man who awaited her at the end of the aisle, but she had no choice. She had measured her options, realistically assessed her situation, and come to one conclusion. It was idiocy to say no. There would be no other offers. It was either him or no one, and he was a good, gentle man, a friend. He worked hard and could provide for a family. He would make a good father. In a way, she did love him, and this way would have to be enough.

Somehow, she'd already walked the length of the aisle and now stood facing her groom. He took her hands lovingly and stared into her eyes. Did he find anything there resembling love?

"Do you, Charles Leroy Keane, take Margaret Catherine Gerhardt, to be your lawfully wedded wife?" The pronunciation of their names was jarring, and Peg could focus on nothing else as the preacher continued the vows. She was the wrong bride, and he was the wrong groom. Her name was Marguerithe, not Margaret, and his name was Cop, Willem Copley. Peg suddenly could not feel her legs, and a great hollowness billowed in her stomach. She scratched the side of her face, thinking there must be tears to wipe away, but there were none. Her eyes and face were dry.

The same question that had plagued her for months screamed now across her mind. *Why?* Why had he stopped writing? Was it his God who had at last convinced him of her wrongness, or perhaps Claire Wards herself? Had another woman caught his eye and stolen his heart? Or, worst of all, had he simply realized his error and made no effort to explain? After his initial correspondence, she'd heard nothing in response to her news that she'd at last told her mother of their engagement and would be able to return by mid fall. It took at least five weeks to receive the post from Singapore, and so she'd optimistically attributed the lapse to the perils of the international mail system. She'd written again, wanting to spare them both unfounded anxiety. This letter, too, went unanswered. She tried once more. After six months with no reply, she'd finally accepted the truth, the only answer to the terrible question she could not escape—whatever the reason, he had changed his mind.

Three months before she and Charles had left for Nevada, she'd written Sue, who'd married Fred a few weeks after the *Asama* left port. Her response had arrived yesterday. Cop had been reassigned, and he and Fred had lost touch. He'd not responded to any of their letters or phone calls. Cop did not seem to want to be found. Peg swallowed down the word she wanted to scream—*coward*.

It was on February 4, 1932, two weeks before her twenty-eighth birthday, that she finally removed the engagement ring from her finger and put it away in the Hong Kong coin purse in her top dresser drawer. It was a Thursday, and that same afternoon, the photograph of Cop kissing her at the base of St. Paul's had cruelly arrived in the mail. She'd held it in her lap and stared at it until her room grew too dark to see.

Friday morning, she phoned her principal and pleaded for her job back. Charles had waited a respectful duration before reappearing, Marie having conspiratorially told him that the engagement with the foreigner was off. Peg hadn't minded his company, and he had approached her unromantically, as a friend who cared that she was suffering. After a few months of spending more time together, he had kissed her at the movies. A week later, he proposed. Bewildered that he still wanted her, despite his initial misgivings and her pointed rejection, she conceded. She did not even consider whether or not she wished to marry him. Marie was overjoyed, clapping her hands, crying, and showering them both with kisses when they told her the news.

Peg watched Charles's mouth shape the words "I do," and she glanced over her shoulder to see if Cop might somehow appear. The doors did not open. She heard her voice make promises to love, honor and cherish, and a platinum band inset with the smallest diamonds she had ever seen was slipped on her finger. Charles leaned in to kiss her.

"We did it, Magpie. We did it!" he whispered into her ear. She kissed him once on the cheek and handed the flowers back to the preacher. There was nothing to do but look forward. As the chapel doors closed behind them and they reentered the baking Nevada desert, the noonday sun glinted blindingly off the chrome of their parked car. Peg shaded her eyes and looked for shadows on the ground. There were none.

She knew then that she was forever fractured, that the bride she had hoped to be, marrying the man she loved more than any other, would always stand eagerly at the altar, waiting for her true groom to arrive. She would live the rest of her life in that moment of hopeful, blissful anticipation for when they would be joined together, when everything they had felt for one another would be affirmed. Her body, the husk, would be Charles's wife, the mother to his children, Mrs. Keane.

Charles opened the passenger side door for her, and twenty minutes after they'd arrived at the chapel, they were back on the road with rice in their hair driving toward Los Angeles

Printed in Great Britain
by Amazon

69288686R00163